WISDOM SPRING

THE ALASKA THRILLERS SERIES
BOOK ONE

Andrew Cunningham

Books by Andrew Cunningham

Thrillers
Deadly Shore

The Alaska Thrillers Series
Wisdom Spring
Nowhere Alone
The 7th Passenger
Lost Passage

Yestertime Time Travel Series
Yestertime
The Yestertime Effect
The Yestertime Warning
The Yestertime Shift

"Lies" Mystery Series
All Lies
Fatal Lies
Vegas Lies
Secrets & Lies
Blood Lies
Buried Lies
Sea of Lies
Maui Lies

Eden Rising Series
Eden Rising
Eden Lost
Eden's Legacy
Eden's Survival

Children's Mysteries (as A.R Cunningham)
The Arthur MacArthur Mysteries: The Complete Series

To Scott

1960-2003

I think you'd approve

Prologue

Looking like a waterlogged waif in the periphery of my headlights, she couldn't have been much more than five feet tall and had no belongings that I could see. She was standing on the most deserted stretch of highway you could ever imagine, thumb out in a deflated sort of way. In the darkness and the rain, I almost missed her.

It's amazing really, how many things can go through your mind in just a few seconds. In the time it took me to put on my turn signal and pull over, I had already questioned the wisdom of picking her up, flashed to my father's endless stories of hitchhiking in the early sixties as a teenager, and was presented with the sad realization that even if she turned out to be a whack-job, I really didn't care. I no longer cared about much of anything. But I was oddly intrigued. How did she get to this god-forsaken spot? How long had she been standing there?

I stopped the car and waited. Despite it being a major highway, there were few headlights or taillights in either direction. The only sounds were the clicking of the turn signal and the soft swishing of the windshield wipers. I switched off the turn signal. The competing rhythms were going to drive me even crazier than I already was—like two metronomes slightly out of sync. That was better. Without the competition, the windshield wipers were fairly quiet—the advantage of an expensive car.

The passenger door opened, and she got in. Close up, she appeared older than I thought in the brief splash of my headlights. Maybe her late twenties. I was close about the height though. Five-one, at best. Her hair was blonde but looked darker plastered to her head from the rain. Wearing only a thin windbreaker to protect her from the elements, her blouse, jeans, and sneakers were thoroughly soaked. She squished as she sat down on the leather seat.

Mumbling an apology for getting my seat wet, along with a barely audible thank you for picking her up, that's when I noticed the tears. Funny how I was able to see the difference between tears and rain. It wasn't my business though, so I ignored it.

Putting the car in gear, I asked, "Where are you headed?" again knowing that I really didn't care.

She was silent for a few seconds, then shook her head in resignation.

"To Hell," she answered.

I smiled for the first time in weeks. Granted, it wasn't much of one, but for the first time since the funeral, someone said something I could relate to.

"I'll take you," I said. "I'm going that way myself."

Chapter 1

The funeral was everything I expected it to be. Whispered condemnation accompanied by looks of hatred. There was no escaping it. I had to be there. After all, it was my daughter—the love of my life—lying there, looking like Snow White waiting to be awakened by the kiss of a prince. But there would be no prince. After the funeral would be the burial, and that would be the end of her. I would have preferred a cremation, with her ashes spread out under her favorite climbing tree, but her mother wanted it this way, and who was I to argue? I was a pariah. What I thought counted for nothing.

My wife—well, soon to be ex-wife, I'm sure. She would be pushing the divorce through in record time—stayed as far from me as the limits of the chapel allowed, with a throng of friends and family protecting her from me. My only family was a brother in Alaska who I advised to stay home. And it wasn't that I no longer had any friends; there were a couple left, but they were just wise enough not to be seen with me. Who wants to be associated in public with the man who killed his own daughter?

I murdered her. Not intentionally, of course. The police never charged me. But it was I who gave her the shot that killed her, and it was I who went ahead against the advice of Karen's doctors, my wife, and just about everyone else, and made the fatal decision to contact the doctor with the revolutionary cancer drug. Karen was dying anyway. Her doctors wouldn't admit it—they said she had a chance of recovery yet were always hazy with the percentages—but I knew it. I could feel the life very slowly seeping out of her little body. They said to be patient, but they were just hoping for a miracle they knew would never come. So how can you be patient in that kind of situation?

Doctor Hill wasn't a quack. He was just disliked—thoroughly disliked—by the medical community in this country. Despite being an American, he had chosen to do all of his research out of the country and had awarded the manufacturing contract of his cancer drug to a small Swiss company, angering the AMA and the massive pharmaceutical companies. As such, his drug, though wildly successful in the countries that allowed it, hadn't yet been approved by the FDA. They said approval could take years. I couldn't wait years. Karen couldn't wait years. His treatment—a single drug, powerful, but with surprisingly few side-effects—could be taken with just about any other drug safely. "Just about" was the operative phrase.

Because of his outsider status, he couldn't work with Karen's doctors or attend to Karen personally, but he had taken an interest in Karen's case based on an email I sent him. I had read an article about him and knew that he was Karen's last chance. We talked several times, and while he was confident that he could help her, he warned me that any involvement on his part was illegal. If he were to administer the drug to Karen personally, he would be arrested. Doctor Hill explained that the only option would be for him to send me the drug and for me to administer it myself. I provided him with copies of all the paperwork available, which included the list of drugs that Karen was already taking. All the drugs minus one, that is.

We were inundated with paperwork, and I thought I had gathered it all, but one of her drugs never made it on the list I gave Doctor Hill. THE drug. The one drug that reacted to his. He said that he asked me if she was taking it, but I was brain-dead. I don't even remember him asking. It wasn't his fault, although the courts certainly planned to make it his fault—if they could extradite him from whatever country he was now living in, which was doubtful. They would say he preyed on a distraught father. I suppose I could blame the healthcare system in general. But in reality, I gave her the shot that killed her, and I knew I would never be able to forget it. She was dead within minutes. I took away any minute chance she had of survival.

After the funeral, I left. I packed a few items into the car, and just left. I had been let go the week before from my very lucrative job—it was too embarrassing to have me on the staff. I kept the one credit card that was in my name only, but gave my wife everything else; the house, the hefty bank account, all of our investments, and the second car. I wasn't even sure I would be alive in a year. Thoughts of taking my own life at times consumed me. But I refrained.

I did make two selfish decisions; in retrospect, important ones. I had a safe deposit box with almost a hundred thousand dollars in cash that no one knew about. It was money I was putting away in case the economy really tanked and cash became vital to our existence. I'm not totally sure why I didn't tell my wife about it. Maybe I didn't want to worry her. Or maybe I sensed that our marriage was on shaky ground and that somewhere down the line I might really need it. I couldn't have imagined this. Needless to say, I didn't reveal the existence of the box after Karen's death, figuring it might be the only thing I'd have left to draw on if I decided to live. Normally, the vultures would have searched my assets beyond my established accounts and discovered the box, but given the circumstances and the fact that I seemed willing to relinquish everything but the clothes on my back, I don't think they even looked.

The second decision was taking my gun. It was a Sig Sauer .40, my pride and joy. Originally bought for home protection, I had come to value my Thursday nights at the gun range as—oddly enough—my "quiet time." I could get lost in my shooting and totally escape the pressures of my work. I took it with me in my retreat, thinking I might need it down the line—not for self-defense, of course, but for a quick and easy end to my miserable life.

So I left. There were no tears on my part. I had cried myself dry during the week following Karen's death. There was nothing left, for now. I knew it would hit me again and again in the days … the years … to follow. But for now, there was nothing.

*****

Boston was in my rearview mirror as I headed south. I was in Connecticut before I allowed myself the thought that I had absolutely no idea where I was going. I had my credit card, all of the cash from the box, a couple of suitcases, and no place to go. I figured I'd never return to Boston, so if I landed someplace I liked I'd deposit the money there. If I decided to end it all, I'd send it to my brother. So I just drove. I stayed the night in a Hyatt somewhere outside of Baltimore—old habits died hard. No cheap dives for me—but it was wasted money; I barely knew where I was. Again, visions of suicide began to creep in, but the thought of a poor, unsuspecting chambermaid coming across my body in the morning prevented me from following through.

It wasn't until I saw the sign for I-20, near Florence, South

Carolina, that I made yet another life-altering decision. I needed a friendly face and some peace and quiet. I needed to think without the noise of reporters, lawyers, ex-wives, and ex-friends. I needed to come to terms with all that had been thrust upon me. I needed to go to Alaska. My brother would give me the space I craved, and, when the time was right, the slap in the face that would allow me to jump-start my life.

I had been to Alaska enough times to know how beautiful the summer can be, but it was still only May, and I wanted to let the Alaskan spring thaw complete its cycle, so I decided to take my time getting there. I had always loved to drive, so going the long route wouldn't be a problem. After all, for the first time in my adult life, my calendar was clear. In fact, I no longer had a calendar. Time meant nothing to me.

I spent that night in some medium-priced chain hotel off the highway in Georgia. It was only the second night of my banishment from my old life, and already my tastes were cheapening. Would my third night be spent in a seedy cottage motel, set back behind a hubcap stand owned by a cross-eyed family? If so, it would definitely be time to call it quits.

I ate a late dinner in a nearby Denny's. That was a first for me, as my preference had always tended to run toward the Capital Grille and such. But as I looked around me and saw all the happy faces of the kids out for a night on the town, I kind of wished that I had taken Karen to a Denny's. We had wonderful times together, but I had to face the truth. I was a snob. I spoiled her rotten, but she never got to experience some of the things that "normal" American kids did. Sadly, she might have ended up being as much of a snob as her father. But I still wish she had had that chance.

I spent an hour there, watching the families, barely touching my food. My insides were so knotted up I was having trouble breathing. The waitress asked me if there was something wrong with the food. I told her I just wasn't hungry. I had her wrap it up, with the intention of eating it in my room when my stomach settled down. However, as I walked out the door, I stuffed it in a trash can.

I couldn't go on like this. Every waking moment was monopolized with thoughts of Karen. Was I wrong? Would she have lived using the conventional methods? No. There was no doubt in my mind at the time, so it did no good to second-guess it now. I could see it in the doctors' eyes. No matter how often they told us to have faith, they knew what the ultimate result would be.

I got in my car and hunted out a liquor store and bought a bottle of Scotch. Yet another first. Growing up, I had to endure both my parents getting drunk on a nightly basis. They weren't mean drunks, just unhappy drunks. They never hit or yelled at my brother and me, they just quietly drank themselves into oblivion, dying within a year of each other when I was in college.

A lot of people take on the habits of their parents, and my brother did for a few years, before finally sobering up and making something of his life. I went the opposite route. The thought of putting alcohol in my body made me angry, so alcohol was just something I didn't drink, until that night in Georgia.

Maybe I just wanted to see if it would help me forget. But really, is the death of your only child—your princess—something you can forget? I sat in my room, drinking from the bottle. Frankly, it was disgusting, but I kept going. However, I wasn't forgetting. I was remembering to the point of agony. A third of the way into the bottle I ran for the bathroom and vomited. I stayed with my head in the toilet all night, throwing up again and again.

I kept that room for another night. I was feeling so awful, I could barely move. I put the "Do Not Disturb" sign on the door and stayed in bed all day. I ventured out again that evening and found a small pub-style restaurant. I was hungry and tried to replace some of what I had lost from my system. But I was only half aware of where I was and what I was doing. I watched the captioned news on the TV above my table. It was all the same. It never changed. The Middle East was erupting once again; there was a manhunt for the murderer of four political staffers of a U.S. senator; our relations with Mexico had taken a turn for the worse; and I didn't care.

I was in my car the next morning driving west. I caught my reflection in the rearview mirror, or at least from the nose up. That was more than enough. I never considered myself handsome by any means, but now I was almost zombie-like. The stress of the last year had left my once almond-colored hair with streaks of gray. Courtesy of my adventure with the bottle, my eyes were now red-rimmed and bloodshot. Who knows, maybe they were that way before my drinking binge, because I also had bags and dark circles under my eyes from months of sleepless nights. My stomach still felt some of the after-effects of my bout with the bottle. That, I could deal with. The guilt over Karen's death I couldn't. It's all I could think about, and I was driving myself crazy. I desperately needed a diversion.

That's when I met Jess.

I was somewhere west of Sweetwater, Texas. It had to be the ugliest, flattest piece of road I had ever been on. The only saving grace was that once it got dark, I didn't have to look at it anymore. I wasn't tired, so I just kept driving. It was well after midnight on that black, rainy night when I ran across her.

*****

"What's your name?" I asked.

"Jess," she mumbled, wiping away tears.

"Short for Jessica?"

"No, Mary." She had come alive, sort of, enough to be sarcastic. "Sorry," she said.

I mustered up a smile of sorts. "That's okay. I'm Jon."

I was trying to maintain my non-caring demeanor but was losing the battle. Maybe it was too many days alone on the road. Maybe there was a part of me that still had a hint of life trying to burrow up through the sorrow. Whatever the reason, Jess intrigued me.

"I've gotta ask. How is it you came to be standing by the side of the road in the middle of friggin' Texas? There are no towns around there, no off-ramps, almost no dirt roads that I've seen. Just highway. Were you beamed there by a spaceship?"

She smiled. It was a strange smile, as if I had just stumbled onto her secret.

"I got picked up by a family in a truck stop outside Abilene." I had to strain to hear her. "They decided they didn't want me in their car anymore and just dropped me off on the side of the road."

"Just dropped you off?" I asked incredulously.

"Just dropped me off."

"Did it have anything to do with the reason you're headed to Hell?"

"Everything to do with it."

"And just why are you headed there?"

She shook her head. "It's a very long story and I'd rather not get dropped off again because of it."

I had been watching for the last mile or so the flashing lights of a State Trooper coming up quickly behind me. He must've been going north of a hundred miles-per-hour. As he got closer, I saw that he was in the fast lane, so I was pretty sure he wasn't after me. Suddenly, he was close enough for us to hear his siren. As he screamed past, I saw movement out of the corner of my eye. I looked over at Jess and saw her scrunched down in the seat, the purpose obvious. She was also shaking, and it wasn't from the cold.

Maybe I had picked up a whack-job after all.

Chapter 2

She was asleep in minutes. I pulled over to a rest area and searched my trunk for a blanket. I covered her with it and continued on my way. I didn't have to worry about driving past her destination. It was obvious that, like me, she was drifting. I studied her in the passing headlights. She didn't look like a drifter. Her shoulder-length hair was in disarray from the rain, but I could tell that it had been professionally cut. Her fingernails had been manicured fairly recently, and her clothes were a good quality. She was running from something. And what could she have possibly told the family that would scare them enough to let her out in the middle of nowhere, without even waiting for a town or a rest area?

Finally, I pulled into a truck stop, turned off the car, and closed my eyes. I wasn't worried about Jess. My money, gun, and suitcases were locked in the trunk and there was little she could steal in the car. But she didn't seem the type. Most likely, when I awoke, she would just be gone.

She wasn't. We woke up almost simultaneously. The car clock said 6:15. I had slept for over three hours. The sun was shining, and for the first time in a long time, my waking thought wasn't of Karen. Jess seemed better too.

"Thanks again for picking me up," she said.

"You're welcome," I answered. "Can I buy you some

breakfast?"

"I'd really appreciate that. I haven't eaten in a while."

It was a real American truck stop. Tractor trailer trucks filled the expansive parking lot. I had already stopped at a couple on my way west, and there was something about these greasy places that was beginning to appeal to me. I had just hit forty years old and it was like I was letting my hair down for the first time. I was no longer trying to live down my parents' problems or live up to the expectations that earning a half a million dollars a year brought with it.

We found a booth and both ordered large breakfasts. But knowing my emotional state and sensing hers, I predicted that much of it would remain untouched, despite our hunger. As I sipped my coffee, I studied her in the daylight with her disheveled hair and still damp clothes and found her attractive. She wore no make-up, which was probably new for her. And while she had the kind of appearance that didn't really need the addition of makeup, without it, I could see just how worn out she looked, as if something enormous was weighing her down.

"So what was it you said that made the family drop you off?"

She hesitated, but only for a second. "I told them I hear dead people."

I burst out laughing and almost spat my coffee on her. Of all the things she could have said, that was one I wasn't ready for.

After I recovered, I said, "Don't you mean you *see* dead people?"

"That was in the movie," she answered. She smiled, just for the briefest of moments, as if sensing the absurdity of it all. But there was also a rational look about her. "I don't see them. I hear them."

"Gee, and they kicked you out of the car for that?"

"Yeah. Who'd have thought it?" she said. Again, the smile

quickly appeared, this time staying a little longer. "Then they threw a Bible out the window and told me to read it. I mean, who has a Bible so close by that they can throw it out the window at you?"

"But you're serious about all this."

"I am."

"Do you do it for a living, like Whoopie Goldberg, in *Ghost*?"

"No. Nothing like that. It started about a year ago. I almost didn't notice it at first, I just thought I was getting some weird thoughts. But as time's gone on, it's become clear that it's a voice I'm hearing."

"Do you know what started it?" I asked. I was hooked now. She wasn't putting me on.

"I do," she answered. "I'm just not ready to talk about it."

"Are they 'good' voices or 'bad' voices?"

"I told them 'dead people' for effect, but it's actually only one voice and I honestly have no idea where it's coming from. As for good or bad, in the beginning it was just benign. It didn't seem to have a particular purpose. But just recently it seemed to be leading me down a dangerous path. At the same time, it has actually saved my life more than once. In fact..." She stopped and shook her head. "If you want me to catch another ride, I'd understand. But I'd rather you didn't."

"Not at all." I cocked my head. "Why would you rather I didn't?"

"Because I think you are the one I'm supposed to go with."

"Supposed to?"

"It's a really long story, and I'm not trying to scare you."

"You're not scaring me. Frankly, I don't think anything can ever scare me again."

"Why is that?" she asked, and I realized she was trying to take the focus off herself.

I decided that the only way I was going to hear any more of her story was to tell her mine—create a bond of sorts. So I told her. I laid it all out. I told her of Karen getting diagnosed almost a year earlier, the strain it put on my marriage, the doctors, the tests, the sadness, the hope of the new drug, and finally, my injecting her. I shared my innermost thoughts and fears for the first time since Karen got sick, and it was with a total stranger. As I talked, I thought about my wife and how far away we had been from each other emotionally even before Karen's cancer.

When I was done, Jess and I each had tears running down our face, and people from nearby booths were staring at us. It was time to go.

"So where are you heading, really?" I asked as we got into the car.

"I really don't know," she answered. "How about you?"

I had a choice to make. If I told her Alaska, she might want to accompany me the whole way, and I might decide in an hour that I was sick of her. I chose to cross that bridge when I got to it, so I told her. She made it easy on me.

"Can I go with you at least part of the way? And if you decide you'd rather be alone at any point, I'd understand if you wanted to drop me off. Preferably not on a deserted highway." She smiled. I was beginning to like that smile. It was kind of crooked. One side of her mouth would raise a fraction higher than the other.

"Deal." I said. "On the condition that you tell me what you're running from, and more about The Voice."

She was silent for a moment, and I could see her wheels turning. It seemed that whatever she was about to tell me would require trust, and she didn't even know me. She finally made her decision.

"That's fair," she answered. "Just give me some time to work up the courage."

I filled up with gas, and we got on the road. As we were leaving the truck stop, we passed a police cruiser. I watched Jess out of the corner of my eye and once again saw her shrink into the seat. I'd have to see if her story explained her actions.

We drove in silence for a while, which was okay with me. It gave me time to think. Although I had done nothing but think since the moment I left what used to be my home, all my thoughts had been dark, often bordering on the suicidal. For the first time, my interest was piqued, and while Karen would always be in my mind, she wasn't the only thing in there.

I kept glancing at Jess, who was staring out the window, dwelling on her demons. At one point, the tears came again, and she quietly wiped them away. I sized her up as best I could. She was a professional woman of some sort—having been in sales, I could spot one a mile away—but she had a look that told me she would've been more comfortable working on a farm, or in a bookstore, or at just about anything other than corporate America. Time would prove me right or wrong when she decided to tell her story.

We were approaching the junction of Interstates 20 and 10 when she finally spoke. It was almost a whisper, with no preamble.

"I used to work for Massachusetts Senator Gary Hillstrom. Are you familiar with him?"

So I was right about her being a professional woman, but wrong about corporate America. Politics was close though.

"I am. I voted for him a few times."

"So you're from Massachusetts." It wasn't a question, but it seemed significant to her in some way. I could see the "ah ha" go off in her head.

I had always liked Hillstrom. He was originally elected as a

Democrat, which is when I first voted for him. After a couple of terms, he had become wildly popular, but he didn't like the direction the party was headed, so he switched. When election time came, he ran as a Republican and won by a landslide, which included my first non-Democratic Party vote ever. The Democrats didn't know what hit them. A term later, he also became dismayed with the Republican Party, and in the next election, he ran as an Independent, once again blowing away the competition. While his constant change of parties gave him the label of a flip flopper among the most radical minority in each party, it didn't affect his popularity. He had become quite powerful and had become a fixture in the news. More importantly, he was respected on both sides of the aisle and loved by his constituents.

"How long did you work for him?"

"I started about a year ago..."

"About when your "voice" started?"

"Yes, but at the time I didn't really notice it. I just felt like my intuition was working extra hard. I had just been laid off from my job as a research librarian and someone suggested—although, for the life of me, I couldn't tell you who it was—I apply to the senator as part of his research staff. I got the job. All too easy..." She wandered off and was again staring out the window.

I gave her some space. After all, we still had a long drive ahead of us. I could wait.

But I didn't have to wait long. She was back.

"I'm starting to think..."

"That The Voice steered you toward the job?" I asked.

"Yes. I hadn't really thought about it. I had just assumed it was a friend or colleague, but it wasn't. But it doesn't make sense."

I raised my eyebrows.

"Yeah, I know," she said. "You're questioning whether any of this makes sense."

"The jury is still out. Why doesn't this part make sense?"

"I guess it really does. Like I said, it seems The Voice had led me into a dangerous situation. But the thing is, over the last week, The Voice has saved my life a few times. Why would it put me there in the first place if it was just going to save my life?"

"I don't know. Maybe there was something you were supposed to see or uncover?" I just threw it out there. I really had no idea. I was still trying to process it all.

"And I did. And it was big. And Hillstrom is at the center of it. Now my life is effectively over. Really over if they catch me. Because of me four people have lost their lives—good people. And everybody thinks I killed them. And now I've put you in the middle of it."

"I'm sorry," she added. "I'm sorry I didn't tell you sooner. If you want to let me off now, I'll understand."

Strangely enough, I didn't.

All I said was, "So where does The Voice fit in now?"

"It's behind everything. It's the reason I left Washington, the reason I hit the road, and even the reason you picked me up. It's leading me somewhere. I just don't know where."

Chapter 3

She was quiet again, obviously trying to decide how to proceed. This time I broke the silence.

"Before you go on, I've gotta ask, why did you tell the family in the car that you heard dead people? Especially since I assume you are trying to stay under the radar."

Jess's eyes took on a mischievous glint. "They were annoying me. I felt like I had stepped into a revival meeting. They kept telling me that as a single girl hitchhiking, I was going to hell. All they talked about was Jesus, heaven, hell, and eternal damnation. Finally, I just blurted out, 'I hear dead people.' You've never seen a car stop so fast. I figured standing on the side of the road had to be better than that."

She quickly turned serious again. "I say all that, but in reality, I think it was The Voice, and I was just repeating what it was telling me. I think I needed to be dropped off there in order for you to pick me up."

"Do you always listen to The Voice?"

"I'm learning to. As I said, I'm alive because of it."

"So what did you discover working for Hillstrom?" I asked. I was anxious to get to the meat of the story.

"Part of the problem is that I don't really know. I don't know any details. All I know that it involves conspiracies within conspiracies. The worst kind of corruption. Corruption that could have a lasting effect on this country. The scary part? I almost bought into it. In fact," she looked away, "I did buy into it. That's why I signed the death sentences of four really good people. You asked me if I always listened to The Voice. I didn't that day and they are dead because of it."

She took a breath and began. Her story was amazingly simple, and yet, the ramifications it could have on the country were anything but simple. Getting my head around it was going to take some time.

She started with a statement. "Senator Gary Hillstrom doesn't exist."

She hesitated before going on. I don't think it was a dramatic pause—she didn't seem the type—it was more like she thought I was going to laugh at her, like I did at her "I hear dead people" comment. When she realized I was just listening, she continued.

"Gary Hillstrom isn't his real name."

"You mean he changed his name. That's not really uncommon."

"No, I mean his entire history—personal life, work history, everything—is made up."

"Wait a minute." Something wasn't adding up for me. "He was a state senator before running for the U.S. Senate. I remember that much."

"Right, he was," she answered. "What was he before that?"

"I don't know. I think he was in business or something."

"No. Everything prior to his run for the state Senate is fabricated."

"That's pretty hard to believe. He's running for public office.

He can't just make up a resume and hope no one notices. Even if he somehow made it through the process of becoming state senator, his opponent for the U.S. Senate would have scrutinized every aspect of his life. It couldn't happen."

I was beginning to doubt everything about her now.

"I know. It seems impossible. That's why I didn't believe it either. But humor me, because here's the scary part: Let's say his past was made up. What would it mean if the people digging into it uncovered nothing out of the ordinary?"

I had to think about that for a minute.

"It means you would have to have a hell of a lot of people in on the deception. It would be a conspiracy like no other. It would have to be planned years in advance."

"It would, wouldn't it."

"And the cost of creating his 'past' would run well into the millions of dollars. Maybe tens of millions."

"Yup."

"What about his childhood? His school records?"

"Supposedly he went to some church school up through high school. The place burned down and all records were lost. And he didn't go to college. That was part of his appeal—a politician who was really a common man."

"So you're saying this isn't just some guy wanting to get elected and lying about his past. This is a massive conspiracy orchestrated by people with unlimited resources and a long-term goal. Didn't I see that movie?"

Her voice dropped almost to a whisper. "Maybe, but I wasn't in it. I'm in this one and it's very real."

I was quiet for a few minutes while I chewed on it. Finally, I asked, "So where does The Voice fit in?"

"I don't know. I really don't. As overwhelming as all of this is—and I'll go into more detail later about what I do know—that's not the end of the story. There's something much deeper to all this. I think that's the reason I'm hearing The Voice. I think I'm supposed to find something, but I have no idea what."

We stopped at a rest area. I needed to stretch my legs, but more than that, I needed to clear my head. It was a flat, prairie-like rest area with a few rocks, almost no trees, a small restroom building, and lots of open space. Jess went into the restroom while I walked. Eventually I saw her come out of the building and lean against my car, just watching me. I didn't hurry. After about twenty minutes, I went in and relieved myself. When I came out, she was sitting on a bench in front of my car. I walked up to her.

"So, are you saying that the police are looking for you?"

"Not just the police. Hillstrom's men, too."

Then I had a thought. "I have a vague memory of hearing a story a few days ago about a manhunt for the murderer of four political staffers. Is that you?"

"It is. They were each killed by a single shot to the head. They were executed."

"Did they give your name on the news? I wasn't really listening."

"No. Not yet. I think they are trying to make it sound as if they don't have a suspect yet. Maybe to lull me into false sense of security. But they know it's me."

"How do you know?"

"I'll explain that soon. It'll make more sense then. But I think Hillstrom is using his influence to keep my name out of it. I think he wants to get to me first."

"Why? Do you have anything tangible they want? A CD or flash drive with damning evidence?"

"If I did, I would have already gone to the newspapers. No. I have nothing, which gives them time to find me. Without proof, I can't go anywhere. Who's going to believe me? I don't even know if you do."

And that was a good question. It was outlandish, to be sure. On the other hand, I didn't get to the position I had in sales by misreading people. She wasn't lying. The question was: Was she sane? Did it all happen the way she said, or did she just "believe" it happened? No, there was definitely sincerity coupled with sanity there. I believed her.

"Actually, I do, and that means you need some help. And since I have nothing to lose, it may as well be me that helps you. We have to do some planning and figure out the next steps. We'll stop for lunch, drive a few more hours after that, then find a hotel for the night. Hopefully we can come up with a strategy."

I looked over at her and saw misty eyes. "Thank you," she said, softly putting her hand on mine. "I'm sure you still have some doubts, and hopefully I'll be able to dispel them over time. But I don't know what I'd do if you didn't believe me at least a little bit."

We took the next exit and drove a couple of miles until we located a Burger King. Needing to stretch our legs, we opted to go inside. But the minute we walked through the door, Jess's demeanor changed. She looked around nervously and made a beeline for the restroom, leaving me standing there without a clue as to what had just happened.

While nothing about my encounter with Jess could be considered normal, this seemed out of character for the woman I had gotten to know over the last few hours. I could tell it wasn't just a case of an emergency bathroom run. This was something else. I quickly ordered a couple of burgers and fries, having no idea if it was what she might want, but feeling that it would be prudent not to wait for her before placing our order.

They rang up my purchase and handed me the bag of food. Do I wait here, in the car, or close to the bathroom? Taking a seat in the restaurant seemed the best move. Five minutes passed. Various customers came in and out—the normal Burger King crowd. But then two men who had a different appearance about them walked through the door. Yes, they were ordering food, but there was something else. They were looking for something—or someone. They did it furtively, but without a doubt, they were searching the faces of the customers.

They weren't cops. That much was obvious. But they had a "security" aura about them. P.I.'s? Bounty hunters? I couldn't tell. But my gut told me they were looking for Jess. If that was the case, how did she know? We arrived almost ten minutes before them, but she was disturbed from the moment we walked into the place.

I watched them as nonchalantly as they watched others. They were focusing only on the women. Finally, they got their orders, and with a final glance around, they left. I kept watching as they got in their car—a late model Ford—and headed back toward the highway. I waited a couple of minutes, then went back to the restrooms. I hadn't seen any other women go back there, so I was pretty sure Jess was alone.

I knocked on the door and said, "Jess? You okay? They're gone." What made me say that last part was beyond me, but I knew it was the right thing to say.

She opened the door cautiously, saw that I was alone, and came out. She was a mess, visibly shaking and wide-eyed.

"What happened?" I asked. "How did you know?"

"Know what?"

"That two guys were in here looking for you. At least, I think they were."

"Ahh," was her reply.

"Ahh?"

She shook her head as if to say, "not here," so we walked out to the car without speaking. Once we got in and I had locked the doors, she seemed to breathe easier. I moved the car over to a more secluded corner of the lot to make her feel a bit safer. I offered her a burger, but she shook her head.

Finally, she said, "I didn't know anyone was coming in to look for me, but it makes sense. When I walked into the place, I had a message to run to the bathroom…"

"What was the message," I interrupted.

"I can't really tell you. It was just a message. It wasn't anything spoken, no flashing lights, nothing pushed me. I just knew, and I knew that I had to go in there quickly, that I didn't have much time."

"The Voice?"

"Yes, but as is usually the case, I had no idea why. That's why I didn't come out."

"You didn't get an 'all-clear' message?"

She gave me a look, as if I was making fun of her.

"No, I'm serious. You got the message to go in. How would you get a message that it's okay to come out?"

"I did. You called to me."

That made me stop. It was confusing and was becoming more so by the minute. Did that mean I was part of the message? Or did The Voice know that I would let her know? I was feeling a little bit of overload.

"Don't try to find an explanation," she said, looking at my furrowed brow. "I've had a year of this and I still can't explain it."

She seemed better, but still a bit shaky. Again she turned down the burger, so I started the car and pulled out.

"What did they look like?" she asked.

"Pretty average," I answered. "Two white guys, probably mid-thirties, definitely not cops. They were checking out all the women, but not in 'that' way. They were definitely looking for someone. It seemed logical that that person was you."

"Hillstrom's men," she stated.

"But why out here?"

"I don't know. He seems to have unlimited resources and I'm on the run. They probably know that I have no money, so to get anywhere I'd have to hitch, and the highways are the easiest places to get rides that will take you far away. Maybe they did the math and figured how far I could've gotten. I really don't know. I just know they are out there looking for me. I can't help but to think that it's just a matter of time before they find me, and now you."

Chapter 4

Once we were on the road Jess seemed to calm down. I kept an eye out for the Ford, and over the next couple of hours of driving, I got more of the story.

When Jess signed on, Hillstrom had taken an immediate shine to her, and vice-versa. Jess was in an office in a different building from Hillstrom, and so didn't see him on a daily basis, but he made an effort to stop by at least once a week to thank his research staff for all their hard work. Occasionally he would take one or more out for lunch. Over time, the occasional lunch with Jess became the occasional dinner.

"He was absolutely charming," she told me. "He never said or did anything inappropriate, but he made me feel special. I'll admit, I developed a bit of a crush on him."

"Did you sleep with him?" I immediately regretted the question. Was I a little jealous? However, it didn't seem to faze her.

"No, although in all honesty, I was waiting for him to ask. If he had, I think I would have." A little more staring into space, then she returned. "I had a lot of time to think while standing on the side of the road. That was all intentional on his part. He would never have asked me to sleep with him. By keeping me at arm's reach, I was like a school-girl. I would have done anything for him, with the hope that someday ... God, I feel so stupid!"

"Don't," I said. "You were manipulated by a master. You had no control over it. He made sure of that. I was a vice president of sales. I would have given anything to have someone with his skills on my team." I realized that my old profession was seeming rather silly to me now.

"Thank you. But I realize now that, over time, he was subtly dropping hints that some people were out to tarnish his reputation. He must have been good, because I had no idea that he was even doing it. He was developing my loyalty, and I think he was doing the same to others in my office. We were all becoming spies for him and didn't even know it."

"Spies for what?"

"Don't know. Each other? Maybe he did that to all his staffers. Maybe they were all so loyal to him they would rat out a colleague if need be. I think he was just covering all his bases. Maybe he was paranoid. But judging by all that has happened, I think he had deeper reasons for wanting to spy on people. I think he was hiding a lot and wanted to make sure it stayed hidden. Anyway, so when my co-worker Greg came to me with information he said he was going to bring to the press, that's when I made the mistake that got my four co-workers killed."

She explained that Greg had been working on some background material on the senator at the request of Hillstrom's official biographer.

"An autobiography by Hillstrom is due out next year. But by the amount of work this biographer had us doing, I really doubt Hillstrom is writing any of it himself," she said.

Jess said that Greg had run across some fairly obscure inconsistencies in the senator's background.

"Greg was like a bloodhound," she explained. "He was by far the best researcher there. He really should have been a reporter.

Hillstrom loved Greg. Greg did a lot of great work for him, and his research skills were the source of many of the senator's bills in Congress, popular public causes, not to mention dirt on his opponents. But his skill got him in trouble this time."

As Greg dug deeper, more was revealed. Inconsistency led to inconsistency. All minor by themselves, but when put together, they must have set off an alarm in the mind of a master researcher.

"It was obvious for about a month that something was bothering Greg, and as each week went by, he was getting more … well … I don't know if 'agitated' or 'excited' would be the more appropriate word. The loyal staffer was agitated, but I think the researcher part of him was excited. He was getting totally caught up in the process. Finally, a few days ago—maybe a week, I've lost track of time—he had us meet him for dinner at some out of the way restaurant. There were five of us who worked in the office. We were pretty close, as people in a small office sometimes get. I think the four of them were a little closer because they had been together longer. I only say that because the other three believed him immediately, but I was having trouble with it."

"So what did Greg say?" I asked.

"Basically everything I've already told you. He kept in generalities and didn't show us any of his research. He purposely didn't go into specifics. Maybe it was his way of protecting us. He said it was on his laptop and printed copies and flash drive copies were in a safe deposit box somewhere."

"Which," I interrupted, "are probably gone now. If Hillstrom has the reach you say he has, the laptop would be history and finding and accessing his box would be simple for them. That proof is long gone."

"I agree. I came to that conclusion too. Anyway, Greg said he had some reporter friends he was going to give the story to. I asked him if he was sure, because the wrong information could ruin Gary's career—yes, we all called Hillstrom by his first name. He insisted. Greg said the public had a right to know. He had obviously made up his mind."

"And the other three agreed?"

"As I said, I think they believed him, but they had doubts about his plan to make it public. We all really liked Gary, and they weren't sure if Greg had gotten a little too caught up in it all. But in the end, they went along with his decision."

"What did you do?"

"I killed my friends. I went home troubled by all that Greg had said and woke up the next morning with The Voice very emphatically saying, 'Run!' But I didn't. All of Hillstrom's mind control—if you want to call it that—kicked in. I really thought Greg was jumping the gun with his information. And frankly, it really sounded too ridiculous to be true, so my loyalty to Gary kicked in and I called his office from my cell phone when I was on my way to work and asked to speak to him. He was always very accessible, so I got through immediately."

Her eyes misted over again.

"I tried to say it so Greg wouldn't get in trouble. You know, talking about his enthusiasm for his research, and all that. But eventually we got to the part where Greg was going to the newspapers. He took it all in stride and thanked me for my loyalty. He assured me that Greg wouldn't get in trouble, but also let me know what a serious blow to his credibility it would be if Greg passed it on to the newspapers. He said he'd go over to our office and talk to Greg and clear up the details he was mistaken about."

"Did you go to the office?"

"Almost, but no. The Voice came again the minute I hung up. Again it said, 'Run! Now!' As it said it, there was a parking lot sign that read 'Park your car here all day for $15.' I don't know why, but I knew it was a message, so I pulled in and parked my car and hopped on the Metro. I took it to the stop near the office. All of a sudden, I was scared. I had all kinds of chatter in my head. The Voice wasn't exactly saying anything, but it seemed frantic somehow. It was scaring me. So I got off the Metro and went into a Starbucks across the street from the office. I decided to call Greg and confess what I had done, but before I could call, I saw the four of them leaving the office with a couple of guys. They got into a car and that was the last I saw of them."

I could see it was becoming a struggle to control her emotions. "What did you do?"

"Nothing. I sat in that Starbucks for hours, watching the front of my office building, hoping I'd see my friends come back. But I knew they weren't ever coming back. I just felt it. Finally, it had to have been mid-afternoon, I went to the closest ATM and took out a hundred dollars—that's all I had in my account—and hopped back on the Metro to Union Station. I bought the cheapest ticket I could find to someplace as far from Washington as possible, that would still leave me with a few dollars. I ended up going to Charlottesville. Not very far, but at least away from Washington. I've been hitching since then."

"When did you find out about your friends?"

"Late that afternoon. I was in a coffee shop having a muffin— it was about all I could afford—when I saw a police car pull up. Two Virginia State Troopers came in and ordered coffee. As they were leaving, they got a radio call telling them to be on the lookout for me. They actually named me. Do you have any idea what that feels like? Then they described me and called me a fugitive from justice, accused of murdering four people. Because they were members of a senator's staff, Homeland Security was involved, so it became a priority. I heard later on a radio how they were killed."

A thought came to me. "Well, there's no doubt in my mind that you were set up."

"Why?"

"If Hillstrom just wanted to get rid of those four, he would have had them killed and then hidden the bodies—sunk them to the bottom of the Potomac, or something. The fact that they were found so fast, and you were accused so quickly, tells me that this was set up to make you the fall-guy. Spreading the word via the police is the easiest way to catch you."

It was getting dark and I was on the lookout for a hotel.

"The good news," I said, "is that it sounds like you were able to skip town without them noticing, so we'll assume they don't know where you are. The bad news is if they are as powerful as you say, we don't know their reach. But since we don't have any control over that, we'll stick to the things we do have control of." I was trying to think of every spy novel I had ever read. What were the basics for getting lost?

"I left my computer when I said goodbye to my old life," I began, "but I still have my phone. So we can go on the Internet to get more ideas on how to keep you hidden. But a couple of things come to mind. Do you still have your cell phone?"

"No, I thought of that—them tracing my phone's GPS—so I smashed it when I was leaving Washington. I haven't called anyone from anywhere. My parents are both dead, and I have no siblings. I still have my credit card on me, but I haven't used it."

"I've got my credit card and cash, so we should destroy yours anyway, just to be safe—so you don't use it by mistake. You'll have to change your appearance. Change the color of your hair."

She was looking at me.

"What?" I asked. "You don't want to change your hair color?"

She gave that little smile. "I've changed the color of my hair more often than you've brushed your teeth. No, it's not that. I was just trying to figure out … Why are you doing this? You've had every reason in the world to jettison me and move on. You don't know me. You don't know if I'm a total loon, or worse, a con artist. And if I am telling the truth, you now have a bulls-eye on your back. So why are you helping me?"

As I was trying to come up with an answer, I spotted a decent-looking Marriott from the highway and took an exit that said Deming—I guess we were in New Mexico—and pulled into the parking lot, parking a fair distance from the front door. I turned off the engine and sat. After a minute, I responded.

"My life ended with Karen's death. I assume you don't have any children." She shook her head. "There is no way to explain the deep grief you feel when you lose a child. 'Shattered' is the only word that comes to mind, and that doesn't even come close. I have a gun in my trunk. I had visions of pulling off the highway someplace out here, in an area like this—Texas, New Mexico, or Arizona—of walking into the desert, and ending it. Let the buzzards and desert animals take care of my body. The problem is, there is still a tiny particle of me that wants to stay alive. And I have no idea why. When my money runs out, what am going to do? I can't go back to my old life, my old career. I never liked it to begin with. I don't see myself taking a job washing dishes in some small-town diner for the rest of my life, eventually being known as the crazy old guy with the mysterious past. I was hoping my brother could help set me straight when I get up there, but that's expecting a lot. No, until I met you, I was just running out the string, delaying the inevitable."

I paused, then continued, knowing that I had made my decision. "As whacked out as your story is, it gives me some sort of purpose. If you're telling the truth, and God knows, I think you just might be, is it possible that I might be able to redeem myself in some way for Karen's death? All I can say is your 'Voice' steered you in the right direction when it picked me. I have absolutely nothing left to lose. I'm probably the safest person you could be with."

She leaned over and gave me a kiss on the cheek. "Thank you."

"Okay, here's how we should do this. I'm afraid you're going to have to share a room with me. I think you should stay as far off the grid as possible. I don't know what kind of crazy monitoring equipment they have nowadays, but they could be keeping an eye on hotels. If a guy is traveling alone for days, then he suddenly requests two rooms, or a room for two, it might flag something in their supercomputer. So, I'll get a room for one and bring in all the luggage. Then we can go get some dinner. That sound good?"

"I'm still not capable of making decisions, so I'll trust your judgment. I never would have thought about them checking hotel anomalies like that, so I'm comfortable leaving it up to you. In the movies if they are trying to stay anonymous, they pay cash at hotels. Should you do that?"

"That's not as easy as it once was. I will pay cash, but I'll still have to leave my credit card for the deposit. As long as they don't know who I am, I think I'm okay."

I checked in while Jess waited in the car. As they gave me my key card, I heard the name Hillstrom and walked over to the bar, where CNN was displayed on a big screen TV. Staring at me was a 60-inch version of Jess. Luckily, it wasn't a great picture of her—probably her driver's license photo—and she looked like about a million other women. I just caught enough of the report to know that the prime suspect was one Jessica Norton. So far, they seemed to be concentrating their search in the general DC area, but I knew that would expand nationwide soon. Maybe it already had.

"Seems like all the good-looking chicks turn out to be murderers," said the bartender. He was looking at me, and I realized there was no one else in the bar.

"Makes you not want to date anymore," I replied.

"You said it. Can I get you anything?"

"No thanks. I was just checking out the bar. I'll probably stop in later. I gotta go bring in my bags."

"Okay, see you later."

I felt like running to the car, but I restrained myself. When I got there, I said to Jess, "Change of plans. We're doing takeout. And you're going to come in through the side entrance."

"Something's happened."

"Yeah, your picture is front and center on the evening news."

"Oh shit."

"It's not a great picture, so you're probably pretty safe for the moment. Hopefully no one at that truck stop, the Burger King, or your evangelist family, will put two and two together. But I'm going to run into a drugstore and pick up some hair color. Dark brown? Do you wear contacts?" She shook her head. "Okay, I'll pick up some reading glasses that you can wear if you're out in public. I'll get the lowest magnification so you won't trip over things. And some sunglasses. Every little change helps, I suppose. Of course, what do I know? It's not like I've ever done this before. Chinese okay with you?"

She nodded her head dumbly.

It was weird. Jess's life was on the line, and by association, so was mine, and yet, I was excited. I don't know why, but I felt motivated about things again. I was actually getting into this!

Chapter 5

We were sitting in the room an hour later, an array of Chinese food cartons spread out in front of us. I was hungry, but I noticed Jess just picking at her food. I suppose having the whole country on the lookout for you could affect your appetite.

"Maybe I've watched too many movies," I said between bites. "But it occurred to me that just about everything in this country is built around technology, so the safest thing we can do is avoid it as much as possible. Stay away from toll roads—toll booths have cameras—take the smaller roads. If we can get to Alaska without incident, my brother and I can keep you smuggled there until ... well, until something."

"What do we do when we hit the Canadian border?" Jess asked.

"Hadn't thought of that. We'll come up with something, I guess." I changed subjects. "Any peep out of The Voice?"

"Nothing," she answered. "It's not like it carries on conversations with me, but I've kind of gotten used to hearing it."

"So tell me more how it works. I know it told you to run. You said you think the parking sign was another message. How can you be sure? Does it ever talk in complete sentences? Is it male or female?"

"Definitely male. The messages come in lots of different forms, which is why it's so hard to explain. As I said, in the beginning it was more like intuition. It progressed into my dreams at night. I'd wake up knowing that somebody had just told me something. After a minute I'd usually remember it. Sometimes I'll be in a public place and I'll hear someone give me an instruction. I'll quickly look around and realize that no one near me had said it. Sometimes it's a little more emphatic, like it was in Washington, and sometimes I'll just be reading a book or a magazine, or even a menu, and a sentence will pop out at me with some sort of instruction. When I look back down at the page, that sentence isn't there anymore. How did I know about the parking sign, or using the restroom at the Burger King? I can't really tell you. I think I'm just getting used to the communication in all its forms."

"Was the 'run' message typical of the kind you get?" I cut in.

"No. As I said, that was much stronger. In fact, it was almost pleading, now that I reflect back. But usually it's simple messages like, 'Cross the street here' or 'Take the Metro right now.' Usually not words, just images. Sometimes even an image with a word. Some—especially over the last week or so—have kept me hidden or even saved my life, but most of the messages over the last year have been pretty benign. I'm not even sure why many of them came. I mean, I know where to cross a street."

"Could it be that The Voice has been training you to listen to it?" I asked. "Maybe it knew that you had to get used to its presence before it could make any life-changing suggestions. It had to become part of you."

"Funny you say that, because at times The Voice brings me a lot of comfort, like it's a part of me. Maybe you're right and it has been training me."

It was getting late and I suggested we get some sleep. They had given me a king-sized bed and I didn't want to raise any flags with the front desk by asking for two queens. But I figured we were adults and could survive being in the same bed. The truth was, I had become quite attracted to Jess, but this wasn't the time or place to act on it. She had other things to occupy her mind at the moment.

She had run out of her apartment quickly, without packing anything, so I knew tomorrow I would be in the women's section of some department store stocking up on clothes and other items for her. In the meantime, I let her wear one of my shirts to sleep in.

I took a shower first, so as to give Jess all the time she needed when she took hers. I had gotten into the habit over the last couple of weeks of sleeping in my underwear, but for this occasion I dug into my suitcase for my pajamas and put them on in the foggy bathroom.

Jess's shower seemed to go on forever. It must have felt especially good to her. Calming as much as cleansing. I couldn't imagine having to leave home the way she did, without time to think, without time to prepare. But she was doing pretty well, considering. While I, too, had to leave my home under stressful circumstances, it was completely different. Like Jess, I was totally lost, but unlike her, I had had time to prepare—too much time maybe. Anyway, while I was heartbroken, she was scared. Terrified, really.

I thought about The Voice. I'd always been a pretty common-sense kind of guy, and communication from the grave—or wherever it was coming from—didn't fit into the realm of "normal" for me. But what were the odds of someone in her situation, being scared beyond rational thought, meeting up with someone who was no longer afraid of anything? And on the other side of that, her entering my life provided me with a purpose at the exact time I needed one. Okay, it was a little spooky.

Jess finally came out of the bathroom. She was wearing the

shirt I had lent her, but all I could think of was what was under that shirt. Oh, it was going to be a tough sleeping night for me!

She crawled in next to me, again gave me a kiss on the cheek, and thanked me one more time for everything I had done for her. I looked at her again before we turned out the lights. The shower had been cleansing, but the stress in her face was still there. Add to that the sheer exhaustion she must've felt. If anyone needed a good night's sleep, it was Jess.

*****

It turned out not to be a tough night for me after all. I must've fallen asleep the minute my head hit the pillow. I awoke to the smell of coffee. I looked over at Jess, sitting cross-legged on a chair by the window. She was staring into space. It was a dark day, with a light drizzle coming down. There were probably some hills in the distance, but the clouds obscured them. I looked at my watch. Eight-thirty. That was the latest I'd slept in years. Jess heard me moving and came out of her catatonic state.

"The coffee isn't great, but it's coffee," she said, stretching.

"How did you sleep?"

"Like I was in a coma." She paused. "The Voice came just as I was waking up. Kind of a half dream. It was an actual sentence — maybe because I wasn't awake yet."

I was alert now. "What did it ... uh, he ... say?"

"'It all starts in Homer.' I have no idea what it means."

I did. I felt a shiver travel down my spine. "It means that, for whatever reason, I'm not supposed to drop you off along the road. You're definitely coming with me to Alaska."

She cocked her head and looked at me.

"I never told you where in Alaska I was going," I said. "My

brother lives in Homer."

"Whoa."

"Yeah. I guess you're meant to chill out for a while."

"I'm not so sure."

"What do you mean?"

"That Voice has been guiding me toward something. I don't know what yet, but something. To just lead me someplace to hide out doesn't feel right. Maybe there's another reason I was supposed to meet you."

"You mean you think Homer might be hiding a clue?"

"Honestly, I don't know. But it seems to make sense. Also, it said 'it all starts in Homer,' not 'Hide in Homer.' That sounds pretty significant."

"You're right, it does."

I decided right then that I was either all in or all out, and I knew the answer to that. The Homer thing had rattled me. Not only had I not said a word to her about Homer, I had nothing on me or in my luggage about it. It wasn't even in my brother's information on my phone. Only his cell phone number, and that wasn't a Homer exchange. There was absolutely no way she could have known. Add that to all the other little oddities and I had to believe it was happening. She really was hearing a voice.

"We have a couple of hours 'til check-out," I said, looking at my watch. "Will that give you enough time to color your hair?"

"Yeah," she answered, looking at the bottle. "This is a pretty simple process."

"Okay, then tell me what you need for clothes and whatever. I'll go find a Wal-Mart—this is the southwest, there's gotta be a Wal-Mart—and I'll pick it up for you."

"I feel really guilty. You're buying everything for me and you don't even know me. I can't even contribute."

"Jess, look, this is something I can do, and something I want to do. Don't worry about it. So tell me what you need."

We made a list. Jeans, blouses, underwear, hair brush, toiletries, sneakers, and much more. I didn't know how I was going to possibly get it done in two hours, but Jess pointed out the Wal-Mart from her view at the window, so luckily I wouldn't have to waste any time looking for it. Once we were done, Jess headed to the bathroom with the hair color and I grabbed a few hundred dollars—I felt more comfortable paying cash—and went out the door, not looking forward to my shopping spree.

In fact, it wasn't bad at all. I accomplished it in a little more than an hour. I had her sizes written down and grabbed what seemed appropriate. I figured we could fine-tune her wardrobe later. I headed over to the sports department and bought two boxes of .40-caliber ammunition. I really couldn't imagine needing another 200 rounds of ammo, but I also had no idea what I was getting myself into. And being in a state where buying bullets was as easy as buying potato chips, I figured better safe than sorry.

I arrived back at the hotel a few minutes before eleven. I knocked on the door to warn her that I was back, then used my key card to enter. I was greeted by a dark brunette.

· "What do you think?" she asked.

Over the last twenty-four hours, I had become quite attracted to Jess, so blonde or brunette, it didn't matter to me. As far as I was concerned, she was spectacular. I didn't put it quite that way, though.

"Looks great," was my safe response. "So what's your natural color?"

"Beats me. I can't remember that far back," she answered with a laugh. "No, actually, believe it or not, it's blonde. Those stereotypes of 'dumb blondes' are real. Not the dumb part, but the label. People do look at you as if you're stupid. When I turned twenty, I started coloring my hair to escape everything about being a blonde. I wasn't very confident back then. I know who I am now, so I stay my natural color most of the time, unless I get a whim to change it. I haven't been this color in a few years, so nobody really knows me like this. I thought about cutting my hair, but it's actually longer now than normal—I missed my last appointment—so I figure I'm better off letting it grow."

"Well, hopefully I didn't do too badly shopping for you." I put the bags down on the bed.

All in all, I think I did okay. She gave a couple of the tops funny looks, but was way too polite to make any critical comments. The sneakers actually fit—I had been worried about that—as did the sandals. I could tell the shorts weren't exactly her style, but they would do. She was happy with the jeans though.

After thanking me for the tenth time, she retreated to the bathroom with her treasures, especially excited to use the toothbrush. When she came out, she was a new woman.

"I can't tell you how good it feels to be out of the clothes I've been wearing for days now."

I had also picked up a suitcase for her, and she proceeded to carefully pack it.

"I still don't think we should go to a sit-down place for breakfast." I looked at my watch. "Or rather, lunch. I think we should pick up something for the road, then talk about the route we want to take to Alaska."

"Sounds good to me. I can live on take-out for as long as is necessary."

There was an optimistic tone to her voice. It was almost as if she had forgotten there was a massive search on for her. Almost. Or maybe she just wanted to feel normal for a little while and had pushed it all away. It would all come back far too quickly, so I tried not to do or say anything to trigger that reality. Not yet.

We left by way of the side entrance, the fugitive and her accomplice.

*****

I stopped at a Subway and we picked up sandwiches and chips. I think I had now made a total eating transition from my old stodgy life.

She dug into her sandwich with a vengeance. I realized that she had been so upset the night before that she hadn't eaten much of the Chinese food, and she was famished.

She stopped chewing and seemed to be trying to remember something. I was quiet while she went through her exercise.

"I had a dream about Las Vegas last night. I just remembered it." She looked at me. "Think that means anything?"

"Ever been to Vegas?" I asked.

"Nope," she said, taking another bite.

"Then, yeah, I do. Why would you dream about someplace you've never been?"

"I could picture the strip and the hotels. But then, maybe I've just seen too many episodes of *CSI*."

"It kind of makes sense. I was thinking that we should head north before we hit California. Go up through Utah and Idaho. Less congested."

"And you think Vegas is less congested?" she asked.

I chuckled. "No, but it's a great place to get lost in. We can blend into the background. Hey, I'm willing to listen to The Voice, even if it wasn't technically The Voice."

"There is no such thing as 'technically The Voice'," she said. "A dream seems to be as real as an actual voice, and for that matter, a lot more common than an actual voice. I had a feeling it was a message, but I wanted to get your feedback on it."

"Vegas it is. I haven't been there in a couple of years."

"Don't they have cameras all over the place? Could that be dangerous for me?"

"They do, but we'll figure out a way to keep you disguised."

With that decision made, we got on the road.

After she had finished her food, Jess said, "Okay, so you go first."

"For what?"

"Your life story."

"Why, you need something to put you to sleep?"

"No, I want something to keep my mind off the fact that if they find me, I'm dead. Every minute of every waking hour, that's on my mind, and I can't tell you how scared I am. Diversions are very welcome." Her voice was tinged with a fear-based anger—anger at whoever had ruined her life.

She had been able to fake a light persona to some extent up until now, which made me forget just how frightening this was for her. I felt a little embarrassed. I think she sensed this and her mood changed.

"Besides," she added with a slight smile, "I want to know who you are."

A minute went by. She just looked at me expectantly.

"Okay." And I started.

Chapter 6

Talking about your life is supposed to evoke remembrances of a happy childhood—or of a difficult childhood. We have memories of family trips, barbecues, holidays, playing catch, or being read to by our parents. Or, we have memories of abuse—emotional or physical—turmoil, yelling, sadness, and anger. Either way, the memories involve emotion in some way.

Not me. I never realized it at the time, but my home was completely devoid of emotion. You don't necessarily notice these things as a kid. You don't really know what's supposed to be normal. You don't compare your family to your friends' families, at least maybe not until you're a teenager.

So as I described my childhood to Jess, I could see an expression of sympathy forming. Or maybe it was a look of pity. At minimum, it was incomprehension. Could someone really grow up like that?

My father was an Army drill sergeant. My early years were spent going from base to base. Nothing ever felt permanent in those days. Friends never lasted long. Either we'd move or they would. Our house was never "homey", it always had a transient feel to it. When he became a drill sergeant, things seemed to settle down. He was stationed at Fort Jackson, in South Carolina. We were there for what seemed like a long time.

"It's funny," I said to Jess. "On my way here, I passed Fort Jackson when I was on Interstate 20. Okay, maybe my thoughts were elsewhere, but you'd think I would get some sort of feeling of nostalgia. But no. Nothing. Not a thing."

"So what made it emotionless?" she asked. "Whether you know it or not, you are not being emotionless as you describe your childhood. I'm sensing a tremendous amount of sadness."

"Now. Not then. Yes, now I feel sad. For years after my parents died I felt nothing but anger toward them. I guess that's finally dissipated. You're right. Now it's just a profound sadness."

I explained to Jess that the life of a drill sergeant isn't easy. Long hours and a tremendous amount of stress. I didn't see much of my father, but when I did, he really didn't have time for my brother and me. When he was home, he would spend hours washing and waxing his car—a vintage Pontiac Trans Am—usually with a buddy or two.

"He was one of those people who kept everything bottled up. He never talked much. Maybe it's because he talked and yelled so much in his job. When he did talk, it was to reminisce about his teenage years—he seemed to be happiest then—before he had to enter life for real. When he wasn't home, or at work, he'd be at the bar with those same buddies, his fellow drill sergeants. I can't say I really knew my father. Looking back, I think he was really unhappy—unhappy with his career choice, with my mother, with just about everything. Even his Trans Am. He spent a lot of time with it, but it wasn't his 'pride and joy' like you see in the movies. It was just something else to occupy his time."

"Listening to you, I feel like putting a gun to my head," said Jess. "That's really depressing. I get the feeling your mother wasn't much different."

"If there were two people made for each other, it was them. I think they both had a secret death wish. My mother had no personality whatsoever. Again, you really don't notice it as a kid, but looking back I can see it. She went through the motions. She got together with the other Army wives, but I think it was more because she felt she had to. I don't have a lot of memories of the other wives as time went on. I think they slowly distanced themselves from her. She wasn't a horrible mother from the standpoint of keeping us fed and clean, helping us with our homework, things like that, but there wasn't anything behind it. I don't think she ever formed that mother-child bond with us."

"Anyway," I continued, though not enjoying the conversation at all, "my father retired when he hit the twenty-year mark and earned his pension. I think he just wanted out. I was in my teens at that point. We moved up to Massachusetts, where they had both grown up, and my father got a job at a Home Depot. He seemed happier there than in the Army, but he also seemed lost. Maybe he needed the Army structure. I don't know, but by that time I doubt he was able to change—either one of them. I went off to college when I graduated high school, happy to get out of there. They spent their evenings drinking. I think my mother had been a secret drinker for years. A year after I left home, I got word that my mother had liver cancer. She died soon after that. A year later, my father followed. He had pancreatic cancer. Again, it was quick. Age-wise, they were very young—mid-forties—but in reality, they were old. Old and tired."

Jess seemed stunned by my story—obviously very different from her own. "You seem to have come out of it okay," she finally said.

"It's taken a long time. I promised myself I'd never be that kind of parent to Karen, and I wasn't. I loved her with my whole being. But I didn't totally escape my parents' clutches. I've been tightly wound my whole adult life. In my mind, I blamed my wife for the distance between us, but I now know it was me. I've gotta tell you that I feel more free right now than I ever have in my life. I'm finally loosening up."

"I'm glad the whole federal government on my trail could help," replied Jess, trying to inject some much-needed levity into the situation. But I barely heard it.

"I kind of feel guilty saying that. It sounds like I'm saying that I'm free now that my daughter is dead. But I don't mean it like that. I'd like to think that if she was with us right now I'd be feeling the same freedom."

"I didn't take it that way. It's obvious that you loved your daughter very much."

And then out of the blue the tears came and gushed down my face like a flash flood. Luckily, I had just seen a sign for an approaching rest area. I could barely see as I exited off the highway. I pulled into a spot far from any other cars and just sobbed. Jess undid our seatbelts and pulled me over to her, holding me tightly.

Long after the tears had ended, she still held me. Finally, I lifted my head in embarrassment.

"I'm sorry," I said. "You're the one with the world after you. I should be holding you. I don't know what brought that on."

"I do," she answered. "It was partly the death of your daughter, but mostly I think it was the death of your old life—your daughter, your parents, your childhood that really wasn't a childhood at all. It's all gone. And that's why you feel so free now. There's nothing left of who you used to be. You can now be anyone or anything you want to be. But it's also scary for you. There's a lot of loss. It's like your old life ceased to exist."

I put my hand behind her head and guided it down to where our lips met, and I kissed her. I could feel her body relax as she gave in, her tongue touching my lips, then exploring my mouth. The kiss lingered until finally, we came up for air. Nothing was said. We held each other gently, but firmly. We had each found an island of safety in our messed-up lives, and we didn't want to let it go. Eventually, we released each other. But Jess wasn't finished. She leaned over and kissed me again, running her hands across my face, through my hair, and down my back. The second kiss lasted longer than the first. Finally, our lips parted and I looked at Jess, really noticing for the first time the deep blue of her eyes.

"Let's get some air," she said.

We got out of the car and walked, hand in hand, just soaking in the moment. Eventually, we sat under a tree and held each other. We were in no hurry to move. Here, we didn't have to think about who might be after Jess—and me by association—or how to get her out of it. We were sitting under a tree in the middle of nowhere. No one was going to find us here.

Finally, after a couple of hours basking in the sun and in each other's presence, barely saying a dozen words the whole time, we got up and brushed ourselves off.

"We're not going to make Vegas tonight," I said. "We're not too far from Phoenix and Scottsdale, so we can find a place there for the night."

Neither of us voiced it, but there was another reason we didn't want to drive that far.

We found a Sheraton and I repeated the check-in process from the night before. I used the key card to let us into the room and had barely set down the luggage when Jess was in my arms kissing me. She pulled me over to the bed as we frantically tore at each other's clothes. In seconds, we were in bed naked, still clawing, as if there were more clothes to come off. We rolled the length of the bed, frantically kissing and feeling every inch of skin we could find. We were breathing heavily, and the sweat from my body merged with hers, creating a fine sheen between us. Finally, we reined in the pace a bit and took our time exploring. Slowly and tenderly, I ran my hands the length of her body, starting with her toes and moving my way up her legs, thighs, and hips. She was working from the other direction, starting with my head, down to my chest and stomach, until our hands met in the middle. The touching instantly increased to a frantic pace, until finally I entered her and we exploded together.

For a little while our lives were forgotten. No one was chasing us. Shadowy government conspiracies and memories of a lost child didn't exist. It would all still be there when we emerged from our emotional oasis, but for now it was only the two of us.

Afterward, we laid there, completely exhausted. We fell asleep in each other's arms and woke up an hour later craving food.

"What time is it?" I asked softly.

"I don't know," Jess answered. "I don't want to move." She had her head on my chest.

I craned my neck and caught a glimpse of the clock. "It's after nine."

"Can we do Chinese again? I kind of missed out last night."

"Yeah. Most Chinese restaurants are still open this late. Maybe someone delivers."

I called the front desk and was given the name of a close Chinese restaurant that delivered. I called and put in a large order—larger than we'd ever be able to eat, but we just couldn't decide. A combination of hunger and a separation from reality was guiding us.

The scent of sex hung heavily in the air. We took turns in the shower and were reasonably refreshed when the knock on the door came. Jess hid in the bathroom while I paid the man for the boxcar-sized delivery of food, and we quickly dug in, not saying much until we had at least sated the worst of our hunger.

At eleven, we turned on the local news and were immediately brought back to the bad dream Jess's life had become. Jess was the first story, and the news wasn't good. In the thirty hours since I had seen her picture on the TV in the bar at the Marriott, her story had snowballed, catching the American fancy as only a story this sensational—as promoted by the news media—could. The cocoon of relative anonymity that we thought we were living in had broken open, and reality had emerged.

Newscaster: *"We start tonight's broadcast with the Jessica Norton story. Federal authorities have announced that progress is being made in the search for Norton, sought in connection with the brutal slaying of her four co-workers, all staff members of Senator Gary Hillstrom of Massachusetts. Since the story first broke naming her as the suspect, hundreds of calls have come into the FBI tip line with purported sightings of Norton. While most have led nowhere, FBI spokesperson Michelle Carter announced at a press conference this evening that some of the information has proven helpful.*

Carter said that Norton was seen taking a bus from Washington, DC, to Charlottesville, Virginia, the day of the murders. Trucker Wayne Henderson confirms picking up a blonde woman he says was Norton in Charlottesville and dropping her off in Atlanta."

Wayne Henderson: *"She seemed really nervous and didn't talk the entire eight-hour trip. She kinda huddled down in the seat. A couple of times a cop or ambulance went by with their sirens on, and it definitely made her nervous. I was kinda glad to get rid of her in Atlanta."*

Newscaster: *Carter also said Norton was spotted two days ago in a truck stop off Interstate 20 in Texas with a man. Witnesses said she seemed emotional. While the witnesses couldn't provide a description of the man,* *other than that he was white, authorities are hoping he will come forward with more information as to the whereabouts of Norton. No video surveillance was available from the truck stop. Meanwhile, a nationwide search for Norton, thought to be armed and dangerous, continues.*

I looked over at Jess, who was staring at the screen. Finally, she looked at me, fear in her eyes. I put my arm around her.

"You'll be okay. I'm going to keep you as safe as possible. Even more than that, you're going to have to trust in The Voice. It seems to be protecting you."

"I know. This is just so surreal though."

"Well, I've done a complete and thorough search, and I can assure them you are definitely not armed," I said, hoping to break the tension.

It didn't work. She looked at me with a fragility that was positively scary, then put her head down on my lap and started crying. A moment later she jumped up and ran to the bathroom, where she threw up. I followed her in and held her head the way I did when Karen would get sick. In fact, at that moment, she seemed as vulnerable as a child.

It was as if it had all suddenly become all too real to her. We both knew that if she was caught, the Hillstrom machine would never let her live. Or me either, for that matter. We were no longer far off the grid. They were closing in and would soon have us in their sights. She had every right to be sick.

Then it hit me. I cared about something again. Life was worth living, if only to protect Jess. It wasn't fair that she was in this nightmare. She was a good person who had only been doing her job. I was aware that the chances of me being able to help her out of this mess were miniscule, but I had to try. As far as I could tell, my identity was still hidden, especially there being no video from the truck stop. And there was no word about the Burger King, so we may have caught a break there, too. I had to make sure Jess was never seen with me. As long as we could maintain my secrecy, we still had a small chance. A small chance of what, was the question.

After a while, Jess finally stood up shakily and headed for the shower, where she stayed for over half an hour. When she came out, she brushed her teeth and got into bed without a word. Shell-shocked is the only way I could describe it. I could hear her quietly crying into her pillow. I rolled over to put my arms around her, and while she didn't object, she also didn't respond.

*****

In the morning we repeated the now-familiar routine of getting her to the car, then me going back in to pay the bill. We started on our way. She was quiet, but not totally disengaged. I held off suggesting breakfast. Even though she had nothing in her stomach, I knew she wasn't ready to eat. And since I was still full from the night before, I could survive until lunch.

An hour into the journey she turned to me, all of a sudden clear-eyed, and said, "Is there any relationship between Las Vegas and a circus?"

I laughed. "Yeah, Las Vegas *is* a circus."

"No, I'm serious."

"You really don't know much about Vegas, do you?"

"'Fraid not, why?"

"You've never heard of Circus Circus?"

"Uh, no."

"Famous hotel and casino. Not high end like the Mirage or Bellagio, but still popular."

"I think that's where we're supposed to stay. I was sitting here thinking of Las Vegas, when all of a sudden I flashed onto a circus tent. It felt more like a message than just a random thought."

"Circus Circus it is, then."

"I want to apologize," Jess said.

"What could you possibly have to apologize for?" I asked.

"The way I shut you out last night. The way I just kind of shut down altogether. I know how much you're doing for me. It's not fair to you. I just feel like I'm in way over my head."

"That's because you are. We both are. We can't let this guy beat us though. Yeah, the odds are against us, but nothing is impossible. And with that Voice leading the way, you just never know."

"Every once in a while, I get a feeling. Hard to explain, but it's a feeling of … I don't know … warmth maybe? Whatever it is, it gives me hope. And I know it's coming from the source of The Voice. I had that a few minutes ago, right before the circus image. I'm ready to face this. My life isn't what it was, and I just have to accept it. I'm ready to go after this guy. You're right. I don't know how we're going to do it, but we'll just take it one step at a time."

A minute later she said, "I'm hungry."

I smiled. "That's a good sign."

As I looked over at her, I saw her jump, as if an electrical charge went through her body.

"Whoa!" she exclaimed.

"What was that?" I asked, ready to pull the car over.

"It was a message. I've never had one hit me like that. Wow! About as loud and clear as you could get. My whole body is tingling."

"What was the message?"

"'*Find Wolf Run.*' Do you have any idea what it means?"

Chapter 7

"You okay?" I asked. Jess was breathing heavily.

"I think so," she answered. "That was pretty intense, and it's coming back in waves." She took a deep breath and let it out slowly. "It's starting to pass. I think I wasn't meant to ignore that message." She looked at me quizzically. "So does that mean anything to you?"

"Sort of," I replied. "I mean, in relation to Vegas I'm definitely familiar with it, but at the same time, it makes no sense."

"Umm," she began.

I cut her off. "Yeah, I know. That was a little vague."

"A little."

"I've spent a fair amount of time in casinos. I was in sales. Sales conferences take place where people can drink and gamble in the evenings. Sales and gambling seem to go together. As a result, I've played a lot of slot machines."

"And let me guess." It was her turn to interrupt me. "*Wolf Run* is a slot machine."

"It is."

"So we find a *Wolf Run* in the Circus Circus casino and look for the clue." She seemed proud of herself.

"Yeah, well, sorry to burst your bubble, but that's where it makes no sense."

"Why?"

"*Wolf Run* is a really popular machine. Do you have any idea how many they probably have there? And if Circus Circus is like any other casino, they won't all be in one place. You might have a bank of three in one row, a bank of four in another, and then single ones spread out all over the casino floor. I just don't get it."

I added, "Which brings up a sort of related question. If your Voice is supposedly leading you to the source of Hillstrom's secret, or proof of his guilt, why can't he just come out and say it? What's with all these friggin' clues?"

"I know. I've asked the same question. Here's how I see it: First, I'd venture to guess that communicating from the beyond—or from wherever it's coming—is not an easy task."

I gave her a *"how in the world would you know that"* look.

"Hey, I'm speculating here. How many conversations have you had with dead people? For some reason, it's really important for this person ... thing ... voice ... whatever ... to communicate with me. All I'm saying is it's probably not a simple thing to do or else everybody would be hearing voices.

"Second," she said quickly, before I could cut her off, "remember how we decided that it has trained me slowly to recognize it over the last year? This is probably a continuation of that. I have to pick up the clues gradually so it doesn't overwhelm me. Like this last clue. Even a few days ago, to have it shock my body like that would have been too intense for me. Anyway, that's my theory. She looked at me as if to say, *"try to challenge that logic."*

I couldn't argue it, so I just shrugged my shoulders and said, "That could be it. It would just be nice once in a while for The Voice to be specific, like 'Go to Joe's Bar tomorrow at ten and ask for Porky. Tell him The Voice sent you.'"

Jess laughed. "Hey, you never know. Another few weeks of this, and I might be getting that kind of message."

"Not sure we want another few weeks of this."

I instantly regretted the remark because it brought up the question in my mind: Would we be alive in a few weeks? I looked over at Jess and knew the same thought was going through her head. But she covered it well and quickly changed the subject.

"I was thinking about the cameras in the casinos," she said. "Should we start planning how I'm going to get in without being seen?"

"Yeah," I answered. "From what I hear, they also have state of the art facial recognition software these days, so that if they get your face on camera, all different kinds of agencies could tap into it."

"I suppose I could wear a floppy hat and sunglasses."

"Still risky. Eventually you'll look up without knowing it." And then I had an idea. "If you look like you're trying to be anonymous, you never are. Those are the people who tend to stand out. But if you stand out in the first place, nobody really notices you."

"Once again, your vagueness is impressive. And you were in sales?"

"Yeah, well, I never had to sell something like this. Anyway, a wheelchair. You pretend to be handicapped. You know how you often see a handicapped person being wheeled around by a relative? Like someone with severe cerebral palsy. You notice the wheelchair and then look away because you don't want to stare. I could wheel you in and no one would really notice you. A floppy hat wouldn't be out of the ordinary, and if you turn and kind of hang your head over the side, no camera will pick you up. They probably won't even notice me because they'll be looking away. And really, who notices the person pushing the wheelchair anyway?"

"It means you won't be able to check in alone. There will now be someone connected to you."

"Right, but once we leave Vegas, we can go back to the other system. Will they really flag me? I don't know. Maybe I've just been extra cautious. Anyway, I could have been coming here to pick up a relative or an escort and take her out for a couple of nights. People meet other people in Vegas all the time. Hopefully it won't register. It's worth a try."

"We have to find a store that sells wheelchairs. Bet we can find one at Wal-Mart."

"If not, we'll find a medical supply store. Can you look up Circus Circus on my phone and dial it?"

She did and in five minutes I had a handicapped room reserved. The advantage for us of Las Vegas falling on hard times was the abundance of rooms available. An hour later we found a Wal-Mart and I came away with a simple wheelchair for about $200, a floppy hat, and a blanket to add to the illusion.

"Do you feel like we are somehow mocking handicapped people by doing this?" Jess asked.

"No, my goal is to keep you alive. It's as simple as that. And I don't care what I have to do to accomplish it."

She put her hand on mine and squeezed.

We discussed her upcoming acting job and by the time we hit Las Vegas, our plan was clear. Jess put on her hat and draped the blanket over her lap. A moment later, I pulled in to the valet parking at Circus Circus. I got out as the attendant approached and handed me my slip. He opened the door for Jess, and then took a step back. What he encountered was a small woman with her right hand contorted and frozen in place in front of her chest. Her head hung to the left as if she were looking for coins between the seats. The hat covered much of her head, so the attendant couldn't see her face. If he could, he would have seen her eyes closed, her mouth fixed open, and some drool dripping down her lip. I was proud of the job she was doing.

I opened the trunk and pulled out our luggage and her wheelchair and wheeled it up to the passenger door. I reached in and gently picked up Jess and set her down in the chair. She remained in character the whole time.

I had hidden the extra ammunition in the wheel well with the spare tire, but the gun and all the cash were in a small carry-on that I held tightly. I let the bellman take the rest of the luggage. I tipped the valet and wheeled Jess into the hotel.

The check-in clerk took one look at Jess and insisted that if we needed anything, anything at all, to call them and it would be provided. I thanked her, not feeling the least bit guilty for duping her with the charade.

We were on the twentieth floor of the West Tower. As we took the elevator up, Jess still hadn't said a word. The bellman was polite and tried to make small talk, but his discomfort was evident as he was trying a bit too hard. At one point Jess let out a small groan, then made a slurping sound. I thought the bellman was going to heave all over the elevator. He couldn't wait to get to our destination floor and open the doors.

We finally made it to our room and I gave the bellman an extra-large tip for the agony our act had caused him. He went away happy and I closed the door, looked through the peephole and told Jess it was all clear.

"Ugh," she said. "I have to go wash my face. I've got drool all over it." She stood up and was suddenly transformed into the beautiful woman I was beginning to fall for.

It was a nice room, a little larger than most in order to accommodate the wheelchair. As expected, there were two beds. I went over to one and pulled the covers down and messed up the sheet so I wouldn't forget in the morning. Given our situation, it would look a bit strange to a housekeeper if only one bed had been used.

We didn't unpack, as a quick getaway might be needed.

"Sorry you're going to be stuck in the room," I said. "At some point I'll bring you out, but I don't want to overdo the exposure."

"That's okay. I'll watch CNN and learn some things about myself." She walked over and put her arms around me. "I really need a shower, too. Would you like to join me?"

There was no way I was declining that offer.

Forty-five minutes later I was dressing for my foray into the casino in search of a *Wolf Run*. I looked at my watch. It was four o'clock. I promised to be back by six and we'd order room service. We kissed and I headed out on my mission.

I entered into the noise and excitement and chaos that is a casino. Immediately I realized that I should have waited until after to take my shower. Although the ventilation system was better than some casinos I'd been in, it was still smoky.

As hard as it is to do in a casino, I set up a grid system in my head and started to check out every one of their 1500 slot machines (or so their brochure said). I was right about its popularity. I counted twenty-six *Wolf Run* slots, with denominations ranging from one to ten cents. I figured I'd need to try them all, so I allotted five minutes per machine. In the two hours, I was able to play fifteen of them. Some had players entrenched in front of them, with obviously no intention of moving anytime soon, and on two of the machines, I spent a lot longer than expected. I was winning on both of them, and you just don't leave a hot machine. By the time I returned to the room, I reeked of smoke, was $800 richer, and still had no clue.

After I showered — this time solo — and ordered room service, I said to Jess, "I know we weren't led here to win money. I have money already, although I guess every little bit helps. I saw nothing down there that gave me the slightest reason for us being here."

"Maybe the illumination will come later," said Jess. "Meanwhile, you've got to see this," and pointed me toward the TV. "They played it about a half an hour ago, so I'm sure they will repeat it. I don't know whether to laugh or be scared. They located the Bible family who picked me up. Hopefully the authorities will dismiss them as crackpots."

We waited, but the story still hadn't come on when the knock sounded at the door. Jess jumped into the bed I had messed up, turned away from the door, and pulled the covers halfway up her head.

I answered the door and told the waiter that I would bring in the cart, if he would just hold the door. "My sister is asleep," I whispered.

Once he was gone, Jess jumped out of bed, proclaiming herself starved. We had ordered burgers and fries, with a couple of large Caesar salads. Jess took a bite of her burger just as the story came on CNN.

"Watch," said Jess with a mouthful.

· As for breaking news, there was nothing to report. They were still trying to locate the unidentified man who was last seen with her, but so far, no one had come forward.

"Thank you for that," said Jess.

"You're welcome. But if you steal any more of my fries, I'm turning you in."

She threw one at me.

Newscaster: "Harry and Laura Joplin, of San Antonio, claim to have picked up Jessica Norton in a truck stop along I-20 in Texas late in the *evening on May 15th. They let her out along the side of the road an hour later. I asked the Joplins why they let her out."*

Harry Joplin: *"There was something really strange about her…"*
Laura Joplin: *"She was sent by the devil…"*
Harry Joplin: *"Well, I don't know about that, but she was weird. She asked us for a ride, and we figured it was the Christian thing to do. Once we got in the car, she didn't say much at first and was kinda freaking out our two young daughters. She just kinda sat there staring. Then out of the blue she said that she sees dead people. I'll tell you, she scared us."*

"*Hear* dead people, not see dead people. Weren't they even listening?" said Jess.

Laura Joplin: *"I prayed to Jesus that she wouldn't hurt us."*
Harry Joplin: *"That's when I saw the gun sticking out from under her shirt."*

I looked at Jess. She rolled her eyes and shrugged.

Laura Joplin: *"That's when Harry pulled over and asked her to leave."*
Newscaster: *"Did she object or give you any problems?"*
Laura Joplin: *"No. It was almost like she wanted to leave."*

"You got that right," said Jess.

Newscaster: *"Are you sure you saw a gun?"*
Harry Joplin: *"As God is my witness."*

"God must be near-sighted," quipped Jess.

Laura Joplin: *"The weird thing? I looked back as we drove away, and she had disappeared."*

Newscaster: *"The Joplins' supposed sighting of Norton took place the night before she was identified at the truck stop farther along Interstate 20. No other confirmed sightings have been reported."*

"Well, that was … uh … entertaining," I said. "I don't think they came off as overly credible. The damaging part was their lie about the gun. Between that and the other report, people are going to think you are dangerous, and the police don't take that lightly."

I finished my dinner, with the exception of half of my fries, which had mysteriously disappeared, and announced that I was going to see if I could check out the rest of the *Wolf Run* slots.

"Do you want to come?"

"No. You'll go faster without me. And this has been a really tiring day. I'll wait for you here."

I headed down to the casino floor and continued my mission. I spent another hour and a half in vain. I was able to play all but two and lost a hundred dollars for my trouble. No messages appeared, no strange people showed up, and the heavens didn't open up and drop a clue into my lap. So I left the casino to retreat back to the room. I went through the lobby and pressed the button for the elevator. While I waited, I looked at the signs advertising coming attractions. Just as the elevator door opened, one of the attractions caught my eye.

And then I knew it. The reason we were in Las Vegas.

Chapter 8

I stared for a moment longer to make sure I had all the information, then hurried up to the room. I think I scared Jess by not knocking before I used my key card.

She took one look at me and knew I had discovered something. "You found the *Wolf Run*?"

"No, I still don't understand that message, but I may have run across something important. I was going through the lobby, and right there in front of me was a sign. I mean a real sign, not one of your "signs from heaven" or whatever they are. Ever hear of Mill Colson?"

"The celebrity lawyer?"

"Yeah, but he's more than that. He does take on various movie stars, rock stars, and sports stars, so people see him as a celebrity lawyer. And he's definitely colorful and plays up his celebrity connections. But he's actually a real trial lawyer. A good one. He got famous when he took on a couple of high-profile murder cases. That's when the stars started hiring him. It's the trendy thing to do."

"Didn't I read that he's a real asshole?"

"Only to his adversaries. I gather he has an unbelievable ego. But if there is any such thing as earning your ego, he has. On the other hand, the press loves him because he really knows how to work an audience. He can be charming and funny and interesting.

His autobiography has been at the top of the bestseller lists for weeks."

"And we're talking about him why?"

"Guess who's giving a lecture and book signing here at Circus Circus tomorrow in one of the function rooms? And guess who could use a good lawyer?"

"You know how much he probably charges? I have absolutely no money, and I refuse to let you use any of yours. Assuming we could even see him, once he found out how poor I am, his ego would never let him take me on as a client."

"I think it's the opposite. I think his ego is just the reason he would take you on. Right now, you're the ultimate celebrity. You are on every newscast. You're mysterious, because no one knows where you are. You are about as high profile as it gets. He doesn't have to charge you a cent. Because of you, book deals and the lecture circuit will bring him millions. You'd be a cash cow to him."

I paused. "More importantly though. To guarantee all of these riches, he'd have to get you off. I can't think of anyone more capable of doing that."

"Getting me off isn't really the issue, is it? He could get the police and FBI to call off their search, but it wouldn't stop Hillstrom. At some point, he'll catch up to me and I'll be dead."

"But how do you think he would get them to stop looking for you? To prove someone else is guilty. Or at least shift the focus. He's probably got an army of private detectives working for him. Let them try to go after Hillstrom."

"I don't know," she said doubtfully. "I suppose it's worth trying, but I don't hold out a lot of hope."

"We've got to at least try. And I really think this is why you were led here."

"You might be right," she said, shaking her head as if she

couldn't believe what she was agreeing to. "Okay … Mill Colson it is."

Millard (Mill) Colson wasn't a lawyer, he was an institution. A master at self-promotion, Colson came up through the ranks like a comet, not because his skills were necessarily better than other lawyers, but because he made sure no accomplishment went overlooked, be it by a superior, or especially by the news media. He was not above paying reporters to write a piece on him, or to become his own anonymous source to disseminate information on himself. But those were in the early days. The publicity took care of itself now — although he wasn't afraid to manipulate a story or two if he saw fit — because, over time, he truly had become a great lawyer.

It was assumed early on in his career that he was from a dirt-poor family and had put himself through college without any help from the outside. He liked the aura the story provided, and while he didn't confirm it, he never denied it either. That was the way with Colson. He had a charisma that made people want to believe whatever tale he spun. In fact, he came from quite a wealthy family and never had to work hard for anything. Instead, he learned early on that with him using his brains and charm, those around him were more than willing to do all the work. It wasn't laziness on his part, but a superior intellect. When he discovered the law, he went about it like it was a game, and he was a master at his game. He could sway juries with a simple change of expression. He had reporters eating out of his hand. Very simply, he was the best there was. And that was why we needed him to represent Jess, to change public opinion and to make people feel sorry for her. Once the public believed she wasn't capable of murdering four people, then we could start spreading the Hillstrom story. To bring it up now would be premature. Nobody would believe it. Colson was the man who understood that timing and could make it happen.

"What's the plan?" asked Jess.

"I'm going to run out and pick up a video camera. Think about your story. I want you to tell it to the camera. Tomorrow, I'll try to pigeonhole him after his lecture. I'll use the video to close the sale."

I was back an hour later. When I got up to the room, Jess said, "You're not going to believe this. I just saw it on the news. Guess who's going to announce his candidacy for president next week?"

"Hillstrom."

"Yup. He's putting his name in the ring as an independent."

"And that was his plan all along. He's going to run for president, win because he's so popular, and he and his secret organization will be running the country. Well, at least we know the time-frame we're working with."

It took about two hours to get the wording right in Jess's message. When she started talking about her coworkers, she started to cry. Even though it was genuine, Colson would take the tears as theatrics and applaud it. It was almost two in the morning when we finished it, and we collapsed into bed.

*****

Colson's talk and book signing was scheduled for three o'clock. We slept late and ordered room service breakfast. It was still only eleven when we finished, so I decided that it was time Jess got out for a bit. It wasn't comfortable for her in the wheelchair with the way she had to contort her arm and hang her head over the side, but at least she could soak up some of the sounds. I figured I'd also show her a *Wolf Run*, just in case something hit her.

The road trip lasted less than an hour. Between the discomfort of the chair and the fear of being caught full face on camera, she'd had enough. I managed to show her a *Wolf Run,* but to her it wasn't any different from all the other slot machines.

I got her up to the room, where we wasted time waiting for Mill Colson. I knew Jess was nervous, but I was surprised at how nervous I was too.

"You should probably have all the luggage ready to go, in case something goes wrong. If I can't convince him, we should take off."

Finally, 2:15 arrived, and I headed down to get a good seat.

I had to admit, he was good. He was in his late fifties, fit, and well-groomed. He had a full head of hair tinged with gray. His energy was boundless. He was animated as he kept us entertained with stories of old cases, and what it's like traveling the country in his private jet. I looked around. There were probably about a hundred people transfixed on Mill (he insisted people call him that). Occasionally he would touch on serious topics, but he had his patter down so perfectly, he could transition from one story to another, from one emotion to another, without skipping a beat.

He talked for almost an hour, then invited everyone to come meet him at the signing table.

I moved into line with the others, trying to figure out how I could tell him about Jess without the person behind me hearing. That was solved when an assistant walked along the line handing out pieces of paper and pencils.

"It goes a lot faster if you write on the paper what you would like Mill to inscribe in your book," she said.

It seemed a bit egotistical to me, but it also made sense. Famous authors must deal constantly with groupies who just want to talk. There was probably also less chance of the author hearing the name wrong, or spelling it wrong, and wrecking the book. For me, it was perfect.

I wrote: *Jessica Norton needs a lawyer. Interested? She didn't kill those four people.*

I waited in line fifteen minutes before it was my turn. As I moved up to the table he looked at me with a wide friendly smile, but one that also seemed to say, *"I'm really famous, and you're not."*

An assistant handed him a book open to the title page, ready for his signature. At the same time I gave him the paper. He started to read it, pen in hand, then stopped and slowly looked up at me, folding the paper so the assistant couldn't read it. He seemed momentarily confused, but focused quickly.

"This for real?" he whispered.

I nodded my head.

"She here?"

"Around," I answered. I pointed to the small video camera in my left hand. "She recorded you a message."

"Why don't you go have a seat and we can talk after."

I moved off to the side, very aware of dozens of people staring at me. If he took her case and anyone made the connection back to me, my invisibility was history.

It took about a half hour to finish with the line. When he was done, he got up, stretched, and walked over to a smaller room off the main hall and motioned me to follow. When I reached the room, he closed the door behind me. We were bathed in silence.

"I thought a little privacy would be called for." He held out his hand. "Mill Colson. And you are?"

We shook. "For the moment I'm anonymous, if you don't mind."

"Fair enough. You know, people try to entice me to take cases all the time. Some are real cases that don't pique my interest. Most are bogus. People who just want to meet me. Which one are you, Mr. Anonymous?"

"I'm the third kind. I'm the one who can offer you the case that will add to your legacy. Put another star above your name. Jess doesn't have a penny and can't pay you, but you won't care. This case will create so much curiosity for you, you're going to have to take it. Never mind the fact that it will bring in millions for you when it's all over."

"You some kind of salesman?" Mill asked.

"Used to be. Now I'm just a guy trying to keep an innocent woman alive."

"Keep her alive how? Or why?"

"I don't know how. I'm just doing my best. Maybe you should let her tell you why." I handed him the video camera. "It's less than ten minutes long, but she covers the high points."

We both sat down at one of the tables and he turned on the video. It was a small screen and the audio was a bit tinny, but it didn't matter. A minute into it, I knew he was hooked. She told her story as completely as possible, leaving out The Voice, of course. That was strictly between us. At the end, he looked at me, and I could tell the wheels were turning.

"Is she planning to turn herself in?" Mill asked.

"She'd be dead within the hour. No. No way. I just have to keep her hidden."

"Then I can't meet with her. I'd be guilty of harboring a fugitive."

"I understand. You could go through me, or we could set up phone calls between the two of you. It's hard because I don't know if lines are bugged."

"None of mine are," said Mill. "My offices, vehicles, and phones are swept constantly for listening devices."

"So do you believe her?" I asked.

"I'm sure you've seen enough lawyer shows. It's not what I believe, but what I can convince a jury of. But to answer your question: I don't believe she killed her co-workers. But frankly, I haven't believed that from the beginning. It was too professional. I had some of my people check into her, and they found nothing that would lead me to believe she was anything but an average twenty-eight-year-old office worker."

I looked at him quizzically.

"You think I don't have people out there investigating potential big clients? If I get contacted—like I did today—I have to be prepared. For example, I knew that if she asked me to take the case, she had no money to pay me. So if I took it, it would be pro bono. Up til now, there was really nothing about the case to make me drop everything. However, the Hillstrom connection adds an interesting twist. That part of it seems far-fetched, but that doesn't mean it can't be true."

He paused, mulling it all over. I let him think.

"So if I took the case, what would you two be doing?"

"Hiding out. Seeing if we could get proof on Hillstrom on our own."

"Is there something she knows?"

Here was the moment of truth. Do I mention The Voice and risk him walking away?

"Okay, I'm going to be a little vague here, and I apologize. There are a few clues she has that she is determined to follow. They're nothing that would help or interfere with your investigation, and if they led to anything, we would tell you immediately. But for reasons I can't explain.... " I left it hanging.

"I can accept that for now, but not for long."

"Thank you."

"Okay. Let her know I will take her case. I'm going to want to announce it within a few days, minus any mention of Hillstrom. That'll be going on behind the scenes. So I suggest you get as far from here as possible, in case some reporter puts two and two together."

"What's the best way for us to stay in touch?" I asked.

"Give me an hour. There will be a disposable cell phone waiting for you at the front desk. I'll have it programmed with my number and the number of one of my investigators. Use this phone only to call me or the other number on it. Don't use it for anything else. Memorize my number. If you lose the cell, pick up another disposable phone and call me from that. I will always have to know how to get in touch with you. Now, at this point can I have your name, so I can leave it for you at the desk?"

"Jon Harper. J..O..N. Room 2013."

"Okay. Well, nice to meet you Jon. Don't tell me where you're going. Just leave as soon as you get that phone. I have a lot of planning to do, so you might not hear from me for a couple of days. I'll let you know before I go public."

We shook hands and went back out into the main hall, which was still bustling with people, and he took off, his entourage trailing behind.

For the first time, there was a ray of hope in this madness.

Chapter 9

When I got back to the room, I could tell Jess had been nervously pacing. She looked at me expectantly.

"He'll take the case," I said.

She jumped into my arms with a squeal. After she had calmed down a bit, we sat by the window and I covered all the points of my talk with Mill. She had a few questions, but was mostly a little overwhelmed by it all. To go from office worker to client of Mill Colson was mind-boggling. But it didn't take her long to return to the situation at hand.

"Well, we're all packed. Are we still headed for Homer?" she asked.

"We are."

"You should have asked him to fly us there in his jet. We could have avoided dealing with Canada."

"No, it's important that he doesn't know where we are. I get the feeling he was concerned for your safety. I don't think he totally buys the Hillstrom thing, but I do think he knows your life is in danger. He was adamant about us leaving immediately and getting lost." I looked at my watch. "We should head out now."

Once again, we went through the charade of Jess in the wheelchair. At the front desk I paid our bill in cash and picked up the package Mill's people had left for me. The woman at the valet desk called for our car, and fifteen minutes later, we were on the road, heading north on Interstate 15 out of Las Vegas. Since it was already early evening, we knew we'd have to stop somewhere for the night, but it was cool and clear, and the stars filled the expansive sky. We both felt like driving.

"We never did find out where *Wolf Run* fits into all of this," Jess said once we were away from the gaudy lights of the city.

"Could it be you got the wrong message?" I asked.

"It almost electrocuted me. I don't think so. But I also didn't feel any sort of urgency once we were there, so I don't know if we just missed a clue, or if things changed."

"Maybe I should have had you check them all out," I said. "Maybe it was a clue only you would have noticed."

"I doubt it. I wouldn't have had the patience. I don't see how people can just sit there hour after hour. And it was way too noisy for me. Besides, we didn't want my face showing up on a video somewhere."

We both went quiet, appreciating the soothing hum of the tires on the highway.

Finally, Jess broke the silence. "Why couldn't we just find some small town out here in the middle of nowhere to live? We could get lost and no one would ever find us."

While it was an appealing thought, I couldn't tell if fear was creeping back into her consciousness, or just sheer exhaustion. I was learning that being on the run put all of your senses on overload. Adrenaline was constantly flowing, you were always moving—mentally and physically—to the point where you just wanted to sit down and say "Enough! No more of this."

She looked at me with a deep sadness in her eyes. "But I know that's just a pipe dream. They are eventually going to locate us. I don't know how, but it's just a matter of time before I get recognized—somewhere. What then?"

"If it's a cop, we call Mill and just hope he can keep us safe somehow. If it's one of Hillstrom's goons … well … I guess I learn how to kill."

"Could you?"

"Could I kill? A couple of weeks ago I thought my life was over. There was nothing left for me and I was ready to kill myself. Now that I have something to live for, could I kill someone else to survive? Absolutely. I was a parent. To protect Karen's life, I would have done anything I had to in order to keep her safe. Any good parent would.…"

I trailed off, realizing that, in fact, I actually killed my daughter. But Jess knew exactly what I was thinking.

She rested her hand on my arm. "You didn't kill her, Jon. You were doing what you just told me—everything possible to save her."

"Yeah, well, anyway … If someone is threatening our lives, I will kill him."

The fire had gone out of the conversation. My guilt had taken over. We stopped at a service area where I got gas and went into the Burger King and got us some food.

I began to feel better as we ate and apologized to Jess for my mood.

"Jon, you lost a child. You never, ever have to apologize for the darkness that's in your life. Unfortunately, it's always going to be there, some days more than others. The grief will show up when you least expect it. I know that from experience. I still haven't gotten over the death of my parents. Sometimes I would be sitting at my desk at work and just start crying for no reason."

"When did they die?" I asked.

"About a year and a half ago. Remember that ferry accident in

India? Over 600 people died."

Sadly, I only vaguely remembered it. What did it say about me that 600 people could die in an accident in some third world country, and it barely registered with me? What does it say about the news media that they gave it such little coverage, making it inevitable that we would pay little attention? If the same thing had happened here, it would be on the news for weeks.

"And they were on it? What were they doing in India?"

"My parents were writers. My father worked for the *Washington Post* as a travel writer, and my mother was a freelance travel writer. She wrote some guide books for Fodors—mostly the Middle East and Asia, but occasionally some places in Europe. They actually met in India about thirty-five years ago. He was doing a travel piece for the *New York Times*—that's where he worked then—and she was doing research for a guide. They were staying at the same hotel, so they shared a taxi from the airport. The rest was history. I was born a few years later. My father had just gotten a job at the *Post*, and they had moved to northern Virginia. My mother decided to cut back on her writing and be a full-time mother."

She stopped, and I could tell she was reflecting on her childhood. "Anyway," she continued, "when I left home, my mother got right back in the writing saddle. Whenever my dad had an assignment that took him to an interesting place, she went with him. They were so in love and so devoted to each other."

I thought back to my childhood and how completely different my parents were from hers. It was hard for my anger at them not to resurface.

"So, when my father got an assignment to cover modes of travel in India, my mother had to go along. I mean, how romantic to go back to where you first met? I talked to them the night before they were taking the ferry. You know the funny thing? They almost didn't take it. My father had been fighting some sort of stomach thing the whole trip and they were trying to decide whether to go or let him spend the day in bed."

Her eyes were filling up as she talked. "When I saw the ferry accident on the news, I immediately tried calling their phones. When I couldn't get through, I called the *Washington Post* and the U.S. Embassy. A few hours later they confirmed that my parents were supposed to be on the ferry. I flew over and waited with the relatives of all the other missing victims. A week later, each day seeing more dead collected from the bottom of the river, they identified their bodies. They had drowned."

"I don't remember the cause of the accident," I said.

"A fire in the engine room that spread to the fuel tanks and caused an explosion. It sank in minutes. Like many of the boats over there, it was old and a firetrap."

I let a few minutes go by before commenting.

"It sounds like you had a happy childhood," I said, trying to steer her away from death.

"Oh, I did." I saw her eyes brighten. "I really had a magical childhood. My parents were constantly taking me on trips. I saw so much of the world. But it wasn't just that. I always felt we were a threesome. It wasn't just parents with a kid. They included me in everything. We were a team. I had a great childhood." She looked at me, suddenly remembering my story. "Sorry."

I smiled to let her know it was okay. "Hey, we all have different experiences in this life. My childhood sucked. I'm getting over it. But I think most people have decent childhoods. Yours just happened to be particularly outstanding. Don't ever take it for granted."

"I don't."

She told me more about her life. The trips she took with her parents, some of the funny experiences, and holidays in her house. I enjoyed the stories, but more importantly, I was listening to the happiness in her voice, and was hoping she could savor it for a while and forget about the reality that we were living with.

Finally, at about three in the morning, we stopped at a nice but forgettable hotel outside of Provo and checked in. Since it would be harder to sneak her in that time of night, we went with the handicapped charade.

Once we made it to the room and got into bed, as tired as we were, we made love slowly and passionately, holding onto the stories Jess had told of the love between her parents. Maybe we hoped that the love that was growing between us would someday manifest in the same way.

If we weren't dead.

Chapter 10

Things began to unravel the next morning. And yet, thanks to Jess—or The Voice—I had made some decisions the night before that probably saved our lives.

The day started out like a cliché—dark and stormy. We slept in, having arrived so late at night, and didn't get up until almost ten. After a quick shower, I offered to run out for some bagels and coffee. Jess was going to take her shower while I was gone.

I returned in less than half an hour, only to find Jess standing in the back lot where we had parked the night before. Her hair was still wet and hanging off her head in strands. That wasn't a good sign. The couple of bags we had brought in with us were next to her. She frantically waved as she saw me, so I pulled up in front of her.

"We've gotta go," she said, panic in her voice. I opened the trunk and ran around to the rear to help her throw everything in. I heard sirens in the distance.

"What happened?" I asked, as we got in. I slammed the car in Drive, turned it around, and headed out the way I came in.

"I was recognized." Jess was having trouble breathing.

"Give it a minute. Take your time," I said. The highway was only a quarter of a mile down the road. As we approached the entrance ramp, the sirens were right on top of us. From all directions, police cars converged on the hotel. Jess had ducked down the minute she got in the car, just in case. As I got on the highway, I looked over to my right at the hotel and counted at least seven police cars.

"That was way too close," I said. "I think you can get up now. No, wait." A State Police cruiser blew past us on the other side of the highway with its siren blaring. It got off the exit. "I think it's okay now."

Jess raised her head tentatively and slowly got into her seat. She was visibly shaking.

"I came out of the bathroom in my towel after my shower and found the housekeeper had just come in the room. She must have knocked while I was in the shower and came in when she didn't get a response. She quickly apologized, but then I could tell something was wrong. She looked over at the wheelchair with a puzzled expression, then back at me. Her eyes opened wide and I knew immediately that she recognized me. She kept apologizing while she backed out of the room. She looked terrified. I heard her run down the hall, so I threw some clothes on, zipped up our bags, and got out of there."

"Well, we may have just made it."

"And now I know why you checked us in the way you did last night."

"Thanks to you."

*****

When we arrived at the hotel the night before, I looked at Jess and could tell something was troubling her.

"I'm getting that chatter in my head again," she said.

"Is it telling you not to stay here?"

"No, I don't think so. But I think we have to be extra careful for some reason."

So before I got out of the car, I put on a University of Nevada baseball cap I had picked up at a drugstore in Las Vegas, pulling it down on my forehead, and slipped some cash into my shoe. I put Jess in the wheelchair, with her hat and blanket, and told her to moan a little bit, and as time went on, to start moving around and crying out. We got to the front desk and, as I hoped, only one person was on duty, a young guy.

"How much for a double?" I asked, being sure to keep my head down so as not to provide a good angle for any cameras they might have.

"Uh, eighty-nine dollars," he answered, all the while sneaking glances at Jess, who was putting on a great performance of someone who had been up way too long, wanted to go to bed, but couldn't really communicate it. The more uncomfortable he got, the better for us.

"I hope you can help me," I said. "I'm really stuck. I've lost my wallet—I think I left it in the hotel we stayed in in Las Vegas last night. My credit cards were in it."

He was eying me suspiciously, while at the same time obviously bothered by Jess's performance.

"I have cash," I said quickly. "I have some hidden in my shoe— boy, I'm so glad I did that. I thought I was putting it there in case I got mugged. I never thought I'd lose my wallet." I looked down at Jess, who had started moving around and whimpering. "It's okay Denise, I'll get you into bed soon. I promise."

I turned back to the clerk. "Look, I can give you a deposit. I have $300 here, and I'll write down address and license information. I've really got to get my sister into a bed... " I leaned forward in a conspiratorial way and whispered, "and a bathroom.

Oh, it's such an ordeal getting her taken care of in there."

"Well," he started. I swear he was actually sweating. "We're not supposed to without some form of ID…" On cue, Jess let out a howl.

"I don't want you to break any rules," I said, "but things are getting a little desperate here. Please?"

He folded, as I knew he would.

"Okay, I guess I can break the rules just this one time, but it's my ass…" he looked down at Jess and turned pink, "uh, my job on the line, so I'm asking that you take care of the room." He handed me a registration form, which I filled out with completely bogus information. According to the form, my name was Herbert Field, and I now lived in Hannibal, Missouri, with a Missouri license plate on my 2003 red Chevy Impala. I took my shoe off, reached in and pulled out three $100 bills folded together. I dropped them on the counter like that and said, "I'm sorry if they're a little sweaty."

That did it for the clerk. He touched the corners to make sure they were hundreds, then swept them into the drawer with as little skin to money contact as possible. Meanwhile, Jess was making all sorts of weird noises and was thrashing about in the chair. He swiped the key card to activate it.

"Down the hall and to the left," he said, holding out the key card.

"Thank you so much," I said, grabbing his hand in thanks.

As we started down the hall, I could see him making a beeline for the bathroom to wash his hands.

*****

Now we were heading north on I-15, hoping to get far away from the hotel as quickly as possible.

"I was just hoping he wouldn't ask me for my car registration as a form of ID," I said. "That would have taken some fast talking. Poor guy. He didn't know what hit him."

"Take this exit, now!" shouted Jess.

I acted just in time, almost missing the off ramp.

"So, what was that?" I asked.

"Somebody yelling in my ear," she answered.

"Did it … he … say which way?"

"No."

"I think we're on 189. I'll just stay on that and see where it leads us."

We reached a high point on the highway and I happened to look back from where we had come. I quickly pulled over. "Look at that," I said.

Interstate 15 was a sea of flashing lights, and traffic was completely stopped in the northbound lane.

"What do you think?" asked Jess.

"They might have set up a quick roadblock hoping to catch us before we had time to reach Salt Lake City, or they've pulled over someone in a red Chevy Impala. Either way, we would have been screwed stuck in traffic like that. I'll tell you, The Voice is better than GPS."

I started driving again and looked over at Jess, who had started crying.

"You okay?" I asked.

"No, that really scared me. Getting yelled at in my head like that. It made me feel like a little girl getting reprimanded. But it's not just that. Every time I start to feel a little safe, something happens to bring me back to reality. I don't know where we're supposed to go now. I don't know how much longer I can do this."

Once again I pulled over, this time into a strip mall parking lot, and put my arm around her.

"I don't know what to tell you, Jess. You're just going to have to have faith … in me, in The Voice, and mostly, in yourself, that you're going in the right direction. Right now we're on the run. At some point that's going to change. We're going to go on the offensive. We're going to find the information to stop Hillstrom. And when we do, we can stop running. But we have to get there first."

The tears stopped. She sniffed and blew her nose. "I'm sorry. I'm okay now."

"Let's just see where this road takes us," I suggested. It was heading up into the mountains. Getting as far from the highway as possible seemed like a good idea to me.

The rain had stopped and the sun was trying to peek out from the rapidly retreating clouds. However, a dark horizon suggested more bad weather later on. After a few minutes of driving on the new road, we came to a sign pointing to the Scenic Alpine Highway to our left.

"Any gut feeling?" I asked.

"Nope. It says the Sundance Institute is on that road. Probably pretty beautiful up there. I could use some beautiful views to clear my head. This is amazing country."

"Have you ever been out here before?"

"As a kid, I seem to remember. Most of the traveling I did with my parents was overseas. As an adult, I've done very little traveling. Mostly the New York to Washington corridor, and a few trips to Florida with friends."

"Well, you're going to see a lot of beautiful country from here on."

"Wish I could appreciate it. Hard to when you don't know if you are in someone's cross-hairs." She shook her head, as if to erase the thought.

We stopped briefly in Sundance to pick up some food, the bagels no longer appetizing and the coffee long since cold. We drove to the first scenic overlook we found and sat in silence while we ate, taking in the view. There were a couple of other cars parked there, so as much as we would have liked to stretch our legs, we didn't get out. When we were finished eating, we continued on our way. The road was surprisingly empty of traffic, probably from the earlier rain and the threat of more.

After about ten minutes, the view was no longer of interest to me. I was looking in the rearview mirror, concentrating on something else.

"Jess, where did we put the bag with the money and my gun?"

"We threw all the bags in the trunk at the hotel, why?"

"There's a scenic overlook coming up in a second. I'm going to hop out and grab the bag."

"What's wrong?"

"There's a car behind us that doesn't feel right to me."

She turned and looked. "Where?"

"You can't see it right now. It's around one of the turns, about a half mile in back of us. The problem is, it's been about a half mile behind since we got on this road. It was behind us when we stopped to buy the food, then again when we stopped to eat, and now it's back there again, always the same distance."

"Police?"

"I don't think so. It's a tan SUV. If it was police, I think they would have stopped us by now. If it's someone else, maybe they're waiting to catch us alone." We pulled into the overlook. The only other car was just leaving, so we had it to ourselves. "I say, let's stay right here and see what happens. If it is the police, they're going to catch us anyway. If they're from Hillstrom, we may as well find out now."

I jumped out, pulled the bag from the trunk, and quickly got back into the car. I took out the gun and set it on my lap. I always kept a round in the chamber, so when the time came, I would cock the hammer and be ready. I was trying to act like the protector, but in reality, my stomach was halfway up my throat. I was scared to death.

We got out to sit on the rock wall and waited. I sat so I could look out at the view on my right, while still keeping an eye on the road on my left. I kept the gun next to me. After about five minutes, I saw the SUV creep around the bend in the breakdown lane. There was only a driver. Seeing we were alone, he made his decision. He slowly pulled in with his hazard lights on and took a parking spot near us. My sweaty hand was on the gun hidden behind my body. I pulled back the hammer.

I whispered to Jess, "If I say 'go', or if anything happens, jump off the wall and hide behind it." The wall was about three feet high. Beyond the wall was about fifteen feet of rock before it became a cliff.

The driver got out and stretched—the worst acting job I'd ever seen. He was young—mid-twenties—and well built. He was dressed casually, but for the city, not the mountains. Obviously not a tourist. The SUV had a rental look about it. He wore a light jacket, not so much because it was chilly, which it was, but to hide the gun on his belt over his butt. His fake stretch was the stupidest thing he could have done, as it allowed me to catch a glimpse of the gun. Okay, so I wasn't dealing with a mental giant.

"Nice view," he said.

"It is," I answered. I was between him and Jess. She didn't say a word. She was probably petrified, or waiting for the signal to jump behind the wall.

"Car's giving me trouble," he said, rather lamely, I thought. I wondered if he was as nervous as I was. He probably wasn't part of Hillstrom's team. Most likely he was just one of many temporary goons hired for the express purpose of finding and killing Jess. He looked at Jess. "Hey, do I know you?" He was scratching his leg in an obvious attempt to have his hand near his gun.

"Why don't we cut the crap," I said. "Were you sent to kill her?"

Genius that he was though, he decided he had to tell us how smart he was before killing us. He slowly pulled his gun out while he talked.

"Everyone else is looking for you along the highway. I saw you turn off suddenly, so..."

I lifted my gun, aimed, and fired while he was in mid-sentence. His eyes grew wide as he saw my gun a second before crumpling to the ground as the bullet caught him in the chest. The sound of the shot reverberated through the hills.

Jess and I fell behind the wall the moment after the shot. I lifted my head to see where he was, but he wasn't going anywhere. He was sprawled at an unnatural angle on his back on the pavement near his car. A pool of blood had formed on his chest and was dripping down to the concrete.

I knew I had to act quickly. I jumped over the wall and ran to his body. I grabbed him under his armpits and dragged him back to the wall. Jess came alive at that point and jumped over to grab his legs. Together we lifted him over the wall and set him down out of sight of the road.

"You okay?" I asked Jess. The fact that she'd helped with the body surprised me, because she was obviously in shock.

She didn't answer.

"There's a water bottle in the tray between our seats. Can you get it and pour it on the blood drops on the concrete?" She nodded, and without a word ran to the car. There wasn't a lot of blood, and hopefully the coming rain would wash it away, but this would make it harder for someone to notice.

I walked to the cliff and looked over. It dropped about twenty feet to a steep slope leading to another drop-off into a dense forest. I was hoping he would roll into the trees when I dropped him over the edge.

I ran back to the body. A few cars had passed on the road, but luckily none had pulled in. Jess poured water on the stains, rendering them almost invisible. The rain would finish the job. She picked up his gun and dropped it over the wall next to his body. I quickly searched him and found a wallet and a cell phone. Putting those aside with the gun, I checked for traffic and again picked him up by the armpits and dragged him to the ledge, where I set him down and rolled him over the side.

He landed on the slope below with a sickening thud, then slid down and went over the edge into the trees. From where I was standing, I couldn't see his body, but he had left a good amount of blood on the rock. Hopefully the rain would do a cleaning job before the blood dried. I looked back at Jess, who was just staring at me, then I looked over the edge of the cliff again.

I had just killed a man. This was for real now.

Chapter 11

I was waiting for the nausea. Wouldn't that be the natural reaction to your first kill? Shouldn't I have been bent over vomiting and wondering how I could have just done that?

No. Other than a little shortness of breath and some shaking, I felt fine. And those were merely the after-effects of the adrenaline rush. It's amazing what you can do when you've hit rock bottom and no longer care. Of course, that wasn't exactly true. I cared about Jess. But that was simply another reason why the man's death meant nothing to me. I was protecting her. He had come to kill us, for no other purpose than he was paid to do so. Should I have really given a second thought to ending his life? I didn't think so.

For Jess, though, it was a different story. Reality had caught up with her and had hit her hard. She was sitting by the wall hyperventilating. I hurried over to her as she took in great gasps of air. I guided her head between her knees and rubbed her back, trying all the time to talk her down. I spoke in calming tones, telling her it would be alright, dehumanizing the man who had come to kill us, and letting her know that it was our right to fight back.

She was a mess. Tears were flowing and she was sobbing, while at the same time choking on her sobs, unable to breathe. I was afraid I was going to lose her.

"Jess," I continued, "I'm falling in love with you. Do you

understand? You've given me something to live for. There is no way in hell anybody is going to take that away from me. If we're going to win this, we're going to have to be willing to come down to their level. We may have to kill again. We have to take apart their machine piece by piece, coldly and logically, with no emotions. We will win this."

I kept talking, knowing that this was a crucial moment. Her future survival depended on how she made it out of this crisis. After about fifteen minutes the gasps slowly began to lessen, then disappeared altogether. She finally lifted her head and I saw that the tears were gone. But she was fragile, oh so fragile. Her eyes were red-rimmed and she was a mess, but she seemed to be functioning again.

"Do you really love me?" she asked, her voice a hoarse whisper.

"I do."

She put her arms around me and we just sat there behind the wall, not saying a word. I could hear cars come into the overlook parking area and stay for a few minutes, then leave. Occasionally someone would get out and stand by the wall looking out at the view, then it would become quiet again as they left. I glanced up at the sky and saw the dark clouds rolling back in. It would soon be pouring.

"We should go," I said quietly.

"Not yet. I have to tell you something. When you were talking to me, The Voice was also talking—comforting me, just as you were."

"You were being double-teamed?"

She tried to smile, without much success. "Yeah, I guess so."

"What did it say?"

"There weren't many words. It was more feelings and

emotions. While you were using words like 'win' and 'cold' and 'logical', The Voice was sending those sensations through me, as if it was showing me what they would feel like and why they were important. Like a tutorial to go along with the text."

"I'm beginning to really appreciate this Voice," I said.

"Because of the two of you I understand now what has to be done. And…" She hesitated.

"And what?"

She shook her head. "I'll tell you later."

I gave her a look.

"I'm not trying to be mysterious. There's just something I need to let sink in a bit."

The heavens suddenly opened up and the rain came down in buckets. I gathered up the would-be assassin's wallet, keys, and gun, and we ran for the car.

When we had closed the doors, I looked around. The parking lot was empty.

"We should think about getting out of here. You drive my car while I drive his. We'll take it to a parking lot of a hotel and leave it. The car will probably sit there for days before anyone notices it. And who knows when his body will be found, if ever. This rain should get rid of all the blood on the ledge. I'll look at his phone later and we can see if he called anyone when he was following us. Either way, there might be some interesting numbers on the phone. I can pass them on to Mill."

I gave her a kiss and told her to follow me, and I jumped out into the deluge and ran over to his SUV.

The guy was a slob. Fast-food wrappers and bags, soda cans, cigarette butts, and coffee cups were everywhere, and the car had an overpowering stench that made me open the window more than a crack, even with the rain. I quickly looked around for anything of importance, but other than the garbage, the car was empty. I figured he had stashed his stuff in a hotel room somewhere. I was right about it being a rental though. I found the contract in the glove compartment and pocketed it in case it might prove useful.

I backed up and pulled onto the road, making sure Jess was behind me. It led back to I-15, but I took a side road before hitting the highway, eventually ending up in Salt Lake City. I stuck to the smaller streets as we wound our way through the city. I had no idea where I was, but at the same time I didn't think of myself as lost because I didn't know what my immediate destination was either. The downpour had been replaced by drizzle and the driving was easier. I pulled into a good-sized no-name hotel in a rougher-looking section of town and sought out the most remote corner of the parking lot. Jess pulled in next to me and moved over to the passenger seat. I left the SUV's keys on the seat and joined Jess in my car.

"Plates," she said, as we were backing up.

"Huh?"

"The word 'plates' just popped up. I have no idea what it means. License plates, maybe?"

I looked around, and suddenly knew what it meant. I pulled the car back into our original spot and reached into the glove compartment for a pocket knife. I opened it to the screwdriver blade and looked around the parking lot. No one was in sight, and I couldn't detect any cameras either, but I put my hat on just in case and pulled it low.

"We should take the plates, just in case we need to switch them with mine."

"But won't a car with no plates attract more attention?"

"You're right." I looked around for the closest car. It was about a hundred feet away. Checking again to make sure we were alone,

I got out and sprinted over to it and quickly unscrewed the front plate. I ran back and replaced the rear plate on the SUV with the stolen plate, then went to the front of the SUV and removed the front plate. I was back in the car in less than two minutes. I handed the plates to Jess, who stashed them under her seat, and we took off.

"The front of the SUV is up against the wall, so no one will see the missing plate. And with a plate on the back, hopefully the SUV will go unnoticed. Good catch. My real hope is that being in a questionable neighborhood, someone will see the keys on the seat and steal the car."

It was beginning to get dark and we were both exhausted from the stress of the day. We managed to make it as far as Ogden without getting back on the highway and found a nice Hyatt. We had abandoned the wheelchair at the last hotel, which was okay with me as I felt we had taken that act as far as we could, so we reverted back to our original routine.

After we got settled, I ventured out for some food and returned with a pizza and a couple of salads. We decided to make it an early night and were lying in bed after showering off the memories of killing a man. Jess had her head on my chest. We were quiet, just enjoying the closeness. When her hand began to wander, the mood quickly changed and there was no turning back after that.

I was just reaching the point of no return when a phone rang and we both jumped. I rolled off Jess, my body reacting to the sudden change in focus. Jess quickly turned on a light.

It rang again, but I was totally disoriented. It wasn't mine. Was it Mill's or the assassin's? I made my way to the desk where I had put all the phones. It was the disposable from Mill.

"Hello?" I answered out of breath.

"Jon, Mill Colson. You okay?"

"Hi Mill. Yeah, the phone just startled us."

"Well, I just wanted to let you know that I'll be making the announcement tomorrow. Obviously, I'm not going to bring up anything about Hillstrom, but at least we'll get the ball rolling. Is my client there?"

"Sure, just a second."

I handed the phone to Jess. "He'd like to speak to you."

"Hello?"

Jess talked to Mill for about five minutes. Mill, of course, did most of the talking. Jess answered with "okay" and "uh huh" about a dozen times. Finally, when she was able to get in a word, she said, "Mr. Colson … okay, Mill … I just wanted to thank you for taking me on. Between you and Jon, I might just make it through this." Mill said something else. "Uh, I think maybe you should talk to Jon." She handed me the phone. "He wants to know if we've seen any sign of Hillstrom's people."

I got on the phone and proceeded to tell Mill about our hasty departure from the hotel and our encounter with the man at the overlook. I had a feeling it took a lot to surprise Mill, but this bit of news left him almost speechless.

"Do you still have his phone and wallet?" Mill asked, after getting over the shock.

"We do."

"I need to get them from you. The other number programmed in your phone is for Joe Gray. He's my lead investigator. I don't want to know where you are. Deniability and all that, but he's in the general area where I think you might be. Tomorrow morning, I want you to call him and set up a meeting place where you can turn over the dead operative's things."

"Okay. There was also a 9mm semi-auto. I'm keeping that."

"Well, don't give it to Jess, and if you do, don't tell me about it.

I want to be able to tell the public that she is, in fact, not armed and dangerous."

We hung up with him telling us to be careful.

"What do you think?" I asked.

"I think he now believes that someone is after us. Whether he thinks it's Hillstrom or not really doesn't matter. He'll investigate the leads. What?"

I was looking at her and I must have had a strange expression on my face. "Nothing. It's just ... well, this isn't the same person who was hyperventilating a few hours ago. Something has changed."

"What's changed is that I'm now aware of who I have on my side. Between you, Mill, and The Voice, which seems to be getting stronger in me, everything is being done to keep me alive. I'm still scared out of my mind and it's a constant struggle to not fall apart. But I'm also tired of running. What's changed? As scared as I am, I want my life back, and I'm ready to go after them!"

Chapter 12

I called Joe Gray first thing the next morning. He was waiting for my call, and was in Logan, less than an hour north of us. Since we were heading north anyway, we decided to meet in Logan, and he gave us directions to a fairly remote parking lot on the outskirts of Utah State University.

We exited the hotel in the usual way and stopped at a Panera Bread for bagels and coffee. Jess waited in the car while I picked up the food.

"One day, it will be nice to be able to go into a restaurant again," she said when I returned.

"You'll have a life again. I promise." A promise I had no idea if I could keep.

We drove most of the way in relative silence. Jess was deep in thought and I felt it better not to disturb her.

About ten minutes outside of Logan, she asked, "Have you ever ridden a horse?"

The question caught me by surprise. "A horse?"

She laughed. "Yeah, you know, long face, four legs, and a tail. Cowboys ride them."

I gave her a dirty look. "Once or twice, I suppose. Why?"

"My parents loved riding and always took me. I have fond memories of the squeak of the saddle, the bouncing up and down, the sore butt afterward, and the smell. I love the smell of horses."

"So, what brought that question on?"

"I don't know. I was just sitting here and suddenly I thought I could smell horses. Then I started reminiscing."

"A message, maybe?"

"Maybe. Yeah, I think it was. What do you suppose it means?"

"God, I hope it doesn't mean we're supposed to switch to horseback. I said I did it once or twice. I didn't say I liked it."

Logan was located at the base of the Wasatch mountain range. The town itself wasn't anything special, but the hills just outside of town were beautiful. Joe's directions were good, and I found the parking lot with no trouble.

We pulled up next to his non-descript rental car. The spring semester had finished and most of the students were gone, so the small secluded lot had no other cars. I got out and immediately looked around for security cameras.

"Don't worry, I already checked. That's why I chose this spot." He was walking around the front of his car toward me. He put his hand out. "Joe Gray."

We shook. I was momentarily disappointed. I guess I had expected someone who looked like he was ex-cop or FBI, but Joe was the exact opposite. He was short—five-nine or five-ten—in his late forties or early fifties, thin, and dressed in jeans and a flannel shirt. There was nothing about him that stood out—he was as vanilla as the car he was driving. Which, of course, probably made him an excellent investigator. He was totally forgettable.

As we shook, Jess got out of the car and joined us. Joe looked at her closely, then said, "I've seen every picture of you available. Your hair is different, but there's no doubt that you are Jessica Norton."

"Jess is fine," she responded.

"Okay. Jess it is. Nice to meet you." They shook. "Mill has

briefed me on everything you told him. Hard to believe about Hillstrom, but then, if it was easy to believe, his people wouldn't be doing a very good job, would they?"

"I know it seems fantastic, but it's real," said Jess.

"Well, the nice thing about my job," responded Joe, "is that all I do is to collect evidence and follow it. I have no preconceived ideas, no prejudices, and I can leave emotions out of it altogether. It allows me to keep a totally open mind."

He continued. "So, here's how it will work. There's no need to tell me where you are, but you need to keep that phone with you, so I can call you at a moment's notice. A lot of what I do is time-sensitive, and if I discover something that I need to discuss with you, you need to be available. If I find evidence that they are on to you, I'll especially need to get in touch with you. But it goes both ways. I'm available day and night. Call me whenever you need to. For most things, I'll be your contact person. You should call me if you discover something. Mill will be in touch with you on a regular basis, but I'm in charge of the investigation."

Jess and I both nodded our heads in agreement.

"And," he added. "You've done a good job so far of staying under the radar. Jon, other than that vague description of you from the truck stop, so far it seems no one knows about you. You've gotta keep it that way."

"What about the hotel in Provo?" I asked.

"I've been monitoring the news, as well as the police scanner. Again, a description that could apply to ten million men in this country, and a car registration that was bogus. And nobody actually saw your car. They've got nothing. So far you're doing well."

"Unless, of course, the guy I killed managed to tell someone where I was."

"There is that," said Joe. He opened the stolen phone and looked at the recent calls. "The call log is empty. In fact," he was pressing various buttons, "the address book is empty too. There are no numbers in here at all. Do you think he knew it was you, or just suspected it?"

"I think he only ever saw us in the car," I answered, "so my guess is that he suspected it. But he spent a lot of time tailing us, so he must have been pretty sure."

"You're going to have to start being even more vigilant."

"I'm surprised he didn't at least call the police," said Jess.

"They're the last people he'd call," responded Joe. "If Hillstrom is behind all of this, he doesn't want the police to catch you. I'm sure he's got the reach to kill you while in custody, but he doesn't know how much you'd tell the police before he could get to you. No, he's using the police as a tool, but it's to his advantage to catch you first and dispose of you quietly. I'm sorry. That was maybe a little too honest." Jess had turned pale and was leaning against the car for support.

"No, it's okay. I know the reality of it. I saw someone get killed right in front of me and I helped dispose of the body. The thought that they might be converging on us brought it all back too clearly."

"Could I see the other things you got from the guy, including the gun? Also, I need to know exactly where the incident took place, and where you stashed his car."

I told him, then retrieved the items from the trunk and gave them to him.

He studied the gun for a minute, then turned and reached into his car, pulled out a small cloth bag and handed it to Jess. "You've got small hands. A nine-mil is okay, but you're going to have a bit of trouble shooting it, assuming you have to, of course. In the bag is a Sig .380—much smaller than the nine."

Jess reached in the bag and took out the gun, which fit perfectly in the palm of her hand.

"It's easier to conceal and you'll find it more comfortable to shoot. I've included an extra magazine and a box of ammunition. I'd like to keep the nine, if you don't mind. I want to trace it to see if it turns up anything. I'm sure it'll lead to a dead end, but it's worth a try. The Sig is completely untraceable. All I ask is that you don't make any mention of it to Mill. He doesn't want to know, so I'm not telling him that I gave this to you."

"He was pretty insistent about that on the phone last night," I said.

"I'll let him know that I collected the gun from you. That'll keep his conscience clear. He will assume that you are, in fact, unarmed. He's going to be spinning to the media how innocent you are…"

"…which I am," interrupted Jess.

"I know that and he knows that. The public doesn't. If he can feel comfortable telling them that you are not armed, it just adds to the credibility of the story."

"So what now?" I asked.

"Now, you're kind of on your own. I wish I could hide you someplace or provide you with bodyguards, but frankly, if they are as organized as you say, those options wouldn't protect you. You are better off on your own. Besides, my time and the time of my staff, is better spent trying to find something that will implicate Hillstrom. Okay, now get out of here."

We shook again and headed to our cars. As I was getting in, he called out.

"One more thing. The guy you killed was most likely local help, and it doesn't sound like he was particularly good at his job. With him suddenly dropping out of sight they will probably bring in the professionals. They won't be as easy to kill or get away from.

Just be aware of that."

"Pleasant parting words," I mumbled.

We sat in the car and watched Joe drive away. While I had a good feeling about Joe and his abilities, I was feeling suddenly lost. Jess must have been feeling the same way, because she asked, "What now?"

"I know this isn't what you were hoping for, but I haven't got a clue."

I sat with my hands on the steering wheel at a total loss. Neither of us spoke. Finally, I looked at Jess and said, "Something."

"Huh?"

"When in doubt, do something. Anything. We're in a catatonic state right now and we have to jumpstart our brains. So I say we should just start driving. We know what our eventual destination is."

"Can your car's navigation get us to Homer?"

"Sure, but from here, who knows which way it'll take us. It'll give us choices, I've gotta go 'pre-digital age' and find a road atlas somewhere. Do they still make them?"

Jess shrugged. "Beats me."

I started the car and pulled out of the parking lot, slowly making my way back to Interstate 15, and headed north. After crossing over the Idaho border, I pulled into a service area. Lo and behold, they still made road atlases. Jess had fallen asleep— probably emotional exhaustion—and I let her sleep while I pored over the map. Finally making my decision, I got back on the highway and continued north.

Jess slept for almost two hours and was slightly disoriented when she woke up. I let her get her bearings.

"Are we still just driving, or have we made a decision?" she finally asked, after a long stretch in which I could actually hear her joints crack.

"We made a decision."

"Oh good. What did we decide?"

"This road leads us right to the Canadian border, by way of Great Falls, Montana. Once we go over the border, eventually it will lead us to the Alaska Highway, which will take us right into Alaska."

"Great. Did we figure out how to get me across the border?"

"Well, we had a lively discussion about that, but no, we haven't figured it out yet. I'm hoping a solution will come to us when we get close."

After Joe's parting comments, we found ourselves on edge, constantly on the lookout for suspicious vehicles. Every once in a while, a car would get behind us and follow for a few miles. Eventually it would get off at an exit or pass us, but for those few minutes, the stress would build. Frankly, we were driving ourselves crazy. Just for variety, I occasionally got off the highway and followed smaller roads for a while, before connecting back up with I-15.

Late in the afternoon we were sitting in the car at a service area eating takeout when my phone rang. By that point, our nerves were shot, and the suddenness of the ringing had its effect. Jess let out an "Oh," and dropped her water bottle on the floor, and I dropped my burger on my lap. The top half of the bun flew off and the burger landed face down. My crotch was covered in ketchup.

"Mill?" asked Jess.

"No, that's my phone. Probably my brother."

I recognized the number. "Hey Scott."

"Hey bro. Where are you?" I had called my brother back in South Carolina to let him know I was coming.

"I don't know. Idaho, Wyoming, Montana … I've kind of lost

track. Idaho, I think."

"So you're still a few days away."

"Most definitely." I answered.

"How's your mood these days?"

"I'm finding ways to distract myself." I looked over at Jess, who rolled her eyes.

"You sound better. You were in pretty bad shape when we last talked."

"I was, but some things have happened to help change my perspective. I'll tell you when I get there."

"I'm looking forward to your trip stories," he responded.

"Well, you won't be bored. I guarantee it." Jess could hear both ends of the conversation and I thought she was going to burst out laughing.

"Any mail come for me?" I had had all my mail forwarded to my brother.

"A credit card bill. You obviously haven't been using it. There was only a small balance. I went ahead and paid it."

"Thanks. I'll pay you back when I get there."

"You using cash for everything?"

"Yeah, that's another thing I'll explain when I see you." I never told him about my safe deposit box money.

"Um," he started. "I'm sorry Jon, but a package also arrived from your wife's lawyers. Divorce papers."

"Cool, I'll sign them as soon as I get there."

Scott was silent for a moment. "So you're not upset?" he asked in a puzzled voice.

"God, no."

"Wow, this *must* be some trip."

"You have no idea. Um, I'm bringing a friend."

"I figured as much," he responded. "I'm looking forward to

meeting her." Scott could read me like a book. "Give me a call as you get closer."

"I will. And Scott?"

"Yeah?"

"Thanks for all your support. In case I don't get the chance to say it later, I love you."

"Uh, okay. I love you too. You're not planning on dying on me, are you?"

"I sure hope not." I hung up the phone and looked at Jess, tears in my eyes.

"He sounds like a good guy," she said.

"The best. I just hope we're not putting him in danger by going up there."

"Jon, we don't have to go to Homer."

"Yeah, we do. A part of the puzzle is up there, and we're not going to get out of this until the puzzle is solved. Besides, if I can stay anonymous, he won't be in any danger and it'll be a good place for us to be."

We did a lot of driving that day and made it to Great Falls, staying in a decent-looking Best Western. My days of five-star hotels were a thing of the past, but I had come to the conclusion that it no longer mattered. All I was looking for now was a safe haven. When your perspective changes, the hotels all look the same.

We caught a clip of Mill's press conference after we had gotten into bed. As expected, he handled himself well.

Mill Colson: *"I'm here to announce that I have been retained by Jessica Norton to represent her in response to the laughable charges that have been brought against her. She is the victim of an insidious conspiracy, and over time we will prove that."*

Reporter: *"Is she going to give herself up?"*

Mill: *"While I, of course, recommended that option, she feels that she would be putting herself further in harm's way by surrendering to the authorities. And I will respect her decision."*

Reporter: *"Do you know where she is?"*

Mill: *"I honestly have no idea where she is."*

Reporter: *"Did she come to you, or did you seek her out?"*

Mill (with a smirk): *"I don't seek out my clients."*

Laughter from the audience.

Reporter: *"What can you tell us about the rumor that she is traveling with a man?"*

Mill: *"I can't tell you anything about it."*

Reporter: *"Do you know?"*

Mill: *"Next question."*

Reporter: *"What is this conspiracy you talk about? Isn't a conspiracy theory just a convenient way to put the attention on someone else?"*

Mill: *"Yes, but in this case, it's very real. It's too early to go into details."*

Reporter: *"Is she armed and dangerous, as the police are telling us?"*

Mill: *"She is not armed and she has never been dangerous. As I said, she is a victim here, a convenient patsy for an elaborate conspiracy that was about to be revealed. The true story will come out and Jessica Norton will go from feared killer to American hero."*

The story had already exceeded sound bite limits, so the rest of the news conference was cut from the report for a commercial.

"What do you think?" asked Jess

"He's a celebrity lawyer. I think he can't help being dramatic. I didn't think he was going to bring up the conspiracy at all, so that surprises me. He may have just put a bulls-eye on his back. He also put one on yours by calling you an American hero. He's telling them what they could only suspect, that you know even more than they thought. I don't think it was a great news conference, but I still think we picked the right person."

It was the middle of the night when the phone rang. It took me a minute to realize that it was the disposable cell from Mill. I turned the light on and reached for the phone.

"Hello?" I said, my voice thick with sleep.

"You're a dead man."

That woke me up. "What?" Jess was looking over at me with concern on her face. I put the phone on speaker.

"The only way you're going to live is to tell me where she is, then leave her and get in your car and go. Just keep driving. It's only a matter of time before we find out your name. When we do, you will die, but not before you get to witness the very ugly deaths of your family members. I'm sure you have children, a wife, parents. Doesn't matter who. We will find them and kill them."

I disconnected the call without saying a word.

"Do you think they know where we are?" asked Jess.

"No. I think they were fishing, and that wouldn't have been enough time for them to trace it, if they even can. I'm much more worried about something else. That was the disposable phone Mill gave me, which means they have access to that number. That can only mean one thing: Mill Colson has a mole in his office."

Chapter 13

We were too wired to sleep now. I looked at the clock. It was 2:30. There was only one thing I could think of doing. I put the phone on speaker so Jess could hear, and dialed Joe Gray's number. He answered on the second ring, sounding wide awake.

"Hey," he said.

I started right in without a preamble. "Who besides you and Mill knows my name?"

"Nobody. What's going on?" He spoke briskly, instantly alert, as if he was always on the phone at 2:30 in the morning. Maybe he was.

"You're absolutely sure?"

"Absolutely."

"And who has this number?"

"The same two people. Just Mill and me. What's happening?"

I told him about the phone call. I finished by saying, "So somebody else has that number. I'm thinking it's someone in Mill's office."

"Shit."

"So I go back to my other question. Now that it's been determined that you two aren't the only ones with access to this phone, is it possible that someone also has access to my name?"

"No. There is no possible way."

"Why?"

"Because he only ever told me your name once, and in a very secure location. We have systems in place when we have to meet about something highly confidential. You just have to trust me on that one. We've been doing this a long time. When we do have to refer to you, we have a codename for you, and that's all we ever use."

I didn't bother asking him what it was.

"As for the phone," he continued, "that baffles me, but we're talking about electronics and communications. There's always someone who can hack into that stuff. However, I will bring this up with Mill. You could be right. If so, this conspiracy might be enormous. Hillstrom could have tentacles in companies all over the country."

He continued. "Here's what I want you to do. Make sure you have my number and Mill's number memorized. Destroy this phone. Tomorrow, pick up another prepaid phone and call me with its number. Only me. From here on, you communicate only with me. Don't lose Mill's number, but don't call him. Just to be safe, don't ever identify yourself when you call me. I never want your name anywhere out there."

"How do you know the leak isn't in your office?"

"Because my office travels with me. I am my office. When I referred to the people working under me, they are not people I actually see—maybe once or twice a year at most. I pass on the assignments and we communicate by phone and email. However," he said, stopping me before I could interrupt, "the assignments they have now are all related to Hillstrom. Nobody, absolutely nobody, knows about you. Whoever got that number was just hoping they could either scare you enough to give up Jess, or somehow have you reveal something about yourself. I wouldn't worry about your family. They don't know who you are, so they can't get to them."

"That's the funny thing," I answered. "I have no family." I decided not to mention my brother. "There is nobody they could hold over my head, so that doesn't concern me."

"Well, you did the right thing to call me. Call me again when you get your new phone, then become invisible."

After I hung up and smashed the phone, Jess said, "Should we leave tonight? Do you think we're in danger here?"

"No. I really don't think they have a clue as to where we are. In fact, that call assures me that the guy I killed didn't get my plate number. Or if he did get it, he didn't pass it on, as we figured from his empty phone log. If he had, they would have looked it up and the one who called would have referred to me by name. Using my name would have added a whole new dimension of fear to the threats. Besides," I continued, "we can't leave now. We're close to the Canadian border and we haven't figured out yet how to get you across. Whatever we decide to do should be done during a busy time, not in the middle of the night."

Jess seemed to accept my explanation, but logical or not, neither of us slept for the rest of the night. What I didn't say to Jess was that I believed Joe when he told us in the parking lot that the disappearance of the guy I killed would send up a flag. I had no doubt that they knew generally where we were. How many people would they send in to saturate the area? Would they be watching the border?

We left at nine. We stopped at a Radio Shack and I bought a phone. Once it was activated, I called Joe and gave him the number. Lack of sleep and stress from the phone call the night before had us exhausted, and you do stupid things when you are tired.

On our way out of town I stopped at a diner and told Jess I'd order some breakfast and bring it back to the car. Jess had apparently had enough.

"I want to go in too."

"That's not smart."

"I don't care. We're in the middle of nowhere and I look different from my photo. No one will notice. Just once I'd like to sit down at a table for my breakfast. Just today. I need this."

She had a pleading look about her and I couldn't argue any longer. I should have, but frankly, I was just as tired of it all as she was. So I gave in.

There are old "classic" diners—the ones labeled Americana that they write whole books about—and then there are just old diners. This was the latter. There was nothing charming about it. Nothing that made you yearn for the good old days when diners were an American institution (long before I was born). It was actually fairly disgusting. The place reeked of old grease. There were about a dozen customers, not one weighing less than 300 pounds. I immediately saw the source of the weight problem in the cans of lard sitting next to the grill. Five steps in, Jess must have also had enough of the assault on her senses.

"Field trip's over," she declared, and we made a hasty retreat back to the car.

As I was opening my door, I looked over at the diner's entrance and saw two men who had been about to enter staring at Jess. I pegged them immediately as from out of town, given that they each weighed less than 200 pounds. They also weren't dressed like locals and had an air about them that said, "we're on a mission." They discussed something for a moment, then went in, both casting glances back our way.

Fortunately, my car was parked in the furthest corner of the lot away from the door and in such a way as to make my plates unreadable. The best they could have come away with was the fact that they weren't Montana plates.

I didn't want to draw attention to ourselves, so I tried to stay as casual as possible as I pulled out of the lot. Once on the highway though, I accelerated quickly, hoping to put a lot of distance between us.

Jess could sense the change in my demeanor, but wisely said nothing and didn't turn around to see what was scaring me. Once safely away, however, she cast a worried look my way.

"Two guys," I said in response to her stare. "They were entering the diner and looking at you. I'm convinced they were Hillstrom's men."

"Maybe they just like pretty girls," she responded, trying for some levity, but falling flat.

"Those weren't looks of lust," I said.

"Then why didn't they follow?"

"I don't think they were convinced it was you."

"Think it's one of those situations where they'll sit down and midway through their meal they'll decide it was me?"

"That's exactly what I'm thinking. It's why I'm trying to get as far ahead of them as I can."

"Would it help if we put on the stolen license plates?" asked Jess.

"It might help," I answered. "You never know. But I'd rather wait until after I cross into Canada."

"I notice you didn't say 'we'," said Jess.

"We've got to figure out a different way for you to get across. Any messages?" I asked hopefully.

"Nothing. He's been strangely silent."

As I drove, I kept one eye on my rearview mirror. So far, nothing. It was déjà vu. This was exactly like my trip across Texas— ugly flat country, and a long straight road with little traffic. When we reached Shelby, I pulled into a truck stop/motel. I parked in amongst some eighteen-wheelers where we would be hidden from both the highway and the rest of the parking lot.

"Before I saw those guys, I was going to suggest stopping really early and catching up on our sleep. Not now. Now time is not on our side. We have to get you out of this car."

"Maybe I could stow away in one of those trucks."

"Assuming you could get in—and all their cargo doors seem to have locks—it would be too dangerous."

We waited and watched for over an hour. Although we were hidden, I had a view of the highway. About a half an hour into our wait, I saw a newish, black SUV with our two friends get off the exit. I got out of the car to get a better vantage point of the parking lot and saw them pull in. They took two laps around the lot with all the cars, then drove toward the town of Shelby.

"One crisis averted for the moment," I said as I got back in the car.

The waiting was interminable. Absolutely nothing was coming to us.

Finally, Jess said, "Horses."

"Again?"

"I guess it was a message, the thing about horses."

"What do you mean?" I asked.

"Look." She pointed to a large horse trailer being towed by a powerful pickup truck that was making its way around the parking lot, finally settling near a field, and only about a hundred feet away from us.

"It has Alberta plates," she said.

"Yeah, but is it coming from Alberta or going to Alberta?"

"I've gotta trust the message. I have to assume it's going there."

We watched as a man and woman got out of the truck and went

to the back of the trailer, which was facing us. They pulled down the ramp and unlocked the inner door, and the woman checked on the horses.

"They going to take them out, you think?" I asked.

"It's probably too open here, and noisy from the trucks. It would scare the horses. If they got away, they could end up on the highway. They're probably just checking their hay and giving them some water. I'm hoping they're going in for a bite to eat and they'll leave some of it open for air. Then I can sneak in and find someplace to hide."

The idea showed promise. "We don't know how far they're going, but I can just stay within sight of the trailer. You know the number of this phone in case we get separated?"

"I do. If they end up going to a ranch, just park someplace near the entrance in an inconspicuous spot and I'll find you."

"You're sure about this?"

"Absolutely. Those horse thoughts were definitely preparing me for this."

I reached under the seat and pulled out the .380. "Take it. You just never know."

"And if the customs people find me?"

"Ditch it before they come in. Put it under some hay or something. If they find you, they're not going to be interested in looking any further."

She put it in the pocket of her jeans.

We watched and waited. Eventually the woman came out of the trailer and they locked a half door. It was low enough so that the horses could get air, but too high for them to get out. The couple stretched, then walked over to the restaurant.

"Here goes," said Jess.

I kissed her. "Good luck. Keep your head down."

I watched as she looked around. Seeing nobody, she sauntered over, as if taking a walk. When she reached the trailer, I saw her talking to the horses. Then she looked around again and climbed over the door. The horses moved restlessly with a strange presence among them. Slowly though, they calmed down. I could imagine Jess in there talking to them. Soon, all was quiet.

I took that time to get rid of any traces of Jess from the interior of the car. Anything that didn't need to be there I put in the trunk, including my gun and ammo, which I buried deep in my suitcase. I was so intent on my project, I didn't hear the SUV pull up.

"Howdy," came the voice from behind me. I jumped six inches, then turned and found myself facing the two from the diner. They wore basically the same clothes, were about the same height and weight, and both had black hair. They could have been brothers, except for complexion. One was of Latin descent, and the other was a pasty white guy.

"Sorry, you startled me," I said, inwardly swearing because I had just packed my gun away.

"Sorry to bother you. We're looking for a woman, and we realized that she looked amazingly like the woman you were with at the diner in Great Falls."

I hesitated a fraction of a second. "I wasn't with a woman." *Think fast! Think fast!*

"Well, yeah, you were. We saw you."

Then it came to me. My only possible way out.

"Are you cops?"

They looked at each other then back at me. The pasty guy said, "No, of course not." I knew what they were thinking, that I was about to give Jess up and make some excuse for being with her. They were almost salivating as they sensed their prize within their grasp.

114

"Well, that girl…"

"The one from the news?" asked the pasty guy again.

I looked at them, cocked my head, and gave an expression of incomprehension.

"What girl from the news?"

They looked deflated. "Well, who were you with?" asked the other guy.

I looked around, leaned in close, and said, "A hooker."

"A hooker?" asked the white guy in a loud voice.

I tried to shush him while acting uncomfortable.

"Yeah, that's why I thought you were cops. I picked her up at the diner, and came out here where we, uh, did it."

"So where is she now?" asked the one with the darker complexion.

"I don't know. I paid her and she left. Went into the restaurant, I think. My guess is if you look for a truck rocking, you'll find her."

I think I had convinced them. "You say she was on the news?"

"No," said Pasty. "She just looked like someone else. Sorry to bother you." He started walking back to the car, then turned. "Was she any good?"

I just gave him a big wide smile.

They got in their car and drove away and I almost collapsed, my legs were shaking so much. We had dodged a bullet that day. We couldn't keep getting lucky.

Chapter 14

While I was talking to the two goons, the horse trailer couple had come out of the restaurant. I watched them now as they made preparations to leave. The woman went into the trailer to look around. Satisfied that all was in place, she came out and they locked the trailer and put up the ramp. A minute later they were pulling out of the lot. I waited to see what direction they took, my fingers crossed. I wasn't overly worried. Nothing bad would happen if they headed south, it would just delay us getting to Homer. But I didn't know if we would find such a perfect hiding place for Jess again.

However, I needn't have worried. The truck took the northerly route, heading for the border. I waited a few minutes, then followed. The border was only a half an hour away, so I figured I had given them the right head start in order to arrive there at about the same time.

When we got to the border post, I was directly in back of them. They seemed to know the guard who stopped them, as they spent a lot of the time laughing. He moved them on and they waved to him. It was my turn. I was nervous, but other than the gun in the trunk, I had no reason to be. I pulled up.

"Could I see your passport please?" The guard still had a smile on his face from the horse people.

"Sure." I handed it to him.

"Your reason for going into Canada? Business or pleasure."

"I'm heading to Homer, Alaska, to visit my brother. Certainly not business. We'll have to see if it's pleasure when I get there."

He laughed. "Yeah, I have two brothers." He handed me back my passport. "Good luck!"

I waved to him as I took off, now that I was as good a friend as the horse people. I took my time, knowing that the trailer would be going a lot slower. I didn't want to get too close and have it seem obvious that I was following them. I pulled over in the rest area of the border post just to kill a few minutes. I looked cautiously around, but there was no sign of the SUV. I gave it ten minutes, but then was too antsy to wait any longer, and started on my way.

I caught up with the horse trailer fifteen miles up the road. They were moving at a faster clip than I expected, and when I didn't see them at the ten-mile mark, I started to panic and found myself speeding up to catch up with them. I was just starting to wonder if they had pulled off somewhere when I saw them in the distance. I breathed a sigh of relief and slowed down to a reasonable speed. We continued like that for a long time. The road was flat, but I could see mountains in the distance to the west. We passed by Lethbridge and merged onto Route 2 toward Calgary. They stopped for gas once but didn't open the back of the trailer, so Jess had no opportunity to escape.

Somewhere outside of Calgary their turn signal went on and they slowed to a crawl. I accelerated and passed them on the left and watched them in my rearview mirror turn down a dusty road. Jess was right, they were going back to their ranch.

A half a mile past the ranch entrance was a pull-off on the side of the highway. Not a rest area, per se, but enough space to be officially off the road. I pulled onto it and parked as far from the tarmac as possible and turned off the engine. What now? We hadn't really thought it out very well. Jess had suggested I wait at the entrance to the ranch, but that was impossible. The ranch entrance was right off the highway and the ranch buildings were a half mile down a very flat and exposed driveway. I'd be too conspicuous sitting at the end of the driveway and Jess would be out in the open trying to walk back up to the highway. No, there was only one solution.

I started the car and went about a mile, where I took an exit onto a crossroad. I crossed the highway and got back on, this time heading south. A couple of miles later I did the same thing in reverse, going back in the direction I was originally headed, but now south of the ranch. When I reached the driveway, I turned down and headed for the ranch buildings, all the while trying to figure out what I would say when I got there.

I pulled into the ranch yard just as the woman was leading a horse from the trailer into an enormous barn. I snuck a glance into the trailer. It was empty. Either Jess had already gotten out, or she was hiding under something waiting for her opportunity.

I turned off the engine and got out of the car, where I was immediately met by the husband. He looked to be about my age.

"Howdy. Can I help you?" He was friendly, but also a bit wary. "I saw you following me. Was kind of wondering if I was going to see you."

I tried to look embarrassed. "I'm really sorry about that. I actually wasn't following you. I'm headed to Alaska to visit family. I found myself driving a little too fast, so I decided to slow down and start enjoying the ride. It just happened that I slowed down in back of you, so we ended up going the same speed. As I was driving behind you, I started thinking about how this is supposed to be great horse country. Well, when you turned off, I passed you, but pulled over a little way up trying to muster the courage."

"The courage for what?" He was a little friendlier, but the wariness was still there. His wife had joined him.

"My name is Bill Miller. I'm from Boston—born and brought up there, so the only horses I've come in contact with are the police horses on Boston Common. So, I got to thinking how nice it would be to see a real live horse ranch. Might sound weird to you, but this is a life so far out of my realm of experience, I thought, 'what the heck, maybe they'd show me around so I can at least say that I experienced a real ranch'. And as I say it, I realize how stupid it sounds."

I think I had finally won them over. After all, people proud of what they have like to show it off.

"We'd be happy to. Come on inside the barn. We were just taking care of the horses we had in the trailer."

"Do you race them?" I asked as we walked across the parking lot, trying to sound as much like a city slicker as possible.

They laughed. "No, we breed them, and some we take to shows. That's where we were coming back from—a show in Idaho. I'm Norman and this is my wife Suzanne. If we visited you in Boston we'd be the same as you—fish out of water. We'll go into a city if we have to, but we could never live there. We need the open space as much as our horses do."

For the next hour, I learned more about horses than I ever wanted to. But to their credit, they made it interesting. It was a fascinating—but very hard—life. Long hours and a lot of work. But they'd been successful at it, not worried about money and thoroughly enjoying their life. We sat on their porch for a while after they showed me around, and they plied me with lemonade and cookies.

Finally, we said our goodbyes and I got back in my car, turned around, and headed up the driveway. I hadn't looked in the back seat, but just assumed.

"Comfy back there?"

"Not really," came her muffled voice. I had left a blanket on the back seat to cover herself with. "I've been on your back floor for over an hour. I doubt if I'll ever walk again. What took you so long?"

"They offered me lemonade and cookies. Who can pass that up?"

"Did you get a doggie bag? I'm starving."

"Sorry."

We reached the highway. When we were out of sight of the ranch, I gave Jess the all-clear and she poked her head up.

"Whew, fresh air," she said.

"Maybe for you. You're smelling a bit, um, horsey." Getting serious, I asked, "So, how was it?"

"It was okay," she answered, climbing into the passenger seat. She leaned over and gave me a quick kiss on the lips. "We made it."

"We did."

"I think the horses accepted me there pretty quickly. I would have enjoyed interacting more with them, but I think I was too worried about how I was going to get out of there. How did it go with you? I heard those guys come by and could hear some of what was said, but I think I missed a lot."

I caught her up with their "visit."

"So I'm your whore now?" she asked at the end.

"Yup. And you were good, too."

"Well, I know that." She changed the subject. "Any way we could get something to eat? I wasn't kidding back there. I haven't had anything to eat all day. The hay in the trailer was starting to look pretty tasty."

We were close to Red Deer, and as soon as I found a promising exit, we got off the highway. Jess still didn't want to eat in the car, but after the morning's escapade, was gun shy about trying a restaurant again. Since it was already late afternoon, we went ahead and found a hotel. I asked Jess what she wanted to eat, and she responded with, "a lot." So I went for Chinese while she showered the horse smell off.

While we were eating, she told me of her experience in the trailer.

"I've always cursed the fact that I'm short. It's a negative when you are trying to find a guy. It's also a negative in job hunting. People don't seem to respect you if you're short. I wasn't wishing I was tall, just normal. You know, five-five or five-six."

"What you're saying is you were a short dumb blonde. That's two strikes against you right there."

"Yeah, I know. In the scheme of things, it's a petty complaint. People have it a lot worse. But I guess what I was getting to is that today I thanked my lucky stars that I was short. The owners of that trailer were clean-freaks. Once I got in the trailer there was nowhere to hide. I was really panicking. I almost came running back out."

She continued, "I looked up and saw a wire mesh storage shelf with a four- or five-inch lip on the side so things wouldn't fall down on the horses. It just had some blankets on it. It looked like it might be sturdy enough, so I figured I'd give it a try. It must have been not much more than five feet, because I just fit. The blankets were under me, so she couldn't see me through the mesh, and I kind of built them up around the lip. I figured if she didn't look up or need to store anything on it, I'd be okay. I was also crossing my fingers that it would hold my weight, but I figured The Voice wouldn't steer me wrong. It worked. She was so intent on getting the horses secure, she didn't look up. Once we were on our way, I took my time getting down so the horses would get used to me."

We'd had a stressful day and were both tired. We cleaned up the remains of the food and I took a shower, then joined Jess in bed, where we made love before passing out.

*****

We were up early the next morning, anxious to get on our way. I gave Joe a quick call to let him know we might be going into an extended stretch of no cell service. He appreciated the call and said he had no news to pass on. He told us to be cautious and to call him when we could.

We got on the road, figuring we'd stop for breakfast after we'd driven for a while. At about 9:30, we came up to a service area. I pulled in and was about to park when I saw a familiar black SUV in a parking spot in front of the restaurant. I stepped on the gas and kept going out of the lot and right back onto the highway.

Jess looked confused. "What's going on?"

"Our friends were in the restaurant. I'm going to get off at the next town and lay low for a little bit."

"Do you think they saw us?"

"Don't know. I didn't see them, but if they were sitting on that side of the restaurant, they could have. I think it's time to change the plates. We've been fortunate that—to my knowledge anyway—they haven't gotten my license plate number. The car has never been parked so they could see it. If I'm going to stay anonymous, it's time to stop taking chances."

We passed a road sign that told us we were close to Edmonton.

"Nothing like a big city to get lost in," I said, while Jess craned her neck to keep watch out the back window.

We pulled into a restaurant parking lot and I located the most remote corner behind the kitchen. Looking around and seeing no one, I took the stolen plates out from under Jess's seat and hurriedly replaced my Massachusetts plates with those from Utah.

"What do we do if we get pulled over?" asked Jess.

"I don't know. I'll do everything I can to follow the law and not get pulled over."

I got out and opened the trunk to retrieve my gun.

"You still have yours?" I asked when I got back into the car.

"I do."

"Let's just hope we won't have to use them." I put mine under my seat.

It seemed Jess was destined not to have a sit-down meal. We finally stopped at a fast food place just as they finished serving breakfast grease and had just started serving lunch grease. Oh how my eating habits had deteriorated. While we ate, parked in the parking lot, I studied the road atlas. Jess was quiet as she let me plan.

"Here's what I think," I said finally, pointing to the map. "The quickest way out of here and the way I had figured we'd go is over to Route 43, then to the Alaska Highway. But if we go up through St. Albert and catch a little road across to 43, maybe they won't be looking there—especially if it's only the two of them."

Jess agreed and we headed out. We had just started when I noticed we needed gas, so I pulled into a self-serve station and pumped the gas. When I was finished, I got back into the car and shut my door. The instant I did that, the rear passenger door opened, and the pasty guy slid in. In his hand was a gun.

"Just drive," he said.

Chapter 15

He kept the gun down low but pointed between the seats at stomach level.

"A hooker, huh?" he said, looking at Jess. He glanced back at me. "You had us fooled. If you hadn't pulled into that restaurant parking lot, you would have gotten away with it. We got lucky again when you decided to take this route out of Edmonton. I knew you'd try something sneaky, so we headed up this way. God was smiling on us today. He was shitting on you though. You didn't even see us, did you? We were parked two lanes over in the gas station. I saw you drive in and I thought we'd won the lottery."

I cursed myself for putting the gun under the seat and not having it in my belt. But my gun wasn't small like Jess's, and it was uncomfortable to drive with.

He was looking at Jess. "So you're the famous Jessica Norton. You have any idea how many people are looking for you right now? And I'm the one who found you. After I saw your car at the restaurant, I contacted the people who hired me. They just about shit their pants. Who knows how many people they've just sent up here." He turned his attention to me. "My buddy back there is calling in your license plate, so we'll finally know who you are."

Thank God I'd just changed the plates.

"You've been a real pain in the ass," he continued. "My guess is she'd have been caught back in Texas if you hadn't come on the scene."

"Does it really matter how many people they're sending up?" I asked. "You're just taking us to a good spot to kill us, right?"

"You got that right. You're a smart guy. No sense in lying to you. Our boss wants us to hold onto you for him. He wants the credit for killing you. No fucking way! You're mine. If anybody is going to get the credit, it'll be me. But hey, you gave it a good ride. You made it to the middle of fucking nowhere. And that's where you're going to die."

Jess had discreetly pulled the gun out of her pocket.

I said, "So this is the spot in the movies where the bad guy figures that since he's going to kill them anyway, he can tell the good guys the whole story of who hired him and why."

"How the fuck do I know?" he answered. "The guy I work for was contacted by the guy he works for, who was contacted by someone else. I don't know who wants you dead. All I know is that they're paying me to get a job done."

"How much are they paying you?" I asked.

"None of your fucking business."

"I'll give you a hundred thousand to walk away."

"Yeah, right. Like you have it on you?"

"Of course not. But I can get it fast."

It looked to me like he was giving it a fleeting thought, but not much more than that.

"Nah, I'll get a bonus for this. For all I know, it might be a hundred grand. Besides, I don't want the same people looking for me who are looking for you."

Dense woods lined the road and I could see pasty guy looking around for a good spot to pull over. I glanced over at Jess and saw she had her eyes closed. She was working up the courage to do what she knew had to be done.

"Up there," he said. "Take that dirt road."

I slowed and turned down the road. He had a good killer's instinct and had picked well. It wasn't so much a road as a path, one that led directly into the woods. I couldn't believe he actually saw it. I would have passed it right by. It was secluded and literally in the middle of nowhere, like he said. He directed me to pull into a batch of trees totally hidden from the main road.

I had often wondered why people allow themselves to go with someone who has a gun. You have to know that the outcome isn't going to be good. My feeling was that you fight back, even if you got killed in the process. It would still be better than what's waiting for you at the other end. But here we were, in a car with a man holding a gun on us. In this case though, we had a fighting chance. I don't think it even occurred to him that we might be armed.

I stopped the car and looked at Jess. Instantly I knew it. She was getting direction from The Voice. I could just tell. She was going to be told when to fire. The SUV pulled up in back of us and the other guy got out. As he started to walk toward us on my side of the car, pasty guy opened the back door and was about to get out when Jess shot him. She aimed her first shot through her seat and it caught him in the arm. He was too surprised to shoot. Then she turned to face him, aimed at him over the seat, and coolly pulled the trigger five more times. The noise was deafening in the enclosed space.

As she was shooting, I grabbed my gun from under my seat and was out the door. The other guy was reaching for his gun when I shot him. He was about twenty feet away—an exceptionally easy shot for me with all my gun range practice. Except, most of my experience was with a paper target. Shooting at a real body was a lot different. However, I had a vast amount of experience now that

I had already killed once, and it seemed to be easier the second time. I put two more bullets into him as he fell, then checked him. He was dead. I went back to see about Pasty, but I needn't have bothered. He was riddled with Jess's six bullets. There was no doubt as to his status.

I looked in on Jess, vividly remembering her complete breakdown when I killed the guy at the overlook. But it was a very different reaction this time. She was still sitting in her seat, but other than some shaking, she seemed calm—almost at peace. I knew The Voice had something to do with that.

"You okay?" I asked, already knowing the answer.

"Yeah, I am," she answered, putting her hands to her ears to stop the ringing. "You know what I am? I'm tired and I'm pissed. Let them come and get me. They're going to have a fight on their hands."

I smiled at the change. I could tell she was still scared—that wouldn't go away anytime soon—but there was something else now. Slowly the fear was being replaced by anger, and I knew that it might just help keep us alive.

"Let's pull these guys into the woods," I said. "I bet they have bears or wolves or coyotes up here. If we're lucky they'll stay hidden long enough to get eaten."

There was quite a lot of blood and I watched Jess for signs of cracking, but she was fine, for now anyway. I didn't exactly know what it was, but I had no doubt that The Voice was the source. It had gone from guide to confidante, of that I was sure, and at some point she would tell me more about it.

Meanwhile, we had a decision to make. After we had dragged the bodies deep into the woods and had covered them with branches until they were completely hidden, I looked at my car— my beloved Beemer. The back seat and windows were splattered in vast amounts of blood and the front passenger seat had a bullet-sized hole through it. It was time to abandon it. But how?

Plates or no plates, the car could be traced back to me through the vehicle identification number. Jess and I talked about the options and decided to leave the car where it was and take the SUV.

"This road is old and looks like it's rarely used. If we can get this car way into the woods, it could be a long time before it's found. Hopefully by then the two bodies will have decomposed or have been eaten."

"The other thing," said Jess, "is that we took all the identification off those guys. If the police do find the bodies, they might assume one of them is you."

We took everything out of the car and loaded it into the SUV, then I drove the car as deep into the woods as I could, and we spent the next hour hiding it and eliminating all traces of the car ever having been there.

Finally, we were ready.

"Well, they were cleaner than the last guy whose car I had to dispose of," I said. "Not too bad for a couple of guys."

"You must not have very high standards," said Jess. She sniffed the air and frowned.

We turned around. The SUV was a big Nissan Armada. It was owned by the pasty guy—Mitchell Becker—which might have explained why it wasn't a pigpen. He took some pride in it.

We were on the road heading west toward 43 when Becker's phone rang. I looked at Jess then down at the phone. It said, "Unknown Caller."

"What the hell," I said. "Maybe he won't know Becker's voice."

He didn't.

"This Becker?"

"Yeah, who the fuck's this?" I asked in my best Becker

imitation.

"One of the many people who can fire your ass," he responded. "So watch how you talk to me. We just touched down in Calgary. I got word that you've found her."

"Yeah, we're following her right now."

"Where are you?"

I motioned for Jess to open the atlas.

"We are on Route 16 heading east from Edmonton. She's gotta be headed for Saskatoon or Winnipeg. According to my map, if you head east on Route 1 out of Calgary, the two roads converge in Winnipeg. Maybe we can corner her."

"Okay, that's what we're going to do. Call me back at this number if there is any deviation."

"Will do." And I hung up.

I looked at Jess and smiled. "Oh wait. A deviation. We're going west, not east, and we're not on Route 16."

Jess laughed. I still couldn't see any sign that she was bothered by the earlier events, but I knew it was something that could hit at any time.

"We may have just bought ourselves some time. I figure we can talk to him for the next few hours if he calls, then Mitchell Becker is going off the grid. Which reminds me. We should call Joe and let him know what happened."

We didn't know what the laws were in Canada about cell phones and driving, so Jess called him. If Joe was surprised that we had killed two more people, Jess said he didn't sound it. She took him through it step by step and finished with us sending Hillstrom's goons in the opposite direction.

Since we had talked to him not that long ago, he didn't have any updates for us. He told Jess to be careful and they hung up.

We had two more calls that day from the unknown caller, and

we let him know that Jess was still heading east, then I turned the phone off. Mitchell Becker ceased to exist.

We pulled into Grande Prairie that evening and found a decent-looking hotel. We had passed a couple of signs for Alaska, which had excited us. We still had a long way to go to get to Homer, and we had no idea what we would do once we arrived. But with Hillstrom's people converging on Winnipeg, and us in a different vehicle, for the first time since I picked Jess up, we were beginning to feel safe.

Chapter 16

The next day we reached Dawson Creek, the official start of the Alaska Highway. The days following were the closest thing to peace we had experienced since the ordeal began. We drove through some of the most beautiful country I had ever seen, catching glimpses of moose, deer, bears, and even bison. We bought a small tent and spent the nights at some of the many campgrounds along the road. Still careful to keep Jess out of the public eye, we always chose the most remote spot to set up the tent. We were in no hurry, sometimes just pulling over and spending an hour or two looking out at the view. We made love each night, both of us so grateful that I had stopped for her on that rainy night in Texas.

It had been a bad winter, and the higher elevations were still snow-covered even this late in the season. Although normally a busy road filled with RVs and trucks with trailers that time of year, there were also times when we felt all alone travelling through the snowy mountain passes. While serene, it could also be nerve-wracking navigating the curvy roads. Always in the back of our mind was the potential threat of Hillstrom's men cornering us out there in the middle of nowhere.

Jess had changed since the shooting. Although she had moments of anxiety from having killed a man, they mostly appeared in the middle of the night. During the day there were glimmers of a strength about her I hadn't seen before. It was nothing we talked about, and in fact, I'm not sure she wanted to talk about it. There was something else, too. During some of the quiet times, I would see Jess close her eyes for anywhere from ten minutes to a couple of hours. She wasn't sleeping though. The best I could figure was that she was meditating. Whatever it was, something was happening, as she always came out of it with a look of contentment.

Phone service was spotty at best, but I managed to call Scott and let him know where I was. I also called Joe. He said that so much negative information was being put out there about Jess—drug use, alcohol abuse, anger problems and a history of violence, among other things—that Mill decided it was time to present Jess's side of the story. Even though they hadn't yet found anything incriminating on Hillstrom, Mill was going to make the accusations anyway, without being too specific. He had a press conference scheduled in a couple of days.

"They also found the mole in Mill's office," added Joe. "He refused to say who he was working for, but there was enough evidence to prove he was collecting information. Mill threw him out on his butt. So that part's over."

I let him know that we'd be at our destination soon and would call him again then.

At one point I decided to turn Becker's phone back on to see if any messages had been left. I was rewarded with a feast of information. There were close to thirty messages, all from "Unknown Caller." They all started with some variation of "Where the fuck are you?" The early messages asked for an update, but the later ones sounded more desperate. They had reached Winnipeg but had no idea where to look. They had men stationed all over the place trying to spot my Beemer. One message reported that the plates on the car that Becker's buddy had passed on were from a car rented by an operative who had gone missing. It ended with "What the hell is going on?"

I decided to take a chance. At that point it had been three days since I had last talked to him. I pressed the button to return the call and got him immediately.

"Where the fuck have you been?" came the familiar refrain.

"They got the drop on us outside Saskatoon. They came out of fucking nowhere. They had guns. Nothing we could do." I tried to whine a bit. "We just now got free. We're starving."

"I don't care about that, you moron. How could you let yourself get jumped? Do you have any idea how badly you've screwed up this whole operation? Do you know how many people I had to bring up here based on your info. Shit! So where did they go?"

"I don't know for sure, but I heard her saying in the next room something about needing to go back to Washington. Something about that's where the evidence is. I don't know what she was talking about, but it sounds like they're heading back to the states."

"Shit, shit, shit!"

"So what do you want us to do?" I asked.

"You? Go jump off a bridge for all I care. You two are fucking fired! I don't ever want to hear from you again. You may as well get a job at Burger King, 'cuz I'll make sure you never work in this business again." He hung up.

I put the phone down on a rock, and using another rock, smashed it to bits.

"I could hear a lot of yelling," said Jess. "What did he say?"

"We're fucking fired. The good news is that Burger King is hiring."

"Could it be that we might actually be safe for a while? Not only did I hear you steer them back toward Washington, but they're no longer wondering what happened to Becker. Now that he's been fired, nobody is going to be looking for the SUV."

"Exactly," I agreed. "That couldn't have gone any better. I just decided to listen to his messages on a lark. I'm glad I did. We've just bought ourselves even more time."

We needed to start thinking about the border crossing again. I suggested that Jess lie down on the floor behind the passenger seat and I would pile some things on top of her, but she didn't like the idea.

"I know you'll probably make it across the border without them searching your car, but what if you don't. If they find me, we're both in trouble. But if I find some other way to cross and they catch me, you'll still be anonymous. You can continue to find something on Hillstrom."

I didn't like it, but she made sense. So our final day in Canada was spent watching for opportunities for Jess. She had finally agreed that if nothing promising showed up, she would take the chance in the SUV.

Fortune, however, was smiling. At the campground that night we parked again in a remote spot, but across the campground was a humongous RV with a roof rack that was piled high with all kinds of gear. These were some serious RVers. The vehicle held a family of five, usually a safe bet to get across the border without problems. The father was packing things onto the rack when I sauntered over and asked him if he needed any help. He declined, but thanked me for the offer, saying that this was just the stuff they wouldn't need that night, but that they were pulling out in the morning. I engaged him in conversation and discovered that they were heading for Alaska, to a campground in Denali National Park.

We were going to have to time it just right, but knew we had to try to get Jess up the ladder and under something on the roof rack in the morning before they left.

And that's exactly what happened. After he stowed the last of the gear on the roof in the morning, the husband walked over to the camp store to check out. The wife and the three little girls were inside the RV, and the girls were making a racket. Jess looked around to make sure she was alone, then scrambled up the ladder. I saw her fiddle with what looked like a heavy-duty bungee cord, then slip under a tarp. Her hand popped out while she reset the bungee cord.

I didn't wait for them. It would look way too suspicious for me to follow behind them. But I also wouldn't be able to see if Jess got caught. I just had to trust. I hit the Canadian checkpoint soon after I left the campground and made it through using the same line I had used before. This was an odd border post, in that the U.S. post was thirty miles away, over a swampy marshland. Again I sailed through easily. I drove on to the first rest area I could find, and that's where I set up my Jess vigil.

The waiting was interminable. After an hour I found myself pacing the parking lot, which wasn't realistic. I knew full well that they would be longer than an hour. But after two hours, I was seriously worried—and there was nothing I could do about it. My imagination was running wild. I pictured Jess sitting alone in an interrogation room at the border. If she had been discovered, she'd be dead in a matter of days, maybe hours, and there was nothing anyone could do—Mill Colson, Joe Gray, the police, or me— Hillstrom's army would make sure of that.

The three-hour mark was approaching when, in the distance, I saw a massive shape lumbering up the road at about thirty mph. It was them!

Now the big question: Was Jess still on top of the RV?

I was hoping that this being the first rest area since the border crossing, and with an RV full of kids, they would stop. They did. They pulled up close to me, and when the father got out, we greeted each other like long-lost friends.

"Thought that RV looked familiar," I said. "Wasn't that a weird border post? You have to go so far between the Canada and U.S. checkpoints."

"We've done this route a couple of times, so we were prepared. Thought you'd be long gone by now on your way to Anchorage."

"I kept waking up all night, so I was really tired. I pulled over and took a nap. Just woke up about ten minutes ago."

The mother took the kids over to a small playground on the other side of the RV to work off some of their energy. The ladder was on my side, too close to the father for Jess to chance it. Her safest bet was to drop off the back of the RV—a long drop for her—unless the guy decided to join his family. However, he would have none of that. He had just spent three hours—and who knows how many days before that—driving with them. He was finding all kinds of excuses to stick near me and continue the conversation.

Looking over his shoulder, I could see Jess's hand protruding from the tarp, trying to unlatch the bungee cord. Seeing as how he wasn't about to leave, I had an idea.

"Hey, since you've done this route before, would you mind taking a look at my map?" I asked, ushering him over to the SUV. I opened the atlas on the front hood and maneuvered him to stand with his back to the ladder.

I asked him about hotels, national parks, wildlife, and anything else I could think of to give Jess time to extricate herself from the tarp. I could see her from my vantage point. Her head was sticking out and she was looking around to make sure no other cars were entering the rest area. Luckily, it was a quiet road. She squirmed out of the tarp, remembering to hook the bungee cord again, and basically slid down the ladder and scooted around the back of the RV. I thanked Al—we were finally on a first-name basis—and pretended to prepare to leave. At that moment, one of his kids started crying. With a heavy sigh, Al told me to have a nice trip, and made his way around the front of his RV over to the playground.

As soon as he was out of sight, Jess ran over to the SUV. I opened the back door on my side and she jumped in, ducking out of sight. I got back in and we took off. A minute later she was sitting in the passenger seat, trying to stretch. She reached over the seat and grabbed a bottle of water from a bag. She drank half of it before breathing again.

"I'm so thirsty," she said with her next breath. "It was stifling under that tarp. I'm glad they stopped at this rest area. I don't know how much longer I could have stayed under there."

At Tok, we got onto Highway 1 heading south and made it to Anchorage late in the afternoon. We were only a couple of weeks shy of the summer solstice, so the sun hadn't gone down—and probably wouldn't until much later, and even then only for a short time. We stayed the night in a very "Alaska-looking" hotel and were off early the next morning for Homer.

Again, the views were breathtaking and we found ourselves poking along. As anxious as I was to see my brother—it had been almost two years, during a trip he had made back east—we were in no hurry to arrive.

Finally, we reached Scott's house, which was on a hill overlooking Kachemak Bay and the mountains on the other side. We got out of the SUV and Jess just stood and stared in wonderment at the view. She said, "I could live here forever. This is heaven."

"That's what I said when I visited for the first time," I said, my arm around her waist. "Then my brother described the cold dark winters and I wasn't so sure after that."

I hadn't seen this house. The times I visited had been soon after he arrived, and he was renting a house. He bought this one after my last visit. It looked as if it had been put together in pieces over the years. Rooms had been added, and the additions didn't always look like the part of the house they were attached to. It didn't seem overly homey from the outside. It was a "working" house—sheds, stacked wood, a henhouse, even right down to an ax stuck in a log. Then my brother appeared at the door.

Scott had really taken to life in Alaska in his eight years there. He looked as much the part as his house did. He was a bit shorter than I was, probably 5'10" and had gained a fair amount of weight over the years. He had a head of bushy black hair and had grown a full beard that showed the occasional flecks of gray. In all, the perfect Alaska caricature. Once he became sober, he had trained to be an EMT, then had gone off to paramedic school. Upon graduation he got a job as a paramedic in Detroit, working in the worst part of the city, attending to gunshot wounds, stabbings, and drug overdoses, and making a name for himself in the process with his skills and fearlessness. Two years in the battle zone was enough though, and he longed to be away from the city. How he ended up in Homer was still a mystery to me, but he loved it. He cut back somewhat on his paramedic work, now just being on call at the local volunteer fire department. Over the years he had also become a motorcycle mechanic, a chef, a carpenter, and, upon moving to Alaska, had even gotten his pilot's license. Basically, Scott was a jack-of-all-trades, and a master of most of them. He earned enough to get by and was happy. He got along with everybody and loved the little things in life. In so many ways, his life had become much deeper than mine, and I envied him for it. Maybe it was a good time for me to take on some of those qualities.

Standing solemnly next to him was Max, his German Shepherd. I had heard countless stories about Max. He was a former police dog who had been retired with his owner when the cop retired. Within a year of retirement, the cop found out he had lung cancer and was no longer able to care for Max. A friend of his knew Scott and knew he'd be in good hands with him. Max looked the part of a police dog. I wouldn't have been surprised if he asked me for some ID.

"Hey bro," Scott called out, taking in Jess at a glance. "Where's your Beemer?" He bounced down the stairs with an agility that belied his weight, Max close behind, and gave me a bear hug. "I'm really sorry about Karen," he said.

I had a momentary feeling of guilt that I wasn't wallowing in misery about Karen. But circumstances had changed that. Besides, she was always in the back of my mind, and would always be there. Deep down, I knew she forgave me for all that had happened, and that brought me some comfort.

"Thanks. It's getting a little easier."

Scott cocked his head and said, "But I've gotta say you look good ... relaxed."

Jess and I both burst out laughing at that. But the thought was there: Did I really look relaxed? Despite the stress and the violence, did this life really suit me better than my old one?

"Scott, this is Jess."

He enveloped her in his arms and greeted her like she was a long-lost sibling. She gave him a big smile in return.

He looked at me. "I already like her better than your ex." He looked over at Jess. "Victoria. Not Vicky, or Vic, but Victoria." He dragged out the "or" in her name mockingly so that it came out sounding stuffy and stuck-up.

"I didn't know you didn't like her," I said.

"Couldn't stand her, but I wasn't going to tell you that." He pointed to the Armada. "So where did you get that? And where's your Beemer? And what's with the Montana plates?"

I decided to shock him a bit—something I was rarely able to do. "The Beemer is stashed deep in the woods somewhere in Alberta, and we stole this from the two guys we had to kill."

It worked. For the first time ever, Scott was at a loss for words. He wasn't sure whether to laugh or not, so he just looked at me quizzically.

"Are you familiar with the Jessica Norton saga out of DC?" I asked.

"Yeah, the one who killed her co-workers and hired that Hollywood lawyer? We're not totally out of touch up here, you know."

"Well, she didn't kill her co-workers, but yes, the same Jessica Norton."

He looked over at Jess, and for the second time in two minutes, he was speechless.

"Oh, this has gotta be good," he finally said.

"Trust me," I answered. "You'll never hear another story like it. You going to invite us in?"

"Yeah." Suddenly Scott was deep in thought. Then he said, "Have you watched the news or gone online last night or today?"

I looked at Jess, then back at Scott. "No, why?"

"Your Hollywood lawyer—Colson, right?" We nodded. "His plane went down last night. There were no survivors."

Chapter 17

Corbin Mays stared out of his office window on the 67th floor of the Empire State Building. In the distance he could see the green of Central Park. It was a beautiful sunny day, in direct contrast to his mood. Mays was the CEO of Exchange Systems, a manufacturer of computer motherboards. But more importantly, he was also the head of one of the most powerful—but completely unknown—organizations in the country. And it was in that capacity that Mays was angry beyond belief. The Jessica Norton situation never should have happened. She should have been dead with her coworkers. Now she was gone. With all the money and tools at their disposal, how could she have disappeared? At seventy-two, Corbin Mays was a man with a long history of getting what he wanted—and he wanted this girl caught.

He turned and looked at Mel "Hutch" Hutchinson, his head of security. Hutch was an impressive-looking man in his late-forties. Ex-military, ex-CIA, Hutch still worked out two hours a day in a gym he'd built in his house. Recruited directly out of Special Forces by the CIA when he was only twenty-four, he had become a decorated operative, though one frustrated by the limits of his responsibility and by the limits of the CIA itself. He felt there was so much more he could have accomplished if he had just been given a little more free rein. As such, his spying career was short. He left the CIA at the age of thirty, and immediately enrolled in college under the GI Bill, eventually obtaining a master's degree from Stanford, graduating summa cum laude. He started his own small, elite security company, but when the opportunity came to work for Mays and his shadowy organization—especially at the salary he was offered—he jumped at the chance, turning the operations of his company over to his second-in-command.

"So where do things stand with the girl?" asked Mays.

"Nowhere," answered Hutch. "We don't know where she is. A couple of idiot operatives who stumbled upon her by accident and then supposedly got captured by her and her mystery man said she mentioned something about returning to Washington to collect evidence."

"Do you believe them?"

"I think there's something fishy about their story. One of my people contacted their boss to pull them in so we could talk to them but was told he'd fired them. When we tried to find them, they too had dropped out of sight."

"So that's now three operatives, the girl, and her protector, who have all disappeared."

"Yeah."

"Seems we have a little epidemic here. You have any theories?" Mays was fuming but controlled himself with Hutch. The man had done a tremendous job for him over the five years he had worked for Mays. This was just a strange set of events.

"Not yet. I figure they somehow got the first guy, since they were using his plates. But we're still working on the other two. And as far as Norton and her friend...." He let it trail off.

"Hutch, I've been working forty years—more than half my life—helping to put this plan into place. The organization behind it—the sheer power behind it—is so massive it would make your head spin. But as in all organizations, mistakes are made. Stupid mistakes. Hillstrom and your predecessor obviously made one because there is something out there that ties him to this. We just don't know what it is. As far as we know, his past is secure. But here's the thing: could it be that all this work, all this time, all this money, and all this commitment, could be brought to a screeching halt by this insignificant woman? Is this what we have to look forward to?"

There was no answer to that, so Hutch kept his mouth shut.

"What about Joe Gray?"

"Gone."

"Gone as in disappeared, like seemingly everyone else around here? Or gone as in dead?"

"Gone to ground. Running for his life."

"You're shitting me, right? So I can now add him to the ever-expanding tally of people gone missing?" Good employee or not, this was too much for Mays. "I'm beginning to think maybe you don't have as good a handle on all this as I thought you did."

Hutch just stared at his boss for about ten seconds, until Mays took a slight step back. *"And let's not forget who can snap whose neck in a millisecond,"* thought Hutch, then said, "Our guys had him cornered, but he's smart. He managed to slip away. But he doesn't have much more than the shirt on his back. No car, no gun, we'll catch him."

"Did he at least provide you with any information before he got away?"

"We have his notes, but it doesn't look like he'd made any progress."

"Is the mystery man at least mentioned?"

"Yeah, but in code. We'll never get his name from that."

"Why couldn't you have hired some people as smart as him?"

"Being smart is one thing. Being smart and also willing to do some of the … shall we say less savory things we ask … is another."

"And Colson?" asked Mays. "He was positively identified?"

"Well.…" Hutch hesitated.

"Well what? I'm not going to like this, am I?"

"The bodies were burned beyond recognition. Even dental records would be no help here. I have to assume he was in it. If he wasn't on the plane, don't you think he would make it known, seeing as who he is?"

"Not necessarily. The man loves publicity. A grand entrance down the line would be like him. Find out. Assure me that I don't have to worry about this, at least."

"I will. I've got people working on it already." He didn't, but he would as soon as he left Mays's office. He also had no doubt that Mays knew that too.

"Hutch," said Mays, bringing the meeting to a close, "not killing that girl with the others was a gargantuan mistake. We can't let it come back to haunt us. Find her and find the guy she's with. The Republican and Democratic conventions are right around the corner. It all gets serious after that. We can't have these loose ends. Find the girl. Now!"

Chapter 18

I didn't know what to say. "He was on the flight?" I asked my brother, groping for words.

"Yeah. I was just online a few minutes ago and he was listed, along with seven other people."

"Oh my God, it's all my fault," said Jess, tears welling up. I reached out to her and she fell into me, shaking, her face buried in my chest.

"It's not your fault. None of it is your fault. Those people are dead because of Hillstrom, not because of you. Stop blaming yourself." The shaking subsided, but she continued to hold on to me.

"So you don't think it was an accident?" asked Scott.

"Not for a second," I answered. "We'll explain it all to you inside. It'll take a while."

Jess released her grip on me and looked up. "I'm sorry," she said simply, wiping the remaining tears away. "You're right. It's not my fault. I feel awful for those people, but I didn't cause it. Let's hope we can find whatever clue is here. Maybe then we'll know what to do next."

"There's a clue here?" asked Scott.

"Yeah, there might be. It's all part of that long story."

Jess had recovered from her shock and seemed marginally

better, so Scott took us on a tour of his house and grounds, Max constantly at Scott's side. He owned ten acres, most of it untouched woodland. Next to the house was a fairly new barn, and behind the barn was perhaps a half an acre of garden, surrounded by a high wire fence to keep out the deer and moose.

Being high up on the mountain, his views were spectacular, and we spent almost a half an hour gazing out as he pointed out the landmarks. He took his time, knowing we were still coming down from the news about Mill.

As we were about to go in the house, a dog came bounding out of the woods and galloped toward us. It was a mixed breed, large and imposing. I could make out some lab, and maybe a hint of Saint Bernard. Max glared at him but didn't move from Scott's side. The new dog jumped up with his paws on my chest, tail wagging, tongue hanging out, and drooling all over me.

"Down Slob," said Scott firmly. The dog immediately stopped and sat at my feet.

"Slob?" I asked, wiping my hands on my leg.

"Officially Slobber O. Harper is his name."

"What does the 'O' stand for?" asked Jess.

"On."

"At least he's friendly," I said.

"He's a goof," Scott answered, "but don't get on his bad side. I've seen him chase moose and even bears out of the yard. He spends most of his time exploring, so he's not always around."

The inside of his house looked nothing like the outside. It was comfortable and homey. The large living room had an enormous fireplace at one end, and a woodstove at the other. The woodstove was for heat and the fireplace mostly for ambience, Scott explained. A 75-inch flat screen TV sat on one wall, surrounded by a bookcase full of DVDs. He had a large, spacious kitchen that also doubled as a dining room. He showed us to our bedroom, newly made up for our visit, with a queen-sized bed sporting a goose down comforter.

"We'll bring in our stuff later," I said.

"Hungry?" Scott asked.

"Starving," answered Jess.

"Looks like you're doing okay," I said patting Scott's stomach.

"Hey, I get fresh venison, moose, bear, salmon, and halibut constantly. Usually in payment, or as a tip, for jobs I perform for people. A little later in the summer my garden will be thriving. What can I tell you, I eat well."

Scott made us a dish of cold salmon and potato salad, got us drinks, and as we sat down at a beautiful old table he said, "So tell me your story."

And we did. I started with the funeral and turned it over to Jess when I got to the point of picking her up in Texas. She told the story of Hillstrom and how her coworkers were killed. When she reached the same pick up point, we just took turns the rest of the way. It consumed the afternoon and then some, and Scott said very little, asking questions where appropriate, but otherwise letting us tell it the way we needed to.

Jess was hesitant about mentioning The Voice, so I did. I knew my brother. Nothing about The Voice would surprise him and he accepted it as fact without question.

We finally finished at about seven o'clock.

"So, what are your thoughts?" I asked.

"I'm proud of you," he said. "My big brother. Mister corporate America. You actually blew three people away?"

"Two," I interrupted. "Jess took care of the other."

"Well, I don't care what the news people say about you," said Scott, looking at Jess, "you've been a great influence on this guy."

Jess seemed pleased by the remark. I was always amazed at

147

Scott's ability to connect with people. Others put great weight on Scott's opinions, because they felt he considered their thoughts equally important. Yet at the same time, if he didn't like someone—except in the case of Victoria, because he knew it would hurt me—he wasn't afraid to make his feelings known. He had a quick mind and a razor-sharp sarcastic wit. He was also full of surprises.

"And," he said (in retrospect, there should have been a drumroll), "I can put you in the right direction for your first clue."

We just stared at him.

"Your Voice was definitely leading you to the right place. There's an antiques store right on the main drag of Homer. Well, they call it an antiques store, it's really more like a junk shop. It's been around for seventy-five or eighty years. I think you should check it out tomorrow."

"And the reason being?" I asked. Oh, how he loved this shit. He knew he had us sitting on the edge of our seats.

"The name. It's called Wolf Run."

We almost fell out of our chairs. Jess and I looked at each other in shock, then we both looked at Scott.

"You're kidding," was all I could manage.

"Nope. Owned by a crusty old guy in his seventies. We get along though. He inherited it from his father, another crusty old guy, or so I'm told. But if there's a clue to all this, that's where you want to check. It might be under mounds of dust, but it's probably there."

"Wait a minute," I said. "It had to be over three hours ago that we told you about getting the 'Wolf Run' message. I know you didn't just now think of it. You've been holding the information all this time?"

"Well, you know me. I like the spotlight." And he burst into an infectious belly laugh that had us all going. "Well, I'm hungry. Who wants a bear steak?"

After dinner, I tried a couple of times to call Joe on the cell phone, but his phone seemed to be shut off. Could he have been on Mill's plane?

"They gave a list of passengers on the plane, right?" I asked Scott while we ate.

"Yup. There was no Joe Gray on it."

"Weird. Maybe he's just in a bad reception area." But as I said it, I knew there was something more to it than that.

We talked for another couple of hours, shifting the focus onto Scott. He was genuinely happy, the total opposite of the kid who left home with a chip on his shoulder and a full-fledged drinking problem. Besides his carpentry work, he had bought a small plane and four years earlier got his commercial license and had become a part-time bush pilot. He didn't advertise, but his word-of-mouth business had grown rapidly.

"I expect to be busy this summer," he said, and as an afterthought added, "if things get bad, I know some really out of the way places I can fly you where no one will ever find you."

"That's good to know," I said. "Hopefully it won't come to that, but you never know."

His love life was fluid—he was dating a couple of women—and I could tell he wanted to settle down someday, but he said he didn't want to marry the wrong woman. I thought of Victoria as he said that.

It was after midnight when we said our goodnights. Jess and I got into bed naked with great intentions but were asleep in minutes.

We woke up the next morning to the wonderful smell of bacon cooking. We ventured out to the kitchen to find a feast awaiting us. In addition to the bacon were pancakes, hash browns, eggs, homemade bread, and a bowl of strawberries.

"You know that restaurant I never made it to?" said Jess. "Well, this beats anything I could have had there."

I tried Joe again after breakfast. Again, nothing. I didn't want to leave a voicemail.

"I'm worried," I said. "Something has happened to him. He wouldn't keep his phone off like that. To be safe, I think I'll turn mine off and check it briefly every day. He can leave a message if he calls."

"So," said Scott, cleaning up the breakfast dishes. "We going to check out Wolf Run?"

Scott was really getting into this. What worried me though was that he seemed to consider it all a game.

"Scott, this is serious. It's dangerous. What we're doing could get us killed."

"Yeah, I kinda got that from the four dead friends of Jess's and the three you guys blew away. Your point?"

I could tell I had hurt his feelings.

"I guess … well.…"

"You don't want to involve me in something that isn't my problem. That the gist of it?"

"Well, it was, but it sounds kind of lame now."

"Yeah, you think? Jon, I'm your brother. You'd be here for me if I was in trouble. You involved me the minute you showed up, but I wouldn't have it any other way. I'm happy you came up here.

"Besides," he added, "I own half a dozen guns, and at a moment's notice I could fly you out of here." He put his arm around me. "Not to mention I'm a good cook."

"That you are." I was suddenly distracted by Jess's silence. I looked over at her sitting on the couch. She had a faraway look in her eyes.

Scott mouthed "The Voice?" to me. I nodded.

So we waited. About fifteen minutes later, Jess came out of it.

"We're looking for an article," she said.

"On what?" asked Scott.

She shook her head.

"You were under, or gone, or whatever, for all that time and all you got was 'an article'?" Scott said it with humor and Jess didn't take offense.

She smiled at him. "It's not all that simple. It's not like the words are just spoken to me, although that has happened. It's hard to explain. It's feelings. It's emotions. Somehow, they lead me to a message. Oftentimes I can't even remember how I got there. I don't think it's easy for … for The Voice to communicate. I don't understand how it works, just that it does."

"Well then, I say let's go," announced Scott. "Wolf Run is waiting."

As we got into Scott's old Ford F-150, Max jumping in the back, I found myself wondering. Assuming we found whatever it was we were looking for, would it be the answer? Would it be the end of our search, or just the beginning?

Chapter 19

Joe Gray was astonished at the speed with which Hillstrom's people launched their attack. One minute he was hearing about Mill Colson's plane going down, and the next he was being ambushed. Did Jon and Jess escape the massacre? He was sure they did. Hillstrom's goons seemed overly concerned about Joe's knowledge of their whereabouts. Well, there wasn't much he could do. If they were okay, they'd know to hunker down once they heard about Mill and weren't able to contact him. Besides, they were the least of his concerns at the moment.

He had to admit that he had only half believed Jess's story about Hillstrom. He knew that she had people in pursuit of her—there was no question about that—and that she was a victim in all of this, but the Hillstrom angle seemed a little far-fetched. Not anymore. He realized now that there wasn't one mole in Mill's office, there were two. He ... or she ... knew Mill was going to "out" Hillstrom at his press conference, and that just couldn't happen. Even to just have Hillstrom's name mentioned in relation to a scandal could derail his whole campaign. No, Mill—and by association Joe himself—had to go, and quickly.

*****

The "hit" had come out of nowhere. He had flown to Rochester, New York, to check out the company Hillstrom had worked for before moving to Massachusetts and running for office. He hadn't gotten very far in his research. Exchange Systems had been around for almost thirty years making motherboards for personal computers. They started off small but were able to make lucrative deals with some of the largest computer manufacturers with prices the companies couldn't pass up. It was a win-win deal for all concerned. The computer companies got inexpensive, reliable motherboards, and Exchange did well enough to keep expanding. The "well enough" part of it hadn't sat well with Joe. Companies weren't usually content to just do "well enough." They were always searching for ways to cut costs and beef up production. While the company's sales were brisk—their motherboards were everywhere—they seemed happy to sail along with only modest increases in profits from year to year. He had to admit though, if the company was a "front" for something, it was a really good one. It gave off an air of legitimacy.

He hadn't found out too much on Hillstrom. Because of his notoriety, the company had made up a small bio that they passed out to reporters looking to do background on the man. It didn't say much. He had joined the company in the customer affairs department soon after it opened, quickly rising to vice president, and had remained there for ten years, until his move to Massachusetts. Nothing else was available.

That was as far as Joe had gotten. His third night there, just a few hours after Mill had called to tell him he was setting up a news conference, he pulled into his hotel parking lot. As he opened his door he was struck on the head and immediately lost consciousness. When he woke up, his head was pounding and there was a golf ball-sized lump near his left temple. He was in a hotel room—a shabby one—and he was tied to a chair. The minute he opened his eyes, he was punched in the face. He felt his nose break and blood streamed down his chin onto his clothes.

"That's to show we're serious," the attacker had said.

There were three assailants working him over, spending the next two hours asking him questions about Jess and "the man" with her, but he gave them nothing. The questions would be interspersed with beatings. They asked about his research and what he was looking for. They didn't seem to know about Hillstrom. He tried to give them just enough to show that he knew something but was being kept out of the loop for the important stuff.

Finally, they gave up. He had convinced them of his lack of worth. They told him they were going to take him to their boss, but he knew better. They were going to kill him, but just didn't want to do it in the motel. There was no way out and he knew he was going to die. That is, until they made a stupid—and fatal—mistake.

They waited until the middle of the night before transporting him. He was bloody and in a lot of pain, but he noted with a certain amount of satisfaction that they were all nursing bruised knuckles. Two of the three walked him out to the car, and then inexplicably put him in the driver's seat. One got in behind him and the other sat in the passenger seat. Both had guns pointed at him. Before he could touch anything, they had him put on surgical gloves. They wanted no one's fingerprints in the car.

So why did they have him drive? Joe could only guess. Most likely, his death was going to appear accidental and they needed him in the driver's seat. Regardless, five minutes into the drive, Joe saw his way out. In a deserted section of the warehouse district they instructed him to turn left at the next stop sign. Halfway through the turn, Joe floored the gas and drove straight into a concrete retaining wall at sixty mph. The guy next to him got off a shot, but it missed Joe and embedded itself in Joe's door.

Joe had fastened his seatbelt the moment he got in the car. He knew the other two wouldn't. At impact the airbags went off. The combination of the seatbelt and the airbag saved Joe from serious harm. The other two, however, weren't so lucky. The one behind him sailed past his head, through the broken windshield, headfirst into the retaining wall. The one next to him had been saved by his airbag, but the bag had cracked his head against the passenger window, leaving him dazed. Joe grabbed the man's head from behind and smashed it down into the dashboard several times until he was sure he was dead.

He quickly searched his attacker in the passenger seat for a wallet, pulling out the cash—a total of $160—and putting the wallet back in the dead man's pocket. It would do no good to steal the credit cards. Those would be flagged in no time. Picking up a loose gun, he painfully extracted himself from the driver's side window, falling to the ground with a thud that left him momentarily stunned. Finally, he got up and limped away from the scene. Once away, he looked for a place to clean up. He came across a metal drum filled with rain water and rinsed off his face. His nose was killing him—his whole body was killing him—but there was nothing he could do about that. He just knew he had to get as far away from the crash site as possible.

Should he go to the police? No, too much explaining. And frankly, Hillstrom's men would find him and kill him. He wasn't safe with the police. Near dawn he came across a clothes donation box with bags piled in front. After ten minutes of digging, he found a shirt about his size. He took off his bloody shirt and stuffed it into one of the bags and put the new one on. Not perfect, but it would do. He looked down at his pants. There were only a few flecks of blood. They were okay. Later, he checked into the dump he now called home.

The question Joe found himself asking was, "How in the world am I still alive?" He should have been dead, at the bottom of a river or deep in a landfill somewhere. But no, here he was, holed away in a bed bug motel paid for with what little cash he had in his wallet—which for some reason they hadn't gotten around to taking from him—and money from his attacker's wallet. He couldn't risk using his credit card or going to the ATM. A month earlier he had picked up a fake ID and had applied for a credit card under the new name, but the credit card hadn't arrived before all this happened. No, he was going to have to figure out some way to get cash. And then what? Essentially he was out of business. He couldn't keep researching Hillstrom. He couldn't really do anything. His attackers had made that clear.

He counted his remaining cash. He had enough to pick up a disposable cell phone. Then he'd call Jon and Jess. He wasn't sure if they would tell him where they were, but he had to try. The irony of all this was that if Jon and Jess—the two most sought-after people in the country—were still alive, being with them, wherever they were, would probably be the safest place for him to be right now. He was going on the run.

ANDREW CUNNINGHAM

Chapter 20

Calling Wolf Run Antiques a "junk shop" was being kind. All I
could figure was that the owner also owned the building and it was
long since paid off. It was the only possible way he could have
stayed in business so long. If he did more than fifty dollars a day in
sales, it would have shocked me. He kept the newer items, which
were probably all he ever sold, near the counter. Scott was right
about the dust, which lay over the rest of the store. It was obvious
some of it hadn't been touched in years. The store was a hodge-
podge of knick-knacks, books, tools, magazines, newspapers, and
furniture. Somewhere in there might have existed a real antique,
but most of the items were just "old."

Scott, who had left Max to guard the truck, introduced us.
"Elmer," his name even seemed old, "this is my brother Jon, and his
wife Marie."

Elmer nodded his head and mumbled a "hey."

"They want to look through your magazines and newspapers."

"That's fine. Just don't make a mess while you do it." Could it
be he had a sense of humor?

We turned and looked around the store.

"So where do we start?" I asked.

"Article? That was it?" asked Scott. "You're sure there was
nothing more specific?"

"Sorry," replied Jess.

He sighed and the three of us wandered through the piles for the next hour, picking up magazines and flipping through them, looking at headlines in old issues of the local newspaper, and generally being unproductive.

Finally, Jess looked over at me with a pained expression. "I've been getting a message for the last fifteen minutes. Basically, it's just 'no, no, no'. I thought maybe it was a kind of 'you're getting cold' message, so I'd move, hoping I'd start to get hot. Now I'm not so sure what it means."

I could see Elmer looking at Jess over his glasses. It must have sounded a bit odd.

"Maybe this isn't the place at all," she said.

"Gotta be," I answered. "It couldn't possibly be a coincidence."

"Then we're missing something," she said.

"This article," asked Scott, "has gotta be about Hillstrom, right?"

"I suppose it doesn't have to be," answered Jess, "but I'd guess that's the best bet. Why?"

But Scott was on a mission and had already walked away. He went up to Elmer.

"So, Elmer, have you read all these magazines and newspapers?" Scott had learned how to communicate with the man. Starting off with a joke that he hoped would lead to an answer was obviously his method.

Elmer just gave him a dirty look.

"Ever run across anything in here about Gary Hillstrom?"

"What the hell is a Gary Hillstrom?"

"You know, he's a senator. Just decided to run for president?"

"There's a reason I live in Alaska. It's about as far away from Washington as I can get. I don't know who's running for president, and I couldn't give a shit. I might know the name of our governor if you give me a second to think."

Although Scott and Elmer were doing some friendly sparring, I had no doubt that Elmer was telling the truth. He probably wanted to stay as far away from the lower forty-eight as he could. Their problems were not his problems.

"Marie," Scott pointed to Jess, "does some writing, and had heard somewhere that Hillstrom had some ties to Homer. I've never heard of it, but you've been here a bit longer."

"About four generations longer," interrupted Elmer.

"Yeah. Well, now that Hillstrom is running and she was going to be here anyway, she figured she'd see if it was true. Obviously not."

"Obviously." Elmer was done.

Scott motioned for us to follow. "I'll see you later," he said.

"Not if I see you first." His joke was as old as he was.

We were standing in front of the store trying to figure out our next step, when there came a banging from Elmer's window. We looked in and he crooked his finger toward Scott. Scott looked at us and went back into the store. We were close behind.

We stood in front of the counter while Elmer rummaged through his bulging desk. He didn't say anything but held up a finger to say wait a minute. Finally, he grunted and emerged with a single sheet of paper that looked like it came off a stenographer's pad.

"That name Hillstrom. It suddenly rang a bell as you were going out the door. I had a guy a year, maybe two years ago, ask me about him. I wrote down the name 'Hillstrom' and the guy's name and phone number."

I was excited, but I already knew better than to interrupt Elmer. Scott, on the other hand, had no problem.

"Why was he asking you about him," asked Scott.

"Beats the crap out of me. He saw a picture and got all excited about something. It'll take me a minute to remember where I put that photo. It was in a frame."

"Do you know who the man was who asked?" said Jess.

"Yeah, it was him." He pointed to a framed article hanging on the wall near his desk. We quickly crowded around while Elmer painfully got out of his chair to go find the photo.

It was a travel piece from the *Washington Post Magazine* on Homer, with a good-sized section on Wolf Run and Elmer, as the resident expert on the history of the town.

Suddenly Jess gasped, then turned white. They always talk about people suddenly turning white, and I thought it was an exaggeration. But I had just witnessed it in person.

"You okay?" I asked.

"Look at the author of the article," she whispered. Right under the title was the name Robert Norton.

"My father," she said simply.

"Yeah, that's the name on the piece of paper," said Scott, reading Elmer's note.

"Did you know he was here?" I asked.

She shook her head. "I had no idea. I didn't always know where he was going, and sometimes he combined trips to save the paper some money."

"So, obviously he was here to write a travel piece about Homer," said Scott. "So what do you think got him interested in Hillstrom? Had he ever mentioned him to you?"

"Never. He was a *Post* reporter, and although he didn't do hard news, he was obviously familiar with the politicians in Washington. But I wouldn't think he'd have any interest in any of them."

"Here it is," called out Elmer. It was the most animated I'd seen him. He was winding his way through the junk with a picture frame in his hand. "I used to have this hung up where that article is now. The reporter got so excited when he saw the picture, he asked to take it to make a copy. I let him. But he returned it promptly. Nice guy. Don't meet a lot of nice people from the lower forty-eight."

He handed the picture to Scott, who showed it to us.

"Oh my God!" exclaimed Jess.

It was a picture dated thirty years earlier of a group of twelve people, all with smiles and their arms around each other, standing around an outdoor grill. Looking to be about twenty-five years old, was Gary Hillstrom! There was no question in my mind that I was looking at a young Hillstrom.

"So, what's so interesting about the picture?" chimed in Elmer, oblivious to the silence that had suddenly come over us.

I slowly turned the picture toward him and pointed to Hillstrom. "Do you know who that is?"

"Of course. That's Ben Fremont."

"Not Gary Hillstrom?"

"Hell, no. I could never forget Ben, or any of them, for that matter. They're all dead—well, except for Clyde," he pointed to an older man. "He's still alive, but about ninety now and crazy as a loon." *Takes one to know one*, I thought.

"What do you mean they're all dead," asked Scott.

"How long have you been here?" asked Elmer, implying that Scott was either stupid or deaf. "You've never heard the story?"

"I guess not," answered Scott patiently.

"Goddamn flatlanders," said Elmer to the air, referring to Scott. "Why do we let them come here?" He addressed us all. "Well, find a pile to sit on, and I'll tell you all about it."

We found small tables and broken chairs to sit on and dragged them over to Elmer's desk. Jess had discovered an empty wine barrel and ended up with the highest seat in the house. As we got settled, the door opened and a local guy, obviously familiar to Elmer, started to walk in.

"Get out, I'm closed!" Elmer shouted, and the man turned tail and literally ran out of the store.

"That must've come as a shock to him," I said to Scott.

"Probably," Scott answered. "That was the mayor."

"Are you two done?" asked Elmer, glaring at us.

"Go ahead," said Scott.

He started, almost cutting Scott off. "This was the last picture taken of the Wilcox family and their employees. Mort Wilcox owned the Moose Antlers Restaurant—a stupid name, if you ask me—the most popular eating spot in town. On a Saturday night you had to wait in line to get in, and you saw everyone you knew there. Food was good, and it was cheap. Nobody had much money back then—Homer wasn't the thriving metropolis it is now—and if you weren't at the Porthole Bar, that's where you were."

He continued, "So you had Mort and Sally Wilcox, their two sons, Pete and Aaron, and their daughter Erin. Tell me, what kind of brains does it take to name your kids Aaron and Erin? You say those two names and tell me if you hear a difference? And they didn't even come up with a nickname for one of them. They just lived with the confusion. Anyway, they had seven workers besides the family. I can't remember most of them, 'cept your boy Ben, and Clyde, the dummy."

"Dummy?" asked Jess.

"Yeah, he wasn't right. A little slow. Actually, a lot slow. He did odd jobs there. Some people made fun of him and called him a dummy. Not your friend Ben. The two of them were close. Strange, 'cuz Ben was smart, really smart, but it was like he had a soft spot for Clyde. He was very patient with him."

"Was Ben from here?" I asked, taking the chance that I would incur Elmer's wrath for interrupting him. But he seemed to have mellowed out.

"No. Showed up about three years before. He was probably about twenty-one or twenty-two at the time. Don't know his story. Never did. But the Wilcox family took him in. Gave him a job and found a small room for him. Over time he and Erin, who was about his age, became sweet on each other. Mort and Sally seemed okay with it. They liked him."

He took a sip of ice-cold coffee that had a look of sludge about it.

"Then one day—almost thirty years now—Clyde walked into the restaurant early in the morning to clean, and discovered Mort, Sally, Pete, Aaron, and one of the employees dead. They'd all had their throats slit. Must've made the national news." He looked at us expectantly.

We looked at each other and shook our heads.

"I would've been about ten," I said. "And Scott would've been seven."

"I wasn't even born yet," said Jess.

Elmer made a disgusted sound. "Well, anyway, they were dead, and Erin, Ben, and the other employees were all missing. State Police came in, but they had nothing to go on. Then a few days later, another body—Smitty, that's right, I'd forgotten about him—anyway, they found Smitty's body up in the hills off a trail. Again, his throat slit. A month later they found Erin's remains. Not much left. The animals had done a pretty good job. They never found the bodies of Ben or the other three. I think they just assumed they went by way of the animals."

"Did they ever suspect anyone?" asked Scott.

"For a time they wondered about Erin and Ben, 'cuz Clyde told 'em that Erin had a knock-down drag-out argument with her parents the day before. He didn't know why. Some people wondered if it was about her seeing Ben. The cops wondered—as sick as it was—if Erin had enlisted Ben's help in killing her family, then they took off. Wasn't much of a theory, especially since Ben and Erin had been going together for over a year with Mort and Sally's blessing. When they found Erin's body, that was the end of that theory."

"Did you tell my f... the *Washington Post* reporter the story?" asked Jess.

"Oh yeah. He asked a lot of the same questions. Like you, he was convinced Ben was this guy Hillstrom. I don't see how. I think he was killed along with the others."

Elmer was finished with his story, and Scott asked to borrow the picture so we could copy it.

We went back to Scott's house for a bite to eat, each of us deep in our thoughts. When we arrived, Scott made us lunch and we sat around the table looking at each other.

"So," said Scott, breaking the ice. "Does that help or just make it more confusing?"

"It's gotta help somehow," I said. "I think that was the article we were supposed to see, as a link to the picture. What do you think, Jess?"

I looked over at her and saw a tear running down her face.

"It clears up some things for me," she said quietly. "There's something I've known for a while, but I didn't want to tell you until I understood why. Now I do. It all makes sense now why I was led here."

"You see," she continued. "The Voice is my father."

Chapter 21

"Your father?" I asked, dumbfounded.

Scott just raised his eyebrows. Never one to jump to conclusions, he wanted to hear this one out.

"I began to realize it after you killed the man in Utah. When I had my breakdown and you were trying to talk me through it, remember I told you that I was getting feelings and emotions coming from The Voice that kind of matched your words?"

I nodded.

"Well, that wasn't all. Two real words also came through from The Voice, and they were repeated a few times. The words were "punkin" and "persevere." My father always called me Punkin. He also refused to let me give up and was always telling me to persevere when I was going through a difficult time. It also explains why The Voice is always so comforting, and why it seems to know me. I always feel a tenderness coming from it, even when it's yelling at me."

"And now we know why you were set on this path a year ago," I said. "You were the only person your father could communicate with, as fragmented as it is."

"Why would he bother, though?" asked Scott. "Why would he get his own daughter involved in something like this and put her life in danger?"

I couldn't believe we were talking about a dead guy as if he were alive and in the next room.

"Unless the consequences of Hillstrom going through with this were worse than any danger she could be in," I said.

Jess let out a little gasp, then looked at me. "Do you think it's possible that my parents' death on that ferry wasn't an accident?"

I quickly filled Scott in on the details of their demise.

Jess continued, "What if the picture my father saw prompted him to contact Hillstrom? Especially if Elmer told him the story he told us. My father wasn't an investigative reporter, but any good journalist would follow up on that. What if he uncovered other things too? Hillstrom would have had to have him killed. Oh my God. This is just too much."

She stopped and thought for a moment, trying to slow down her breathing. I could see her shaking and I reached out and held one of her hands. Finally she said, "The whole last year is now beginning to make sense. And now I know why I was led here. This is where it all began."

"I can't believe he passed on too much information about his suspicions," said Scott. "If he had, Elmer would probably be long-since dead and his business burned to the ground. I'd guess your father just asked a few questions about Hillstrom's past. Maybe enough to worry them."

"And maybe enough to get him killed," Jess said quietly, with a deep sadness in her eyes.

"Let's assume," I said, trying to move on, "that Hillstrom *is* the man in the picture. He showed up here at the age of twenty-one, or thereabouts, but from where? Elmer didn't know, but did someone?"

"If Elmer didn't know, the chances of anyone else knowing, are slim," said Scott. "He pretty much knows everything that is happening or did happen in this town."

"We've gotta try," I said. "Maybe you could ask Elmer if Hillstrom … Ben … hung out with anyone else."

"If he did kill everyone," said Jess, "why not Clyde?"

I could see that Jess was struggling to maintain her composure. The idea that her parents might have been murdered had really thrown her for a loop.

"Elmer said Ben had a soft spot for Clyde," said Scott. "Maybe because Clyde was slow, Ben spared him."

"I wonder how communicative Clyde is. Should we try to see him?" I asked.

"Can't hurt," answered Scott. "I'll ask Elmer where he is. Meanwhile, I suggest we knock off for the rest of the day. Let me show you some of my property."

I looked at Jess. The diversion would do us good. She nodded.

"Before we go, I should check my phone," I said. I turned it on and discovered a voicemail waiting for me. I looked at Jess and Scott, put the phone on speaker, and played the message.

"You know who this is. I'm in a tough spot. You heard about the plane going down, I'm sure. Same time as that, they got me. I escaped because I was dealing with morons, but I have no place to go. They are looking for me and I'm down to just a few dollars. I can't go home and I can't access my accounts without them finding me. If you're open to it, I think it's time we work together. But I don't know how I can get to wherever you are. I know you're suspicious, but call me and I'll try to convince you that I'm alone. Please call me. I just hope you two are okay.

He left his number and hung up. I looked at the time. He had left it three hours earlier.

"What do you think?" I asked.

"I don't know the guy," said Scott, "but that sounded genuine to me. I have a little cash, I could probably wire him. We could have him come to Alaska, someplace remote, then I could pick him up in my plane. That would give me time to check him out."

"That works for me," I said. "How about you?" I looked at Jess.

"I agree with Scott. It sounded genuine."

"Let's do it then." I turned to Scott. "You don't have to worry about the money. There's something I haven't told you." I went into the bedroom and emerged with my briefcase full of cash. I thought Scott's eyes would fall out. I told him about my safe deposit box.

"Well, that says a lot, doesn't it," he said.

"What do you mean?"

"Obviously, consciously or subconsciously you had doubts about your marriage. No one in a happy marriage has this much cash hidden away from his spouse. I'd say the only thing holding you two together was Karen. I knew all along that Victoria was no good for you. You never seemed like a couple. Now this one," he pointed to Jess, "she's a keeper."

Jess actually blushed.

"You have a connection, a communication that you and Victoria never had, and never would have."

I didn't know what to say. Once again Scott nailed it.

I cleared my throat. "I guess I should call Joe."

We agreed on a plan and I dialed Joe's number. He answered on the fourth ring.

"You're okay," he began.

"We are," I responded. All this secrecy of not using names and saying as little as possible would have been almost comical if it wasn't so dangerous for us all. "You hurt?"

"Nothing that won't heal."

"Not that I don't believe that you're alone, but just as some proof, where did we first meet?" Before calling Joe, we had decided to ask him that question. If he wasn't alone, he could lie and we could decide where to go from there. I felt confident that Joe wouldn't lead us in the wrong direction.

"No, that's smart. Utah State University parking lot."

"So what happened? Just to let you know, I have this on speaker and my friend is with me." Despite knowing it was safe, I felt it was still better not to use names. Again, I didn't trust modern technology in the wrong hands. "Also, there is a third party with us whom I trust with my life, and you can too. You'll meet him soon enough."

"Well, it's not like I have any choice at this point. I welcome all the help I can get." He proceeded to give us what I assumed to be an abbreviated version of all that had happened to him. "So, here I am," he finished, "in a fair amount of pain, stuck in a seedy motel in Rochester, New York, with thirteen dollars to my name."

"You were right in your message. It's time we get together. Is there a Western Union counter around there someplace where I could wire you some money?"

"Yeah, I scouted that out this morning on the off chance that you would call back and could help."

"Would two thousand cover things for now?"

"It would. I'm sorry to ask this of you."

"Not a problem. Give me the location and I'll get it off to you today."

"Okay." He provided me with the details, then said, "I have a fake name and identification that no one knows about—Terry Landers. Send it to that."

"Fine." I wrote it down. "Do you have a passport under that name?"

"Uh, no. Do I need one to get to you?"

"Maybe, maybe not." I took a breath. I was about to narrow down our position, but it couldn't be helped. I just had to hope no one was listening. "We're in Alaska. Under your new identity I suppose you could take a commercial flight, but they might be watching for you."

"No, I'm not going to do that. I know they are watching. Luckily, I've been doing this a long time. I've got contacts who can get me over the border on both ends for a little cash. I might need another couple of thousand if you can spare it."

"No problem. Just get into Alaska as quietly as you can. Wherever you end up, preferably some out of the way little place, give me a call and we'll get you."

"I really appreciate this. I'll call you when I get there." He hung up.

My hands were shaking. This covert-ops stuff was foreign to me. I was getting better at it, but it was still going to take a while. I knew that Scott, on the other hand, was thriving on it.

"Let's go find the Western Union office here, then take our walk," said Scott. "I think you guys need it.

He was right. When we got back from town, we headed out into the woods.

"Should we bring our guns?" I asked before we left. "Just in case we run into a bear?"

"You can," he said. "We won't run into one, and they are scared of Slob, but I often bring a rifle just in case. Your gun," he said, pointing to my Sig .40, "will just make the bear mad. Yours," he picked up Jess's .380 and made a face, "might tickle him. However, it's not the bears I'm worried about, but the people following you. From this point on, don't go anywhere unarmed."

Funny, he was my little brother, but he didn't seem that way now. There was a quiet confidence in him that created an aura of a protector, our protector. I just hoped I hadn't signed his death warrant by coming up here.

We spent the afternoon tromping through the woods, occasionally reaching a quiet meadow that allowed us to see far beyond the coast. Max took up his usual post next to Scott, and Slob joined us within minutes of leaving the house. He would run up ahead, scouting the way, then gallop back expecting to be thrown a stick.

Jess and I walked hand in hand. I thought a lot about what Scott had said about Karen being the only bond between Victoria and me. I thought about Karen every day. Despite all Jess and I had been through, Karen was still close by, during every waking minute. She would never be anything but.

The time spent exploring Scott's property was like a wonderful drug that made us forget everything else and appreciate the Shangri-La in which we now found ourselves. We were learning to appreciate each moment's respite from the horror we had entered. Those moments were few and far between, but when they presented themselves, we grabbed them and held on as long as we could. This was one of them and we were reluctant for it to end. Luckily, it was the time of year when the sun only went down for a few hours a night, and even then only to resemble dusk. So when we got back from our walk, we sat around a fire pit Scott had built, while he brought out steaks to grill. When we finally went in, it was after midnight.

For now, we were able to forget. Tomorrow we knew, it would all come back.

Chapter 22

Clyde Merriman was the happiest resident of the Kenai Nursing Home, or so the nursing staff said. My experience with nursing homes told me that he was probably the only happy resident. He had entered the facility when he was seventy-five, fifteen years earlier, courtesy of the state of Alaska, after he had been found for the third time sleeping outside in February. Too old for an institution, the nursing home seemed the best choice.

Everybody loved Clyde, and at ninety, his mental acuity was as good as it was when he was sixty. Which meant that he was just as slow now as he was then.

"Clyde, you have visitors," the nurse announced, ushering us in. I got the feeling that while he was well-liked in the home, visits from outside were rare.

"Hey, who are you?" he asked with a big wide grin. He was sitting in a comfortable chair with the TV on. "You're visiting Clyde? People don't come to see Clyde." He pointed to Jess. "You. You can visit. You're pretty."

"Thank you, Clyde," said Jess. "You're a handsome guy yourself."

Clyde turned red and looked away.

It was obvious to us who should do the talking; the woman he had the crush on. Scott and I sat in uncomfortable chairs in the corner, while Jess took a seat next to Clyde.

"I've come to talk to you," she said. "Is that okay? My name is Jess."

He looked at her and made a face. "You're not here from the state to talk to Clyde, are you? You're too pretty to be from the state. You're not, are you?

"Oh heavens, no. I wouldn't work there. Yuck!"

That tickled Clyde's funny bone. He giggled, then said, "Clyde likes you if you're not from the state."

Okay, that third-person talk was going to drive me crazy.

"You're funny, Clyde. I can't believe you don't get a lot of visitors."

"No, Clyde doesn't have too many friends. All Clyde's friends live here."

"I bet you've had lots of friends in your life."

"No. People don't like Clyde. People are mean to him."

"Not even one friend?"

She was good. She figured out right away that if she brought up Ben, Clyde would get suspicious, so she had to coax him to bring him up.

Clyde's face lit up. "Clyde had a good friend once. Ben Fremont was Clyde's friend." A sad look came over him. "But that was a long time ago."

"Tell me about Ben."

"You're not from the police, are you? If you are Ben Fremont told Clyde to close his mouth and not say anything."

"No, I'm not from the police either. I just wanted to come visit you." She put her hand in his. He liked it.

"Ben Fremont is gone. A long time ago."

"What happened?"

"He told Clyde not to be sad. He said that he had to go far

away, but that he would come back to visit Clyde someday. He never did."

"Why not?"

"They said that Ben Fremont died. Clyde doesn't believe them. They said he died when Mr. Mort and Miss Sally were killed, but Clyde doesn't think he did. He told Clyde he was going away."

"When did he tell you that?"

"Before all the people were killed at Mr. Mort's."

"The night before?"

"No, before that. Ben Fremont was having breakfast with Clyde. He told Clyde not to be sad, but Clyde was."

"Was Ben from Homer?"

"He lived here."

"No, I mean, did he live here as a little boy too?"

"No. He was from far away."

"Did he tell you where?"

"Yes."

Jess changed tactics. "Was it pretty where he grew up?"

"No. It was cold."

"Colder than Homer?"

"Yes."

"Was he from Alaska?"

"Yes."

"Did he ever tell you the name of the town?"

"No, but he told Clyde the town is full of ghosts."

Clyde was losing steam, and now seemed uncomfortable, so Jess quickly changed the subject. As much as her job was to pry information out of him, she appeared to be also genuinely taken by him.

"Do you like ice cream?" she asked.

He perked up. "Clyde loves ice cream."

They kept up like that for another ten minutes before Clyde started to get tired. Jess promised to come back and visit him.

"Not like Ben Fremont," he said sadly.

"No, not like Ben," she answered affectionately, then gave him a kiss on the forehead. Again he turned red and looked away.

"Bye Clyde, I'll see you soon."

"Goodbye Jess."

We got out to the curb and I said to Jess, "Should I be jealous?"

"I would be, if I were you," said Scott. "I mean, c'mon, Jon, he's everything you're not."

"He is cute," admitted Jess.

"You were good with him," I said, turning serious.

"He's a sweet old guy who never had a break in life," she answered. "You heard him. People were mean to him, and it was just because he was slow. It's just so unfair. When we make it through this, I want to keep my promise to him and visit him regularly."

I caught the "when." That was a good sign.

"So, do you think he was talking about a ghost town?" asked Scott.

"It makes sense," I said. "But it's hard to believe he was living *in* a ghost town. But if it's true, why did it become a ghost town? I've got to think that's significant somehow."

"Did you get the feeling that Ben Fremont was a sad person?" Scott asked.

"I think there was a part of him that still retained some humanity, some sensitivity," said Jess. "He was nice to Clyde when no one else was. I think he was also lonely. He needed someone to talk to, and I don't think Erin was that person. He needed someone like Clyde—appreciative of the attention and friendship, but also easy to mold. I have a feeling that if Ben told him to do something or not to do it, he would obey. But I don't think Ben was using him. I think the friendship was genuine."

"The fact that he cared enough for Clyde to tell him not to be sad when he left confirms that, I think," added Scott.

"So what's next?" asked Jess.

"I think we research ghost towns in Alaska," I said. "I'm sure there are websites devoted to them, and I doubt it would raise any electronic flags. I'm sure plenty of people look that stuff up.

"While we're checking on ghost towns," I continued, "we should see what's happening in the news. See if there is any update on the search for you or on Hillstrom's presidential bid."

"Do we have to?" asked Jess.

"Jon's right," said Scott. "If we're going to stay ahead of them, we have to know what they're doing. Or at least, what they are telling the media."

"Any word from your father?" I asked. It seemed natural to now give The Voice an identity.

"No, I think he's giving me a break."

"It could also be that he didn't get much further than discovering Hillstrom in the photo," suggested Scott. "He brought you here. Maybe there isn't a lot more he can do."

Jess thought about that. "It's possible, I suppose. Although I hope not. Even if he didn't go any further in the physical, maybe he can still guide us somehow ... or warn us ... or something. Remember he warned me a lot in DC—which train to take; which way to turn; things like that."

My phone rang. It was Joe.

"I've got a ride. I'll be flying in tomorrow. I have no idea where, but my contact says he knows a good out-of-the-way place."

"Good. Call me when you arrive. Depending on where it is, you may have to wait a while."

"No problem. I'll call you tomorrow."

Scott said he had to run to the airport for a few minutes to make sure his plane was ready, so we went with him. Scott was a popular figure at the Homer airport, so the few minutes became two hours.

He proudly showed us his plane, an old four-seater, twin-engine Piper Apache. After giving his baby the appropriate oohs and aahs, I said, "I hesitate to mention this, but it looks kind of old and a little beat-up."

"It is old," replied Scott, "but it runs great. I keep this thing in perfect condition. Besides," he added with a wink, "hunters and fishermen going into the bush expect their transportation to look the part."

After the airport, we stopped for some groceries, then went home, where Scott created a feast for dinner that included halibut, homemade bread, and a delicious vegetable casserole, followed by hand-cranked ice cream.

"Another month of this," I said to him, so full I couldn't move, "And I'll look like you."

We checked the news, but there was nothing about Jess—she was no longer a high priority—and the only news about Hillstrom was his surge in the polls. A lot was being made of the fact that he was a third-party candidate who was actually polling higher than the Republican and Democratic nominees.

We had just fallen asleep when my phone rang. I reached for it saying, "It must be Joe."

It wasn't. The reception was terrible and the voice was hard to hear, but it definitely wasn't Joe. I could barely make it out, but the voice was saying, "Jon? That you, Jon?" And then the line went dead. I had goose bumps all over my body, and my heart was pounding.

"Was that Joe?" Jess said sleepily. Then she looked at me and sat up. "Jon, what's wrong?"

"You're not the only one hearing dead people," I said. "I know I'm not imagining this. I'd know that voice anywhere. That was Mill Colson!"

Chapter 23

Scott looked down at the mountainous terrain slipping by beneath his Apache. Joe had called early in the morning to say he was in a remote place called Rocky Hole. Scott was familiar with Rocky Hole, having flown there about a dozen times. It was a privately-owned airstrip in the middle of nowhere that catered to hunters and fishermen. How in the world did Joe get there? It was good, though. He would be hard to locate. Rocky Hole consisted of one runway and a bar/general store. It sat at the edge of a large lake, and most of the traffic consisted of seaplanes. He was close now. It had taken him about three hours to get there, but he knew Joe would be fine waiting.

What he was worried about was Jon. His brother, he felt, had no skills for this. Going up against some shadowy, but obviously powerful organization was way beyond Jon's experience. He was a salesman, for God's sake. He couldn't blame Jess for it though. As screwed up as this whole situation was, he recognized that Jess was Jon's savior, of sorts. He knew that Jon had decided to come up and spend some time with him, but what he hadn't been convinced of was whether Jon would actually make it. He knew his brother was devastated by the loss of his daughter and that he blamed himself. He also knew that Jon owned a gun. Was he capable of using it on himself? Until Jon met Jess, Scott thought the answer was yes.

He had to admit though, Jess was something special. He wasn't feeding them both a line; Jess had a spark. She had life, and there was truly a connection between them that Scott had rarely seen between two people. They just had to make it through alive. A tall order, from the sound of things.

He wasn't concerned about his own life. Jon and Jess had both apologized numerous times for getting him involved, and he had assured them that he was glad to be involved. And he was. Life was fleeting as it was. If he was meant to die, so be it. But he would go fighting. He was angry that someone was trying to kill his brother. And like Elmer, he had little use for the goings-on in Washington, so if he could help expose some of its scummier aspects, he was happy to help.

Jon had described Joe in detail, and he sounded like a capable guy. He had no idea how Joe could help, if at all, but here was another person who was about to fall victim to Hillstrom's machine, and Scott wasn't going to let that happen.

Approaching Rocky Hole, he radioed in to let them know he was starting his approach. He pictured the radio sitting on the bar, between the clean glasses and the draft beer. A high-tech operation, it wasn't. Everything went through Fister, the bar owner. Nobody knew if Fister was his first name or last; he was only ever known as Fister, or Fist. Fister informed him that he had a package that would be waiting outside for him. Scott okayed that, asked Fister to make him a burger and fries to go, and began his descent. Although he often took Max flying with him, this time he left Max at home, not knowing what he was going to encounter and figuring Jon could feed him.

After landing, he taxied up to the gas pumps, where Butch, Fister's son, stood ready to fill the tank. Scott could see a smallish, nondescript man standing off to the side. Had to be Joe. Scott slid his .45 into his belt. You just never knew....

Scott climbed out and was approached by the stranger, who held out his hand. "I'm Joe," he said.

"Scott."

"I appreciate you coming to get me."

"My pleasure. As soon as I'm filled up, we can get out of here. Let me pick up my food. Have you eaten?"

"Constantly. Had nothing else to do here."

"Looks like you went through the wringer," said Scott. Joe was covered in yellowed bruises and scabs. He was missing a lower tooth on his left side and had some tape across the bridge of his nose.

"Yeah, it wasn't pleasant. Can't believe I'm alive to see this." He swept his hand around to the surrounding mountains.

"Stupid question, but I assume you weren't followed."

"God, no."

"How'd your contact know about this place?"

"He said he's flown in here twice before. I don't think your friend Fister likes him very much. And knowing this guy, I'm sure he wasn't transporting hunters when he came."

"Fist is pretty picky about the type of lowlife that is acceptable. Okay, give me a minute to pick up my food and say hi to Fist."

Scott went into the building. It was just what the average tourist would expect a remote hunting outpost to look like. Bearskins and moose heads lined the walls. There were three rows of camping and fishing supplies, and a glass counter filled with knives of all sizes. Behind the counter was a small selection of rifles and rods and reels. On the other side of the store was the bar. The smell of Scott's burger hung in the air.

"Hey, Fist," said Scott.

"Hey. Didn't expect to see you this early in the season."

"Special trip. Had to pick up your guest of the last few hours."

"He's not up here to hunt or fish, I can tell you that."

"Nah," answered Scott. "Kind of a special situation."

Fister said no more. He had seen enough in his years to know when to stop with the questions.

Scott picked up his food and a bottle of water and made his way back out to the plane. Butch had finished fueling it and Scott paid him, got in, then helped Joe into the co-pilot's seat.

"Gets pretty loud with the engines on, so you'll need to wear the headphones in front of you. They will dampen the noise and allow us to talk."

Joe nodded his agreement and slipped the headset on. Scott tested it out to make sure they could communicate, then started the engines. Within minutes they were in the air. They circled Rocky Hole once, then headed south toward Homer. Scott ate while he flew, and in no time the cockpit smelled like a burger joint. If it bothered Joe, he didn't let on. He let Scott finish his meal before talking.

"One of the questions I was going to ask you was how you knew Jon and Jess, but having met you, it's pretty obvious. Is Jon your older brother?"

"By three years. But I'm better looking, so that evens things out."

Suddenly, from the headset Scott heard, *"Apache 214, Apache 214, you out there?"*

"Apache 214 here. What's up Fist?"

"Five minutes after you left, a chopper set down. New and fast. Two slick operators on board. Wanted to know if your package was on the plane that just left. Butch, well, he's my son and all, but he's dumb as a stump, and told them he was. They wanted to know where you were heading. Butch doesn't know where you're from, but he told them he saw you

heading south. Anyway, I'd suggest putting down somewhere real soon, 'cuz they're going to catch up to you in no time."

Scott made a sharp turn to the northwest.

"Fist, can you do me a favor?"

"Name it."

"Can you call Pete and Ollie over at Piney Lake and let them know I'm on my way? Ask them to round up any of the boys who might be there. I might need some help. I'll call in to them when I'm closer."

"Roger. I'll get back to you."

The two things Scott knew he could count on were the help locals gave their own up in the wilderness, and the disdain they held for slick strangers. Even though Scott had only lived in Alaska for eight years, and had been flying for only half of that, he had been fully accepted as "one of them."

"Thought you weren't followed."

"I wasn't. They're probably coming in from somewhere else. Unfortunately, the people I get to help me are usually swayed by the almighty buck. Word is probably out about me, and I'm sure it's made its way to all the people who have reputations for transporting "packages." In fact, he probably heard the word even before he agreed to take me here. I bet he double-crossed me even before I was in his plane. Gave them the coordinates of where he was going to drop me off. I tried to use the least sleazy of the sleazebags. The joke's on him though. I know these guys. He'll never get his payment from them. He'll be dead soon after he lands. I'm sorry though. I didn't mean to bring trouble with me."

"Trouble seems to be the word of the week, so don't worry about it. Let's just hope we can make it. Piney Lake is a good ten minutes from here, and I've just spotted the chopper in back of us."

Joe turned to look.

"It's still a ways back," said Scott, "But Fister was right. It's fast."

"Apache 214, you still out there?"

"Talk to me."

"Talked to Pete. Besides him and Ollie, they've got two other boys there. They'll be concealed in the woods. This better be good. They're so excited, I think they've all got hard-ons. They haven't done any flatlander hunting in a while. Don't disappoint them."

"Thanks, Fist, I owe you."

"You sure do. Out."

The chopper was gaining. Scott knew it was going to be close. There was going to be no leisurely landing this time.

"You armed?" he asked Joe.

"Stole one from one of the guys who did this." He pointed to his face.

"Well, then, let's do it." They were still five minutes out and the chopper was getting closer. Scott banked slowly to his right, then a sharp turn to his left. His intention wasn't to outrun the chopper, but to put himself in the best spot possible for landing. He was now in position to come right into the Piney Lake runway without any more major course adjustments.

Many of the backwoods lake guide posts didn't have runways. They relied on the seaplane business. But like Rocky Hole, Piney Lake was an exception.

"Joe, take a look at them. Anything about the chopper I should know?"

Joe had been gazing back almost constantly, trying to gauge how close they could come to landing before the helicopter was on top of them.

"Well, it's not a gunship, if that's what you were worried about, so I don't think they're going to blow us out of the sky. Even if one of them has a high-powered rifle, the chances of him hitting us are slim. That only works in the movies. My guess is that they want to force you down so that you crash in the woods. I don't know if they've figured out yet that you have a plan to land."

"And if we make it?" asked Scott.

"You can bet they'll come in heavily armed."

"Well, besides being a hunting camp, Piney Lake is a survivalist community. They'll take out anyone in their way."

Scott keyed the radio. "Piney Lake, this is Apache 214, over."

"Yo Scott, this is Ollie. We're all set for you here. I can see you in the distance. You've got a big bad bird following you. A little too close."

"Thanks Ollie. I can feel his breath. I'm coming in fast. These guys mean business and are going to have some impressive hardware."

"Roger that. My boys are safe. Any instructions?"

Scott looked at Joe. "Questioning them will be worthless," Joe said. "Nobody seems to know much of anything. At best, they might know who hired them, but even that person is too low on the totem pole."

Scott keyed the mic again. "You do whatever you need to. You've got free rein."

"The boys will be happy to hear that. You get in here quick."

"They're here," said Joe. "Right over us and coming lower."

"Got it," Scott answered. He could see the runway. "I'm going in." It was one of the shorter runways around, and not one that Scott liked to land on even in the best of times. It was not going to be fun.

Meanwhile, the helicopter, whose crew probably thought they were bringing Scott's plane down, suddenly pulled back, now that it was obvious to them Scott was going to land safely. Scott figured they were discussing their options.

Despite the chopper being less than a hundred feet behind him, and his plane coming in a little faster than was advised, his landing was surprisingly smooth. He applied the flaps and brakes and came to a stop with twenty feet to spare. He looked over at Joe, who was clutching the sides of his seat.

"Piece of cake," said Scott, grinning.

"I think I wet your seat," croaked Joe.

As Scott taxied the plane around, he saw the chopper at the top of the runway sitting on the ground. Two men with what looked like M-16s had stepped out of the chopper and were motioning for Scott to approach. The pilot was still at the controls, keeping the blades turning, ready for a quick getaway. Unbeknownst to the men from the chopper, but in plain sight to Scott and Joe, three men with rifles were sneaking up from the rear, taking care to stay behind cover the whole time.

Scott and Joe cocked their pistols at almost the same moment and Scott worked the throttle so they were slowly creeping back up the runway toward the chopper. He saw one of the men from the chopper quickly turn his head toward a shed. Then they both turned in the other direction. Scott could see one of Ollie's men—it might have been Ollie himself—hiding behind a knoll at the edge of the runway, a shotgun pointed at the two men.

Scott stopped the plane. It was obvious a yelling match was going on, and the two from the chopper weren't looking very confident. Suddenly, one raised his M-16, and got off one burst before dropping to the ground, his gun flying from his hands. The second man also raised his gun, but Scott wasn't so sure it wasn't the beginning of putting his hands up to surrender. It didn't matter. He, too, went down.

Scott gunned the motor and headed up the runway, stopping just short of the two bodies. He turned off the engines—thankful for the sudden quiet—and he and Joe got out, guns drawn.

The others had gathered around the two downed men. Both had leg wounds but were very much alive.

Pete sidled up to Scott. "That was some flying."

"I appreciate the help," answered Scott.

"Mind telling us what this is all about?"

"A very large and complicated conspiracy of some major terrorists"—he used the word for effect—"to take over the government. A lot of people have died—some probably at the hands of these two—and a lot more will die unless we can stop it. You think you've got no freedoms now, wait 'til these people take over."

"Hey," said Pete, "I may not like the assholes in Washington, but I served in Iraq, and I don't take kindly to terrorists."

Scott knew that as much as these backwoods guys derided the government, most had fought for it. They didn't mind talking about taking over the government. They just wanted to be the ones to do it. A little terrorist talk would get their blood boiling.

Suddenly he heard a shout, followed by two gunshots, and felt a bullet whiz past his ear. He looked up to see the pilot, whom everyone had forgotten about, pointing a large handgun out his window. He pulled in the gun and revved the motor. At that moment though, two of Ollie's men blasted the cockpit with buckshot and the pilot slumped forward, the engine cycling down. One of the men jumped into the cockpit and turned off the engine.

The two on the ground were crying out in pain. Both had major wounds and blood was pooling up on the runway around them.

"What'll we do with them?" asked Ollie. "You're a paramedic, right? Should you try to save them?"

"Yeah, I guess I don't have much choice," Scott said, and headed to his plane for his medical kit.

A lone shot rang out from behind him. He turned quickly to see Joe point his gun at the second man's head and pull the trigger. A second shot reverberated off the surrounding mountains.

"Shit!" he exclaimed. Nobody else said anything.

Joe looked up at the shocked faces around him. "It was the only option," he said. "If we had let these guys live, you'd all be dead by tomorrow, and we wouldn't be far behind. You have no idea how powerful the people behind this are. They have tentacles everywhere. You call the Alaska State Police and within an hour these people know about it. The only way that seems to work—your brother discovered that," he said to Scott—"is to make the hirelings disappear altogether. Make the ones at the top wonder what became of their men. I suggest what happened here stays here. You talk about it and somehow it's going to get back to them. Scott can let you know when it's all over and okay to talk about."

"Jon pegged you as a mild-mannered type," said Scott.

"Yeah, well, your brother isn't aware of my past." He left it at that.

Ollie said to his two men, "You guys okay hauling some trash?"

"Not a problem," said one.

"Take my pickup down the old logging trail to bear hollow. Take 'em as far in as you can. Watch out for the bears. Strip 'em naked. Any cash in their wallets is yours. We'll burn their clothes, credit cards, and I.D.'s when you get back." He turned to Scott. "What'll we do about their chopper?"

"You want to strip it and sell the parts?"

"Hell, yeah. I can make a fortune off this. I'll tow it over to the big shed. It'll fit. We can dismantle it in there. Pete, when they leave with the bodies, can you wash the blood off the runway?" He turned to Joe. "So these are some serious bad guys? Think they contacted anyone before they set down?"

"I doubt it," responded Joe. "These are hired guns. As such, they want to get full credit for their kills. They're not going to have told anyone where they are until they have proof that they've done their job. No, I think you're all pretty safe."

An hour later, after repeatedly thanking Pete, Ollie, and the other two for their help, Scott and Joe were back on their way.

Scott radioed Fister to let him know that "everything was taken care of" and to thank him again for his assistance. He promised to tell him the whole story at a later date.

"You think Ollie and his friends are going to be okay?" asked Joe.

"Yeah. Like I said, they're survivalists. They all have military backgrounds—most with extensive combat experience—and they're used to skirting the law. They don't see something like this out here, so down the line when they can talk about it, they'll go to town with it. I think your actions shocked them a little bit, but they're not virgins. If they think something needs to be done, they'll do it. Uh, but Joe, when we tell Jon and Jess about it, let's leave out that last part."

Joe smiled. "Yeah, no problem."

Chapter 24

Scott had just left to pick up Joe, and Jess and I sat at the kitchen table trying to make sense of the phone call a few hours earlier. I mentioned it to Scott before he left but asked him not to say anything to Joe until he got here.

It had taken us over an hour to get back to sleep, as we debated the odds that it was actually Mill. Here we were again, this time more awake, but coming to the same conclusion: we still had no idea.

"Okay," began Jess. "Let's assume for a moment that it was Mill, how did he get your number? If you remember, when you gave it to Joe, he said he was going to be the only person who had it, that we were to go through him for everything."

"That's why it'll be good to talk to Joe about this. If Mill is in hiding," I continued, "couldn't he contact one of his press buddies and tell them about Hillstrom? At least get the word out?"

"He probably doesn't know who to trust anymore. I'm sure he's scared out of his mind. If he shows himself, they'll find a way to kill him."

"You're right. I guess we really can't do anything else until, or if, he calls again."

"So where does that leave us?" asked Jess. "Scott won't be back with Joe for hours."

"Let's look into the ghost town theory. If it's true that he was brought up in a town now abandoned, is there some significance to it? I mean, did he leave because the town was going under, or was he somehow responsible for it becoming a ghost town?"

We cleaned up the breakfast dishes and were about to move to the computer when we heard a yelping outside. We rushed to the door, only to see Max and Slob wrestling in the dirt. They would roll over, then hop up and take turns chasing each other. They were having the time of their lives.

"Remember how Max looked at Slob with disdain when Slob greeted us?" I asked. "It was all an act."

At that moment, Max caught sight of us standing in the doorway and suddenly stopped and looked at us as if to say, *"You're not going to tell Scott you saw me doing this, right?"*

"Don't worry, Max," I said aloud. "Your secret is safe with us."

Satisfied, Max nipped Slob, and the games continued.

We went back in and sat at the computer. We started the search just by typing "ghost towns Alaska" into Google. I figured we could narrow it down as needed.

The information was fascinating, and we found ourselves getting caught up in the romance of Alaska during the gold rush days and forgetting our real purpose. There were numerous websites that brought the history to life. While many of the towns were former gold camps or mining towns started in the late 1890s, some didn't lose their last residents until the 1940s and 1950s. What kept the people there all that time?

As we read the accounts of the Klondike Gold Rush, and the 100,000 people who ventured there to make their fortune, we were both feeling a little embarrassed at our lack of knowledge about this part of America's history. Neither of us had ever read *The Call of the Wild*, or anything by Jack London, and couldn't remember learning anything about that fascinating era in history class. Were we just not interested when they taught it, or had it become a footnote, one that was no longer as important as our involvement in wars, and not worth teaching? I could somehow understand Alaskans' disdain for the rest of the country. Other than the focus on its oil, what did we really know about the state?

Finally, we began to focus in on the task at hand and were able to sort our way through the towns, eventually discarding the more famous ghost towns, and those on the official "ghost town tour map." Even so, nothing seemed to fit our criteria. There were a few towns—not necessarily related to the gold rush—that lost their last residents as recently as the early seventies, but upon further investigation, just didn't seem "right." No, we were missing something.

"After all this, do you think Ben was telling Clyde the truth?" asked Jess.

"I think we have to follow it up, just in case. There's something about that story that makes sense, but maybe we have to go about it another way. Why did Ben grow up in a soon-to-be-abandoned town? Why did he leave when he was twenty-one? Is that significant somehow? Then we go back to why he killed all those people. Is he just homicidal in nature or was he hiding something? What was so important in his past that he needed to wipe out all memory of his existence? If this town exists, what deep dark secret does it hold?"

"Just for the sake of argument," said Jess, "a young person stuck in a small Alaska town—obviously it must have had a tiny population—people are either lifers in those towns, or they can't wait to leave. But according to Elmer, he was an adult when he came to Homer, so he couldn't have been too anxious to get out of there."

"Something doesn't feel right. If you are legally an adult at eighteen, and you are living in a town you hate, or one that stifles you, you leave as quickly as you can. But he didn't. He waited until he was an 'accepted' adult. And while there might be legitimate reasons why he would wait until he was twenty-one, I think the age is somehow significant."

"Maturity," blurted out Jess. She gave a half-smile. "Um, that was my father speaking, not me."

"Right. At the age of eighteen, not only did he probably look too young, he wouldn't have had the cunning or the life experience to go into a town, set himself up as someone he wasn't, murder ten people and make it look like he was murdered too, then move across country right into a good job."

"But if he grew up in a small, remote village, where would the life experience come from?" asked Jess.

"And that's the question," I said. "You mentioned at one point that his school records are gone, that the school burned to the ground. Do you remember where that supposedly was?"

"In the mid-west someplace. Ohio, I think."

"Whoever was vetting him would have then checked into that. Ah, screw it." I turned back to the computer and typed "Senator Gary Hillstrom" into Google.

"We're taking a chance Googling him," Jess said. "Wouldn't that raise a flag in their system?"

"Maybe. But he's running for president. You don't think there are thousands of other people looking him up on the computer? I've got to see what it says about his childhood."

The search took me to Wikipedia. I printed out two copies and we sat back and read about Gary Hillstrom.

Ten minutes later we were convinced that the man who lived in Homer for four years as Ben Fremont was, in fact, Hillstrom. To the average person reading his history it would seem fascinating, or sad, or unique. For us, it just helped confirm everything we had suspected.

According to the posted history, Hillstrom was born in Youngstown, Ohio to Maggie and Peter Baker, who died in a car accident within days of his birth. He was adopted by Ronald and Lisa Hillstrom of Akron. He spent his whole childhood in Akron and went from grade school through high school at the Heavenly Father Church School. His adopted parents died soon after his graduation—no cause of death was listed. Several years ago, the school burned down and all of its records were destroyed. No back-up records existed.

He "bounced around"—his own words—for a while, before getting a job with Exchange Systems and, as we already knew, had risen to vice president. After ten years, he moved to Massachusetts, started his own small high-tech company, then ran for office. When he won the state Senate job, he sold his business and went into politics full-time.

I looked up information on his own company, Hillstrom Products, only to find out that it went under within months of him selling it.

"That alone is pretty suspicious," I said to Jess.

"It is," she agreed. "Almost like the company was fake to begin with, so it was 'sold'," she held up her hands like quotation marks, "to a crony, someone who could quietly make the company disappear."

"I wonder if anyone from that church school is still living," I said. "Someone who could confirm that he actually went there, because I don't think he did."

"What do you want to bet there isn't anyone. I bet everyone who taught at that school has since died, probably in a variety of non-suspicious ways. Is it even worth checking?"

"Probably not," I answered. "I'm sure you're right. If need be, we can sic Joe on that. So, you want to hear my theory?"

"I do."

"There is no doubt in my mind that Ben killed those people, but I don't think it was a whim, or him going whacko all of a sudden. I think it was calculated. In fact, I think it was all calculated. I think everything in Gary Hillstrom's life has been calculated. Coming to Homer served a purpose. I don't yet know what the purpose was, but he was definitely here for a reason. Getting the job at Exchange Systems was part of the plan, as was moving to Massachusetts and starting a business. What better way to gain residency and establish yourself so you can run for office?"

"If all that's true," began Jess, "at what point did he stop working alone and start to develop this organization? We're pretty sure Exchange Systems is a front, and it sounds as if his own company was a front. We're missing a step."

We looked at each other, neither one really sure where to go. And then I saw Jess shake. Her face suddenly looked flush, and I thought she was going to throw up. But she didn't, and she slowly regained her color.

When she could finally speak, she said, "Some of these messages actually hurt when they come in. It's almost like the more urgent they are, there's no subtlety. It's almost violent. Anyway, look up 'nobbas' on Google."

"'Nobbas'?" I asked. "Did you get a spelling?"

"No. Try all different ways. I have no idea."

So I did. We spent the next half hour trying different variations in Google, with nothing significant showing up.

Finally Jess sighed and said, "I could have sworn that was a message. In fact, I know it was, but..."

She stopped because I had started laughing.

"What?" she asked.

It had just come to me what "nobbas" meant, and it struck me funny that we had spent so long on it trying to come up with a meaning for it without taking a moment to think about the actual word.

"It's not 'nobbas'," I said. "It's 'not boss'. That's the step we're missing. We've figured all along that this was Hillstrom's show. But in fact, maybe it's not. Maybe Hillstrom is just one of the players. Your father is saying 'not boss', meaning, Hillstrom might not be the boss. This may go back farther than we think, and it may have started before Homer. I think the answer lies in that ghost town. We have to find it."

Chapter 25

Mel Hutchinson was sweating. His ability to intimidate Corbin Mays was slipping away. For the first time since joining Mays's staff, he felt vulnerable. Mays definitely now had the upper hand, and he knew it. Frankly, Hutch had to admit to himself that he wasn't doing a very good job. The people he had hired to carry out some pretty simple assignments—kill the girl and her companion; find out who her companion was; kill Joe Gray; kill Mill Colson— were failing miserably. Colson was the only success, and even that wasn't confirmed yet. What the fuck was going on?

"Update me," said Mays. "Give me some good news."

"We know that Gray was headed for Alaska," Hutch was trying to sound as confident as possible. "I got word from two of my operatives that Gray hired a lowlife to fly him somewhere in Alaska. My guys were flying up from Seattle to intercept them."

"And?"

"And I haven't heard back from them yet." The truth was, he should have heard hours ago.

"Do we know where?"

"No. The lowlife was directed to the guys in Seattle. He must've told them. Nothing was ever passed up the chain."

"Was he going to Alaska to hide out or to meet the girl?"

"I don't know."

"What's the latest on the girl? Do you have any clue as to where she is?"

"No."

"Exactly what *do* you have for me?"

Hutch hesitated, and he knew Mays caught it. He had to be honest, but he wasn't going to accept too much of the blame.

"The truth is, they've dropped off the face of the earth. Nobody has seen or heard from them since the fiasco in Canada. They could be anywhere. Canada is a big country."

"No shit, Sherlock. Well, what's your gut say? Do you think Gray is heading to Alaska to meet Norton and her protector?"

"It's certainly a possibility."

"Anything is a possibility. That's not an answer."

"I don't believe the girl and her friend were coming back to Washington. It's possible my men were decoyed into going east in Canada. It could be the girl headed west instead. Yes, they could be in Alaska."

"Another big fucking place," said Mays.

Hutch's cell phone rang. Please let it be good news, he thought.

It wasn't. He listened for a minute, then told the caller to keep him abreast of any developments.

"Something else I'm not going to like, right?" asked Mays.

"It seems the helicopter has disappeared. As I said, the guys going after Gray never told anyone exactly where they were going. All they told their contact up the ladder was that they were going to some out of the way outpost in Alaska. That's it. Now nobody can reach them by radio."

"How about the lowlife who took him?"

"Dead. Nobody had any reason to question him. Their orders were to get rid of him when he landed back in the states."

Mays was ready to burst, but he was trying to keep his

emotions under control. Could things get any worse?

"Do you think Gray found out about the town?"

"No way. That would be impossible. There is nothing that leads back to the town."

"Somehow that doesn't give me a lot of confidence. How many men do we have there?"

"We always keep two. We rotate them out every few weeks. There's nothing to do there except to chase away the occasional tourist."

"Send four more men. I want six there at all times."

"Isn't that overkill?"

"Judging by the total fuck-ups of your crack team? I'd say no. Maybe Gray doesn't know about the town, but we have too much still there to take a chance, so I'm certainly not going to leave it unguarded."

"Okay, I'll send some more guys up there. I've never been there, but isn't it possible to just remove all the evidence and destroy the town?"

"It's the safest and most remote place for the records. Nobody would ever look there. Besides, you don't just destroy a town. It may be uninhabited, but we'd still catch hell from the authorities. Too much explaining and it might set off some red flags as to who actually owns the property. Someday, when the time is right, we'll destroy all the records, but that day hasn't come. We might still need them."

Hutch's phone rang again. He had never been so reluctant to answer, but Mays was staring at him expectantly.

"Yeah?" he said as confidently as possible and listened as he was delivered the worst news yet that day. When he hung up, he felt like throwing up.

"I can tell by your face, the sweat dripping off your forehead, and your shaking hand that that was another wonderful call. The only thing missing is a growing stain in your crotch," said Mays.

"One of my guys," Hutch was hoarse now, "the one Gray didn't kill in Rochester, still has Gray's phone. He said he turned it on, got a call on it last night, and answered it." The idiot should have let it go to voicemail to get the full message, he thought. "Before the caller on the other end realized that my guy wasn't Gray and hung up, he said, 'This is Mill.' My guy doesn't know anything about Colson but figured a call on Gray's phone was important enough to let us know."

"Well this day is fucking complete. Obviously, I was wrong when I hired you to be in charge of security. But I'm kind of stuck with you now, aren't I? Would you go do your fucking job and come back here with some good news?"

After Hutch had left, Corbin Mays sat at his desk contemplating the recent events. He looked down at his hands and realized he was shaking. So many years in the making, and now, when it was so close to fruition, the whole thing could come tumbling down. All because of an insignificant girl who knew too much.

Chapter 26

We took a break to get a snack and use the bathroom. I brewed coffee, poured two cups, and made my way back to the computer, where Jess was already back at work. As I handed Jess her cup, I said, "I had an idea. We've been looking for ghost towns, because that's supposedly how Ben described it to Clyde. But what if it's not exactly a ghost town? What if there is still a population listed? After all, if Ben lived there, it couldn't have been a *real* ghost town."

Jess typed "list of Alaska towns" into Google and clicked onto a site.

"Then it could be any one of close to 400 towns," she said.

"Let's narrow it down. We're going to have to make some assumptions. I think we can safely rule out the larger, more established towns, so for now, let's say we keep only towns under 200 people, although I think we're going to find that it's far below that number."

While I was talking, Jess was plugging information into Google.

"There are all kinds of sites," she said. "The information isn't exactly consistent from one site to the next, but for the moment, we can use Wikipedia, which lists them in order of size, and has links to census information and the town description."

"The census information could be good," I replied. "That will be helpful for the next part of the process. For now, we can make use of the town information."

"Okay, then," she said, "out of the 400 or so towns, we can now eliminate about half. That's still a lot left."

"And here's the slow part," I said. "Out of the 200 left, let's click onto each link and see how the town is described. If it's a seasonal fishing or hunting village, or a pipeline village, we can eliminate them. I think native villages as well—this is definitely a white man conspiracy. If they are too close to one of the larger towns, those can be crossed off, or on a major road. Anything with a historical significance won't work. We just want something anonymous and out of the way. I know it's a lot of towns, but I think we can eliminate them pretty fast."

We got to it. She printed out the entire list of 400 towns, and we crossed off the top 200. It was time-consuming at first, but once we had the hang of it and knew where to look on the linked page, each one only took a couple of minutes. As we eliminated towns, we crossed them off the hard copy. A couple of hours later, we had narrowed the list down to eighteen towns.

"That's not bad," I said, sitting back in my chair. I looked at the clock. It was two o'clock. Scott had said not to bother calling. If he was in the air I wouldn't get through, and if he was on the ground he probably wouldn't have service. So I had no idea where they were. "The next step is less clear, so it's good that we only have eighteen to work with. I want to look at the census information and see if there's anything that doesn't seem right—population swings or sudden drops—anything that sends up a flag. We need to go back ten or twenty years before Ben came to Homer, so let's examine the census information for the last fifty years for each town."

That was a much slower process, and it was almost five o'clock when we had narrowed it down to three towns, all with populations under ten: Hidden Ridge, Moose Hollow, and Wisdom Spring. Each one had an anomaly that warranted further research.

Hidden Ridge's population had peaked in 1948 with a population close to 300. A small zinc mining operation had been going on since the early '20s, and by the late '40s production was at its highest level. But the mine played out over the next twenty years, and by the late '60s it was boarded up and abandoned. At that point the population had sunk to just over sixty residents. In 1980, there was a sudden surge, and the population almost doubled. We couldn't find the reason for it. Then in 2000, the population was listed as twenty-four. In 2010, it was eight. The timing of the surge fit within the timeframe and was certainly curious.

Moose Hollow was suspicious in another way. The oldest of the three towns, Moose Hollow started out as a hunting camp—mainly for moose hunting, as the name implied—back around the turn of the twentieth century. In the 1930s a lumber mill was built and workers were brought in. By 1960 the records showed a population of 225. In the early '70s, they were bought out by a larger corporation, but the population actually decreased to about 150. That raised a flag for me. In 2005, the mill burned down and most of the population left. The current population was listed as six.

My money, though, was on Wisdom Spring, for a couple of reasons. First, each of the other towns had an easy link from the list to their Wikipedia site. Wisdom Spring had no link, as if it was removed altogether from Wikipedia. We found the information on a personal web page of the grandson of one of the town's former residents. Luckily Jess, being a researcher, investigated further than most people would have. I never would have found it. Hillstrom's people probably hadn't yet either.

The other reason was its story. Like Hidden Ridge, it was once the home to a fairly thriving zinc mine. Opened in 1917, the mine went through its growing pains. In a remote section of central Alaska, its first obstacle was transportation. The road leading to the mine was hardly more than an animal trail. It took them two years to clear a road leading to a "main" road. They also weren't totally prepared for the Alaskan winters and many workers died in those early years. They eventually got their act together, and by 1930 were actually making a profit. A typical mining town, it consisted of forty or fifty houses—some not much more than shacks—a general store, a stable and blacksmith (in its early days), a bar, a hotel, a small church that was also a school, and little else. Population-wise, its high point came in 1953 when it topped out at just over 200. It maintained a steady population for about ten years when, like Hidden Ridge, the mine finally played out. The people left and for the next five years it lay dormant. But like Moose Hollow, a company swooped in in the late '60s and this time bought not just the mine, but the whole town. By then the state owned the land and the buildings and sold it to the company for pennies. Supposedly the company—the name of which we couldn't find—was going to reopen the mine, but the writer of the story wasn't aware of any mining activity there. The 1970 census showed the town's population at ninety. The 1980 census had it at 110. By 1990, the population was down to a dozen, and by 2000 and 2010, it was listed as zero.

"What are your thoughts?" I asked.

"I have good feelings about this one. I'd love to talk to the owner of that website to get some firsthand opinions, but also to warn him to take down the site just in case Hillstrom's people run across it. His life could be in danger."

She searched his main website until she uncovered an address to go with his name, Carl Jenkins.

"He's in Fairbanks, which is quite a ways from here," she said. "How about we call him?"

"Let me do it," I said. "We don't know if the powers in charge have your voice programmed into their computers and can do a voice match. We could be taking all of these precautions for nothing, but better safe than sorry."

We found his number online and I dialed from my cell phone. I didn't want Scott's number to appear. I looked at the clock. Six o'clock and Scott still wasn't back. Should I be worried?

"Hello?"

"Hi, is this Carl Jenkins?"

"It is."

"My name is Harry Coleman. I wonder if you could help me. I'm calling from Missouri. My wife and I have become fascinated with the lore of Alaska and have been researching ghost towns and abandoned mines. We ran across your website about Wisdom Spring and were wondering if we could ask you a few questions."

"Sure, I'd be happy to answer any questions."

"Thank you so much. It was hard finding information on Wisdom Spring. Most other towns have a link in Wikipedia, but not this one." I'd found from my sales days that the secret to effective lying—or exaggerating—is to stay as close to the truth as possible.

"That is strange. I noticed it myself. It had a link until just a couple of years ago, then it disappeared. I even wrote an entry and sent it in. It appeared, then was gone a few days later. Must be a glitch in the system."

"Have you ever visited the town?" I asked.

"Three times. Once when I was ten. That would've been 1962. Again in the late '70s, around '78, I'd guess. Then again a couple of years ago."

"Sounds like you liked the place."

"Well, my grandfather was a miner there, and after the mine closed in '63, he came to live with us. He died in '75. You know how sometimes you just want to go back to your roots? That's why I went back in '78. I wanted to see how the town compared to my memory of it, what buildings were still there, that kind of thing."

"Was it how you remembered it?"

He hesitated. "Well, kind of. I mean, most of the buildings were still there just how I remembered them. The houses that were being lived in—probably about half—had been fixed up nicely, as had some of the businesses. There were even a couple of newer buildings. Any building that wasn't being used, however, was falling apart. So it was a strange combination of well-kept and dilapidated."

"Was the mine up and running?"

"I can't tell you that. I took the road down to the mine and about halfway there the way was blocked with a sign that said 'No Trespassing'. But I could see some trucks and heavy equipment down the road, so they were doing something. I don't know if it was up and running."

"What were the people like?" This, to me, was one of the crucial questions, and might tell us something about Hillstrom.

"Well," he kind of dragged the word out. "I didn't put it in my website, but here's what I think. I think the town was bought by one of those cults."

"Why do you say that?"

"Kids. The place was full of kids. When my grandfather lived there, it was a mining town. Obviously, some of the miners had kids, but it was a normal number for that kind of town. But when I went back, it seemed there were two kids to every adult. Maybe three. One of the new buildings looked like a school, although it didn't have a name on it like most schools. I can't say anyone was particularly unfriendly to me, but they certainly weren't welcoming me with open arms. It was kind of … spooky … I guess. I didn't stay long. Drove around a bit. Stopped in the store, then headed out disappointed that it didn't bring back the memories I'd hoped for."

"And what about the last time?"

"That wasn't much of a visit. I'd seen the census listing a population of zero and thought I'd check it out. I like ghost towns too, and in this case, especially because I had known it before it became a ghost town. Anyway, I got there and started driving through the streets when a guy came out of a building and flagged me down. He told me that it was private property and asked me to leave. He was pleasant about it, but I had an eerie feeling he wasn't alone. There was something dangerous about him, so I skedaddled."

"Did you get to see the mine?"

"No, I didn't get that far. I'm sorry to say that I'm going to have to go. My wife just put dinner on the table."

"Well, Mr. Jenkins, I really appreciate your help." I looked at Jess, who had been close enough to hear much of what he was saying. She nodded her head, as if to say, *tell him*. "Mr. Jenkins, I know you have to leave, but if I could have just one more minute. This is kind of important."

"Uh, sure."

"Everything you just told me confirms things we had suspected. You're probably not going to believe me, and that's okay, as long as I can convince you of one thing. For the time being, I think you should take down your site on Wisdom Spring."

"And why would that be?" His voice had taken on a suspicious tone.

"My name isn't really Harry Coleman, and I'm not calling from

Missouri. I'm not married, but I am traveling with a friend. I say traveling, but it's really running. She uncovered a massive plot against this country by accident, and now a number of people have died as a result of her discovery."

"What are you…"

"Please hear me out. I know it sounds fantastic, and it would to me too. But we are living it and it's real. The reason I asked you about Wisdom Spring is because it plays a part in all this. We don't yet know what part, but that's what we have to find out. Your information was crucial, and I can't tell you how much I appreciate it. The reason the Wikipedia entry on the town disappeared is because they made it disappear. They can and have made a lot of things … and people … disappear. All we can figure is that they haven't come upon your site yet, because it was a little harder to find. All I'm asking is that you take down your site for now, for your own good. If they discover it, they will take it down, and probably you with it because it's obvious that you know too much about the town. Please Mr. Jenkins. You'll know when to put it back up. If we live through this, we're bringing them down and you'll hear about it on the news. If you never hear about it, it means they got to us first. I'm not being melodramatic. Please take it down."

I hung up before he could say anything more.

Chapter 27

Scott showed up with Joe an hour later. They both looked exhausted and Joe looked terrible. Jess and I made them some dinner and we all sat down while they ate and took turns relating the events at Piney Lake. At first, they seemed to be glossing over some of the details, probably for Jess's sake, but when Jess began asking questions, they gave a full accounting. I had a feeling, however, that there was an aspect to the story they were still holding back on, but I let it slide.

When they finished, Jess said, "Your story isn't as disturbing to me as you may have thought it would be. Nothing about it bothers me. I seem to have lost some of my innocence over the past few weeks. What does bother me is getting all of you involved. I can't have any more deaths on my conscience."

"Jess," I said, "you've got to keep the thought in your head that it's not you. You didn't get any of us involved. Hillstrom and his minions did. Also, your father wouldn't have sent you in this direction unless he thought we could help."

"Father?" asked Joe.

"Right," I said. "There's a whole aspect to this that we haven't told you."

Between us, Jess and I proceeded to tell Joe about the mystical part of the whole story. When we were done, he just looked at us.

"Look," he finally said. "I'm just a simple PI. I work with facts. I follow the clues until I solve the mystery. The only way a dead person can lead me in the right direction is if there is evidence left behind on his body. Dead is dead. I'm sorry Jess, I don't mean to make you upset."

Joe saw Jess's face in her hands and assumed she was crying about her father, or about Joe's disbelief. In reality, she was laughing. When she stopped, she looked up at Joe and said, "I'm fine with that. Trust me, I didn't believe it either, and I don't need you to believe it. That's okay."

"Why were you laughing?" he asked.

"Because dead isn't dead. At least, it might not be."

Joe cocked his head, obviously confused. "You've lost me."

Jess looked at me to take over.

"Mill Colson might still be alive," I said simply. I told him the story of the phone call. Joe's mouth hung open. "Now the question is," I continued, "did he have my phone number?"

"He did," answered Joe, a little shell-shocked. "I know I told you that I would be the only one with your number, but Mill insisted. He said that a lawyer needed to be able to contact his client at a moment's notice. He promised that he would memorize the number and not write it down anywhere."

"Well, we can't do any more about it until—or if—he calls again. For now, we have a lot to catch you up on. Even you, Scott. A lot has happened."

They insisted they were awake enough to hear it all that night, so we filled Joe in on our journeys since we last talked, and then told them both the progress we had made that day. Joe, meanwhile, related the details of his Rochester encounter. After that, we all went to bed exhausted.

My cell phone rang at 2:30. Jess heard it first and shook me from my coma. We had made a deal that she wouldn't answer it. As long as I was still anonymous, it was safer for her not to talk, and therefore connect me to her.

I answered it on the fifth ring, just before it would bounce to voicemail.

"Hello." It was a statement, not a question, the best I could muster at that time of the morning.

"Where did we first meet?" Mill's voice came across much stronger than it had the night before. I woke up quickly.

"Las Vegas."

"Specifically."

"Circus Circus."

"Okay. I'm satisfied."

"Not okay," I said. "My turn. Where in Circus Circus?" He was checking not only if he had the right person, but if I was free and safe. If I gave the wrong answer, he'd know I'd been captured. But it could work in reverse. He might actually be in Hillstrom's hands, so I needed him to answer correctly.

"In one of the ballrooms. I was giving a talk and pushing my book. You stood in line."

"How did I tell you about our mutual friend?"

"You gave me a note."

"Okay. Now I'm satisfied." I lost the suspicious tone. "Where are you? What happened?"

"I'm safe. I'm hiding out at a friend's house. I was having a, shall we say rendezvous, and was going to miss my flight. I called Sean, my personal aide, to let him know. We had other people who had to get to New York, so I told them to go without me and I'd catch up."

"Where did the eighth body come from?"

"I'm sick about that. I'm sick about the whole thing. It was the boyfriend of one of my secretaries. When I called to say I wouldn't make it, Sean asked me if this guy could take my place on the plane, so I said sure. Now he's dead. Now they're all dead. All because of Hillstrom."

"You think he was behind it?"

"Absolutely! I had a call earlier in the day telling me to drop Jess as a client or I was a dead man. The caller didn't say who he represented, obviously, but who else could it be? I told him to go fuck himself and hung up. That same night my plane goes down."

"Does anyone else know you're alive?" I asked.

"The friend I'm staying with and my lawyer. My lawyer is going to stall things as long as he can regarding my estate and my firm. I tried to call Joe, but someone else answered. I don't know if they got to him."

"They almost did, and he's a little worse for wear, but he's okay. We just picked him up today. He's with us."

"Thank God. I'm not going to ask you where you are, but I assume you are safe."

"We are. We have another person working with us—totally trustworthy—and between us, we are actually making progress. We've discovered some of Hillstrom's history that you'll never read anywhere, and we've just discovered a clue that may lead us to some of the big answers."

"That's great. I wish I could be of help, but at the moment I'm hiding for my life. I feel ashamed to be hiding, but I don't know what else to do."

"Nothing. There may come a time when we will need your legal expertise, and hopefully you'll be able to come out of hiding, but not yet. When we're ready, we'll let you know. I need a phone number for you."

He gave it and I told him I'd pass everything on to Joe. After we hung up, I filled Jess in on anything she wasn't able to hear and then we went back to bed. There was really nothing for us to discuss, and sleep was more important.

The next morning at breakfast Scott and Joe listened intently as we related Mill's call.

"I'm happy he's alive," said Joe. "He can be arrogant when he wants to be, blustery sometimes, and a showman all of the time, but deep down he has a really good heart. He was good to his employees and genuinely cared about them. This must be eating at him something fierce. I can guarantee that when we need him to do something about Hillstrom from his end, there will be no hesitation—no matter what danger he's in."

"So what's our next step?" asked Scott.

"Clyde!" blurted out Jess.

We all responded with some form of "huh?"

Jess had an embarrassed smile. "Sorry, that was my dad."

Out of the corner of my eye I could see Joe looking a little uncomfortable.

"I think he wants me to go see Clyde again."

"To what purpose?" I asked.

"I think now that we know a little bit more about the town, it might be good to question Clyde about things Ben might have said."

"Do you think Hillst ... Ben ... would have shared that much information with him?" asked Joe.

"He might have," I answered. "He seems to have confided in Clyde a lot. Now maybe he just kept it as general as possible, but maybe he let things slip."

"And," added Jess, "Clyde may be slow, but I don't think there is anything wrong with his memory, even after all this time. He gets tired because of his age and the mental stimulation, but I think if I go in there knowing what to ask, I can get answers while he's still fresh. It's worth a try."

"What are you hoping to get?" asked Joe, who seemed to have moved on from his discomfort.

"I don't know," she answered.

"I do," I said. "If he gave any information at all about his childhood, we might start to understand something about the town. I'd like to go up to the town, but are we going to find anything there that can help us? Clyde might give us more information than the town does—there may be nothing much left there. Or, he might give us information that will help us know what to look for when we do get there. Normally I wouldn't hold out a lot of hope that Clyde could help us, but if Jess's dad suggests we see him, then there has to be something to it."

Joe rolled his eyes.

"Enough!" I shouted at Joe, who almost fell over backwards off his chair. "You may not believe in any of this ghost business. I know you think it's all shit, and if you had asked me a few weeks ago, I might have agreed with you. But Jess is not making this stuff up. Meeting Mill, getting across the Canadian border, even Jess and me meeting up in the first place, was all his doing. I've witnessed it. So if you don't think it's possible, that's fine, I respect that. But don't roll your eyes, and don't question it. Got it?"

Joe softened. "Yeah." He turned to Jess. "I'm sorry, Jess. No, I don't believe in all this. It goes against everything I'm about. It's like asking me to add two plus two and get five. But obviously something is happening that seems to be working, so who am I to question it? I'll keep my opinions to myself."

I held out my hand and we shook, and Jess went over and gave him a hug. The issue was now in the past.

We called the nursing home to make sure Clyde was up for

visitors and they told us he'd be most alert around eleven, just before lunch. We decided that I'd go with Jess into his room, but like before, I'd stay in the background.

We arrived at eleven. We had asked on the phone if it was okay if we brought a small ice cream for him. Despite the fact that it might spoil his lunch, they responded with, "Sure, why not. At ninety he deserves some treats." So Jess walked in with Clyde's favorite dessert and I slipped in behind and quietly sat on the couch.

Clyde's face lit up when he saw Jess and the ice cream.

"Clyde's friend Jess is back. Yay!" he said. "You brought Clyde ice cream. You're Clyde's best friend."

"I told you I'd come back," replied Jess. "How are you doing today?"

"Doing good today. Clyde's best friend is back."

Jess talked small talk with him for a few minutes—not too long, knowing that he tired easily. Jess did most of the talking, as Clyde was busy savoring his ice cream. Finally, when he was done, she segued into the subject of Ben.

"When I was here last, you told me that your friend Ben Fremont might still be alive. So I thought I would try to see if he was so I could find him and maybe I could bring him to see you."

Clyde's face lit up, and I could tell Jess was sorry she used that line.

"Now, I don't know if he's alive, so don't get your hopes up, but I thought I'd try. Is that okay that I try?"

"Clyde understands. Clyde's friend Ben Fremont has been gone a long time."

"Well, maybe you can help me find him. Can you think of anything he told you about the town he grew up in?"

"Bobby asked Clyde to think about that too."

Jess looked back at me, puzzled.

"Who's Bobby?" she asked.

Clyde looked back at her as if she were crazy. "You know. He told Clyde that he was your friend. That made him Clyde's friend."

Again, she glanced back at me, this time with a look of panic. Had somebody discovered us? It was all I could do to not interject in the conversation, but it was important that Jess do this alone. Clyde trusted her.

She turned back to Clyde. "When did you see Bobby?" she asked.

"Last night, when Clyde was sleeping. He told Clyde that it was important to help you find Ben, so Clyde thought and thought and thought."

The Voice! Jess's father. His name was Robert. He would have been 'Bobby' to someone like Clyde. Jess got it too. I could see her shoulders relax and a smile appear on her face.

"Yes," she said, "Bobby and I are good friends, just like you and me. Did you think of anything?"

"Clyde remembers that Ben had lots of friends when he was a boy."

"Did he say anything about his mother and father?"

"No, but Clyde thinks Ben was sad," he said.

"Did he say why?"

"His friends left all the time. He had to keep making new friends."

"Did he say anything else?"

"He was cold."

"Cold?"

"All the time. He told Clyde that he liked Homer because it was warm. Clyde told him he was crazy. Homer was cold. But Ben said his town was colder."

"Did Ben say anything about a mine?"

Clyde stared at Jess blankly.

"I guess not," she muttered, directed toward me.

"Clyde needs to get ready for lunch now," he said.

"Okay," said Jess. "You were very helpful. I'm going to try to find Ben." Her voice choked a bit. "Say hi to Bobby for me."

"Okay, Jess. Clyde will. Bye." And with that, Clyde moved his attention to preparing to go for lunch.

As we walked out, I said, "Really cold and lots of kids. That would fit Wisdom Spring. I thought it was interesting that the kids kept leaving. I wonder why."

But Jess wasn't listening. She was obviously thinking about "Bobby."

"It sounded like he really talked to Clyde," said Jess. "Why would he be able to do that with Clyde, but have so much trouble communicating to me?"

"Maybe it has to do with filters. Because our brains work to capacity, we filter everything that comes in—sort of like a spam filter—but Clyde's mind isn't busy and has none of those filters. He's so simple that whatever comes in comes in. Maybe it was a more direct flow from your father to Clyde."

"Funny," she replied. "I actually envy Clyde right now."

"Yeah, I know." I took her hand and let her have her quiet moment before changing the subject back to her conversation with Clyde. "Thanks to your father—again—and Clyde, I think we've got some of what we were looking for. It's time to go to Wisdom Spring."

Chapter 28

"You're shitting me, right?"

"I wish." This was painful. Hutch knew he should have quit a long time ago. He'd never want to admit that he was out of his league, but the fact was, he was out of his league. There were just too many fires to put out—some of his own making, but many that would have appeared no matter who was in the position. There was too much secrecy. In fact, that was all there was. Even after all this time, he still hadn't been given the full picture. He knew the organization was decades old. He knew that the current project— the one involving Hillstrom—was its "greatest" yet. But he knew that it was far from its only project. He had worked on some of the others. The projects had been going on from the moment of the organization's inception. He saw the money changing hands, the blackmail, and the threats, many of which he was directly involved in. Some had failed, but most had been unqualified successes. The organization reached far into all branches of government, the military, and the private sector. Hillstrom was his first "homegrown" experience. As such, he was seeing a different side of the organization, one that you couldn't walk away from. No, he was in way too deep. He couldn't even attempt to leave now. To do so would be a death sentence.

He continued, "Colson wasn't on that flight. My source tells me that some nothing kid was given the seat at the last minute."

"Did your source tell you where we could find Colson?" asked Mays.

"He's gone underground. We're looking."

"And now he suspects that it was sabotage."

"Probably. As you suggested," Hutch wanted to make sure Mays knew that he was responsible for this one, "I called and told him to drop the girl as a client, but, as I suspected, there was no way he'd do that. It just got him all the more committed."

Mays ignored the transparent criticism. Who did this guy think he was? "Does anyone else know that he wasn't on the flight?"

"I suspect that the media will pick up on it in a few days. Hard to say. Which brings up a question: You've spent a lot of years grooming Hillstrom for the presidency. Wouldn't it have been easier to buy someone?"

"Don't try to teach me my business. I've bought more people than you could ever imagine. Although we've made it almost impossible to do so, people can always follow the money, and this one was too important. It's the final brick in a massive foundation. I needed someone totally dedicated to the cause—someone homegrown."

"And if the girl told Colson enough that he's now aware of our plan? If he does rear his head and goes to the media with it? Hillstrom's run is over. Your greatest project is over."

"My, you're negative. While it would certainly be inconvenient, what proof would he have? Hillstrom is loved, Colson is not. People would laugh at him. You got rid of that researcher kid's laptop and notes, right?"

"I did."

"So anything the girl knows—and she may know next to nothing—is purely second-hand. Which means anything Colson knows is third-hand."

"What if somebody believes him and researches Hillstrom like the kid did?"

Mays was tiring of the conversation. "First of all, that kid was a fluke. Hillstrom never should have used him for his autobiography. He should have used us, and only us. He got a little cocky, which I can assure you will never happen again. You never actually saw the notes, right?"

In fact, Hutch had, but he'd never tell his boss that.

"No."

"The kid had precious little. He had just enough to make him question things and to know that something fishy was going on. That was it. The information just isn't out there."

Hutch silently agreed that the kid's information was sketchy, at best. Easy enough to explain away, assuming the girl hadn't found anything more.

"Hutch, do you get it now why when everyone else in the world transferred everything to computer, we chose not to? It's too vulnerable. So even now, when it would be so much easier, cheaper, and faster to run this organization in cyberspace, I've chosen not to. Sure, we use all the latest technology for surveillance and anything that can't come back to us, but for everything else, including communicating amongst ourselves, we do everything the old-fashioned way and stay well under the radar."

"Hence Wisdom Spring," said Hutch.

"Hence Wisdom Spring," repeated Mays.

Chapter 29

"Here's Wisdom Spring," I said, placing a finger on our road atlas to indicate a spot southeast of Fairbanks in the mountains north of Delta Junction. "It's way in the middle of nowhere. Any suggestions on how we get there?"

"I could fly us in," said Scott. "Delta Junction has an airstrip, but we'd have to arrange some ground transportation after that."

"I was thinking maybe driving up," I said.

"How about both?" asked Jess.

"Jess is right," said Joe. "If Scott and I fly up and you and Jess drive your SUV, it gives us options. If we need a fast getaway, the plane is available and we can ditch the Armada. But that will give us a good vehicle to head into the mountains with."

"It's a good twelve-hour drive," said Jess, who was on the computer getting the directions. "And that's just to Delta Junction."

"Means I can sleep longer than you before flying up," said Scott. "So, the question is," he continued, "what exactly are we looking for? And," he added, "how do we deal with the guards? Your Internet buddy told you he saw one guard, but he thought there were more."

"I don't know the answer to the second part of your question," I said, "But as to the first, just something that is going to give us a clue to Hillstrom's background. Something that might help us solve this."

"Jon?" Jess was still at the computer. "Your warning worked. Carl Jenkins took down his site on Wisdom Spring."

"That's a relief," I said. "Remind me, assuming we make it through this and bring down Hillstrom, to call Carl and tell him why we rattled his world."

"What do we have for weapons?" asked Joe.

"Did you guys keep any of the chopper guys' guns?" I asked.

"I helped myself to the pilot's .45," said Joe. "Figured they owed me. But we left the rest for Scott's friends."

"They went out on a limb for us," said Scott. "It was the least we could do. Besides, there's no place in town that sells ammo for an M-16. Okay, so Joe, you have a .45, and whatever you picked up from the guys in Rochester."

"A 9-mil," said Joe.

"Okay, and Jon, you still have your .40, right?"

"Right. And Jess has her .380."

"I think I could handle something bigger," she said.

"Most of the guns I have would be way too big for you," said Scott, "but I think I have a solution. Wait here."

We waited for him as he went into a small storage room.

"Christmas in Homer!" he called out. "We'll open presents one at a time."

We all looked at each other. What was Scott going to produce?

"Okay," he said, coming out with the first item. "Jess, instead of something bigger, how about a second gun in addition to your .380? I have here a .22," handing it to her. "The magazine holds a lot of rounds and it's easy to shoot. It's not as powerful as the other guns, so instead of bringing someone down with one shot, you might have to bring him down with three."

"I like it," she replied, caressing it. "It feels good. Thanks,

Santa."

He went back in for more. He was enjoying this. "I've got some rifles in here. Jon, you always enjoyed playing cowboys when you were a kid, so how about a lever-action Winchester .45 caliber? You'll feel like Jimmy Stewart in *Winchester 73*."

He passed it out to me. It was beautiful. I *did* feel like Jimmy Stewart.

"Joe, I assume you have some shady military background." Jess and I looked at each other. "Did it involve any sniper duty."

"Some." He left it at that.

"How about this?" Scott handed Joe a high-powered rifle with a scope.

"Perfect," said Joe. He looked at it admiringly.

"Something about your past you want to tell us?" I asked.

"Let's just say I wasn't always a PI and leave it at that."

"And Santa gives himself some presents." Scott emerged from the storage room with two more items. "A Kimber 1911 .45 semi-auto, and a 12-gauge shotgun. You just can't miss with a shotgun."

"Where in the world did you come up with all these?" I asked.

"Ha, this is nothing. You should see the collections of some of my friends. What can I tell you? I live in Alaska."

He continued. "You still have any of that money left, Jon? Because we have to buy a shitload of ammunition."

"I do. I've gotta say that we're going to feel pretty foolish if we arrive in Wisdom Spring and find an abandoned shell of a town with no guards."

"You're getting pretty bloodthirsty all of a sudden," said Scott.

I felt embarrassed. "Well, that's not exactly what I meant."

Scott smacked me on the arm. "I know, bro. I'm just giving you a hard time." He looked at his watch. "The gun store is still open. I'll head down there with Joe. You guys want to make dinner? After we eat, we can come up with a plan. We can leave tomorrow, if you want."

I was glad Scott asked Joe to go with him. Jess had suddenly gone quiet and I wanted a few minutes alone with her. Knowing Scott, he saw that, which is why he invited Joe.

I gave Scott a few hundred dollars and they went out the door. I said to Jess, "Let's sit."

We went over to the couch and I put my arm around her as she snuggled into me.

"What's wrong?" I asked.

"I guess I just needed a moment to step back from all this," she answered. "I'm a normal person. I've always done normal things. How did all this happen? In the last month I've been accused of murder and have half the police in the country looking for me; I've killed a man; I've snuck across the border … twice; I've stolen a car; I have my dead father talking to me. What else? And now we're talking about going to a ghost town looking for information on a man who supposedly killed a lot of people here and is now running for president. And, we're going up heavily armed with the possibility of blowing away some guards. Have I covered everything?"

"You forgot the part about falling in love with your knight in shining armor—a guy whose life had fallen apart and was contemplating suicide before he met you."

"Yeah," she snuggled in closer. "There's that, too."

"All we can do Jess, is follow this through. It's possible that we are the only people in the world able to stop Hillstrom, and whoever might control him. If that's the case, we have a responsibility to stop him."

"I know." We sat in silence for a while. Finally, she said, "Jon, I listed all of the things I've gone through, but I didn't take into account all that you've had to endure, starting with the death of Karen, then the breakup of your marriage and the loss of your job. You've had to deal with a lot, as well. I can tell that you hurt so much about Karen, but you try not to show it."

"Sometimes it's really hard. It hasn't been that long since she died, but it's getting a little easier and having you in my life has been a lifesaver. Losing my wife and my job were blessings. Frankly, my life was going nowhere. All of this stuff—the hiding, the killing—has brought out a side of me I didn't know existed. It makes me realize that I could never go back to even a semblance of my old life. When this is all over—assuming, again, that we make it through—I have no idea what I'm going to do. I just know that it will be different. It'll be a conscious life. Never again will I be a drone. I have a feeling that the same applies to you."

"It does. Together we can be truly alive. Assuming, of course, that we're not dead."

We were ready for this mission to get on its way. We went into the kitchen and prepared dinner, and an hour later Scott and Joe showed up with ammunition for all. After dinner, we sorted through the boxes. Scott had bought some extra magazines for all of the pistols, so we didn't have to worry about reloading as often.

We spent a couple of hours discussing the plan, which was fairly loose. Only two of us would actually drive into the town. We decided on Jess and me. If they recognized Jess, all the better. At least we'd know we'd come to the right place. We would drop Scott and Joe off on the outskirts of town. It would give them the opportunity to observe from a different angle and to serve as cavalry in case we ran into trouble.

"I'm hoping that the first time through we can just get an idea of how many guards they have," I said. "The eventual goal is to capture the guards."

"Or kill them," added Joe.

"Or kill them," I agreed. "Then we would have free rein to search the town."

"If these people are as sophisticated as you say," warned Scott, "they might have cameras surrounding the town. We have to be aware of that. "What do we expect to find?"

"Expect?" I said. "I really don't know. I hope we'll find something that will explain all this. It's possible that this is all a wild goose chase."

"If they have guards," said Joe, "then there is something there. It might be small and hard to find, but there is something they don't want us to discover."

We packed the car that night in anticipation of an early departure. Scott figured out how far behind us he'd have to leave, and the plan was in place. Max was going to go with Scott and Joe, and Slob—as was the custom—would stay and guard the place. Scott called one of his girlfriends to stop over and feed Slob while he was away.

Jess and I left at six the next morning. It was early-summer, and the air was crisp. Neither of us had slept much, but we weren't tired as we pulled out of Scott's driveway.

For the first time since this ordeal began, we weren't running or hiding. We were bringing it right to them, and hopefully it would be the last thing they would ever expect.

Chapter 30

We headed north out of Homer, taking the same route, in reverse, that we had taken the previous week, and once again were completely overwhelmed by our surroundings. It was tempting to pull off the road and just sit for hours listening to the sounds of nature, but we couldn't. We had a job to do. If we were successful, maybe we could come back this way and take our time.

But while it was spectacular country, I wasn't sure I could see myself living there. It had worked out beautifully for Scott. His enthusiasm for his lifestyle made me happy for my brother. However, it was just a bit too remote for me. I was in no way a city person—I had hated working in downtown Boston—but neither was I ready to give up the conveniences of civilization to live in a cabin in the middle of nowhere. Jess and I discussed it for a while and, while we acknowledged the romance in the idea of chucking it all for wilderness living, she seemed to be of the same mind about it. And yet, at the same time, this whole experience had soured us on civilization. The need for privacy—especially now—was strong in us. Would we come around to the idea of living someplace so remote? Could we find a happy medium? Seeing as how we first had to live through this, I knew it might all be moot.

We took turns driving. Luckily, we didn't have to worry about getting to Delta Junction after dark, as there was almost no dark this time of year. Scott said he was going to find a motel online and call ahead and reserve two rooms.

Every once in a while, Jess would lapse into one of her quiet periods. After the third one I asked if she was in contact with her father.

"No," she answered. "I wish. But I have been thinking about him. I was thinking about his communication with Clyde. As strong as it is, I wonder if I could actually use Clyde as a channel. When this is all over, do you think I could have a conversation with my father through Clyde?"

She wanted so badly for her parents not to be dead—the same feeling I had about Karen—that she was soaking in this communication with her father. My fear was that it was eventually going to eat her up.

"I suppose it's possible," I said, trying to remain as neutral as I could. "But I wouldn't want you to get your hopes up. Already you've had more contact with a deceased loved-one than almost anybody. Try to appreciate that." She nodded in agreement, a tear in the corner of her eye slowly forming enough to finally escape down her cheek. "What I wouldn't give to be able to talk to Karen. But I'm not so lucky. You have to think of Clyde, too. He's over ninety years old and tires easily. Trying to channel your father might just be too much for him. It's one thing for Clyde to dream about him and converse that way. But fully awake? I'm not so sure."

"You're right. I should appreciate what I have. It's just that I've been given a taste and I want more. Is that so bad?"

The last part of that she wasn't really asking of me, so I didn't answer.

We occasionally stopped for breaks and finally rolled into Delta Junction a little after eight. Scott and Joe had arrived about two hours earlier and were waiting for us at the motel.

It wasn't a bad place. It was clean, comfortable, and had a small family restaurant across the parking lot. Scott and Joe had already eaten, but Jess and I were famished, so they sat with us as we ate.

But we were all too tired to talk much about the next day, so we agreed to meet at nine the next morning. There was a tenseness to go along with our weariness. We all felt it, and when Jess and I were settled in bed, we made love with a frenetic energy. There was a desperate quality to it, as if we both sensed that it could be our last. Finally spent, we fell asleep in each other's arms.

The next morning was dreary with a light mist in the air, and it had gotten much cooler. We all met in the restaurant, a little on edge, barely touching our food. We were anxious to get on our way, but at the same time, were stalling. There wasn't much to talk about concerning the course of action. All the planning had been done at Scott's house.

We finally took off at ten, travelling about a half an hour on Route 2 before seeing the turnoff for Wisdom Spring. There was no sign—I'm sure there had been one once—but I knew from the map that this was the road. It was a dirt road, as I expected, but not in too bad shape, and the Armada had no problems with it. Although the road was overgrown to an extent, I sensed that it had enough occasional traffic to keep it from vanishing completely. Once we were out of sight of the highway, we pulled off to the side and armed ourselves.

According to the map, Wisdom Spring was almost ten miles from the highway. We drove it slowly, constantly on the lookout for cameras. We didn't expect any armed guards to be this far from the town, but surveillance cameras were a real worry. For that reason, Scott and Joe stayed hidden in the back seat. When I figured we were less than a quarter of a mile from the town, I pulled over. Jess and I looked carefully for electronics of any kind. Seeing none,

Joe opened the rear passenger door, and he and Scott slipped out and disappeared into the woods, with Max close behind. From behind a tree, Scott gave me a thumbs up.

"Here we go," I said to Jess. I had my Sig next to me on the seat and Jess was holding the .22 under a sweater on her lap. Her .380 was tucked in her belt. I put the SUV in gear and we crept down the road. After a couple of minutes, the trees parted, and we found ourselves overlooking a valley. We stopped to survey the scene.

A hundred years ago, the valley—without the signs of civilization—must have been spectacular. At the far end, a couple of miles away, and at the base of a mountain, was a pristine lake, fed most likely by snow run-off. To our left was a massive forest a few miles wide and deep, butting up against more mountains. We were entering on the right-hand side of the valley—more mountains to our immediate right, and a clearing below us. Part of the clearing was natural, but it had been expanded at different points in the town's history. The edge of the forest had an unnatural look, the result of man's interference. Acres of forest had been clear-cut to make room for the buildings. The wood from the trees probably made up most of the buildings. Below us lay the town. It was ugly, ugly the way I would have imagined a mining town. None of the roads were paved, but it had a real downtown, of sorts. It was a block long and had a half a dozen brick buildings. Both sides of the street were edged with raised wooden sidewalks. Surrounding the downtown were several short streets with cheaply-made houses. The yards were overgrown and some of the roofs had begun to collapse. But at one time the houses were probably decent. Comfortable, at least.

The outskirts of the town were a different story. For a half a mile beyond the end of the downtown, scattered on the hilly landscape, were shacks—three dozen or more. Originally, there were roads connecting the shacks, but they were almost unrecognizable now. Many of the shacks had fallen in on themselves, but there were still a few standing. This was the town that Carl Jenkins remembered as a child—a real mining town. When he went back years after the mine had closed, it was the newer part of the town he encountered. Now it was all dead.

Well, not completely. There were three black Jeeps parked in front of one of the buildings. Obviously, nobody had been alerted to our presence. Maybe our fears of surveillance cameras were unfounded, otherwise they would have intercepted us by now. But if I had any question about whether or not this was the correct town, the identical Jeeps clinched it. There was something quasi-military about their presence.

The only thing missing from the town was the mine. It wasn't anywhere in sight. The right-hand cliffs curved around a bend at one point, so I had to assume the mine was there.

I gave Jess a look and started the SUV down the hill. It wasn't steep, but it was long, and its gradual grade had put us fairly high over the valley. I drove slowly, partly to give Scott and Joe time to catch up, partly to look like tourists, and partly to not give the owners of the Jeeps too much warning. In my rearview mirror, I saw Scott and Joe emerge from the woods. Joe went straight down the hill on our right, which consisted of large rocks that would give him cover and offer him a good view of the street in case he had to do some long-distance shooting. Scott headed off to our left to try to get down in back of the buildings—closer for his shotgun. I was a little worried about Scott. He was hefty these days and I didn't want him taxing himself too much. But I had to give him credit, he was looking pretty nimble. Max followed close behind. I gave thanks that Max wasn't a barker. I had wondered about the wisdom of Scott bringing Max along, but as I saw them heading down the hill, I could see the dog's enthusiasm and the way they worked together. Maybe a police dog would come in handy.

Still creeping along, the road began to level off and we were approaching the official start of the town. We could now see the buildings up close. Being brick, they hadn't suffered as much as the houses. The first building on the left was missing its sign but could have been the mine office. Attached to that was a much smaller building that housed the jail. This had been a mining town, after all, and a jail was probably needed, especially on payday. The reason for the jail was right next door. A sign over the door read "Spring Bar," and the door and large picture window were very much intact. I could see through the window a standard bar to the right and a few tables to the left. There were some bottles behind the bar. Did they still have alcohol? Did the security guards use this in their down time?

On the right-hand side of the street was a general store with half its sign still attached, followed by a drugstore, a clothing store, and a restaurant. Across from the restaurant and set a little bit away from the bar was a hotel. The Jeeps were parked in front, obviously their base of operation. Beyond the hotel and set farther back was the nondescript building that Carl Jenkins had assumed was a school. He was probably right.

No one had stopped us yet, so we continued on. Where were they? If there had been only one guard, like Carl had encountered, I could understand. He might be in the kitchen eating. But there were three Jeeps, which to me meant the possibility of as many as six men, two to a Jeep. You'd think someone would be watching. But then again, how many visitors did they actually get here? One a week? One a month? It would be so easy for them to become lazy and careless.

The main street rounded a bend and continued down through

a copse of trees. From up above I hadn't been able to see where the road went because of the trees. As it emerged from the copse, it dropped another hundred feet to a plateau. From there I could see the road wind around the corner of the mountain.

I realized that I was holding my breath, and could see Jess was doing the same. We had been, from the moment we entered the town. Out of sight of the buildings, we exhaled.

"We made it through stage one anyway," I said.

"Can you imagine growing up here? It's depressing," remarked Jess. "It's one thing to choose a life in the mines, but at least in places like West Virginia they are near real towns. They are not so cut off from civilization. This seems like the end of the earth."

"I can better understand the early days of the town when it was all about getting the mine up and running," I said, "but I don't understand the more recent incarnation, the one Carl saw with all of the children. I can see his assumption that it was some cult that had taken over the town."

"And maybe he was right."

After five minutes of driving, we arrived at the mine entrance and were immediately disappointed. I'm not sure what we were expecting, but I had assumed that the mine played a part in the story. It was time to change my thinking. Littering the perimeter were a half a dozen rusted hulks. Knowing nothing about mining, I had no idea what some of them were for, although there were a couple of long-deceased trucks in the mess. I could still read the words "Wisdom Spring Mining Company" on the side of one. A couple more years and that would be unreadable.

The entrance to the mine was a mess. There was an iron gate that hadn't been opened in years, with a rusted padlock securing it in place. But even if the gate were gone, we wouldn't have been able to see anything. The whole front of the mine was caved in, making it impassable.

We looked at each other, the dismay showing in our faces. Had we come all this way for nothing?

Chapter 31

We hadn't.

The security guards convinced us of that.

Not knowing what was going on with Scott and Joe, we decided to make our way back to the town. If we were lucky enough to make it through unseen, we could pick up the two others — three including Max — and head back to the motel to regroup. But being lucky twice in a row was a little much to expect.

As we came out of the trees heading back into the downtown, a guy was standing outside the hotel smoking. He looked up, saw us, and his jaw dropped. His cigarette fell to the ground. He stepped out into the street and motioned for us to stop, saying something over his shoulder to his partners in the hotel. I could see a holster on his belt. I slowed down and rolled down my window.

"Where the hell did you come from?" he demanded.

"Hey," I replied with a wide smile. "Name's Larry. This is my wife Marie." I held out my right hand to shake, having transferred the Sig to my left.

He ignored my hand. Meanwhile, five others had piled out of the building, all with the same confused expression, probably thinking, how could we have possibly made it past them?

"You know this is private property, right?" asked the first man.

"Golly, no," I answered in my best hick voice. "The wife and I are checkin' out Alaska ghost towns. I knew there was one around here someplace. Had no idea it was private property. We'll get out of your way."

"Frank, hold on," one of the other guards said to the man on my side. "I think it's her."

Two of the guards had wandered over to my side, which made me happy. I didn't want them all on Jess's side of the car.

"You think?" said one of the others.

"Positive."

"Do you mind getting out of the car?" asked Frank.

"Kind of," I answered, making a face. "Look, I don't know who you think she is, but she's my wife, Marie."

Out of the corner of my eye, I could see the other man shake his head no, to indicate that I was lying. Two of the men were carrying rifles, and two had their hands on their gun butts, ready to pull them out of the holsters.

Frank reached down for his and I said, not in a hick voice, "I wouldn't suggest you do that." I brought my gun up and pointed it at him. He froze. The one next to him, however, didn't. He raised his rifle and I shot him in the chest.

Chaos ensued. I heard Jess snap off three quick shots, heard the boom of Scott's shotgun, and looked back at Frank, but he had disappeared. The third man on my side, however, was raising his pistol toward me when I heard a different boom. It was Joe. He had climbed down much closer to the town and was right in front of the general store. The man on my side flew five feet before landing crumpled in the road. Two more shots from Jess and another shotgun blast and it was over.

Not quite. I heard a Jeep start up. Somehow Frank had made it over to the vehicles in the confusion of the gunfire. The Jeep peeled out in reverse, then I heard him shift, jamming it into gear, and he took off down the road in a cloud of dust. We all took shots at him and missed.

"Should we go after him?" I asked.

"Waste of time and too risky," said Joe. "He'll make it to the highway before we can catch him, then what? A high-speed chase? I don't think so. Once he gets closer to Delta Junction or Fairbanks and has cell phone coverage he'll put in a call for reinforcements, but I can't imagine that they are anywhere close. I'd guess that we have a few hours, so we'd better make the most of it."

I looked over at Jess. "You okay?"

"Surprisingly, I'm fine. Second time I've killed someone, and I'm fine."

She actually looked fine.

Scott stepped out into the street from the corner of the building. He had accounted for two of the hits, obvious from the state of the bodies. I think I was the only one shaking.

We dragged the bodies from the street and hid them behind one of the buildings. Eventually they'd become bear or wolf food.

"So, what's our plan?" asked Scott.

"Why don't we work in teams," I answered. "Jess and I will start with the school—if that's what it is—while you and Joe check out the hotel. Then we'll just keep on going through the buildings until we find something. I don't know what we're looking for. Go through everything you can. Basically, we need to discover what this town was used for and some answer as to what is going on. What's the story behind Hillstrom and who's behind the story."

Jess and I walked over to the large building and found it secured with a padlock on a chain. The windows had been boarded up. After some searching, I came up with a metal bar and used it to break the chain. The door opened with a screech. The hinges hadn't been oiled in a few decades. Second nature caused me to flick the light switch. Much to our surprise, the lights went on—a few of them anyway.

I looked at Jess and cocked my head. "How much sense does that make?" I asked. "It means they have some major generator someplace powering this town."

"But why this building?" asked Jess. "It's obvious that it hasn't been used, or even entered for that matter, in many years. Why not disconnect it?"

It definitely was a school. Desks were still in place and blackboards were still attached to the wall. Anything that could provide information was missing, however. No papers, no books, nothing written on the blackboard.

The school had four classrooms, a small gym, a small cafeteria and restrooms for each sex. We spent forty-five minutes searching every nook and cranny. Our only success was the discovery of "Ben F" written on the wall of a stall in the boys' room.

"Ben Fremont?" I asked.

"That would be my guess," said Jess.

"Then we can be pretty sure he was here."

Other than that, the school held no clues. We were about to head out the front door when Jess stopped. She put her hand to her head, as if she had a headache.

"We're not done here," she said.

"Do you know what we're looking for?"

"Nope. Just that there is something here to find."

I squatted, leaning against the wall and just stared down the hallway.

Five minutes of staring and it came to me.

"Wait a minute," I said. "It's right in front of our faces. Do you remember what the population of Wisdom Spring was in 1980, around the time Ben was here?"

"Something like 110," said Jess.

"Let's count the desks in the classrooms."

We came up with sixty desks.

"Doesn't it strike you odd that a town with 110 people would have a school this size?" I asked. "We have to assume that if they had fifteen desks in each room, chances are most of them were being used. Sixty children in a town with just over a hundred residents? Either those women were really fertile or the children in this school didn't belong to the adults in the town. I think this whole town was a school of some sort. But for what?"

As we started back out the door, I asked, "Was that what we were supposed to find?"

Jess stopped and closed her eyes, then nodded. "I think so."

We could hear Scott and Joe in the hotel, so we hit up the other side of the street, starting with the diner, which took about ten minutes. Other than few discarded kitchen machines and the tables, chairs and counter, indicating that it had, indeed, been a diner, there was nothing of interest. The same was true of the clothing store, with one exception.

The store had been cleaned out of all of its stock and nothing was left on the shelves. However, Jess discovered the one clue that remained.

"Do you notice something odd in here?" she asked.

"Not really," I answered.

"No, of course not," she said. "You're a guy. I wouldn't expect that you would."

"I will ignore the insult. What am I not seeing?"

"The shelves still have the shelf markers indicating clothing size. Other than a small section of men's clothes and an even smaller section of women's, ninety percent of this store was devoted to kids' clothes. I'd say about five years old to early teens. That fits with what we came up with in the school."

The same theme presented itself in the general store, an inordinately large amount of space devoted to candy and toys. From what we could determine from the remaining shelf markers, the toys were simple ones—balls, dolls, jigsaw puzzles, and games. The store had a back room with a faded sign that read "Mining Supplies." Like the rest of the store, it was empty.

We walked outside and sat down on the edge of the raised sidewalk. We could hear the two others now in the building we assumed was the mine office across the street.

"Something I don't get," said Jess. "Let's work on the assumption that the whole town was some sort of school, based on the ratio of kids to adults. So there is no way the adults could have been the real parents to all these kids. That would tell me that the adults were here to do a job, that of raising the kids. If that were the case, why would they need stores? Wouldn't everything be supplied to them?"

"One would think. Maybe for appearances? After all, this was a town. If people like Carl Jenkins could just show up, why couldn't other people? It would make visitors suspicious if they couldn't buy something in the store."

Scott and Joe emerged from the mine office and walked across the street to where we were sitting. They sank down next to us.

"Well we found a few interesting things, but not the smoking gun you were hoping for," said Scott.

"So did we," I said. Jess and I proceeded to tell them our theory.

"That theory might answer one question we had," said Joe. "Follow us."

They led us over to the jail. While it looked small from the outside, it extended farther back than it appeared. The front entrance gave way to a small outer office, which was connected to the jail area by a door. The jail consisted of twelve cells, although I hesitated calling them that. These were not cells separated by bars but were individual rooms not much bigger than a closet. I opened the first one and was appalled by the lack of space. "Closet" might have been generous. The cell was three feet wide and five feet deep, with a ceiling only five feet high.

"A man would be seriously cramped in there," I said. "And why so many?"

Jess's eyes became wide and her mouth dropped open. She grabbed my arm. "Oh my God! They weren't meant for men. They put kids in here!"

Chapter 32

After I had gotten over my shock, I asked Scott, "What else did you find?"

"Nothing related to kids," he replied, "but a couple of interesting things and one pretty significant thing, we think. I'll save that for last. The building next door, the one you think was the mine office, was completely cleaned out. The bar really was a bar. The bottles you saw through the window were empty, but we did find a few—more recent—bottles of the hard stuff, as well as a lot of bottled beer. I get the feeling that these guys were pretty bored here and had brought in their own liquor. Probably kept it there and not in the hotel because they just liked the idea of sitting in a bar. They had cleaned it up pretty well. The hotel was where we found the significant item, but the hotel was also kind of interesting mainly for what wasn't there."

"What wasn't there?"

"A computer. Everybody has a computer nowadays. The idea that the guards were out here in the middle of nowhere without one is odd, to say the least."

"No Internet out here?" suggested Jess.

"Easy enough to get around," I said. "Besides, look." I pointed to the hotel. "They have a satellite dish right on the roof. Probably for TV, so Internet wouldn't be a problem. You checked for laptops?"

"We checked for everything," said Scott. "We found a satellite phone in the kitchen, but no computers or tablets of any kind. Even their cell phones were basic vanilla. Identical phones, in fact. No smart phones. No ability to connect to the Internet. And other than the IDs we took off them, the men had nothing in their belongings that would indicate who they worked for. There were no phone numbers stored on the phones, and no call history listed. Not that there is any service out here anyway, which is probably why they had the satellite phone. The only thing we did find was a notebook that seemed to serve as a daily diary or ledger of the activities here. Based on that, there is *no* activity at all here. It basically listed each day, and whether or not any visitors had driven through. This book started about four months ago—maybe when this group started their shift here, since I imagine they have to rotate guards, otherwise they'd go crazy—and in that time a total of two couples came through looking for ghost towns."

He continued, "The only entry of interest was from a few days ago, announcing the arrival of four more guards. That tells me that Hillstrom, or whoever is behind this, is scared. The fact that they can't find you worries them."

"They're scared so they send more people to this godforsaken place? That tells us that this town is hiding something," said Jess. "Why in the world would they need six security people? They've barely needed the two up til now. So there is still something we haven't found."

"I think the whole notebook thing is interesting," I said. "In this age of computers, it's almost unheard of to be using a manual system. Anyway, I agree with Jess. There's something we haven't found. I think it's time to take a closer look at the mine."

"Which brings us to the final item, the one of significance," said

Scott. "It does have to do with the mine, but it's a little scary and we decided not to touch it. Hidden in the pantry is a box attached to the wall. It has a sign that reads, 'Mine closure instructions. Break glass only upon authorization.' Now, my guess is that it includes some sort of codes. I think 'closure' is a euphemism for 'destroy.' We didn't open it for two reasons: First, we assume it has instructions inside, but on the off chance that it starts the sequence, we thought it prudent to wait; Second, there are some wires coming out of the box. We both agreed that it is probably some sort of alarm. If you were to break the glass, an alarm would go off somewhere, maybe using the satellite phone line, letting someone know that the first steps to mine closure have begun."

"Assuming we find an entrance to the mine, it probably has a pretty sophisticated lock," I said. "Would you guess that the key or combination is in there, or do you think the security guards have it?"

"The guards definitely would not have it," piped in Joe. "If this mine contains information that would put a whole plan in jeopardy, they wouldn't give ready access to some low-level guards. If destroying the mine requires entering it, then the combination or key would be in that box. However, if it can be detonated remotely, I think we'll be out of luck."

"You want to guess?" I asked.

"It's just a guess," he answered. "I'd say you have to start the detonation sequence from inside the mine. That box hasn't been touched in a long, long, time. Maybe the guards don't even know about it. It was well hidden."

"But if we break the glass, you're saying that we might be sending a signal to whoever put it there, warning them that we're here?"

"Maybe. But again, we're dealing with the remoteness of this place. It's still going to take a while for someone to get here. I suggest we look at the mine, find the entrance if we can, then make our decision based on that."

I looked at my watch. About an hour and a half had passed since Frank escaped. I found myself looking up the road.

Joe caught me looking. "We're okay for a while," he said. "We'll have plenty of time to check out the mine."

"Do you think Frank will come back to try to pick us off?"

"No. Unless he had a high-powered rifle stashed in the Jeep, which is doubtful, at best all he has is his pistol. You're not going to pick anyone off with that. No, he'll wait for reinforcements so he can lead them here. He's probably keeping watch on the road's entrance from the highway so he can follow us if we leave."

"Which brings up the question," said Jess, "how do we get out of here without being seen? The road looks like the only way out."

Silence.

"I made a big mistake showing myself," said Jess. "I should have hidden under something. They would have let you drive out."

"And then where would we be?" I asked. "We'd still have to come back here and deal with the guards. There's nothing to suggest that the result would be any better. I'm not sure any plan would have been perfect. We just need to move on. I suggest we go to the mine and look quickly and then get out of here as fast as we can."

"Actually," said Scott quietly. "Jess brings up a real concern. Frank could be waiting somewhere at the head of the road, not to follow us, but to get as many bullets into our car as he can. So driving out of here really isn't an option at any point."

More silence.

"Then here's the plan," said Joe. "Jon, you and Jess go to the mine. You don't need us. Scott and I will head up the road. We'll stash the Jeep when we get close to the road entrance. If Frank is there, we'll take him out. If not, we'll wait and see if reinforcements arrive. But whatever we do, we should do it now and not spend our time talking."

Jess and I nodded. "Okay," he said. "Whatever you find down there, find fast."

Scott came over and hugged Jess and me. "Good luck, bro," he said.

Scott, Joe, and Max hopped into one of the Jeeps while we turned the Armada around and went back down the road to the mine.

"Hope they're going to be okay," said Jess.

"I'm not sure you'll find two more capable people," I said. "Plus, there's Max, the brains of the group."

Jess smiled to be polite, but she was definitely worried—more worried about them, I think, than about us.

We arrived at the mine a couple of minutes later, presented again with what looked like an impassable entrance. This time we got out of the SUV for a closer look.

Finding the true entrance turned out to not be as difficult as we had thought. The gate with the rusted padlock was all for show. The rocks covering the entrance were real, but upon closer inspection had been piled very strategically to look like a cave-in. We found a clasp at the bottom of the gate that, when unlatched, allowed us to lift up the gate entirely and move it out of the way. Once we did that, we were able to go behind the rock pile, where we encountered a substantial steel door with a keypad. The door was about the size of one you'd find on a commercial freezer. It had a handle similar to that of a freezer door. The keypad was set back in the door, with a clear cover, but insulated against the harsh Alaska winter.

Jess suddenly backed away from the door and leaned against the rock wall.

"Oh!" she exclaimed.

"What's wrong?"

She held her head as if it would stop the message.

"There's death in there. My father is very disturbed."

"What kind of death? Like a disease? Are we in danger?"

She was quiet for a minute. "No," she said, almost out of breath. "There's no danger to us, that much is clear. I just can't get the message." She stopped holding her head. "I'm sorry, there are too many emotions coming through. A tremendous anger and sadness. I think though that whatever it is, he wants us to see it, or experience it."

"I think we're going to have to take the chance on the thing in the pantry at the hotel. We'll just have to hope it doesn't start the countdown."

Jess was feeling better, so we got in the Armada and headed back to the hotel. We found the pantry with no trouble, and the box attached to the wall. It was exactly as Scott had described it.

"What do you think?" I asked.

"We really have no choice."

"Okay," I said. "Here goes." I found a large kitchen knife and, turning it around, smashed the glass with the butt.

We listened for a moment. "Well, nothing blew up, anyway."

Chapter 33

Hutch answered the phone in his office.

"Hutch? Carver here. Remember that alarm you said is real important? The one you said would probably never go off? Well, it just went off. Figured you'd want to know."

Hutch's blood ran cold. The only person who could approve the mine's destruction was Mays, and he was pretty sure he wouldn't have done that.

"Another thing," said Carver. "My office got a call just a couple of minutes before the alarm. It was from one of the guards in Wisdom Spring. The reception was not very good…"

"Why didn't he use the satellite phone?" interrupted Hutch.

"He was saying something about him being the last one alive. Then he mentioned the girl."

"The girl is there," Hutch responded. "She's gotta be. And I bet Joe Gray is helping her. Who do we have close?"

"We have four guys in Anchorage. Not the best of the best, but better than nothing. They can probably be there in three hours."

"Get them. How long til we can get the best of the best up there?"

"Eight hours, anyway. Maybe a little more."

"Scramble them. Get 'em moving now!"

He hung up, seriously reluctant to make the next call. He took a breath and dialed.

Mays picked up.

"What?" This wasn't going to help his mood.

"The mine alarm in Wisdom Spring just went off."

"Oh my God! What are those fucking guards doing? Did you call them? I don't want them in the mine. I want them fired. Replace them with some people you can trust. No, I don't want them fired, I want them dead." Hutch had never heard him so out of control.

"Well, you got your wish. They're dead. Five of them anyway."

That stopped Mays's ranting.

Hutch explained the phone call that came from the remaining guard.

"The girl. She's there," replied Mays.

"I figure she's got her mystery man and probably Joe Gray."

"I want you to get up there yourself. I want everybody up there. I want her dead. I need her dead. Then I want you to blow the mine. Should have done it a long time ago."

"Why…"

"Because it wasn't my call. Just get up there!"

Hutch hung up the phone. All this time he thought Mays was top dog. "'Wasn't my call.'" How far up did this thing go?

Chapter 34

There was a small handle on the other side of the broken glass. I pushed it down and the whole outer casing swung open revealing a single envelope. I would have expected a fancy document with a wax seal, stamped: "Secret: For Your Eyes Only," or something equally as sexy. No, it was a plain white number ten envelope with no writing on it whatsoever. Inside was a single sheet of white paper with a short typewritten note: *Door code: 8,6,8,9,7,1,4,0,#.* *Document room code: 4,4,D,S,F,9,9,0,#. Mine destruction box is in second* *chamber on right-hand wall. After activating code, mine will self-destruct* *in ten minutes. Code: 4,A,G,6,9,F,#,#,1.*

In many ways it was disappointing. I came from a generation of advanced technology, illustrated by over-the-top spy movies that had to outdo the ones that came before them. Yet, here I was with a single piece of paper with a simple message probably typewritten on an old IBM Selectric. I won't say it was without its own share of drama, though. As boring as it was, this paper held what could be the answer to the biggest conspiracy in history. Kind of scary, really. I copied down all of the numbers then left the envelope in the box and closed the outer casing. The broken glass was a clue that someone had opened it, but I felt more comfortable leaving the original document in place.

We went back out to the SUV, both of us sneaking glances up

the road, looking for some sign that Scott and Joe were okay. The road was empty. We drove back to the mine and approached the door.

My hands were actually shaking as I punched in the code. As I hit the pound sign, a little light turned from red to green. I shot Jess a glance, pushed down on the handle and pulled the door open.

We were immediately struck by the dampness and smell. It was a true cave. A dim emergency light lit the entranceway. I looked around for a light switch and found an industrial-size lever. I pulled it down and we were suddenly bathed in a bright light. After determining that we could get out the door again, we shut it securely. Someone would need the code to get to us.

We were in the entrance to the mine. To our right was a rickety-looking elevator, obviously used to take miners down to some lower level. It was chained off—real chains this time—and hadn't been used in forty or fifty years. Directly in front of us was a different entrance to the lower levels. It was a road of sorts, wide enough for a vehicle with about seven feet of clearance. It went down a mild slope. I could make out a switchback about two hundred feet down. The whole descent was probably a series of switchbacks.

To our left was the second chamber mentioned in the note. We walked through it and, sure enough, on the right-hand wall was a box. Much bigger than the box in the pantry, this one was serious. I opened the outer covering and saw a keypad. I closed the door quickly, not really wanting to touch it.

This section was small and led into a third and final chamber. At the end of the third chamber was a door—a regular-size door but made of steel. Near the handle was a small keypad.

"The document room?" I asked.

Jess didn't need to answer.

I punched in the code and opened the door. I flicked the light switch and we just stopped and stared. The room was small, maybe 15x20, with tables lining the walls. Stacked on the tables were about a dozen large storage boxes. An industrial-size dehumidifier with a hose leading to a drain hole in the rock chugged along under one of the tables, and a lone, nearly empty smaller table sat in the middle of the room, a can of pens and markers on one corner. A cheap desk chair was pushed under the table. Once again, my disappointment at the cheesiness of it all was palpable.

Each of the stacked boxes was labeled with a series of letters and numbers—meaningless to us. I opened one and found it full of manila folders, each one with a name of a person or a company.

"How do we want to do this?" I asked.

"We just have to go through them, I guess."

"We don't have a lot of time," I said. "Suppose I take one side of the room and you take the other. We open each box and pull out a folder if we recognize the name or it looks interesting. It would be a start at least."

Jess began on the right side of the room, and I started on the left. The boxes were stacked three high. I put the top two of the first stack on the floor and started on the bottom box on the table.

The files were neat, which helped a lot. There were no bulging folders; all of them were thin. In fact, some of them were so thin I had to pull one out to see why. The name on the folder was "Alice Palmer," a name that meant nothing to me. I opened it to find a single page of ledger paper with a picture attached and just a few entries. The picture was of a cute little girl with blonde curls. The entry read:

Alice Palmer
Entered Wisdom Spring 10-4-71, approx. age: 7
Obtained from Ukraine National Orphanage

Deceased 11-6-72

That was it. I put it back in and continued my search. I pulled out a second similarly thin folder. This one had a picture of a younger child.

Jeffrey Lamp

Entered Wisdom Spring 6-5-72, approx. age: 5

Obtained from Ukraine National Orphanage

Returned to orphanage 12-14-72

I looked at a few more. Two more were deceased and three more were returned to the orphanage. I pulled out my phone—my own smartphone, not one of the cheap ones—and took pictures of some of the pages.

The second box was similar to the first but had a few folders that were thicker. All this time we were quietly going about our business. I saw Jess occasionally open a folder, then close it again and put it back in the box. We were working quickly, knowing time wasn't on our side. I looked at one of the thicker ones. There was a name I recognized—a foreign name—but I couldn't place it. I pulled out the folder and put it aside.

"Any folder that is somewhat thick, we should put aside," I said, my voice disturbing the eerie silence of the room.

"There are a lot of kids listed here," said Jess. "Some are dead. A lot of them weren't here more than a year."

"I've taken a picture of some of them," I answered. "Open a few more and see if you can see a pattern."

I was beginning to panic, time-wise, though, and found myself going through the boxes even faster. I was starting to recognize some names. Some were politicians from the '80s and '90s, recognizable names, but otherwise fairly obscure.

"It's obvious that we're going to have to take some of this with us. I suggest some boxes of the thicker folders, then a box of the thin ones. The thin ones might tell a whole different aspect of this story. Whatever this story is," I added. "Just pick those at random, I guess."

"We could take them all," suggested Jess.

"I think we should leave some," I answered. "If they send someone to check on it, maybe they won't know how many boxes are supposed to be here and won't notice any missing. If we take them all, it'll be obvious we were here."

Jess agreed and we got back to work. She found our smoking gun a few minutes later.

"Ben Fremont!" she exclaimed. I was there in a second.

We knew we couldn't take the time to go through it carefully, so we quickly turned the pages while I snapped a picture of each one. Some of it was information we already knew, and some of it was going to require much more attention. The first page, though, told us some things we didn't know.

Ben Fremont

Entered Wisdom Spring 12-2-69, age 7

Obtained from Nevada Camp for Boys

Original name: Nicholas Spencer, changed 2-12-70

Graduated 12-2-83

Name changed to Gary Hillstrom, 1987

"We were right," said Jess. "He was twenty-one when he left."

"Let's put it in our keeper box and try to get through the rest of these," I suggested. As much as we wanted to study Ben's file, the very information we came for, there was just too much to absorb. It was also important to finish going through the other folders. I was starting to see more names I recognized. Some of them were politicians still in office, including a current Congressman from Arizona—Hillstrom's running mate. I started sweating. I came across another name I knew, and I could feel the hairs on the back of my neck stand up.

"Is Mario Pecorelli one of our Supreme Court justices?" I asked.

"Beats me," Jess answered. "I might be able to tell you two or three of them, but not all eight."

"Nine."

"See?"

I was pretty sure he was, so I went through the folder at a rapid pace. Yes, appointed to the U.S. Supreme Court in 2005. He wasn't a former resident of Wisdom Spring, but I got the impression that he was part of the conspiracy, whether he had been bought or threatened. I'd have to read closer for that. There was a ledger sheet full of numbers. I had a feeling they were maybe offshore bank accounts and payments, but we'd have to look more closely later.

We finished in about two and a half hours, much longer than I had hoped. We had come upon a who's who of world politicians and business leaders. At quick glance, a few of them had graduated from Wisdom Spring like Ben Fremont, while with most of the others, it was unclear as to the connection. We ended up with six boxes, five crammed with the larger folders and one with the very thin ones.

"We've got to get out of here," I said, and Jess agreed. We carried the boxes out and I took a picture of the room before we turned out the light and closed the door.

We made it to the main door when Jess said, "No, not yet."

"What?"

"There's something else we need to see, and it's important."

I had learned not to question her, so I just said, "Okay, lead me. But," I said, looking at my watch, "we need to go quickly."

"It's down this ramp," she said, pointing to the road. She led the way and we started our descent. It was easy walking. At about the two-hundred-foot point, the road switched back the other way.

We did two more switches before Jess stopped at a door. It was just set in the rock wall. There was no lock or keypad. The road continued on, but Jess made it clear that this was our destination.

"Any hint as to what's behind this door?" I asked.

"Not really. I just know that it's not good." I put my hand on my gun in my belt. "You won't need that," she said, and opened the door.

We were immediately hit with a strange smell—sort of musty and sort of sour. I found the light switch and illuminated the room.

As if on cue, we both bent over and heaved up the contents of our stomachs.

We had stepped into a chamber about the size of a small warehouse, and in front of us were dozens of dead bodies in various stages of mummification.

Many of them were young children.

Chapter 35

After leaving Jon and Jess in the town, Scott and Joe headed up the hill in one of the Jeeps, two warriors in search of a battle. Even Max seemed keyed up. He knew something big was going down. They drove in silence, each man deep in his own thoughts, until they reached a point approximately two miles from the highway. Scott found a small clearing on the right and backed the Jeep in as far as it would go, partially concealing it under a tree. The woods were dark and the Jeep was black, so they were pretty sure it wouldn't be seen. They started up the road.

"I guess our first job will be to take out the remaining guard, if he's up there," said Joe. "Then we watch and wait for reinforcements. We can figure out what to do next based on the number of people they send."

"If I had to guess," replied Scott, "the reinforcements will probably come in two waves, those close, then those from the lower forty-eight."

"I suppose it's even possible that they don't have anyone close," said Joe.

"Possible. But nothing so far has been that easy."

At about the one quarter mile mark, Joe headed off into the woods on the right and Scott and Max took the left.

As Scott made his way through the trees, he reflected on the change in Jon. Jon had always been sort of straight-laced, unwilling to stretch laws or get wild, while Scott was the exact opposite, known to local cops as a kid on the fringe—not a bad kid, but one capable of getting into trouble and definitely worth watching.

Scott was ecstatic when Jon got into sales, figuring it would loosen him up a bit and help him gain confidence. The confidence part came out loud and clear, which helped him work his way up the ladder to the kick-ass highly paid job he ended up with. He even loosened up when it came to business, learning how to cut the right corners. His personal life, though, was a different story. If anything, he became more rigid. Marrying Victoria was a major mistake. Scott knew it from the beginning, and he suspected others did too.

Then Victoria got pregnant. She was obviously happy about it. Jon, on the other hand, was probably beginning to sense his dissatisfaction with his marriage, and a child meant that he was stuck in it for the next fifteen to twenty years at least. But when Karen was born, he embraced her with all of his heart—that much was obvious to Scott. In some ways, she became a surrogate for Victoria. The more attention he gave Karen, the less he had to interact with Victoria.

But this was a new Jon. Forceful, creative, and much looser. He knew that Jess played a big part in Jon's resurgence, but the other factor was this situation itself. Jon had adapted to it with an ease that surprised Scott.

He reached the edge of the woods near the highway. There was no Jeep. He waited quietly anyway, Max stoically by his side. They had figured Frank would have to go into town to make a phone call to his bosses. The question was, would he come back?

He did. After fifteen minutes of waiting, the Jeep turned off the highway and slowly pulled into a half-moon shaped open space next to the entrance to the road. He parked on Joe's side, face out, but just sat in the Jeep. It would be more difficult to take care of him unless he got out.

After about twenty minutes, Frank emerged from the Jeep, stretched, and came over closer to Scott's side, where he unzipped his pants and started to relieve himself. In deference to his manhood—no guy should be attacked while taking a leak—Scott waited for him to finish. While Frank was zipping up, Scott gave Max the signal to attack.

Max was a blur of gray as he shot out of the woods and landed on the guard. Frank's hand wasn't even off his zipper yet. Max had him pinned down and was growling, as if to say, "*Your ass is mine. You're under arrest.*"

Scott and Joe hurried out from their hiding places and approached the guard, who had an expression of sheer terror, Max's face two inches from his own. Scott gave Max the necessary positive reinforcement while Joe slipped the guard's pistol from its holster.

"Off, Max," said Scott, and Max got off the guard, but still watched him warily.

"Get up," said Joe.

Frank got up slowly and Joe grabbed him by the neck and pulled him into the woods. Scott had found a small trail off the road on his way up, so he jumped in the Jeep, leaving Max to help guard Frank, and drove it down to the path and stashed it deep in the woods. He made his way back up to Joe, his gun pointed at his prisoner, who sat by a tree.

Joe was asking, "How many are coming?"

"Don't know what you're talking about," replied Frank in a surly voice.

"You have a chance to live," said Joe. "Just give us the information we need."

"What chance? You're going to kill me no matter what. Doesn't really matter. Even if you don't kill me, my employer will. He already said that if we screw up, we're dead."

"Then why'd you come back here?" Scott asked. "If they'd already threatened you, why didn't you just keep on driving?"

"You're joking, right?"

"Uh, no."

"I wouldn't last a day. Do you have any idea who you're up against?"

"No, tell us."

"That's the thing. I don't know. I just know they are as powerful as shit and taking a job with them was the worst thing I ever did. I figured that if I stayed the course, maybe I could talk my way out of it. But at the end of the day, it doesn't matter. I'm a dead man."

Scott was starting to feel sorry for the guy. But when he remembered that he was ready to kill any one of them—especially Jess—down in the town, his sensitivity toward him lessened.

"What's in the mine?" he asked.

"Beats the hell out of me. We weren't allowed to go in."

"So I'll ask again," said Joe. "How many are coming?"

"I don't know who they're sending. What I can tell you is that you're dead too. No way are you going to get out of here alive."

"So basically," began Joe. "You're just a grunt who was hired to kill people."

"I was hired to keep people out of Wisdom Spring."

"Right," said Joe. He looked at Scott, "You want to check the highway and make sure no one is coming."

"Sure." Scott wasn't stupid. Looking down the highway would be useless. It was too early for reinforcements to arrive. He knew why he was going. He also knew there was no way to stop what was about to happen. And he wouldn't stop it even if he could. People make their own futures.

After he performed his farcical mission, he returned back to Joe, who was pulling the lifeless body of Frank deeper into the woods. Frank's head hung at a funny angle. Scott momentarily felt bile rising in his throat, but he willed it down. Joe came out of the woods.

"So let me guess," said Scott. "CIA?"

"For a while. Special Forces before that."

"And you're happy being a solitary PI?"

Joe threw up his hands. "What can I tell you? You get a little tired of killing." He looked back to where he left Frank. "But I guess you never lose the skill."

"Should we wait or go down and help Jon and Jess?" asked Scott.

"I've been thinking about that," answered Joe. "I think we should split up. Someone should stay here just in case they leave a guard … or guards. And if one of us is down there, he can catch them from behind."

"I'll go down," said Scott.

"I figured as much. I'll stay here. If they leave people, I'll take care of them and then head down. If they don't, I'll follow them to the town and find a way to get behind them. I'll take the first Jeep you stashed a couple of miles down. You take the one you just hid."

They shook hands, wished each other good luck, and Scott, with Max close by his side, went to get the Jeep. Joe, meanwhile, hid behind some rocks and closed his eyes for a catnap.

*****

Fifteen minutes later, Scott parked the Jeep in front of the hotel and crossed the street to wait in the diner. He sat in a chair, put his legs on a table, laid his shotgun across his knees, and tried to get comfortable.

*****

A couple of hours after Scott left, Joe perked up from behind the rocks. A vehicle was coming. Just one? He expected more. But after all, these were only the reinforcements close by. He moved a little farther away from the rocks and into the trees. They turned onto the road, slowed down for a moment—maybe thinking Frank would be waiting—then picked up speed and headed for Wisdom Spring. They were driving an SUV, rented he was sure, and he saw four heads.

If he had known there would only be one car, he thought, he would have been prepared and would have taken out the whole carload right then. He ran down the hill toward the Jeep hidden two miles away.

*****

A few minutes later Scott heard the SUV drive into town. He, too, was surprised at only one vehicle. He knelt down and watched through the window as the car came to a stop. Four men cautiously got out to search the buildings. Scott slipped out the back door with Max and hid behind a shed. He heard someone shout that they must be at the mine, then heard them get back into the SUV and head down the road.

Scott jumped up and ran through the woods, Max close at his side. A few minutes later he heard a gunshot. The fleeting thought went through his head that he should have been waiting at the mine the whole time, not in town, or that he should have opened fire on them in the town. Because he didn't, Jon might already be dead. He had dropped the ball, and he knew it.

He reached the line of trees in front of the mine. Jon and Jess were standing by the Armada with their hands up. The truck's back was open, with some boxes piled inside. The four men were all pointing guns, and he heard one of them say, "Kill them, then blow the mine."

Chapter 36

"Oh my God, what happened here?" cried Jess. "Look at all these bodies, and so many of them children."

"These must be the 'deceased' children in the folders," I said, my stomach still churning.

"But why are they mummified? And why wouldn't they just bury them?"

"The cool temperature of the cave kept them from decomposing," I said. "I think they chose to 'store' them here because they knew that someday they would blow the mine. They couldn't bury them in a mass grave because—if the folders of the kids are right—they died over a period of several years. They'd have to bury them individually, and a graveyard that size would tend to raise questions. Also, my guess is that they probably didn't want the other kids to know that they had died. Storing them here made sense. Remember when Clyde said that Ben was sad because kids would always be leaving, so he couldn't make friends? This is where they went, or some of them, anyway."

"I wonder if he knows, even to this day, exactly what happened to them."

"I guess it depends on how close to the top he is."

As we talked, I was edging closer to the bodies. It was the last thing I wanted to do, but I knew I had to. I would stop short of actually touching any of them, though.

"What are you doing?" Jess asked.

"I want to see if there is any evidence of how they died." I still couldn't place the smell. It was unpleasant, but not a decomposition smell. I finally decided it must be the smell of mummification.

I bent over a little boy and could see no obvious marks. I checked a few others without success. There were quite a few adults—more adults than children—and it was obvious how they had died. Each one had a single knife slit from ear to ear.

"If I had to guess, they probably poisoned the kids. They slit the adults' throats. All the same way. Why not a bullet? Were they afraid of someone hearing? They were probably dissenters or people in the wrong place at the wrong time. The adults weren't killed in here, though. There's no sign of blood."

"Can we go?" asked Jess.

"Yeah. I just want to take some pictures. If they end up destroying the mine, we'll need some sort of proof."

I first counted the bodies. There were seventeen children and thirty-six adults. I quickly took a couple of dozen shots from all angles, then we left the room. I held Jess as we walked back up the road through the mine, neither of us talking. We got back to the first chamber and each picked up a box. I opened the door cautiously but saw nobody around. We walked them over to the Armada and stashed them in the back.

We took two more trips. When we came out with the final boxes a black SUV sat behind the Armada and four men were getting out. I dropped the box and reached for my Sig. One of the men shot and the bullet hit at my feet, showering me with dirt.

"Don't try it," he said.

"Wow, it really is the girl. What're we supposed to do?"

The obvious leader of the group said, "They told us that no one should be left alive. Even the girl. Especially the girl. Kill them, then blow the mine."

A streak of gray shot out of the woods and landed on one of the men. It was Max. The man screamed. Max had already disarmed him—almost literally—when I heard the sound of Scott's shotgun. A second man went flying. Another blast and all of the windows on the passenger side of their SUV blew out. The two remaining men were running for cover, so I scooped up my Sig and shot the keypad on the outer door, which had closed behind us. Then I followed Jess, who was almost in the woods.

Scott called Max back so he wouldn't get shot. The man he had attacked was not going anywhere anytime soon. The remaining two hunkered down behind their SUV, throwing the occasional wild shot over the hood. Jess and I had hidden behind an old piece of machinery.

"Stay down," I said. "I'm going on the other side of Scott."

Jess nodded her agreement and I moved back further into the woods, then came around behind Scott, eventually parking myself about twenty feet to his left. We were now in a position to cover any escape attempt on their part into the woods behind them. Nevertheless, one of them tried it. All three of our guns went off at once and the man dropped to the ground.

A pistol flew over the top of the SUV and the remaining man raised his hands. "I'm done. I'm coming out."

At that point, Joe emerged from the woods thirty yards up the road, ready to start shooting. Seeing the situation, he lowered his rifle and sauntered in.

Scott already had the man—the one who had ordered us killed—spread-eagled on the ground. Jess was checking on Max's victim, who was alive but not moving.

"If you want even the chance of living, you're going to tell us everything you know about your bosses," said Scott. He gave Joe a glance that I tried to figure out.

"I can't tell you much, honest," said the man. "We were hired a couple of years ago to be on call. They paid us well for almost no work. The only stipulation was that if they called, we were to drop everything and move quickly. This was the first time I got the call."

"How'd they find you?" I asked. "How did you get hired?"

"The four of us are all ex-cons. They approached me in prison and told me that they could get me out. They'd pay me, but I'd owe them. It seemed like a good deal. I still had another five years on my sentence."

"How'd they get you out?"

"I have no idea. One day the guards came to my cell and told me that I'd been paroled. I didn't ask questions."

"So who are 'they'?" asked Scott.

"No clue. I was told someone would contact me and he did. He met with all four of us. He gave us our guns and some shitty cell phones and told us to carry the phones with us at all times. They could only be used to call him or to get a call from him. We had to memorize his number and delete it from our call log if we ever got a call from him."

"Did he give you his name?" asked Jess.

"Yeah, Mr. Smith. Real cloak and dagger shit."

"Did they tell you others were on their way today?" asked Scott.

"Yeah, but he said it would take them hours to get here. If you leave now, they'll never catch you and I won't say anything."

Joe motioned to me and we walked out of hearing distance.

"We can make use of him," he said, and told me his idea. I liked it. It had the chance of actually keeping them off our tail while we sorted things out.

We walked back to the prisoner.

"We'll see how willing you are to cooperate," said Joe. "You're going to make a phone call. You're going to call that number and tell them that you found us and killed us."

"And," I added, "that you put our bodies in the mine and blew it." Joe hadn't been there to hear that part of the command. "Those were their instructions," I said to him.

Joe nodded. "You hold the phone so I can hear them. You better sound as natural as you normally would, or you'll be dead. What's your name?"

"Billy."

"Okay Billy, do it and don't screw up."

Billy sat up against the SUV and dialed the number.

"Hey, it's Billy. We got 'em."

I couldn't hear the other end of the conversation, but Joe seemed satisfied with what he was hearing.

"There were four of them." Pause. "Yeah, the girl was one of them." Pause. "Oh yeah, it was definitely her. We all recognized her." Pause. "Joe Gray? I don't know. We didn't ask their names. We just shot them." Pause. "It's gone. We put their bodies in the mine so there would be no trace of them. Then we blew it up." Pause. "Thanks." Longer pause. Joe shook his head no. "No, it would be a waste of time. There's nothing for them to do here." Pause. Joe nodded. "Yeah, we took care of him." Pause. "Okay. We'll get rid of the Jeeps and destroy the satellite phone." Pause. "Yeah, we'll go through the buildings and get rid of any evidence of the other guys being here. That shouldn't take long." Pause. "Okay, thanks." He hung up.

Joe took the phone from him and handed it to me. The number was in the call log. I wasn't sure how, but that could prove useful.

"Sounds like they are calling off the reinforcements," said Joe.

"Maybe I destroyed the keypad for nothing," I said.

"No," said Joe. "It was probably still a good idea. Why don't you guys head back up to the town and I'll follow you up."

Billy suddenly had a wary expression on his face. "You said you'd let us go."

"And that's what I'm going to do."

We got in the Armada, backed up and turned around. As we rounded the bend, I heard a shot, then another. I braked.

"Did Joe just kill them?" I asked.

"It's what Joe does," said Scott.

Chapter 37

We were back in Scott's house, decompressing. We had all come back in Scott's plane. The Armada had outlived its usefulness. It was a hot vehicle and it was time to get rid of it. I parked it in the small airport parking lot and Scott called his friends Pete and Ollie at Piney Lake, asking them if they wanted an SUV of questionable ownership. As expected, they were happy to take it on. Piney Lake was only a couple of hours away, so we knew it would be picked up in no time and all evidence of our existence up here would be gone. I left the keys under the seat and said goodbye to the Armada.

It was a tight fit getting all six boxes in the plane, but we did it. Because of the lack of room, Max ended up sitting on my lap. He eyed me suspiciously until Jess finally offered to take a turn. He seemed much happier on her lap, which I could understand. I would be too.

It was too loud and distracting in the plane to have a decent conversation, so now, with an ocean of Chinese take-out in front of us, Scott asked, "So exactly what is in the boxes?"

"We only had time to give them a cursory glance, but they contain files on hundreds of people, some famous and some not, all of whom seem to have some connection with all of this. We did find Ben Fremont in there." I gave them a quick recap of the little bit we read on him. "I think after we eat—or while we eat—we should each take a box and go through the files more carefully. We're not rushed for time, and as far as I know, nobody has a clue as to where we are. That work for everyone?"

Joe looked at his watch. "It's late, but if everyone is as keyed up as I am, we should at least get a start on it."

"Sounds good to me. Jess?" asked Scott, looking over at Jess, who had been quiet.

The reason for her silence became apparent the minute I looked at her. She was "gone" again. I put my fingers to my lips to motion Scott and Joe not to talk and they nodded. We probably could have talked though, as noise didn't seem to disrupt her sessions, but it just seemed more natural to me to give her the space. Even Max sensed it, getting down on his haunches and staring at her. Finally, she came out of it and saw us looking at her.

"Sorry," she said, a little embarrassed by the stares. "I never quite know when a message is going to come."

"Anything good?" I asked quietly.

"Reception—if you want to call it that—wasn't very good, but I sensed the message was important. It had something to do with 'replacement' or 'replacing' or 'exchanging.' Sorry, that's the best I could do."

"Okay," I said. "So we keep aware of that." I gave Joe a glance.

"Hey, don't look at me," he said. "I don't understand it, but I'm starting to respect it." He added, "Hillstrom worked for Exchange Systems. Something to do with that?"

"Maybe," answered Jess. "But we already knew that, so maybe this is something else."

"Well then, let's each grab a box and get started," I said.

We began the project with hope and enthusiasm, despite the daunting nature of what lay before us. For Jess and me in particular, if this didn't provide the answers—and even more importantly, the proof—to clear her name and expose Hillstrom, we had no idea what we'd do. During some quiet moments we had touched on the subject and found the alternatives grim. We would probably have to buy a remote piece of land in Alaska and live the rest of our days in hiding. Some people would give their right arm for an opportunity like that. For us, we'd do it if we had to, and we'd be happy being with each other, but it wasn't how either of us envisioned our ideal future.

Along with one of the boxes bursting with files, we each also grabbed a handful of the folders from the box of thin ones. Those were the ones we were going through first.

"So why did they—for lack of a better term—dispose of all those children?" asked Jess. "And why were some of them killed and others sent away?"

"I may have come upon the answer to the second part of that," said Scott. "I've been making a separate pile for each, deceased and sent away. The ones they gave back to an orphanage all appeared to be under the age of six. Anyone older than that they killed."

Immediately we all made piles like Scott's.

"You're right," I said. "I wonder why?"

"I can take a guess," answered Jess. "Whether it was a financial decision or a moral one—I seriously doubt the latter—they probably felt that anyone under six could go back where they came from and probably soon forget all about the town. In other words, they didn't worry about them becoming a risk to their operation. By the age of six or seven the kids were probably too old and would be more likely to describe life in the town. They'd be a security risk."

"Makes sense to me," said Joe. "And I'm guessing that they went through so many kids because they were looking for a specific type. They had to match certain criteria."

"Such as?" I asked.

"Don't know. If we use Ben Fremont as an example of a success story, then they were trying to find people with certain sociopathic tendencies, people they could mold into whatever they needed. What we're looking at here is a good old-fashioned 'Charm School'."

"You mean like the old book by Nelson DeMille?" I asked. "I've read articles over the years that suggested these training schools really do exist."

"They do," said Joe flatly.

I looked at him with a "how do you know that" expression.

"Joe used to be CIA," answered Scott in response to my look.

"Training facilities like this exist all over the world in varying forms, rarely this coordinated though," said Joe. "Spies have had to infiltrate other countries ever since the advent of … well, spies. It would be to differing degrees, depending on the purpose. Sometimes they are already adults and just need to learn the ways of a country before they can take their place in society, and sometimes a bit more intense. If this is really what Wisdom Spring was, then it would be the most extreme example I've ever heard of."

"Wait a minute," I said, barely listening to what he had just said. "You were CIA?"

He nodded.

"And all this time you couldn't have been in touch with one of your contacts there to let them know what was going on? After all, you were one of them. Wouldn't they believe you?"

"No," said Joe, who seemed uncomfortable talking about it. "For two reasons. First, it was over twenty years ago. Most, if not all, of my coworkers have long since retired. Second, I was kind of asked to leave, so I'm not sure how good my contacts would be even if I had them."

He looked down at one of the files.

"You going to leave us hanging?" I asked.

"There was a killing that I was involved in. The death of a woman in North Korea. It wasn't exactly sanctioned. Seemed like the right thing to do at the time. Seemed like the only thing to do at the time, so we … I … did it. They didn't see it that way and to avoid embarrassment, they cut ties with me.

"Anyway," he said, anxious to move on. "I think Wisdom Spring was a training ground. If so, they had a long-range vision because at that age it would take fifteen years or more to graduate the finished product."

It was late and we decided to call it quits for the night. Jess and I were asleep in minutes.

We were all back at it early the next morning. Scott had gotten up before any of us and had gone out for coffee and bagels.

We were each now going through the longer files. Every once in a while, someone would make an exclamation as they came across a familiar name.

"Well, I found the second mole in Mill's office," said Joe at one point. He was holding one of the thin folders. "I remember meeting her not too long ago. Some sort of researcher or gofer. I only remember her because she was cute."

"And I think we can confirm Exchange Systems as a front," said Scott with a mouthful of bagel. "I've found two in a row who worked there."

I was listening, but I was also busy reading Ben Fremont's file and had to keep my mouth from hanging open. "Something mind-boggling here in Hillstrom's folder, labeled Ben Fremont. A lot of it is stuff we already figured out, but there's some new stuff, as well as something that will knock your socks off."

"Which you're going to save for last," stated Scott.

"Just like you did with Wolf Run," I retaliated.

"Oh, no, I approve. I was just checking to see if you had picked up the Harper family trait."

"Their focus for him at Wisdom Spring was politics and business," I said, "and it sounds like they had some good instructors there. When he became Hillstrom the politician, that thing I told you about him," I said, looking at Jess, "about him starting as a Democrat, becoming a Republican, then running as an Independent, developing fierce loyalties from each side? That was planned from the beginning. All of those traits I liked about him when I voted in all those elections were all learned at Wisdom Spring. Not one bit of it was genuine. Not one bit of HIM was genuine."

I continued. "His boss at Exchange, who also seems to be his contact with this organization—I haven't found what it's called yet—is someone by the name of Corbin Mays. He's the CEO of Exchange."

"I've got him in my box," said Jess. "I'll look at him next."

"And now for the big piece of information. Jess, your father was right on with what he was trying to tell you with the 'replacing' or 'exchanging'."

"Oh," exclaimed Jess. "So it is more than just the company name?"

"Yes, this whole operation with Hillstrom is called 'Operation Exchange'. And I think I know why. Once Hillstrom is elected they are going to make an exchange. Sometime next year, Gary Hillstrom is slated to be assassinated."

Chapter 38

They all looked at me in stunned silence.

"Does it actually say that?" asked Joe.

"In so many words. It refers to him taking office in January, and that his mission will 'reach its conclusion,'" I made quotation signs with my fingers, "by the middle part of next year. Does anyone have a folder for Paul Gilmore?"

"He's on the ticket with Hillstrom, right?" asked Scott.

"Yeah. We have to assume he's involved in all this, but to what extent?"

"Found it," said Jess, pulling it from the box. She handed it to me. "You do the honors."

I read out the top matter to the others, which was almost a carbon copy of Ben's:

Paul Gilmore
Entered Wisdom Spring 10-4-76, age 7
Obtained from Nevada Camp for Boys
Original name: Robert Smith, changed 5-10-77
Graduated 3-31-90

"Other than the fact that he's younger than Hillstrom, it was the same procedure. They even came from the same place. They obviously had a deal with this Nevada Camp for Boys, just as they did with the orphanage in the Ukraine. I'm sure there were others."

Jess had gotten up and was tapping on the computer.

"The Nevada Camp for Boys had a major fire in 1988 and went out of business" she said. "Most of the buildings were destroyed, including, I'm sure, the one that housed the records."

"They are good at covering their tracks," I said, looking back at the folder. "Gilmore graduated from Wisdom Spring in 1990. Didn't the 1990 census put Wisdom Spring's population at around twelve? Could it be that Gilmore was their final graduate?"

I studied the material further. The others went back to their boxes in the meantime.

"He knows," I finally said. They all looked up. "He knows he's going to take over as president. It says it right here that his mission includes taking over the presidency from Hillstrom in his first year in office."

"Who exactly is he?" asked Scott. "Until this vice presidency thing, I'd never heard of him."

"He's a Congressman from Arizona. He's served two terms. He doesn't have anywhere near the charisma that Hillstrom has, but he seems to be a lot smarter. He was heavily promoted by Arizona senator Stephen Brice and former Arizona governor Alfred Barlick. I remember all that from the days when I actually cared about politics."

"I have both Brice and Barlick in my box," said Scott. "I already looked at them. I think their only connection with these people is money. Looks like they've been paid off pretty well. It also listed a few of the bills that they've voted on. On another note, I've also found one of the current senators from Alaska in here, and one from California. The Alaskan one went to Wisdom Spring. The other is connected by money."

"I've found a few too," said Joe. "Most seem to be connected by money, but a couple of the younger ones went there."

"And I saw the name of one of the Supreme Court justices." I offered. "There was a ledger full of numbers in his folder. I assume they were bank transactions of some kind."

"The ones I saw who were connected by money had those ledgers too. I'd say you're right."

"Oh … My … God!!!" I suddenly exclaimed. "'Operation Exchange' isn't just about replacing the president. Don't you see what's happening here? Slowly, over the years, they've been replacing members of Congress with their own people! They start by paying off some of the older sleazier ones, then when the time is right, they have them support a Wisdom Spring graduate. Their goal all along has been to take over the U.S. government!"

Dead silence. Then Jess covered her ears and said, "I've got a marching band in my head. The impression I get is that my father is very happy. Hard to explain, but it seems like he's actually celebrating. I think you've nailed it.

"But they can't replace everyone," she said, dropping her hands. "I can't believe, first of all, that they had that many people graduate—especially ones who could become politicians—and second of all, that they could bribe that many members of Congress. After all, they're not ALL crooks."

"Yeah, they are," mumbled Scott.

"They don't need everybody," I said, ignoring Scott. "They just need a few people in key positions. I bet if we found all of the people connected to this in Congress, we'd have most of the important committees covered. And besides, look at how many fellow politicians Hillstrom won over. It doesn't take very many to control Congress."

"Okay then, something else I don't understand," said Jess. "If

Hillstrom is so popular, he could help bring people together to further their cause. Why kill him?"

"Here's my theory," I said. "You worked for him. Would you say he was overly intelligent?"

"Intelligent? I never really noticed one way or the other. He was very charming."

"Right. And that's what got him to where he is. Hell, I voted for him a few times and I couldn't really tell you if he was intelligent. Popularity eventually wears off. At some point the presidency gets real and people are going to want answers. I don't think he's capable of providing those answers. Gilmore, on the other hand, *is* intelligent. So what better way to solidify their mission than to kill off Hillstrom and make him a martyr? Best of both worlds. You still have Hillstrom's popularity working for you, this time from beyond the grave, with the intelligence of Paul Gilmore."

"So who profits?" asked Scott. We looked at him with funny expressions. "Hey, I don't have three heads. It's a legitimate question. It's one thing to have control of Congress, but it won't be forever. So there has to be a plan behind it. Someone has to profit. You know that, down the line, it's going to be all about money. Someone started this. Someone or some group is funding it. They have to get something really good out of this to justify the time and money spent. Who are they and what are they gaining?"

Silence once again.

"And another question." Scott was on a roll. "Okay, so this 'school' at Wisdom Spring began in the late '60s. Are you telling me that forty some-odd years ago they came up with the idea to replace the president with one of their own? How much sense does that make? First of all, the people who came up with the idea are probably dead by now. They sure made out in this deal. They decided that they could grow a president? 'Hey, if we start now, then in forty years or so he'll be ready.' I'm sorry, but that makes no sense at all."

"No, it doesn't," I responded. "But the fact is, there was a school there and one of its graduates is now running for president. I'm sure there's more to this story. There's gotta be. I don't have the answer to it, but I think we're getting closer."

"Just so somebody is thinking how illogical it is."

"Well then it's time to put some logic to it," I said. "I wonder if Hillstrom knows he's going to be assassinated. I bet he doesn't. He doesn't strike me as the willing terrorist martyr type. I wonder how pissed at these people he'd be to find out. Maybe we need to get off the sidelines and get in the game. I think it's time to shake things up a bit."

"And I think," said Joe, "it's time to bring Mill in on all of this. We're going to need his help."

"He's going to have to come up here," I said. "Right now, this is a safe haven. If he can get up here without being seen, he can be right in the middle of it." I looked at Scott. "Do you mind one more person here?"

"He's not sharing my room. He gets the couch."

We talked about it for a few minutes, then Joe dialed Mill's cell phone.

After verifying through a series of questions that he was really Joe and was not under duress, and Mill doing the same, Joe gave him some bare bones information in the unlikely event that someone else was listening. He assured Mill that it was necessary for him to come to us. It was agreed that Mill would borrow a friend's jet and fly to Anchorage, where Scott and Joe would pick him up.

"What's next?" asked Jess.

"We have the phone number of the security guards' boss. I think it's time we use it," I said.

"Who are we calling?" asked Joe.

"How about Hillstrom?"

"We'll never get through to him. Why don't we just call the press now?" asked Jess.

"I'd rather leave that to Mill," I said. "That's his area of expertise. No, I suggest we spend the rest of the day scouring through these files. Pull out the name of every influential person we can find. Somewhere in those boxes is our invitation to Hillstrom."

We got back to work. Occasionally someone would bring up some big-name politician or news reporter. There were a number of news people with folders in the boxes. It just proved to me beyond a doubt that the press was equally involved. Unfortunately, we got no further in figuring out who was behind it. There were no folders on the masterminds, as far as we could see.

About an hour into it, Scott asked, "Has anyone else found any asses?

"What?" I asked.

"So far, three of my files have the word 'ass' somewhere near the end of the file, followed by a colon, then someone's name, with what looks like a date. One of the guys has three asses in his file, followed by names."

"I did see a couple of files that had that in them," I answered. "I kind of dismissed them because I had never heard of the person, and I was trying to concentrate on the files of people I was familiar with." I shuffled through until I found them. "I have three. So far, at least. I still have more files to go."

Meanwhile, Jess and Joe were doing the same. They each found one.

"I was curious about that too," said Jess. "I figured I'd look at it more closely later. So what does it mean?"

We all looked over the eight files. None of the subjects were familiar to us. They weren't politicians or famous businessmen. Joe, however thought two of the names after the "ass:' seemed vaguely familiar.

"Do you mind Googling them?" he asked Jess. She got up, went to the computer and started typing.

"You have a theory?" I asked him.

"I do," was all he would say.

After a few minutes Jess said, "Well, if I have the correct people, both of these guys are dead. One was the president of a big ad agency in England…"

Joe interrupted her. "Did he die on January 7, 2010?"

Jess looked at him, nodded her head, then continued typing. It was beginning to dawn on us all what these were.

"The other guy was the mayor of a small town in Colorado. He died in a car accident May 12, 2011. But then, you already knew that."

"I did."

"Why would the mayor of some hick town be familiar to you?" I asked.

"Because he was in the news. It was a big deal. Some company wanted to buy up water rights in the area and he was leading the fight against it. Then he died in a crash, but I kind of lost track of the story after that."

Jess asked us for the other names and went to work. As we suspected, all of the names following the "ass:" were deceased.

"'Ass:' stands for 'assassinated'," said Joe. "I bet as we go through the files we'll find more names of dead people, and I can guarantee that the subjects of the files will be people we've never heard of. You see, they weren't just training future politicians and corporate heads at Wisdom Spring. They were training assassins."

Chapter 39

This was getting scarier.

"So you're saying that anyone who has an 'ass:' in his file is an assassin, and those are the people he's killed?" I asked.

"That's what it looks like," answered Joe. He had just pulled out another file. "They're not all guys, though. Here's a woman, and she's responsible for two kills."

"I don't see anywhere in these files where they are referred to as assassins," said Jess.

"You have to read between the lines," replied Joe. "And I'm betting if we compared them all, we'd find some consistent label they've all been given. It really doesn't matter though. There is no doubt that they are assassins. And from what I've seen so far, their missions aren't to take out high-profile figures, but more obscure targets."

"Why?" I asked.

"I think if we investigated a bit further, we'd see that whoever took their place was somehow connected to this organization. They've probably discovered that it's important to replace lower-level—but strategically-placed—people, as well. That's probably how most of the Wisdom Spring graduates are being used. Not everything is accomplished at the top."

We needed to stop for a while to absorb it all. Jess and I went for a quick walk to clear our heads, while Joe retreated to his room. Scott, meanwhile, decided it was time to feed us something healthy and got to work in the kitchen on an early dinner. "We've all earned it," he said, and prepared a feast of salmon and crab legs, finishing it up with crème brulee.

The break did us all some good and when the meal was ready, we came to the table in much better moods.

"Is there anything you can't do?" Jess asked Scott, cracking open a crab leg.

"Yeah, find the perfect woman. And now, after watching you and Jon interact, and how perfect you seem for each other, my standards can only go up, which will make it even harder to find the right person."

I felt a little sorry for Scott at that moment. Jess was right, Scott seemed to be without limits. He deserved somebody as amazing as Jess. But in typical brotherly fashion, I could only respond with, "Hey, I think my ex-wife might be available."

He made a face.

"So what did we learn from all the folders?" I asked.

"That we can't trust anybody," answered Joe. "It's as simple as that. I think we need to make a list, filed under categories, of everyone we've found who's involved in this. We have media people, politicians, corporate executives, and now, assassins."

"I'll make the list," said Jess. "After all, I am the researcher."

"No argument there," I said.

"And you say there are more boxes still in the mine?" asked Joe.

"Yeah, six more," I said. "This was all we could take, though. And of course, I shot the keypad, so we can't go back for them. But, all of those contained the really thin folders. Using the thin ones we have here as examples, some are the children who died or were sent away, but most seem to be those from the lowest level of the organization—insignificant, for the most part. If I had to guess, I'd say we've got most of the important ones right here."

Jess and I went to work. I read out the names and categories, while she typed. If I had never heard of them and we couldn't determine a category, we put them under "unknown." Scott and Joe cleaned up after dinner, then read through files after we listed the names, hoping to find something we had missed the first time.

It was seven o'clock. We had done enough for one day and were all slumped in chairs in the living room. Jess and I had the couch and I was massaging her feet.

"Well, there was no clear link to Hillstrom," said Joe. "The only avenues we seem to have to contact him are through the guard's cell phone, or this Corbin Mays guy, the head of Exchange Systems. I think we'd get the furthest by calling the number the guards had to call. By the way, I checked Billy's phone. It doesn't have any kind of GPS on it. It's real basic, and nothing has been added. So they can't find us that way."

"Then I say we should get this ball rolling," said Scott. "Let's call the number."

We discussed the strategy for a few minutes and decided Jess should be the one to make the call, that Hillstrom would be more likely to respond to her.

Jess took a deep breath and dialed the number listed in the recent calls. She put it on speaker. It rang twice before it was picked up.

"Yeah?"

"This is Jessica Norton. You know who I am?"

There was silence. He was deciding how to respond. Finally, he said, "Yes."

"I'm calling from outside Wisdom Spring. You're familiar with that, right?"

"I am."

"Before your people destroyed the mine, I made it out with a box of very interesting material."

The longer we could keep them thinking the mine was destroyed, the longer it would take them to send someone to check it out, we hoped.

The person on the other end said nothing.

"I want to talk to Gary Hillstrom."

"Who?"

"Don't play stupid."

"I'm not. Do you mean the guy who's running for president?"

"I do. I want you to have him call me at this number."

"Why me? I don't know that guy. How the hell would I get in touch with him?"

Obviously, this contact was way down on the ladder, told only what he needed to know.

"You can't, but your boss can, or his boss, or his boss's boss. Somewhere up your chain of command, someone has direct contact with Hillstrom."

"I don't thi…"

"Trust me," she interrupted. "They do, and I suggest you get started. You had orders to have me killed, and you've got to know from the news reports that I worked for Hillstrom. That should give you a hint. So here's what you tell them: I want to hear from Hillstrom himself within twenty-four hours on this line. That's seven o'clock tomorrow night Alaska time. If he doesn't call me directly by that deadline, I make the contents of this box known. Got that?"

"I'll pass along the message."

"You do that. Remember, twenty-four hours or everything is going to come tumbling down."

Chapter 40

At two o'clock in the morning Florida time, Mays and Hutch sat uncomfortably in Hillstrom's suite at the Tampa Marriott Waterside Hotel. They were alone. Hillstrom had finished off a campaign speech in downtown Tampa and was huddled with his advisers twenty-seven floors below them. The two men were watching the replay of Hillstrom's speech on local TV. The rally ended amid thunderous applause. Like the other candidates, Hillstrom's handlers had made sure his followers were out in force. Unlike the other candidates, they didn't have to work very hard to keep out the detractors. Hillstrom seemed to have very few. Although not everyone would vote for him, even those who opposed his message seemed to like Hillstrom the man.

"Why are you nervous?" asked Hutch. "Haven't you known him for years?"

"I mentored him for years," corrected Mays. "In many ways I probably know him better than anyone. I'm not nervous about seeing him. I'm nervous about the message. This is going to be my call, and I'm not sure yet how I'm going to call it."

He must be nervous, thought Hutch. With just that one sentence Mays had opened up more to Hutch than he ever had in the past.

"How could you have let her escape from there?" asked Mays.

He's back, thought Hutch. "The word I got was that she was dead and sealed in the mine. Why should I have doubted it? It came through the regular channel. The guy who took the call didn't sense any problems."

"Have you talked to the guy who made the call from the mine?"

"No. He was one of the back-ups from Anchorage. He, along with the others, seems to have disappeared."

"And that doesn't raise a red flag for you?"

"It's not uncommon for some of those low-level guys to quit and take off. They don't have the same loyalty as some of the other employees, and they've learned that the best way to quit this organization is just to vanish."

"And you canceled the second group that were on their way up there?"

"I did. Based on the information, there was no reason for them to be there."

"May I suggest that you send someone up there to check anyway?"

"I will."

Five minutes later Hillstrom opened the door. Knowing Mays and Hutch were in the room, he had instructed his security staff to wait outside.

"Awesome event," he said, closing the door and shaking hands with both men. "Did you watch it on TV? They loved me." Getting no response, he looked quizzically at them. Then he turned serious. "There's something wrong, isn't there?"

"Jessica Norton is still alive," said Mays. Hutch had decided to let Mays do all the talking. "And she wants to speak to you."

Hillstrom sat down. He felt a sudden knot in the pit of his stomach.

"How? I thought…"

"Yeah, we did too. But that's not important now. What is important is that I have to decide whether to let you talk to her. She says she has a box of the material from the mine, and if she doesn't hear from you by," he looked at his watch, "eleven o'clock our time tomorrow night—or rather, tonight, she says she'll release it."

"Why does she want to talk to me? Why doesn't she just release it now?"

"I don't know. That's why you're probably going to have to talk to her."

"What if she wants to meet?"

"We'll set it up. And if she doesn't suggest it, you will. Then Hutch, here, will take care of it. Of course you're not actually going to meet with her—we just want her to think that. But we have to find out what she wants."

"It's a little more than four months 'til the election," said Hillstrom. "I'm a third-party candidate in the lead. It's unprecedented. No, it's amazing. And yet, because of your inept people," he was looking at Hutch, "it may all go down the tubes. Unbelievable! Such a screw-up."

"Fuck you," said Hutch. "You talk to me like I'm your lackey. The only reason you're even in this election is because of this organization. Your whole political career is a sham, and if you hadn't let your ego get the best of you and let that researcher do background material on you for your biography—something you were supposed to let us take care of—we wouldn't be dealing with Jessica Norton right now."

"Enough!" shouted Mays. "Face it, you both screwed up. Hell, we've all screwed up. So let's take care of her, for good!"

"So how are we going to do this?" asked Hutch.

"You," Mays said, looking at Hillstrom, "will call her about an hour or two before her deadline. We don't want to appear anxious.

You want to get her to meet with you in person."

"Where?" asked Hutch.

"She says she's somewhere outside of Wisdom Spring. How about there? It's remote, and somehow appropriate. It's a good place for her to die."

Chapter 41

"They're going to want to meet," I said over breakfast.

"Yes, they will," said Joe. "And you know where, of course."

"Wisdom Spring."

"They would consider it poetic justice."

"So we can't meet there," I said.

"Absolutely not. Besides, they're not going to want to send Hillstrom. They're going to send a goon squad. So, we're going to have to keep them guessing until the last minute. Bring them somewhere close, then give them the final location when we're ready for them, not vice-versa."

Joe added, "It's imperative that we convince Hillstrom to come himself. Unless he comes and we can get photographic—and hopefully audio—proof, they can deny any involvement on his part. I think the important thing is for you, Jess, to get Hillstrom talking on the phone. Re-establish your rapport with him, then break the news to him about the assassination. But make sure no one else is listening. You need to start sowing the seeds of doubt, because that might be just the thing that will make him want to meet with you himself."

"When do you think they'll call?" asked Jess.

"That one's easy," I said. "They'll call right before the deadline." Joe nodded his agreement and I continued, "They'll want to give the appearance of not caring, but by waiting that long, it shows how desperate they really are."

We discussed strategy for a while longer, until I could see Jess becoming overwhelmed. I suggested a walk, which she gratefully accepted. I figured there was no way they would call this early, and besides, I refused to let them dictate my actions. We grabbed our guns and headed out the door. We followed the same path Scott took us on when we had first arrived. We knew where we were going. There was a cliff overlooking the bay, with a view of the volcanoes on the distant coast. We walked hand in hand, just enjoying the silence. At one point I heard a snuffling sound behind us and turned quickly, only to find Slob following along.

We reached the cliff and sat, soaking in the warmth of the sun. At that point Jess began to cry. She had to let it out, and I just held her. It was fear, it was stress, it was death. It was the realization that her parents could still be alive if her father hadn't stumbled onto all of this. It was the knowledge that she had killed people. It didn't matter that they deserved it, she had taken lives. As she cried, I began to think about Karen and tears began to roll down my cheeks as well. Soon, we were shaking in each other's arms. I caught a glimpse of Slob, who was just curiously staring at us.

It was twenty minutes before Jess finally wiped her eyes. She then looked up at me with the most amazing expression of love. It sent a charge through me. Everything we'd been through washed away, leaving only the love between us. This was what it was all about. This is what everything was leading to. It didn't matter what came next. Somehow, we had each made it through our hurt and pain. We were on the other side.

We kissed. Deep, intense kisses. We moved over to a patch of grass and Jess lay on her back while I straddled her. I took off her shirt and the morning sun bounced off her smooth skin. A chilly breeze came up and goose bumps appeared. I ran my hand over her arms and stomach, enjoying the feel of the goose bumps. A few minutes later we hungrily made love.

We got back to the house totally recharged. If Scott and Joe sensed a change, they didn't mention it. During the walk back we hadn't said a word, a silence that was power in and of itself.

Even after arriving, we still didn't say much. We just held on to each other. Eventually the high began to wear down and we found ourselves re-entering the life from which we had escaped. Conversation picked up and we had finally returned. But we were different. We couldn't have been gone more than two hours, but we came back calmer, stronger, and with a dual confidence—we not only trusted each other, we had the ultimate faith in ourselves. Bring on Hillstrom.

"Joe and I have to head up to Anchorage," said Scott. "We got a call from Mill while you were gone. He'll be landing in a couple of hours."

"Hopefully we'll make it back in time for your call with Hillstrom," added Joe, "but if not, do you feel comfortable talking to him?"

Jess nodded. "Absolutely. He won't know what hit him."

Scott eyed her. "What happened out there?"

"Just recharging our batteries," I said.

"Uh huh."

Jess and I looked at each other and smiled.

Scott and Joe left a few minutes later.

We had a late lunch, then went on the computer to finish the list of names, and to go online and get any updates on the world. There was nothing much going on. Mill Colson's lawyer was stalling the courts in allowing them to declare Mill officially dead. Hillstrom was leading his closest challenger by ten points. Jess had dropped off the news cycle. Her fifteen minutes of fame was done for the moment.

At about four o'clock, the cell phone rang. Jess was so pumped for this she didn't even have to take a breath. She gave it two rings so as not to appear too anxious, then answered, putting it on speaker.

"Hello." Her voice was strong.

"Jess. Gary Hillstrom." The voice was somewhat distant.

"Hi Gary. Take it off speakerphone."

"Um."

"You want to talk to me, you talk to me alone."

"You requested the call, if I'm not mistaken." He was smooth, like a therapist talking to a patient.

Jess hung up.

"Wow," I said. "I'm impressed."

"He's such a bullshit artist," she said.

The phone rang again five minutes later. Jess answered it.

"I'm not kidding, Gary. If I hang up on you again, the game's over."

"Sorry, Jess. The people with me thought it best that they hear what you said. Obviously it was a mistake."

"You could say that."

"It sounds like you have it on speakerphone, though."

"I do. A friend of mine is listening in."

"The mysterious man who came to your aid?"

"Yes. And just to let you know, I'm not taping this. With the information I have, I don't need this call taped. I sure hope no one on your end is taping, or listening in by some other method, because some of what I'm going to say, you really don't want them to hear. Seriously, you can tape it or you can tell them everything I say, if you want. I don't care. But I'm thinking that you might want to keep much of this to yourself, and you'll understand why."

"I promise you, it's just me. You sound well. You sound strong." Which might have been a euphemism for, "*You don't sound like the starry-eyed girl I used to put things over on.*"

"I am. Killing people can do that."

"Ah, so you admit you killed your friends." I didn't think he was taping it, but he may have been afraid she was, despite her assurances.

"No, I'm talking about the people you've sent to kill me."

"Jess, you know I'd never…"

"Oh shut up, Gary. How I was ever deceived by you, I'll never know. You're so slimy."

"How dare you…"

"Yo, Gary," she interrupted again. "This is my show, not yours. Now, would you like to know why I'm calling?"

"I would," he calmed down. "But do you think we should meet instead?"

I had always given Hillstrom credit for having some brains, but I wasn't so sure now. With that one comment, he had tipped his hand. He was too anxious to meet. I could imagine his handlers cringing in the background.

"I do, but we'll come to that. Here's the thing, I know all about you. Your real name is Ben Fremont. Actually, it's not your real name, it's the name they gave you when you came to Wisdom Spring."

It was dead quiet on the other end. Then I thought I could make out Hillstrom whispering that she knew his name.

"I know all about Wisdom Spring. I actually spent a good deal of time there. Your friends tried to blow me up in the mine. They got the mine all right, which is too bad, but they missed me. I also know that you brutally murdered ten people in Homer."

I thought I heard Hillstrom suck in his breath quickly.

"I could go on and on, Gary. But here's the thing I really wanted to tell you, because I bet you don't know it. And it's up to you as to whether you want to pass this along to your handlers. Did you know that the same people who are behind your sure-win victory of the presidency are the same ones who plan to assassinate you next year?"

He didn't say anything. She had him hooked.

"It's all in the material we got from Wisdom Spring. It goes into it in quite a bit of detail. It seems that they like all the charisma you exude, and that is what's going to get you elected, but they really don't think you'll be the kind of president they need. So, once they get you in office, they plan to replace you—to 'exchange' you, you might say—with your vice president, who, as I'm sure you know, grew up in Wisdom Spring, as well. You see, they think he's really smart. You? Not so much. Tell me to go to hell if you understand what I'm saying."

A pause, then, "Go to hell."

"Good. So now you know why we want to meet with you and not with an army of your hit men. It might be the only way you come out of this whole thing alive. Keep that in mind when we set up a meeting place."

"Since you know so much about Wisdom Spring, how about there?" It was obviously what he was supposed to say, but he didn't say it with much conviction, as if he was trying to think about the merits of meeting with her alone.

"A little too much of a hick town for me. No, here's how we'll work it. You fly into Anchorage the day after tomorrow at noon and give me a call. I'll tell you where we'll meet."

"But I have a rally that day."

"You have a rally every day. Cancel it. If you don't show up, the media gets it all. There's enough proof in here to get you arrested, but even if you somehow were able to talk your way out of it, your campaign would be dead. But better your campaign than you. You meet with us, you might just live through this. That's the offer, Gary. Your choice."

Chapter 42

Hillstrom, ever the optimist, was desperately trying to find a way out. Was the information about his impending assassination real, or was she just using a scare tactic to get him to meet? And if he did meet, was it the same as admitting guilt? Twenty-four hours ago, he was at the top of the world. How could it have all changed so quickly?

"You're not going," said Mays.

"I think I need to," answered Hillstrom. "If I don't show up, they'll turn it all over to the media."

"They'll be dead," said Hutch. "We'll send an army in and blow them away. They won't know what hit them. You don't need to go up."

"They'll expect your people," said Hillstrom. "Jess practically said as much. And what if your army doesn't get there right away? Or what if they disable them?"

"Yeah, right," answered Hutch.

"I suppose we could let him do it," said Mays. "Don't forget, we'll have a second wave coming just in case. They won't be expecting that. She knows him. He might learn things from her that we should know."

"But what if it's a ruse?" asked Hutch. "What if they have the media waiting for us? Just showing up admits guilt."

"They won't," responded Mays. "If they contact the media, I'll know it within minutes. Then we use it to our advantage somehow."

"Why are you so anxious to meet her?" asked Hutch.

Hillstrom knew this question was coming. They had no idea what Jess said to him about the assassination. It had to sound plausible.

"It all started for me in Alaska. It seems appropriate that this part of it ends there. We don't know how this is going to go down." He looked at Hutch. "I know you have a lot of faith in your men, but you've got to admit, they don't have a great success rate of late." Hutch just glared at him. "If something goes wrong, she'll be expecting me. We don't know yet where we're supposed to meet. If she doesn't see me, they'll split and we'll have lost our chance. If I go in first, I can talk to her. As Corbin said, she knows me. We had a good relationship. She trusted me. Okay, she doesn't now, but I think I can keep her occupied until your second force arrives. I can spin a good story that I didn't know most of what was going on and will offer to form an alliance with her to get to the bottom of it. That'll keep her attention long enough for me to learn what she knows."

"She'll believe that shit?" asked Hutch.

"Why was I put here to begin with? Because I have a gift. I know how to work people. Look at my track record. Hell," he said, turning to Mays, "you people saw that gift when I was a kid."

"Okay, we'll do it," said Mays. "But Hutch will be with you." Hillstrom cringed inside. "And we have to know exactly where we're going ahead of time. You have to insist on that. Otherwise you're not going to be there."

*****

Hillstrom was lying in bed, unable to sleep. He could see the beginnings of dawn through the crack in the curtain. All of the Wisdom Spring talk had brought him back to a time he had chosen to forget. For so long it had been wiped from the forefront of his mind. Even the Homer experience was just a distant memory. But now, it had all come roaring back. Here he was, in the middle of summer in Florida, and he found himself shivering. All of his memories of Wisdom Spring were cold ones. Unhappy ones. He had hated his life there, and yet, it was the only life he had known. He had only the vaguest of memories of the boy's camp in Nevada.

Now, what he could remember the most about Wisdom Spring was the loneliness. When he was young—seven or eight or nine—it seemed that every time he made a friend, he or she would be gone within a couple of months. He never understood that. He asked Corbin about it once and Mays explained that some of the children only needed partial training, then went to live with some of their people on the outside. They enrolled them in public schools and integrated them into society, all the while training them at home on the future roles they'd play. Hillstrom asked him why he wasn't one of those kids. Mays just responded by saying that he had a gift, a gift better taught right in Wisdom Spring. They had plans for him, special plans. Yeah, to get assassinated?

Hillstrom had believed him to a point, because he had, in fact, seen the files on a couple of former Wisdom Spring kids who had gone to the outside. But there was something Mays wasn't telling him. There was something more, he just didn't know what it was.

He asked if all of the kids who had transferred to the outside were used by the organization. "Less than ten percent," was the answer, "and none of them even knew they were being used." Hillstrom asked what happened to the ninety percent who weren't needed, and Mays told him that they just lived their lives none the wiser. After all, the in-home training didn't reveal any secrets. The goal was to be successful without any of the subjects even knowing what they had been trained for.

He wasn't so lucky. He cursed the fact that he was one of the "special" ones. He remembered Paul Gilmore from his days there. A real asshole. He was quite a bit younger than Hillstrom, but he was also one of the "special ones," so they spent a lot of time together, despite the age difference. Now he was his running-mate. He couldn't stand him as a kid and couldn't stand him now. And if Jess was right, a year from now, Gilmore would be president and he would be dead.

The memories poured in, none of them good. He never knew his real parents. At Wisdom Spring, he lived with the Fremonts—hence his name change—a middle-aged couple with an accent. He never did find out where they were from. His relationship with his "parents" was distant. There was no love coming from them. He knew now that they were there to do a job. His mother taught history in the school. His father came and went—he had no idea where—but when he was there, he taught Ben the art of lying. He brought back stories of the outside world, a dog-eat-dog world where no one was to be trusted. The only way to survive was to take care of yourself. Relationships were simply ways to get what you needed. That made perfect sense to Ben, seeing the life he had in Wisdom Spring.

This man—he had trouble thinking of him as his father—also taught him how to kill. They started with animals they used for food. Ben became adept with a knife and could slit a pig's throat in a second. Moving on to humans was easy. He watched his first man being killed when he was eleven. It was part of his training. He killed his first man when he was thirteen. There were traitors, or so he was told, who couldn't be allowed to leave and tell the outside world about Wisdom Spring. Men were tried and found guilty. Part of reaching manhood was to kill a convicted traitor in front of your teachers and town officials. By then he was so desensitized that he only hesitated for a moment before slitting the man's throat. That hesitation, though, cost him three days in jail, in the cramped cell with one tasteless meal a day. The next time he had to kill, the hesitation was gone. In all, he killed three men and two women in that fashion during his Wisdom Spring days. He spent another three days in jail for his first woman. Again he hesitated. But not the next time.

His early years at school in Wisdom Spring were spent learning the basics: math, English, history, and foreign languages. He became fluent in Russian, Spanish, and German, and had some knowledge of Chinese and Japanese—all skills he kept from the American people. They would want to know how he learned the languages. But he was also taught loyalty. Someday he would go out into the world and make a name for himself, but loyalty to those who had trained him was to be utmost in his life. He had seen what happened to traitors.

It was a hard life, with school being the focus. Classes would begin early in the morning and go until five or six at night. As he thought about the other children, he had trouble remembering anyone smiling. What was there to smile about? Sometimes they played games in school—word games, board games, sporting events—but it became apparent to all that the games weren't for fun, there was always a lesson behind them. So instead of looking forward to game time, it was dreaded as much as math.

What was also dreaded was the winter. The summer was bad

enough, having to put heavy curtains on his bedroom window to keep the room dark from the constant summer light. And no matter how hard he tried, the light always peeked through. No, it was the winter. That was the worst. The cold and the snow were awful, but it was the dark that almost did him in every year. To not see the sun for months at a time left him in a constant state of depression. Who knows? Maybe they wanted him that way.

In his early years there, he tried to make up for everything else by forming friendships, clinging to every friend he could gather close. But then they would disappear. Eventually he no longer cared. By the time he reached his teens, all of his interactions with the other kids were superficial at best, conniving at worst. This was when he learned about his gift of influence. He would use it on others simply as an experiment. Sometimes his actions caused the other person to disappear. That was not a concern to him. His relationships allowed him to refine his skills, his calling.

As he thought back he realized—maybe for the first time—that there was an inordinate amount of attention in school placed on history. World history was studied for the wars and the conquests. What made a country strong, what made it weak. The conquests of Napoleon, of Alexander the Great, and of Hitler. While Hitler was derided for his tactics and his mental instability, he was to be admired for his ability to sway people to his cause.

As for U.S. history, much attention was placed on the wealthy men who helped shape the country, especially during the 1800s and early 1900s—the bankers, steel moguls, and railroad tycoons. He learned to admire them. In fact, he remembered once being told that Wisdom Spring was descended from these men. He wasn't sure then what it meant. He wasn't exactly sure now either, for that matter.

He did know that there was a plan, and he was a big part of it.

He was never told exactly what the plan was, only that it was the job of the Wisdom Spring graduates to change how this country worked. In turn, it would change the world. There were others—people high up—who were controlling the plan. Ben was one of the chosen ones. He would help make it come to fruition. But what exactly was he making come to fruition? He thought of all the politicians who were controlled by this organization. Exactly what was the plan, the long-term goal? Whatever it was, his role in the creation of it was soon coming to an end, if Jess was right.

He had given his whole life to this. He wasn't a traitor. He wasn't a screw-up. He was loyal. Was this how they were going to reward his loyalty? All of a sudden, he was angry. It wasn't going to end this way.

Chapter 43

Jess hung up the phone.

"Whoa," I said.

"I do okay?"

"You're kidding, right? Hillstrom is going to have to change his underwear because of you."

Scott and Joe arrived with Mill Colson an hour after Jess's phone call. Although still well-groomed, Mill had lost a lot weight from the events surrounding the plane crash. He held out his hand to me.

"Jon, good to see you again, and in one piece." He looked over at Jess, then gave her a hug.

"Good to finally meet you. You're much more attractive than your picture."

"Thank you. It's good to finally meet you, too."

"We've brought him up to speed," said Joe. "Did you talk with Hillstrom?"

"I did."

"Wish you could have heard her," I added. "She blew him away." I told them the whole conversation.

"You hung up on Gary Hillstrom and made him call you

back?" asked Mill incredulously. "That's not something you see every day."

"I suggest we have dinner, relax a bit, then go at this tomorrow," I said.

"That sounds good to me," said Scott. "I don't have anything defrosted. We'll have to order out."

We couldn't ignore the subject and spent much of dinner and after talking about Wisdom Spring, with Mill insisting on hearing all about our adventures getting there.

Finally, we all headed to bed. Joe graciously gave his up for Mill and slept on the couch.

The next day was busy for all of us. Jess sat with Mill, going over every file in the six boxes. Sometimes I would pass them and see Mill just shaking his head in disbelief. I asked him about the legality of him meeting with Jess. After all, she was still a fugitive.

"The rules have changed," was his answer. "I look at all of the politicians and lawyers involved in this and it makes me sick. You think I'm going to get sanctioned for this when a U.S. Supreme Court justice is involved? I think not."

Scott, Joe, and I had a different job. We needed to find a good spot to have the meeting with Hillstrom, or whoever they decided to send in his place. I knew that Hillstrom wanted to come, simply because he now had doubts about his future. But would they let him?

"They're going to send an army with him or without him," I said. "How do we get around that?"

"I think I know," answered Scott. "In fact, I also know the perfect place." He turned to me. "You have enough of that money left to spare about $25,000?"

"Sure. What do you need it for?"

"I want to hire some friends."

"Your survivalist friends?

"Right up their alley. They get to go up against the government and corporate America and play with guns. They'll jump at the chance."

"So where is this place?" asked Joe.

"Right here in Homer. On my property, to be specific."

"Isn't that a bit close to home?" I asked.

"It's actually not the property I live on. I own twenty-five acres on the other side of town. Pretty remote, and in the middle of it is a quarry. At least, it used to be a quarry. I use it to shoot in. Nobody else goes in there. I could station my guys around the rim of the quarry and they'll put a quick stop to any army that shows up."

"You realize," began Joe, "that they are not going to all come at once. My guess is that Hillstrom will have a second plane up there somewhere. Maybe a third. As soon as you tell him where to meet, he'll have the other plane headed here. They'll either get here early and try to ambush you, or if you don't give them the final location when they're in Anchorage, they'll follow them up here and try to ambush you after you've already started your meeting with Hillstrom, assuming he comes."

"So let's set them up," I answered. "Let's tell them the location and give them time to send their men here. We'll have your survivalist friends waiting for them and they can, um, disarm them. Then when Hillstrom arrives, we'll have the advantage."

"Sounds reasonable," said Joe. "It might just work. Let's see the spot."

Scott drove us over. Getting off the main road, we took a dirt road up a long hill, then got off onto a smaller dirt road.

"This is all my property around here. If you and Jess ever want to build a house away from the rest of the world, you're welcome to."

"Thank you. It's becoming more tempting every day."

We reached a small grassy area and Scott stopped the truck. We got out and made our way down a wide trail, Max leading the procession. It was obvious that he had been there many times before. About a quarter of a mile down the path, we reached a large open area surrounded on three sides by sheer rock cliffs about fifty feet high. Running along the base of the wall at the far end was a pile of sand about four feet high. Targets had been set up in front of the sand.

"Pretty much a box canyon," said Scott.

"Perfect," added Joe. "Ollie and his group could position themselves on top of the canyon walls, or hide in the woods and flank Hillstrom's men, cornering them in here."

"I'd let Ollie figure that one out," said Scott. "So are we agreed? This the spot?"

"I'm good," answered Joe.

"I only have one concern," I said. "This land is under your name. If it doesn't work, someone could trace it to you."

"Aw, always looking out for me," said Scott, slapping me on the back. "Bro, it's twenty-five acres of remote Alaskan wilderness. I don't know who comes here. Just because I own it doesn't mean I spend any time on it. And that would be my answer. Don't worry about it."

We got home to find Mill pacing the floor, all keyed up.

"This is unbelievable," he said as we came in. "When we get the word out, this is going to be one of the most significant events in U.S. history. I figure about fifty members of the House and another twenty in the Senate are going to have to resign, if they're not indicted. That's to say nothing of Pecorelli and his Supreme Court seat. Emergency elections are going to be held all over the country. And all of these assassins running around. They've taken out targets all over the world." He asked me, "So when is all this going down?"

"Tomorrow sometime."

"The minute it does, I'm calling a press conference. I'll entice them by emailing them the photos of the dead in the mine. Did you know there are over thirty members of the press on Hillstrom's payroll that we know about? I'm actually friends with some of them."

He continued to talk while Scott called Ollie. Ollie accepted the offer and promised to have six or seven guys leave at sun up. Scott would meet them at the airport in his truck and transport them over to the quarry.

We spent the rest of the day planning our strategy. Mill finally calmed down close to dinnertime when Scott presented us with a banquet of venison, bear, salmon, crab, and halibut. Later that night, we watched the news and heard that Hillstrom had come down with laryngitis and was cancelling his events for the following two days.

At noon the next day, the call came. Jess had rehearsed the spiel. Earlier that morning, Scott had picked up Ollie and six others, all loaded for bear with M-16s, sniper rifles, hand grenades, and an assortment of handguns.

Jess answered and put the phone on speaker.

"Hi Jess, this is Gary. I'm in Anchorage."

"Okay, get back on your plane and head down to Homer." I heard Hillstrom's hand cover the phone, letting his people know where to direct their men. "When you land in Homer, I'll give you instructions where to go. And just you. No security." We knew it wouldn't just be him, but we felt we needed to give him some bargaining room.

"Nope. No way. Here's how it's going to work. You will give

me instructions now where to go once I land in Homer. I need to know where I'm going. And as for security, I'm bringing four of my own. I'm sure you know that I declined Secret Service protection. It's because I trust my own men. You won't be alone, and neither will I. The fact is, I am a United States Senator and a presidential candidate, and I need my security. Take it or I turn around and go home."

"You really don't want to do that," said Jess, keeping to the script.

"I'll take my chances. But I'm not going to walk into a shooting gallery. Take it or leave it, Jess."

"Um, hold on," she said, trying to sound indecisive. Then she and I had a heated discussion in the background. When it seemed like enough time, she said, "Okay, you win, but you better not screw me."

"Funny you should say that, because when you worked for me, I had that thought often." He was so smooth, he was somehow able to make a particularly sleazy comment sound almost sexy.

Jess turned red. He had hit a nerve.

"Do you want the directions?" Jess asked. Her throat suddenly dry. I squeezed her hand in support.

She gave them to him and said, "Four o'clock sharp."

Chapter 44

We waited. There was nothing more we could do. Certain things had to fall into place before we could take our turn onstage. Forty-five minutes after Jess's talk with Hillstrom, the phone rang. It was a friend of Scott's from the airport. Scott had asked him to call if a planeload of men showed up. He told Scott that a private jet had just landed and fourteen men with rifle cases had gotten out and rented three vehicles, then sped off. Scott thanked him and radioed Ollie. Cell phone coverage was nonexistent in the quarry, so Ollie had brought down some state-of-the-art communication equipment. Ollie thanked him and said he'd be in touch.

At two o'clock Ollie radioed back.

"Position secure," he reported. "Three enemy dead, the rest are piled up in a corner, hands, feet, and mouths all duct taped."

"Piled?" I asked.

"Yeah," said Scott. "He probably really means piled. Time for us to head out. Mill, I want you to stay here and listen for a call. I'm expecting there will be another plane on its way before or after Hillstrom comes in. My friend at the airport will call if they land. You'll have to radio Ollie immediately."

"I think I can handle that. Be careful, all of you."

Scott let Ollie know we were on our way, and then we set off. We arrived at 3:30 and parked next to the three rented vehicles. Before we headed down to the quarry, Scott took off his license plates. He put them under his seat, covered up the vehicle identification number in the windshield, and locked the doors.

"I could wiggle out of any questions about my land," said Scott. "My truck being here is another story. Better to remain as anonymous as possible."

We walked to the quarry, once again Max leading the way. When we arrived, Ollie came out of hiding from behind a rock. There was no evidence of the three dead or the 'pile' of live ones. Scott shook Ollie's hand.

"It go okay?" he asked.

"And here I thought you had given us a challenge," answered Ollie. "I don't know what they were thinking. I would check out a position before just walking in."

"I think they were figuring on getting here before anyone else, and at the most, just Jon and Jess being here." He introduced us and Ollie took a long look at Jess.

"Read about you online. These people are stupid. Anyone with any sense would know by looking at you that you didn't kill those four people. Anyway, nice to meet you." He shook Joe's hand, greeting him like an old friend. Joe had more than proven himself in Ollie's eyes.

"We have four people on the walls and three, including me, in the woods. You guys don't have anything to worry about. Besides, the group you're waiting for are going to expect you to be dead or captured."

His radio clicked twice. "They just pulled in. We've got your back."

I was a little nervous. I was finally going to meet the famous

Gary Hillstrom.

Five minutes later, six people walked into the open quarry area. Four were obviously security personnel, with Hillstrom in the middle. The one in front, however, was different. He was dressed casually, but there was nothing casual about him. Former military, I figured. Maybe even former spy. He was definitely in charge.

I glanced at Joe. He had a high-quality video camera hidden in his hand to document the event. He glanced back with an almost imperceptible nod.

They looked around in surprise. All but the leader. He just looked wary. With no cell service in the area to be able to check in with their men, and with the three rentals in the parking area, I'm sure they were expecting everything to be secure.

"Hi Gary," said Jess. "I'm sure this isn't exactly what you were expecting."

"I'm not sure what you mean, Jess," responded Hillstrom in an innocent voice tinged with a fair amount of fear. "Anyway, you got us here, so what do you have to say?"

"I'd like to know who this guy is," I said, pointing to the one in front.

"Who are you?" asked Hillstrom.

"Jon."

"You must be the mysterious good Samaritan."

I saw a slight movement from one of the guards. He had something in his hand. It wasn't a gun. I suddenly realized what it was.

"Tell your man to throw his camera over here right now." He must have been told to get a camera shot of me, probably to send back to their headquarters.

No one moved or said anything.

"You sent fourteen men up here ahead of you. Do you see those men? Your man has until the count of three to throw me the camera or he will be lying in a pool of blood, his brains splattered all over you. One ... two ... "The camera flew in my direction and landed at my feet. I picked it up and threw it against the rocks, smashing it.

"Smart choice." Focusing on the leader, I said, "Again, tell me who you are."

"Mel Hutchinson. Head of security for Senator Hillstrom."

"Yeah, and probably some other duties as well. All yours." I motioned to Jess.

"Are you sure you want to hear all this in front of your security?" Jess asked. "Probably better to hear it alone."

It was clear that Hillstrom wanted exactly that, but he looked at Hutchinson.

His security chief answered for him. "You can tell us all."

"Maybe I should meet them alone," said Hillstrom, a slight quaver in his voice.

"They can tell us all," Hutchinson repeated.

Hillstrom looked scared, but he didn't protest.

"Okay, your choice," said Jess. "First of all, the mine at Wisdom Spring wasn't blown up. It's very much in one piece."

I saw Hutchinson's expression and could tell it was news to them. They obviously hadn't sent anyone to check it out, relying on bad information. Part of me could understand. Down in the states it would have been simple to verify. But the remoteness of Wisdom Spring made everything just that much more difficult. If they were sure of the validity of the information, checking it out could go on the back burner.

Jess continued. "We brought out six boxes of the most important files. We saw all the dead people too.

Now this was interesting, I thought. The response from both

Hillstrom and Hutchinson was one of genuine surprise. Hutchinson was being kept in the dark about some aspects of the organization. Jess caught the reaction, too.

"Hmm. Neither of you knew about it, did you?"

They didn't respond.

"Gary, back when you were Ben Fremont, you once told someone that the hardest part of living in Wisdom Spring was that as soon as you would make a friend, the friend would be gone."

"Who did I tell that to?" That caught his attention.

"Your only friend in Homer. The only one you didn't kill, that is."

Hutchinson looked at him as if to say, "*You left someone alive?*"

"Clyde?" Hillstrom's eyes were far away.

"The one and the same. He wonders why you never came back to see him, by the way. But back to the point: Do you know why those kids went away? Many of them were murdered. Their bodies are stored in the mine. A lot of adults too. The climate in there has kept them from decomposing. They are sort of mummified now." She reached into her jacket and pulled out some of the pictures I had taken and handed them to him. "Anyone you recognize there? Any old friends?"

Jess was really taking it to him, pulling no punches. Hillstrom and Hutchinson both looked at the pictures in amazement. Hutchinson didn't seem bothered by them, just annoyed that he hadn't known.

"You're disturbed by the pictures, Gary, aren't you? What baffles me is why these pictures can disturb you but killing ten people in Homer was so easy."

Hillstrom started to say something and Hutchinson said, "Shut up, Gary."

"That's fine," said Jess. "I'm sure you'll tell us later."

I was amazed. Jess was relentless. After weeks on the run, this was cathartic for her. She proceeded to tell him a few more of the facts we had uncovered, and then came to the part we were hoping would break him.

"I told you on the phone that you were in line to be assassinated by your own people."

Hutchinson whirled his head to look at Hillstrom.

"My guess," I spoke up, "is that your friend Hutchinson, here, is deeply involved. Maybe he's the one who was going to deliver the shot."

"You see," continued Jess, "once you are elected, you have no more value. They probably consider you way too soft for the job, and maybe a little too popular. By killing you, they achieve two purposes: First, they can blame whoever they want—whatever foreign government they want eliminated. The American people will be behind the new president all the way. Second, they put someone in office who can do the job the way they want it done. Maybe someone a little more in line with their goals, and not his own. See, we came to the conclusion that they must have known early on what your strengths and weaknesses were. We don't know if they pegged you to take the presidency right away, or—the more likely scenario—they figured that as a senator your charm could sway almost anyone in Congress. And as they added more and more of their own people in the House and Senate, your influence would grow. We think it was only after seeing your following did they realize your presidential possibilities. Basically, Gary, you were used. You were used from the time you arrived at Wisdom Spring. You knew you had a mission. You just didn't know that they were going to double-cross you. The fact is, you were destined to die, just like your friends. It just took another fifty years or so for them to get around to it."

Jess suddenly put her hands to her head and squatted down. I knew what was happening, as did Scott and the formerly disbelieving Joe, but the others looked confused.

"Don't anyone move," I said. "You just stand and wait."

It didn't take long, only three or four minutes. Jess took her hands away and stood up.

"What I'd like to know is this. Which one of you ordered the death of my parents?"

Hillstrom looked confused. "Who are your parents?"

Hutchinson didn't say a word.

"My father came across information linking you to Homer. He left me clues, and after you killed my friends, I discovered those clues. So, which one of you killed them, along with hundreds of others on that ferry boat in India?"

Jess by this time knew it wasn't Hillstrom, but she was hoping she could get a name from him.

Hillstrom wheeled around to face Hutchinson. "So the ferry boat wasn't an accident! I suspected you had a hand in it, I just didn't know why."

"Shut up!"

"Why? It's all going to come out now. This campaign is shot to hell. As is the organization. Why did you do it?" He turned to Jess. "I didn't kill them, Jess. And I didn't kill your friends."

"You idiot," shouted Hutchinson. Realizing himself now that it was all coming to an end, he lowered his head and said, "Mays was responsible for the ferry. I had nothing to do with that. I also had no idea that that reporter was your father. As I said, that was Mays's work."

All of a sudden, we heard sounds from the path. A half a dozen men emerged, some in a panic mode as they saw the men on the cliff. A few raised their weapons.

Gunfire rained down from the top of the cliff and the six were cut to ribbons. The four with Hillstrom made the mistake of raising their guns, and they too went down. Hutchinson hurriedly raised his pistol and shot Hillstrom in the stomach. He got off a second round as I pushed Jess down and fell on her. Hutchinson was taken out with a fusillade of bullets from Ollie's men on the cliff. And then it was silent.

I looked over to make sure Scott was okay and started to get up. Scott looked back at me with an expression of horror.

"Jon, you're hit!" He came running over.

I couldn't feel any pain, but my shirt was covered in blood. I looked down at Jess and found the source. She was lying there white as a ghost, eyes closed and head turned to the side. A red stain originating from the center of her chest had already soaked her shirt. A small pool of blood was beginning to form next to her body.

"Noooooooo!" I screamed.

Scott pushed me out of the way and started methodically working on Jess. He handed me his keys and told me to run to the truck and get his medical kit. I didn't want to leave Jess but knew there was nothing I could do. Joe, meanwhile, was checking Hillstrom. I didn't bother to see how badly he had been shot—I really didn't care—but I heard Joe say that he was still alive. It took forever to go the quarter of a mile to the truck. When I got there, I was shaking so badly, I couldn't get the key in the lock. Finally, I got the door open and found the case behind the driver's seat. It was heavy and going back seemed to take twice the time. Ollie and his men passed me as I reached the quarry. I heard Ollie yell out a "Good luck." When I made it to them, Scott was covered in Jess's blood.

He opened the kit and took out bandages and other items. He

worked quickly and talked while he worked.

"I told Ollie to call EMS on his radio and explain that I was here and needed a couple of ambulances and that Jess might need to be airlifted to Anchorage. I haven't had time to check on Hillstrom. Joe is doing what he can. Jess needs my full attention. I told Ollie to get his guys out of here and get home before the police arrive. As far as I'm concerned, they didn't exist. They're going to take the rentals Hillstrom's men used to get back to the airport." He looked at me intently, "Jon, Jess is in really bad shape. She's stopped breathing twice already."

Chapter 45

"Daddy?"

"Hi Punkin."

He was in front of her, looking wonderful. There was a calmness about him. A confidence that comforted her. She knew though, that she couldn't hug him. It had been so long though....

"I don't ... I don't ... understand. Where am I?"

"I know it's a little confusing, but I can't really tell you."

"Can't, or won't?"

"A little bit of each."

"What happened?"

"You were shot." There was a sadness in his voice and face that she picked up on.

"Am I dead?"

"That's up to you."

It didn't make sense to her. How could it be up to her?

"Is this heaven?"

"No, but some people mistake it for heaven."

"Daddy, I'm not understanding any of this."

"I know, and I'm sorry about that. If you were staying, you would understand, but you are not staying. It's important that

you go back."

"But I want to be with you. I want to stay."

"You can't. You need to go back. It's not your time yet. And Jon needs you."

"But you said it's up to me."

"Ultimately it is. I'm asking you to go back. Listen to your father."

He used to say that, and always followed it with a grin. The grin appeared, and she felt a warmth course through her body. Was it a body? It seemed lighter somehow, and brighter. Was that why she knew she couldn't hug him?

"But before you go back, I wanted to tell you how proud your mom and I are of you. This wasn't easy, but you fought your way through it."

"Where is mom?"

"She's close. But we don't have a lot of time. Do you have any questions for me?"

He was referring to the Hillstrom affair. She was obviously not going to get any more information about where she was.

"How much did you know?" she asked.

"Not as much as you might think, but in some ways more than you could imagine."

"A riddle?"

"Sort of. I learned about Ben Fremont when I was in Homer strictly by accident, as you discovered. I found out about the deaths of his co-workers and was able to do a little research, where I learned of his association with Exchange Systems. I wondered if it was a front for something else, but I couldn't prove anything. I went to a colleague at the Post, someone more suited for this kind of research. He died in a car accident a month later. Another death on the heads of this group. Let the authorities know that George

Simpson was another murder they should look into. At that point, I didn't realize he'd been murdered and I kind of dropped it, figuring I'd investigate it here and there in my spare time. That's when your mom and I went to India. You know what happened then."

Jess could feel tears streaming down her face.

"Don't cry, Punkin. We're really very happy."

Jess tried to compose herself.

"But how were you able to lead me up to Alaska?"

"That's a little harder to explain. There are some things that even I don't fully understand. Instead of moving on, as I normally would and as your mom did, I was given a choice to stay here. I was able to watch you, and the things happening around you."

"You could see everything?" Was it possible to blush where she was?

"I closed my eyes when I had to." He had that grin again. "No, it's not like I was watching you. I didn't word that right. It's more like I was with you in spirit. But I was aware of the things you were facing—anything that might affect you. It's why I was able to keep you from going into your office that morning. It's why I was able to get you onto that highway in time for Jon to drive by. Jon picking you up was totally his choice. I had nothing to do with that. And yet, I knew he would."

"Getting you to Vegas so you could meet Mill Colson," he continued, "directing you to Wisdom Spring, and then to the room in the mine with the bodies, and other things, those were all events surrounding you in some way, so I was able to pick up on them and guide you."

"It seemed hard for you to communicate," said Jess.

"Incredibly hard. Much harder than I would have thought. I guess it's why more souls don't stick around. I was able to pick up *certain 'tricks,' shall we say, but it wasn't easy. And a lot depended on you. There were certain times that were easier for me because of the mental or emotional state you were in."*

"Do you know who's behind it all?"

"It doesn't really matter at this point. It's over. I don't know any names, but what I do know is that if you dig into Corbin Mays's past, three names will come out."

"Do you miss me?"

"I love you, more than you could ever imagine. But you don't feel the same earthly emotions here. So I don't 'miss' you from the human perspective, but I love you deeply and I will always carry that love with me. Now it's time for you to go."

"Will I hear from you again?"

"No. It's time for me to move on, too. There's so much ahead for me."

"Thank you, Daddy. I love you."

"Just know how proud we are of you. We love you, Punkin. You have a great life ahead of you"

Her father faded from view and she was overcome with a darkness.

Chapter 46

The next few days were a blur for me. Luckily, there was very little need for my involvement. Mill was hard at work, and with Joe's help with the details, he sorted out the legal entanglements. He sent long emails out to media people he knew and trusted, the FBI, the Department of Justice, the Secret Service, the White House, and others. He had scanned in and attached some of the important documents, as well as attaching some of the pictures I took inside the mine, and the video Joe had taken at the quarry. The FBI was sent the list of politicians, corporate executives, and members of the media who were involved. They were also sent the names of the assassins, along with their victims. Then, Mill released an announcement of a press conference he was giving in two days outside Jess's hospital. The fact that Mill was still alive caused a furor in and of itself.

Corbin Mays was arrested the next day, and Hillstrom was placed under arrest in the hospital, with guards stationed at his door. Hillstrom's wounds were bad enough that he had also been airlifted to Anchorage. The men Ollie had captured were also arrested. Questions abounded regarding all the dead men at the quarry and who was responsible. Scott and Joe refused to say, and

Mill ran interference with the authorities. The current president and his challenger in the presidential race immediately took advantage of Hillstrom no longer being in the hunt and proceeded to attack each other with renewed vigor.

I watched the news from Jess's bedside at Anchorage Regional Hospital. The government was in turmoil. Dozens of members of Congress had resigned their posts, as had Supreme Court Justice Pecorelli. Indictments would probably follow, but not until sense had been made of it all. Mill hooked up with a local law firm and had all of the files in our possession copied by their assistants. Now that the media had caught on, there was little chance the files would disappear, but Mill was taking no chances.

Wisdom Spring was suddenly bustling again, this time with dozens of federal agents. The mine door was opened and the rest of the files, as well as the bodies, were removed. Nothing was done until the bomb squad had disarmed all of the bombs that had been planted. It turned out that Mays hadn't been to Wisdom Spring in more than a year. As it was his job to create and update files, a year's worth of information was found in his office safe, further incriminating him. Based on the files in his safe and the boxes of files recovered by the authorities from the mine, over the next few weeks, scores of arrests were made of the lesser members of the organization—the hired help.

Jess was in a coma, but the doctors were "cautiously optimistic." Without a doubt, Scott had saved her life. He had taken charge in the ambulance and had been with her until the med flight plane arrived and he could turn her over to them.

Charges against Jess were quickly dropped, although that wasn't enough for Mill. He planned a lawsuit against the government on her behalf and was going to talk about her in his press conference. When he was done, she'd be a national hero.

I appreciated Mill and all the details he was taking care of, but I was only concerned with one thing: Jess staying alive. I didn't leave her bedside except to use the bathroom and to meet with the FBI. But even that I cut short, wanting to be there if Jess woke up. I let Mill deal with their anger. The nurses were fabulous and brought me food and drinks, although much of it went untouched. Sitting with Jess brought all of the memories flooding back of doing the same with Karen. I couldn't lose another one. Not again.

I watched Mill's press conference on TV. The official FBI press briefing had come the day before and several updates had followed. There was no new information. I wouldn't have expected anything new so quickly, considering the authorities were still trying to get their heads around it. My name had finally come out, as had my life history, including the story of Karen. I wasn't portrayed in a bad light, however, and one report even had Victoria saying kind things about me. It probably wasn't politically correct for her to slam someone who was holding vigil for an American hero. Mill had also received a lot of publicity, making his briefing a highly sought-after event.

The press conference was taking place three stories below Jess's room, and the streets surrounding the hospital were choked with media vehicles and people.

"Thank you all for coming," Mill began. "Three stories above me lies a very brave young woman with a gunshot wound to her chest. I'm told the bullet missed her heart by less than an inch, and she is now clinging to life. Jessica Norton had been accused of killing four of her co-workers execution-style back in Washington, DC. As you all know by now, the charges have been dropped. But what you don't know is the story behind her courageous attempt to clear her name. With the help of a stranger, Jon Harper, someone already dealing with his own devastating loss, and later, the help of my lead investigator, Joe Gray, and Jon's brother, Scott Harper,

Jessica entered into a morass of political and financial corruption that goes back more than forty years."

He went on … and on … from there. I was afraid his talk would go for another forty years, so I turned the TV off. After all, I knew the story.

Epilogue

Jess woke up four days later, then spent the next month recuperating. They had to open her up and go in twice more to fix some internal bleeding, but finally she was steadily healing. She was in a great deal of pain those first couple of weeks, and the doctors informed her that she'd have a pretty visible scar between her breasts. But neither of us cared.

She told me about her experience with her father—an encounter she never would have had if she hadn't been close to death. I passed on the news about George Simpson and the instructions to check Mays's past to learn about his present employers. Of course, they wanted to know how I got that information, so I told them the truth. For some reason they didn't believe me—no imagination, I guess—but they investigated it anyway. Indeed, upon checking the medical examiner's report from a different perspective, George Simpson's death was definitely ruled a homicide.

They found the people behind the conspiracy by checking Mays's employment history. It seems that early in his career—in his mid-twenties—he was a hotshot consultant to some of the largest corporations in America. He was smart and ambitious, with a decided lack of ethics, willing to do whatever was necessary to bring success to his clients. Three CEOs caught a whiff of his true character, combined with his skills, and brought him on board.

One CEO was the head of a gas and electric energy conglomerate, another the head of one of the largest oil companies in the world, and the third in charge of a conglomerate that had bought up water rights all over the country (including that small Colorado town, I learned). Between energy, oil, and water rights, with the appropriate people in Congress, these three men could control America. The plan had been successful and thanks to their influence in Congress and their ability to control some of the media, they possessed much of the power in the country. Two of the three had long since died, and the third was near death, but their empires had been passed on to their sons and daughters, who proved equally as greedy and corrupt. The only thing they didn't have was the White House, which is why they enacted this part of the plan.

I found out that it was the sons and daughters who came up with the idea of starting a training school at Wisdom Spring. Paying off politicians was fine, but what if they could create their own? They were young. They had the luxury of buying politicians now and growing their own for later. Not all of the children at Wisdom Spring were brought in at an age as young as Ben. Most of the older kids' files were in the folders we had left in the cave. All were from orphanages or youth camps, and were chosen for Wisdom Spring for their intelligence, but more importantly, for their moral character, or lack thereof. By starting out with children of all ages, they could start fitting some of them into their roles within just a few years. The younger ones gave them fodder for the future.

Even many children who didn't show any moral defects early were kept. A childhood in Wisdom Spring was enough to turn even the best child into someone they could mold. Corbin Mays was brought in early on to act as an instructor and mentor for the older students. He saw the potential in Ben almost immediately and mentored him for his last couple of years there.

Mays had been offered a deal by federal prosecutors where they would take the death penalty off the table if he named his bosses. He refused. But when he realized they had the means to find them by digging into his past, he quickly tried to accept the offer. By then it was too late. When his case eventually went to trial, who knows how far down the line, I was confident they would convict him. If so, he would be sentenced to death. The Indian government was hot to try him as well, and negotiations were in place to let them have their piece of him.

The bodies in the cave were enough to sicken most people. It was bad enough when it was revealed that the adults in the cave were simply part of the assassins' training—learning to kill quickly and cleanly. But when it came out that the children—the school rejects—also died as a part of the assassins' schooling, the nation was outraged. The assassins-in-training were learning the most effective places to inject poison into their victims, and the children became the test subjects. And when it was learned that Hillstrom himself had killed some of the adults, as well as the ten people in Homer, extra guards and police had to be put on to stop people from storming the hospital in search of the previously much-loved politician.

The most amazing thing to come out was how deeply entrenched in American history this plan was. Although the organization was a fairly recent invention—recent in historical terms—the seeds of the plan went back to the mid-1800s with the heads of some of the most powerful monopolies in the country. Their ambition even then was one of total control, and they worked in much the same way as the Wisdom Spring crowd to buy politicians. They just weren't able to own enough of them. However, their dream lived on in secret writings to their children, and it was those children, and after them their children and others who had gained equal power and total trust who first formed the organization as it was now. They had developed deep ties to corporate heads and heads of state in several other countries. As soon as Hillstrom—and then Gilmore—had the presidency, the dominoes long in place would have begun to fall and one by one those countries, in addition to the U.S., would have come under the control of the Wisdom Spring organization.

Early on, that group—to keep its secrecy, it had never been given a formal name—had decided to stick with the tried and true forms of record-keeping and steered clear of computers. As a result, there was nothing to hack, nothing to accidentally appear on the Internet, and no trails to follow. It was perfect in its simplicity.

As promised, I called Carl Jenkins and told him he could put his website back up, but he was way ahead of me, adding to his history of Wisdom Spring every day as he learned more about it from the news. He thanked me for the warning, saying that, even though he had viewed me as a crackpot, he had followed my advice—advice he was now grateful for. I steered the media his way as the local authority on the history of Wisdom Spring, pre-Exchange.

Hillstrom's wounds were not as life-threatening as Jess's, but took just as long to heal. He had been shot in the stomach, which caused all kinds of problems and necessitated numerous surgeries.

One day he asked to see Jess. At first she was reluctant, but then, at my suggestion, agreed to see him. They wheeled him into her room, handcuffed to his wheelchair, with two U.S. Marshals at his side.

"Thank you for talking to me," he said. "Jess, I'm sorry you were hurt. I truly liked you."

"I'm not looking for an apology," she answered, stony-faced. "My parents are dead because of you. My friends, too. Maybe you didn't do it yourself, but you were involved."

"I know it means nothing to you, but I never knew about your father. I had an inkling from Hutch that someone had found something about my past. And after the ferry accident he made a reference to that person being gone."

Jess started to interrupt, but Hillstrom held up his hand to stop her.

"But that's not why I came. You asked me something back at the quarry that I feel a need to answer. You asked me why I was disturbed by the pictures you showed me of the people in the mine but could so easily kill the ten people in Homer. The fact is, it wasn't easy to kill those people, especially Erin, whom I was quite fond of. It should have been easy. It was the kind of thing I was trained for. I was in touch with my handlers on a regular basis, and they are the ones who told me I'd have to kill those I was closest to because I couldn't have them identifying me later. My history had to stay a secret. The rest of the town didn't really know me—it was only my co-workers who knew me well—so they were the only ones who had to go. I didn't think it would bother me, that I would be ready to kill them when the time came. But I wasn't. I hesitated with each one. That will mean nothing to you, but it means everything to me. Hesitation was something that wasn't an option. Someday I'll write about my life in Wisdom Spring and maybe you'll understand."

He was already thinking book contract, I observed. Forever the narcissist.

"I won't read it," answered Jess.

A momentary silence. "Early on in Homer I started talking to Clyde. He was more of a sounding board for me. I couldn't have any deep conversations with him, but in his own way he was deep. He was just a simple, kind man. In many ways he was the friend I had always wanted as a kid. It's why when the word came down, I couldn't kill Clyde. And now, to know that he was a key in the downfall of this operation kind of makes me almost smile. Old simple Clyde. Clyde, 'the dummy'. Boy, if that isn't karma...."

I had my own question I needed an answer to. "When you told Clyde where you had come from, you referred to it as a ghost town. Why, when in fact, there were a hundred or more people there?" I asked.

"It was a ghost town to *me*. It had been throughout my whole childhood. It could have had a thousand people and it wouldn't have changed anything. Besides," he added, "by the time I left, I knew they were planning to shut it down in a few years. It was only a matter of time before it would become a real ghost town."

"Why Homer," I asked. "Why were you there?"

"I had been trained well at Wisdom Spring, but before I could proceed with the ultimate goal of getting into politics, I needed some real-life experience working and interacting with others. The few years in Homer taught me much of what I needed."

He moved uncomfortably in his wheelchair, still in a fair amount of pain, and focused his attention back on Jess. "The fact is, there's no doubt about the kind of person I am. I don't have any illusions there. But you were right. I was being used from the time I was very young. As I got older, I was able to put the killings behind me, knowing that I would never have to personally bloody my hands again. I was being controlled, there's no doubt about that. But I also deceived myself into thinking that my past was all necessary. I knew that Corbin and his gang didn't have the best interests of the country in mind, and yet, I really thought I was doing something good in Congress. I really thought that I could be a good president."

There was a surprising sincerity to his words, but I also knew he would use those same words at trial to win over the jury. Sincerity only went so far with him.

Getting no response from Jess, he continued. "The reason those pictures from the mine bothered me so much was because they made it all clear. To them, we were all disposable. For a brief minute it brought me back to my childhood and how sad I was. These kids, they were my friends, my only friends until I met Clyde. They meant something to me and they were tossed away like trash. Jess, I'm not a good person, but I'm also not a monster. I performed one monstrous act of violence thirty years ago, but I'm not ... I'm not ..." Tears had welled up in his eyes. He looked down, then back at Jess. "I'd like to see Clyde. Is there anything you can do to help arrange it?"

I could tell what Jess was thinking. It was the same as I was thinking. Despite his narcissism and ability to sway people, here was a man who never had any kind of control in his life. He never had a chance. We all have the freedom to do the right thing, but for Hillstrom it was made almost impossible by this organization. Maybe for the first time in his life, he was telling the truth. And for only the second time maybe since his early childhood was he feeling a genuine emotion.

"I think I could arrange that," answered Jess. Her hatred of the man was still there, but now I could tell she also felt a little sorry for him. "Providing Jon and I are there as well."

At the five-week mark, Jess and Hillstrom were released within days of each other. Jess, because of her celebrity status, was able to get Hillstrom in to see Clyde. She went in first, with me pushing her in the wheelchair. Clyde was watching TV, as usual.

"Hi Clyde."

Clyde's eyes lit up. "It's Clyde's friend Jess. Yay. Why are you in a wheelchair, Jess?"

"I had an accident, Clyde. That's why I haven't visited you for a while."

"That's okay. Clyde knew you would come back."

"Clyde, I have a surprise for you."

"Ice cream?"

"No, something else." She waved toward the door.

A nurse pushed Hillstrom in. I could see the wary U.S. Marshals standing at the door, watching.

"It's Clyde's friend Ben Fremont! You came back. Jess said she'd find you."

"She did, Clyde. How did you know it was me after all these years?"

"Clyde would remember Ben. They were friends." He looked concerned. "Did you have an accident too?"

"I did. Jess and I had the same accident. How are you, Clyde?"

"Clyde is good now that his two friends are here. Where were you, Ben?" He spied the handcuffs. "Did you do something wrong?"

"I did, Clyde. I did many things wrong. I'm going away to jail and I'm afraid this is the only time I will be able to see you."

"Why, Ben Fremont? Why did you do things wrong?"

"It's a long story. But here is the important thing, Clyde. You saved me."

"Clyde couldn't have saved you, Ben. Clyde was right here."

Hillstrom smiled. "I know you were right here, Clyde, but you saved me anyway. Your friendship saved me. Even though I did some bad things, what is going to save me are my memories of my friendship with you. That was the best thing that ever happened to me. I know some people have called you names over the years, but you remember something: You are kind and a good friend. I will always remember that. Thank you, Clyde."

He held out his hand and they shook. Clyde had tears in his eyes. When I looked back at Hillstrom, he actually had tears running down his cheeks.

*****

It was a month later. Jess was finally out of her wheelchair. She wasn't pain-free, but was well on the mend. We were still staying with Scott, who was fussing over Jess like a mother hen. Mill had gone home, as had Joe. Mill had a lot of work to do to rebuild his business, and Joe had promised Mill he would be the head of his security. Mill was also writing another book about his experiences as a lawyer, with a large part dedicated to this case. Numerous publishers had offered Jess an obscene amount of money for the rights to her story. At first she declined, but after we talked about it, decided it would be a good way to put closure on the whole event, not to mention provide us with enough to never have to worry about money again. But she agreed only if I would write it with her.

"You know," said Scott over dinner one night. "I renew my offer. How about you guys build a house on my twenty-five acres. I know the quarry might bring some bad memories, but hell, it's twenty-five acres. You don't have to go anywhere near it."

"Actually, I don't have a problem with the quarry," said Jess. "We talked about living up here once, but decided we needed more civilization." She looked at me. "I'm not so sure that's still true. How about you?"

"Not at all. I know it's not fun here in the winter, but we'll have enough money to go anywhere we want in the cold weather. We could buy property in Hawaii or the Caribbean."

I looked at Jess, the top of her scar peeking through above her cleavage. She said the scar represented healing for both of us. Healing and the beginning of a new life.

The End

ABOUT THE AUTHOR

Andrew Cunningham is the author of 21 novels, including the *"Lies" Mystery Series*: **All Lies, Fatal Lies, Vegas Lies, Secrets & Lies, Blood Lies, Buried Lies, Sea of Lies,** and **Maui Lies;** the post-apocalyptic *Eden Rising Series*: **Eden Rising, Eden Lost, Eden's Legacy,** and **Eden's Survival;** the *Yestertime Time Travel Series*: **Yestertime, The Yestertime Effect, The Yestertime Warning,** and **The Yestertime Shift;** the disaster/terrorist thriller **Deadly Shore,** and *The Alaska Thrillers,* **Wisdom Spring, Nowhere Alone, The 7th Passenger,** and **Lost Passage.** As A.R. Cunningham, he has written a series of five children's mysteries in the *Arthur MacArthur* series. Born in England, Andrew was a long-time resident of Cape Cod. He and his wife now live in Florida. Please visit his website at *arcnovels.com,* or his Facebook page, *Author Andrew Cunningham.*

Made in United States
Cleveland, OH
06 June 2025

17526387R00190